HER RUSSIAN SURRENDER

50 Loving States, Indiana

THEODORA TAYLOR

D1713907

HER RUSSIAN SURRENDER

This Ruthless Russian Plays to Win!

When social worker, Sam McKinley meets hockey player, Nikolai Rustanov, it's fire at first sight—a fire Sam totally runs away from as quickly as her heels can carry her.

All Sam has ever wanted is a nice, normal family with a nice, normal man. The arrogant Russian hockey player who claims he doesn't believe in love right before he offers to "eat her for breakfast," is about as far from that as a girl can get.

But some fires just can't be put out.

Soon after meeting Nikolai, Sam forms an unexpected bond with a tragically orphaned boy who turns out to be his nephew. And did we mention, Nikolai is ruthless?

Determined to acquire the beautiful social worker as a caretaker for his previously unknown ward and a conquest for his bed, Nikolai moves Sam and her useless dog into his mansion.

Sam is dead-set on running, but Nikolai is determined to catch her. And when he does, he'll do just about anything to make her finally surrender to their blazing passion.

Chapter One

"EXCUSE ME, miss. Sorry to interrupt. Is this your jacket?"

Sam McKinley turned from her conversation with a cater-waiter named Husik to see a young man wearing circular glasses. Like many of the men at the Hockey Ices Cancer Gala, he had on a tux, but unlike those other men, his face still had a bit of pudge to it, the baby fat that dogged some guys into their twenties.

He extended her coat, a banged up, brown leather number she'd scored at a thrift store for thirty bucks back in grad school. It didn't really go with the emerald floor length gown she was wearing, but hey, at least it did its job. Nearly ten years later and it was still keeping her warm, even here in Indiana with its brutal winters.

"Yes, that's my jacket," she answered without embarrassment. "Is there something wrong?"

Sam fully expected to be kicked out of this party. She'd only been here for thirty minutes, but she hadn't exactly been invited. Unless using the name of your best friend's husband's former teammate to get inside could be considered an "invitation"—because in that case, she totally was invited.

But she knew not everyone would consider her presence at the event legit, so she braced herself, hoping the man's polite tone meant he'd let her go quietly without calling security.

"No, no, not at all," he answered quickly, his face flushing. "I just wanted to make sure. The woman at coat check assured me this was yours, but I, ah..." He seemed to be searching for a polite way to say that most people didn't attend galas in beat up jackets that were probably older than he was. "I wasn't sure," he finished weakly.

He then rushed in to say, "But there's nothing to be worried about. I'm actually here to extend an invitation. Nikolai Rustanov would like the pleasure of your company on the balcony. I retrieved your jacket so you'd be warm."

Sam breathed a mental sigh of relief that she wasn't getting kicked out but...

"Who's Nikolai Rustanov?" she asked, scanning the room from side to side.

The man's eyes widened as if she had asked him who the President of the United States was.

"Nikolai Rustanov? One of the best hockey players the NHL has ever seen? The new owner of the Indiana Polar?"

The young man seemed to be waiting for Sam to make the connection, but she shook her head with an apologetic shrug.

"Sorry. Never heard of him." She turned to look at Husik, the Armenian cater-waiter she'd spent most of the party talking with so far. "But the Indiana Polar is the state's hockey team, right?"

Husik winced as if he was just plain embarrassed for her.

"Yes, ma'am," he answered. "Nikolai Rustanov--they call him Mount Nik--owns it, and you should probably know... this is his house."

"Oh!" Sam took a closer look around the large, opulent room. The ceilings were covered with intricately carved crown molding, and the ivory walls were filled with luxurious gilt pieces Sam couldn't have pegged on a specific era or design, but they put her in mind of words like "baroque" and "rococo." Every room she'd seen in the place so far was done up in this way, and ever since she'd walked in, she'd felt like she was standing in the middle of a set piece for one of the historical romance novels she used to read back when she was a teenager.

Whoever this hockey player was, his home was beautiful, but way over the top, like Peter the Great and Josephine Bonaparte had hooked up and decided to build a home together in Indiana.

"Wow! Well, thanks for the invitation to join your boss…" Sam smiled at the bespectacled representative of the hockey player with baroque tastes.

"No, need to thank me," the man assured her, lightly cupping her elbow. "If you'll just follow me, the balcony is right this way."

Sam didn't budge. "As I was saying, thanks for the invitation but…" she carefully removed her elbow from his grasp, "…please tell Mr. Mount Nik the answer is no."

The young man blinked. "The answer is no?" He was clearly not used to this response.

"Yes, the answer is no." She held up her coat. "But thanks for the coat! I'll probably be heading out soon anyway, so you saved me a trip."

"But… I don't understand!" the young man's eyes traveled from her ragged coat to her bare ring finger as if he were trying to piece together the answer to a complex puzzle.

"I don't really think there's anything to understand," she answered. "He invited me, and I'm saying no. It's really pretty simple. Now, if you'll excuse me, I was in the middle of a conversation with Husik."

Having nipped that in the bud, she presented the younger man with her back. But she waited until he'd moved away to say, "Actually, I'm glad that guy brought me my coat because I left my business card holder in it." She took out the flat metal case and handed Husik one of the small cards tucked inside. "If you think your niece is in trouble, give her my card. It doesn't have anything but my name and number on it, so even if her boyfriend finds it, it shouldn't cause her any problems. Sometimes just having my card at the right time is enough to get someone out of a bad situation."

Husik took her card with the hand that wasn't holding a tray of appetizers, his eyes running over her name, "Ms. Sam McKinley," before he pocketed it.

"Thanks, but…" His voice dropped to a whisper. "I can't believe you just turned down Nikolai Rustanov!"

"Why not?" she asked.

"Because he's Mount Nik!" The man seemed genuinely perplexed.

Sam resisted the temptation to roll her eyes. So yeah, the hockey player with the hyperbolic nickname was probably a big deal in Husik's mind. And obviously the representative he'd sent over wasn't used to women turning down his boss's balcony invitations. But Sam wasn't here to meet up with hockey players on balconies. She was here to start making contacts, like she promised her partner, Josie, she would. And in her experience, athletes preferred to sponsor splashy causes like cancer and homelessness. Domestic violence, not so much.

Husik was still babbling on. "I mean, he dominates at a face off, and he gets to rebounds faster than anyone you've ever seen. Plus, he leads the league in shots on goal. But you turned him down!"

Sam really had no idea what any of that meant, and she was a little dismayed Husik seemed more concerned that she'd rejected some hockey player's advances than he was about his niece's relationship, which he'd been telling her he suspected had turned violent before they'd been interrupted.

But keeping judgment on a minimum setting was part of her job, so instead of chastising him, she smiled tightly and replied, "Yes, well, I'm just not interested, even if he's really good at hitting balls with his stick."

"Pucks," a deep, heavily accented voice said behind her. "I'm very good at hitting pucks with my stick."

This time when she turned she had to look up, then up some more, to find a pair of cool, green eyes staring down at her from under heavy lids. And suddenly, she understood why the young man he'd sent over had been confused about her response. Nikolai Rustanov was insanely, outrageously gorgeous, with a face and jaw that looked like it had been hand carved by someone with a high appreciation for asymmetry and a body so large, she knew immediately it was muscle and not padding filling out the shoulders of his tuxedo. Suddenly, the nickname "Mount Nik" didn't seem quite so hyperbolic anymore.

And yes, she admitted to herself, any woman would be happy to receive a balcony invitation from a man who looked like this. At least at first glance. But she wasn't like most women, and quickly zeroed in on his faults. His eyes, she noticed, where a total blank, and his lips had a hard twist to them, like they we're in permanent prep mode for sneering.

Cruel. The word appeared inside her mind like a poisonous warning label. He had icy eyes and cruel lips. And even though his hair was light brown, falling in tousled strands past his ears —not military short and bleach blond like the only Russian she remembered from her childhood movie days—the *Rocky IV* theme song totally went off inside her head

Chapter Two

NIKOLAI STARED down at the woman who—much to his cousin, Alexei's, amusement—had spurned his balcony invitation. She was even more beautiful up close than she'd been from across the room where he'd been standing when he first spotted her, dressed in an ethereal, deep green evening gown and talking to one of the cater-waiters. Her hair—which he could see now consisted neither of dreadlocks nor braids but some kind of long twists—was pulled back into a large bun, giving her face perfect visibility. Wide set eyes, shining with good humor, flawless dark brown skin that seemed to glow as if she were lit from the inside, dimpled cheeks, and—his eyes drifted downward—lush curves, very lush curves that were making the dress work hard to keep her contained.

The dimples were a little much, he thought, now that he could see her up close. His usual conquests, who tended to have sharper cheekbones and more skillfully applied makeup, didn't usually sport indents in their cheeks. But in this case she'd sparked his curiosity enough to overlook them. Also, he wanted to see what was underneath that dress. In fact, he decided then and there, he wanted her. In his bed. Tonight.

"You have something else you should be doing," he informed the cater-waiter without taking his eyes off the woman.

"Yes, sorry," the cater-waiter mumbled. "Big fan by the way!"

Nikolai didn't answer, just waited for the smaller man to go away so he could make his next move on the woman in the green dress. She looked slightly disconcerted as she watched the cater-waiter leave. Like she didn't know quite what to do with Nikolai. Or herself.

Good, Nikolai thought. It served her right for turning down his balcony invitation. Apparently, even though she was at a hockey fundraiser, she didn't know enough about the sport to distinguish a ball from a puck. Or him from any of the average, anonymous suitors she might have encountered before.

"Hello," he said now that he had the woman's full attention. "I am Nikolai Rustanov, and you are very beautiful."

He waited for her to preen, but his words only seemed to fluster her more.

"Thanks! So are you... I guess." She had a soft lilt to her voice that made her words sound almost overly cheery.

"Beautiful?" he said after a moment of confusion. Even after nearly two decades in the States, his English was still not the best. Maybe he was misunderstanding her. "You think I am beautiful?"

"Yes, really beautiful," she answered with a nod. "Good job on that front!"

Nikolai faltered a bit. Had she just congratulated him on being beautiful? Like a woman? He reset.

"I'm glad you think so. You and I have—how you say—mutual admiration."

"Oh, well, kind of, but I mean... maybe not really," she answered. She now looked around the room as if she were desperately searching for someone else to talk to. Anybody other than him. "I'm not really into that kind of stuff."

English was his second language, true, but every single thing that came out of this woman's mouth so far had only served to confuse him, making him wonder if it wasn't her first language either.

"Beauty—you don't like it? You are not 'into' it?" he posed the question very slowly just in case, like him, she was still having trouble with the English language.

She shrugged. "I mean beauty can come in handy. Like when I'm arguing with a man and he's all hyped up and security's not available, sometimes he won't act as much of a fool because I'm pretty, I guess. But a few times it's made things more difficult. Like sometimes men underestimate me because of it, and that's no good."

Her answer brought up so many more questions that Nikolai's mind temporarily stalled out. Why was she arguing with so many men to the point that she had to call security? And why did she care if anyone underestimated her?

She glanced up at him. "Do you feel like that too, sometimes? Like being all hot and hunky gets in your way?"

"No," he answered truthfully. "It only helps. Especially with women."

"Woooow! That must be so nice for you!"

She gave him an impressed look, but it felt to Nikolai like she was laughing at him. He did not like this feeling.

"It is," he replied. Usually, he added silently with grim annoyance.

"Your calendar's stuffed with dates I bet. How great!"

He regarded her coolly for a second, trying to figure out if he was really supposed to respond to that. But Black Americans, he knew, could be different. His cousin, Alexei, was married to one who insisted on calling him Nikki and conversations with her were often confusing like the one he was having with this woman now.

"I do not go on dates," he informed her, deciding to indulge the conversation topic, more out of curiosity than anything else. The woman was strange but she was engaging, and Nikolai found himself wanting to stay in her company despite the many bizarre things that had come out of her mouth over the course of their short conversation.

"Seriously?" she asked. "Why not?"

"Dates are not necessary. They are silly custom. If a woman wants one, I say to her, we are both adults, why waste time with silly custom?"

She looked enrapt now, like she was hanging on every word he was saying. "And what do they say?"

"They agree of course, and then we have very pleasurable time together."

The look she gave him now was the opposite of impressed. In fact, he could have sworn he saw pity in her eyes.

She shrugged and said, "I guess we don't have much in common then. When I'm working late, I'm always like, wouldn't it be cool to be one of those people who goes on dates? Seriously, how nice would that be? To like, you know, go to dinner and a movie. But here you are with plenty of women to date, and you don't even take advantage of all your opportunities." She shook her head. "What a waste."

Nikolai narrowed his eyes at her, not knowing whether to be confused or insulted or both. "You are…" he informed her, "strange. Very strange."

"Yes, I know," she answered with that odd lilt of hers. "But it sounds like you've got a little strange going on yourself. Like, is that seriously all you do? Not go on dates with the women you invite out to your balcony? How does that work out for you love wise?"

"I do not love," he answered. "Love is another silly custom. I don't—how you say—believe in it."

She raised her eyebrows. "Love? *Love* is a silly custom you don't believe in? You seriously just said that? How can you not believe in love?!?!"

Nikolai inwardly grunted, happy he only wanted this woman for a one-night stand. She was obviously a romantic. One who would be much more trouble than she was worth if he were the sort who took women out on dates.

He stepped closer to her and said, "Trust me, you do not have to believe in silly customs to give woman much pleasure. Come upstairs. I will show you."

His words must have had some affect on her, because she waved a hand in front of her face, like she was trying to cool herself down.

"Okay, you spit amazing game. Well played, Mount Nik. You're like an expert in getting women all hot and bothered, I can tell."

"Thank you," he said carefully, because he had no idea how else to respond to that seeming compliment.

She slightly turned away from him, her eyes scanning the party.

"Hold on, I have someone I want you to meet."

"You have someone you want me to meet," he repeated. "Who?"

"I'm not sure yet," she answered, her eyes still surveying the room. But then her face lit up. "No, no, no, I take that back. I see her. She's definitely the one."

She waved enthusiastically at a tall, beautiful brunette in a black evening dress who was standing with a couple of blondes also wearing black evening dresses. When she got the brunette's attention, she motioned for her to join them like they were long, lost buddies.

Nikolai's curiosity was fully piqued at this point. The truth was, the brunette, with her high cheekbones and classic features, was much more his usual type, but why would the woman in the green dress be calling her over? Perhaps for a threesome?

"Hi! Hi! Hi!" the minx in the green dress said when the brunette reached them. "What's your name?"

"Katrina," the brunette answered, smiling cautiously as if she weren't sure if the woman who'd called her over was just friendly or insane.

Nikolai was beginning to wonder the same thing.

"Katrina. That's a beautiful name," the woman whose name he still didn't know said. She looked up at Nikolai. "That's Russian, right? Like you?"

"Yes, but I'm American," Katrina answered, throwing Nikolai a flirty smile.

"Well, Katrina, let me introduce you to Nikolai Rustanov. He's a fan of private conversations on balconies, and pleasurable times with ladies, and, and…" She looked up at him, her face and tone completely serious. "What else?"

"Hockey," Nikolai answered, wondering what she was getting at.

The woman in the green dress snapped her fingers, like he'd just given her the perfect answer. "And hockey! Do you like hockey, Katrina?"

"I love hockey," Katrina answered. She turned fully toward Nikolai now. "I have season passes for the Indiana Polar, and you're actually one of my favorite players."

"That's awesome," the woman said, patting Katrina on the shoulder. "I'll just leave you two to it, then."

"Oh, okay," Katrina answered with a wave, seeming more than happy to be alone with him.

"So is that a friend of yours? Someone who works for you?" she whisper-asked Nikolai when the woman in the green dress was out of earshot.

Nikolai didn't answer, just watched the strange woman walk away with a scowl on his face.

"Excuse me," he began to say, preparing to go after her, but then his cousin Alexei appeared and got in front of him.

Alexei was a businessman, not a hockey player, but his face was a match to Nikolai's in that moment. Same Rustanov bone structure, same green eyes, and for some reason, the same grim look.

"What is it?" he asked, immediately knowing something must be wrong. The Alexei he knew would have teased him mercilessly about getting turned down in such a ridiculous fashion by the minx in the green dress.

"Fedya is here," Alexei answered, his voice low. "Your assistant came to me since you were... otherwise engaged."

Nikolai inwardly cursed as he watched the beautiful woman disappear into the crowd. No, he wouldn't be going after her right away as planned.

He'd have to deal with his brother first.

Chapter Three

SAY what you want about the crazy palatial design scheme of Nikolai's Rustanov's house—and its owner, Sam thought, but at least it had lots of nooks and crannies for hiding.

She knew this, because she was currently nestled in a little laundry alcove just off the kitchen. From what she'd seen of the house, it might be the only "normal" room in the place, with straight ahead white clapboard cabinets and the same kind of front loading washer and dryer sets that could be bought at any major appliance store in America.

The regular room with its ungilded anything brought back some measure of the inner peace she'd lost during her conversation with Nikolai Rustanov. Also, it was just far enough away to be out of earshot from the catering staff, and hidden enough that no one would bother to look for her here, including the house's hulking owner—well, not unless he just really, really felt the need to do some laundry in the middle of his party. But mostly it was perfect for a secluded phone conversation with her best friend, Josie.

"You did WHAT?" Josie yelled on the other end of the phone.

"Josie, Josie, it made total sense. He was coming on way too strong, right? So I thought, why not set him up with someone else, and you know... run? Like, really fast."

"Sam..." she could almost see her friend rubbing her temple in exasperation. "We've talked about this. If someone at one of these parties starts flirting with you because you're wonderful and gorgeous, what are you supposed to do?"

"Hit him up for a donation," Sam answered glumly. "But this wasn't some old money millionaire! The guy is fry your brain hot. And huge. Seriously, the locals call him Mount Nik! It was hard to even look at him. Matter of fact, I'm surprised I was able to talk to him as long as I did, because all my alarm bells were going off."

"Alarm bells, like you think he might be abusive?" Josie asked, sounding worried.

"No, not abusive... just scary... you know... alarm bells scary."

Josie let out an audible sigh. "Okay, I know you don't get out much, which makes me wonder about this cop you've been seeing..."

"It's not his fault," Sam quickly said, defending the local beat cop she'd eaten takeout with three times over the past month. "It's early days and Marco is really respectful of my schedule. Plus, it's not like we don't see each other every day when he's doing his rounds. He always makes sure to text me, so I can come out and say hi."

"And do you?" Josie asked.

Ugh, her bestie was so good at asking the questions Sam didn't want her to ask. "When I'm not too busy, I do."

"So that would be like, what? Once a week?"

"Sometimes twice," Sam said. "And more over the next few weeks, since the shelter's empty and I'll just be catching up on paperwork. My point is you shouldn't blame Marco for not taking me out. I'm sure he would if I wasn't so busy."

"And my point is when someone sets off alarm bells inside of you—not because they're abusive or about to punch you out for harboring their wife—then that usually means you like the guy."

"Really?" Sam asked.

"Yes, Sam, really," Josie answered, like she was talking to an idiot. "I still get all goosey inside if I let myself look at Beau too long."

"Yeah, me, too. No rando, but your husband's crazy hot."

Josie laughed. "See, why can't you be like that with this guy?"

"I told him he was beautiful!"

"And then you told him being attractive wasn't all that great."

Sam screwed up her mouth. "Yeah, I guess I did say that."

She sighed into the phone, a wave of homesickness washing over her. "I'm just no good at this, at flirting or fundraising. Can I just come home to Alabama now? The shelter's already open and doing great. And Nyla is doing a terrific job. She could easily take over as director." She could hear the slight hysteria in her voice now, but kept on going. "Plus, I'll be such a good play auntie to that baby you have on the way. I'll babysit whenever you want, just please let me come home?"

Josie laughed. "Nyla is only an intern. You don't even pay her!"

"I didn't even pay you at first, but now you're running Ruth's House Alabama!" Sam reminded her.

"Yes, and you made me at least get my college degree before you felt safe enough to leave it in my hands. This is your dream, Sam. You're back in Indiana where it all started, opening another shelter. At least give it a year before you give up on it."

"I'm not giving up on it, I'm just..." Sam trailed off, not exactly knowing how to finish that sentence.

"Homesick," Josie supplied for her. "And a little scared about being back in Indiana, even if you are making your dreams come true."

Exactly. That's what she loved about Josie. She got her. Really got her. "This conversation isn't making me any less homesick. I miss you so much, girl."

"I miss you, too," Josie told her. "But Beau and I went through a lot of trouble to get you into that party, so go back out there and flirt with the money like a good non-profit director."

"Well, I've already got my coat thanks to the hockey player's assistant. If I go home now, I can probably get some to work done on another grant application."

"Or maybe you could get your Russian hockey player to fund the Indiana Ruth's House like Beau funds our Alabama location."

"Beau does that because you're his wife. The Russian hockey player was all, like…" Sam pulled out her best Swedish Dolph Lundgren pretending to be a Russian accent, "'I do not date. I just want to bone you down.'"

"He said that?!?!"

"No, not exactly," Sam admitted. "It was more like a bunch of stuff about pleasure, then I called the other woman over so he could bone her instead of me."

"You are a trip and you have me down here rolling on the floor, but I'm going to cut you off now because I know you're just using me to avoid hobnobbing with the people who could be giving Ruth's House Indiana donations."

"I'm totally not," she protested. She totally was, but she thought it was truly unkind of Josie to point that out.

"Good, then you won't mind if I hang up. Bye, Sam!"

"No, Josie, don't hang up. Don't—"

The phone went dead.

"…hang up," Sam finished with a sad sigh.

She started to stand, but then stopped mid-crouch when the alcove's door swung open with a quiet creak.

Sam's heart froze. Was it Mount Nik? Had he found her?

But no… it was a boy, creeping through the open door into the dimly lit room.

A bi-racial boy, Sam realized when the light from the next room hit his face. He had golden brown skin and a wide nose that spoke to his African-American ancestry.

Sam took him in with wide eyes. He was painfully thin, but tall. Six, seven, maybe even eight or nine years old. His clothes, she could see even in the low light, were also dirty, covered in various stains. Further signs of neglect could be found in his hair, a mad nest of kinky brown and blond curls that looked like they'd never seen a pair of scissors, much less hair product. And even though he was ten feet away from her, he smelled, to use one of her Alabama bestie's terms, "like a billy goat." Like his current living situation didn't give him regular access to a bath or shower. Like true neglect.

He froze like a deer in the headlights when he saw her crouched down next to the washing machine.

"Hey, buddy, whatcha up to?" she asked with a bright smile.

One that apparently disarmed him, because he didn't immediately turn tail and run, like she'd suspected he might if she'd shown how concerned she was for his well-being.

"Nothing," he answered quickly, his eyes darting from side to side as if he were looking for an excuse to bolt.

"Are you playing a game of hide-and-seek?" she asked. "Because not to brag, but growing up, I was the hide-and-seek queen."

The boy's stance relaxed. But just a little.

"You're not better than me. I'm the best at it."

"No, no… pretty sure it's me." Sam answered. "But I'm

always looking for pointers. Do you live here? Where are the other good places to hide?"

He shook his head. "I don't live here. This is my first time being here."

"Mine, too!" Sam said, keeping her voice light, although the social worker in her was frantically scrambling to figure out who he belonged to and how she could help him. "Did you walk here from your place?"

"No, it's too far." He gave her a quizzical look, as if he were wondering how a grown-up could be so silly. "I drove here with my papa," the boy told her. Then he looked away from her guiltily. "He told me to wait in the truck, but Mount Nik's my favorite hockey player in the world. I wanted to see his house. Just once." He sounded apologetic, and Sam could tell he wasn't normally the kind of kid who disobeyed orders from his father.

"I don't blame you," Sam said cheerfully, all the while wondering what kind of asshole would leave a child in his truck in the middle of one of the coldest Januarys on record. "Can I show you around? I just met the guy who owns this house so I can vouch for you."

"You know Mount Nik?" the boy said, his voice going a few octaves higher, as if she'd just announced she was close personal friends with the King of the Universe.

"Sure do. Want to come meet him?"

The boy immediately stepped forward, the prospect of meeting his hero apparently enough to get him over his fear of the strange woman he'd just met in a dimly lit alcove.

He wasn't six, she could tell that immediately as he moved closer, because at full height he nearly came up to her chest. She also noted that he looked even scrawnier up close than she'd originally thought. She could easily see the outline of his ribs through his thin, long-sleeved cotton shirt.

Sam, as she often did when she encountered children who

had been neglected or abused by their parents, had to tamp down the urge to go after the kid's father and punch him in the face. What kind of man didn't feed his child? Didn't bathe him? Who would leave him in a cold truck without even a winter coat!?

Just the thought of this child's father was enough to completely enrage her, but she kept her face calm and composed as she stuck out her hand to the boy.

"Hiya, name's Sam. What's your name?"

He not only didn't take her hand, he frowned in a way that oddly reminded Sam of the house's owner.

"Sam is a boy's name," he informed her.

"Most of the time, yes, but in this case, it's short for Samantha," she explained.

"May I call you Samantha?" the boy asked.

Sam was impressed by how politely he asked, but nonetheless responded with a firm, "No."

"Why not?" he asked, his voice more curious than petulant.

Normally Sam skirted this question, but she decided to tell him the truth.

"Because that's what my stepfather used to call me."

The boy nodded, an expression of understanding coming over his face.

"You didn't like your stepfather?"

That was the understatement of the century, but Sam just answered, "No," before changing the subject. "What should I call you when I introduce you to Mount Nik?"

The boy opened his mouth, just as a one of the cater-waiters in the kitchen shouted at someone to bring out some more of the garlic roasted shrimp.

Those had been delicious, Sam acknowledged. She'd had a few when she first arrived at the party. But she cursed the unseen waiter when the boy began to back away from her, as if he'd just come out of a spell.

"I've gotta go," he said. "I've been in here too long. My papa might be looking for me."

"Okay," Sam said, keeping her voice as light as possible under the circumstances. "How about if I go with you? You can introduce me to your dad."

The boy shook his head, like what she was suggesting was crazy.

"No. I'm sorry, but I'd get in trouble if he knew I got out of the car and was talking to somebody. I've got to go."

He turned to leave, and Sam caught him by the wrist. Time for Plan B. This wasn't the first time one of her careful interventions had been cut short by the intervenee's impending sense that they'd get in trouble.

"Please, let me go," the boy said, his voice urgent and distressed.

"I am going to let you go. I am," Sam assured him. "Just…"

She pressed her old coat into his hand. "Just take this, please."

"It's a girl's coat," he answered, his eyes going from scared to indignant.

"It's totally gender neutral and it will keep you warm," she answered right back. "The Indiana winter's nothing to mess with."

He bunched the jacket in his fist. "Fine, I'll take it. Let me go now, please."

"Okay, I'm going to, but first let me tell you about the cards in the pocket. They have my name on them. Just my name and telephone number. If you ever need anything, if there's anything at all I can do for you, just give me a call, okay?"

The boy didn't answer, just yanked backwards trying to get away from her.

"Let me go, please. I don't want to get in trouble. Please, let me go!"

Sam reluctantly released him, knowing that keeping him there against his will wouldn't make her any more trustworthy in his eyes.

The boy took off, pushing out of the alcove door so fast, it felt to Sam like watching a boy-sized rabbit sprint away from a possible predator—which was obviously what he now considered her, even though she'd only been trying to help.

A wave of exhaustion passed over Sam, so extreme, she knew for sure she wouldn't be going back to the ballroom for more networking with the Richie Riches as she'd promised Josie she would. Maybe next week or next month or next year... yeah, maybe then she'd feel up to it. But not tonight. No, tonight she was taking her tired butt home.

Chapter Four

"WHAT DO you mean I can't go home?" Sam demanded, her teeth chattering. She was standing underneath a covered carport, which extended out from the brick Colonial mansion on white column legs. The structure, like the rest of the house, was extremely stately, but it did nothing to protect her from the cold night wind, thrashing against her bare arms with no mercy whatsoever.

"I'm sorry, miss," the middle aged valet with the handlebar mustache and a nametag that said "Jose" answered. His expression became apologetic as he took in her shivering form. "We were told to keep you here for a bit when you came for your car. But why don't you go wait back inside? I'm sure he didn't know you'd be without a coat."

"Who didn't know?" Sam demanded, even though she was already beginning to suspect, even before the hockey player emerged from the house, closing its crimson red door behind him before once again coming to stand in front of her, large and imposing. It was like getting rolled up on by a tank.

"Mr. Rustanov," Jose said. "She doesn't have a coat. Can I go get her car?"

"*Da*, I will talk with her while we wait," the hockey player answered, like he was doing her and Jose a favor by only holding her up a little bit, when he never should have given the order in the first place.

"Exactly who the h-heck do you t-think you are?" she demanded after Jose had gone. Her words would have sounded a lot more aggressive if her teeth weren't chattering, she thought.

"Nikolai Rustanov," he answered. "I already told you this. However, my assistant can't find for sure who you are. Maybe you weren't invited to my party? Maybe you, how Americans say, crashed?"

"No, I didn't c-crash," Sam answered, knowing it would be too complicated to explain that she came as the plus one of an Indiana football player who couldn't attend, but used to be on the L.A. Sun's with Josie's husband and hadn't minded letting her use his wife's name to get into the event.

He regarded her shivering form with thinned lips.

"Where is your coat?" he asked, unbuttoning his tux jacket.

"I g-gave it away," she answered.

"Why?" He took his jacket off and wrapped it around her shivering shoulders. "It is very cold."

The large jacket was surprisingly heavy and even though she probably should have told him straight away that she didn't need it, Sam found herself reflexively pulling its front panels across her chest like a blanket. It was just so warm, radiating heat like it'd just come off a furnace.

"How about you?" she asked him with a worried look.

He looked back at her, confused. "How about me, what?"

"Don't you need your jacket? Like you said, it's very cold outside."

"Da, but I am Russian," he answered, as if that explained everything about everything.

"Okay, well, maybe I should thank you for loaning me this

jacket, but I would have been fine if you hadn't made sure I had to wait here outside for my car."

He frowned down at her from his great height.

"Tell me why you gave away your coat."

She shook her head with a sad sigh, thinking of the poor boy she'd met in the alcove. Who had he belonged to? Someone who worked for the man standing in front of her? One of the fans who had been milling around the front gates at the bottom of the long hill when she arrived?

"Do you know any little boys?" she asked. "Like one who's maybe a tall seven or eight years old?"

Another confused look from the big guy. "Why would I know little boy?"

"Because…" she trailed off, her instincts telling her a man like this probably didn't have any children he was close to in his life. And even if the boy had belonged to someone on his staff, Nikolai didn't seem like the type who would ask after his employee's families.

"It's nothing. Nothing you'd understand anyway."

With a bracing breath, she took off his coat and held it out for him to take back.

He just stared at her. Hard. "You should come back inside my house and explain to me your missing coat."

She gave him a sad smile. "No, I don't think so. It's been a long night and yeah, you're really hot. So hot, part of me is very flattered you went through all this trouble just to spit some more game. But I can already tell. You…" she circled the palm of her hand in his general direction, "…you're the kind of guy who would chew me up and eat me for breakfast. So as cute as you are, I have less than zero desire to go there with you."

To make her point final, she waved his jacket towards him, clearly signaling he just needed to take the damn thing, already. "I'm calling it a night. A really long night."

But he didn't take the jacket. In fact, he stepped closer to her, his hard tank of a body pushing the arm holding the jacket back. So close, she could feel the heat coming off him.

"I only agree with one thing you said." His eyes bore into hers. "The part about eating you for breakfast. But I think you will like the way I eat you for breakfast."

A hot chill ran over her, despite the cold, and she felt herself clench down below as the image of his face between her legs barged its way into her mind without invitation.

And suddenly he was no longer high above her. Suddenly, his mouth was coming down on hers, a hot shock of an invasion on a cold winter's night.

Her first thought was that his lips, which she remembered thinking were set in harsh, cruel lines, were actually much softer than they appeared. Her second thought was that he was kissing her. Kissing her! Why was he kissing her? And why wasn't she stopping him?

Maybe because it was cold and he was warm. Actually, make that hot, throwing off heat like a furnace as his lips took easy possession of hers.

Yeah, that had to be it.

Luckily her Prius pulled up in front of them at that moment with a whisper of tires coming to a stop underneath the low hum of its electric engine.

"Okay, okay…" she said, pushing away from him. Though only their lips had been touching, it somehow felt like she was ungluing herself from him, and she had to resist the urge to come right on back for another hot kiss.

"You spit great game and your kissing business is on lock, but here's my car." She seemed to be pointing this little factoid out to both herself and him. "So, I'll be going now. Take your jacket, please."

She held it out to him, this time with insistence.

He stared at her for what felt like eons, before he finally reached out and took the jacket from her.

"I will see you again," he said, his eyes so hooded now, they almost seemed sleepy.

"No, you probably won't," she answered, heading for the car as quickly as her strappy heels would let her. She mentally made a decision to double the number of grant applications she'd been planning to write away for this year, because she wouldn't be attending any more of these charity events, especially if there was any chance of him being there.

"I will see you again," he repeated to her retreating back, not like it was a request or even a desire, but something that was inevitably going to happen. Whether she liked it or not.

Sam didn't answer this time, just took the keys from the valet and got into her Prius. She didn't even bother to crank up the heat before pulling forward out of the carport, insanely wishing she had one of those superhero cars that turned into a high-speed jet with the push of a button.

Sam risked a peek into her rearview mirror and yes, there he was... staring after her. Though she should have been relieved by her successful exit, she had an uneasy suspicion that she hadn't truly escaped.

It was more like he'd decided to let her go. For now.

Chapter Five

HERE WAS all Sam wanted by the time she got home to her cozy two-bedroom cottage (conveniently located directly behind Ruth's House Indiana): lots of love from her dog, who she could already hear on the other side of the door, panting in excitement over Sam's arrival. She'd let the sweet girl get in a few licks before she settled down with the next two things on her list: a HUGE glass of wine and an old episode of *Veronica Mars*.

She'd recently splurged, downloading all three seasons to the Apple TV device Josie bought her for Christmas, and she'd been enjoying re-watching her favorite television show from back in the day—this time without any commercial interruptions. Maybe tonight she'd watch the one where Veronica kisses the good guy cop (who eventually went on to play Schmidt in New Girl) at the school dance after taking down members of the Russian mafia.

Sam thought of Marco, the real life good guy cop she was sort of, kind of, maybe seeing a little bit. He'd also kissed her. A few days ago on the their third takeout date after work. And it had been nice. Really nice. It hadn't set her on fire like the kiss with Mount Nik, but in all fairness, she'd been wearing her jacket and distracted by the prospect of having to get up early to lead a Mindfulness Class at Ruth's House.

She put her key into the lock. Yeah, that episode of *Veronica Mars* would help her put what happened with that super intense Russian hockey player in perspective.

But just as she was about to turn the lock, her phone went off, the screen lighting up with a 3-1-7 number.

"Hello?" she said tentatively, thinking the Russian might have tracked her down somehow, despite not knowing her name.

"Sam from the party, is that you?"

It was a child's voice. A boy's voice. The one she'd met earlier. And he sounded scared.

"Hi!" she said, trying to hide her alarm. "Is everything okay?"

"No!" he answered. "Some bad men are here. Knocking on the door. Telling Papa to let them in."

Sam's heart went tight with fear for the boy. "And is he…?"

"No, he's yelling for them to go away! But I don't think they're going away. They're yelling about some money for drugs. I think he was supposed to sell them but he used them instead. They are Russian, like us."

She hadn't known the little boy was Russian. Just like Nikolai Rustanov, she thought to herself. But he'd claimed not to know any children when she'd asked him about it. Had he been lying or was this a case of coincidence? Like how all black people didn't know each other, and neither did all Russians?

It didn't matter, Sam decided. There was a way bigger matter at hand.

"Okay, listen to me carefully…" She paused realizing she still didn't know his name, even though he knew hers.

"Pavel," he supplied on the other side of the line. "My name's Pavel."

Wow, he hadn't been kidding about the Russian stuff.

"Okay, Pavel, I need you to go somewhere and hide. Somewhere good, not under a bed or in a closet. Like in a cabinet if there's one you can fit into. Stay there until I come for you."

There came the sound of a lot of shuffling, and then Pavel whispered, "Okay, I'm hiding."

"Good, good, Pavel," she said, allowing herself a little breath of relief. "Now just give me your address and I'll get there as quickly as I can."

"Just you. No police!" Pavel said. "Papa will be very angry if you bring police."

"Fine, no police," Sam lied, knowing full well she was going to be calling Marco as soon as she got off the phone. But she didn't want Pavel to freak out about the possibility of police coming to his home, especially before he let her know where he was.

"Pavel, I need your address. I can't help you if I don't have it."

Silence, and in the background she heard the muffled sounds of a door crashing open and angry voices, speaking in a hard language she guessed to be Russian.

"They're here," Pavel whispered. "They're inside."

SAM KNEW IT WOULD BE BAD EVEN BEFORE SHE DECIDED TO GO in on her own. The house she was now parked in front of looked even more neglected than Pavel, with peeling paint and boarded up windows, all telling Sam that the little boy's current residence might not exactly be "on the books," with a proper lease agreement and all that. It also explained why Pavel didn't seem to have much access to water for a bath or a shower. No, Citizens Energy Group wasn't running water through this place for sure.

A shiver of fear ran down her back as she took in the dilapidated building. A home invasion had obviously taken place. The door at the top of the cracked, grey cement steps was standing halfway open, despite the fact that it was deeply cold outside and the house wasn't in one of Indiana's best neighborhoods. She should know... it was just a few blocks from Ruth's House, and she'd purposefully chosen the downtown Indianapolis location for its proximity to both upper and lower class neighborhoods. This one definitely qualified as the latter.

Sam got out of her car anyway. She couldn't just not go in. Poor Pavel was in there somewhere and Marco still hadn't returned any of the messages she'd left him on the way over, even though this was technically one of the neighborhoods he was supposed to be serving. She'd also put in a call to the local police department, but they hadn't seemed all that excited about the prospect of coming out to one of Indianapolis' worst neighborhoods based on a phone call she'd gotten from a kid she'd just met at a party.

No, she had to go in there herself. But Sam wasn't a complete idiot. She wouldn't go in without Back Up.

She came around the car to the sidewalk and whistled, "Hey, Back Up! Come with me, girl!"

Her dark, grey Staffordshire Bull Terrier immediately leapt through the open passenger window of Sam's Prius. She bent down to scratch behind her ears. "Good girl," she said. "But try to look a little more menacing, okay?"

Back Up just smiled up her, tongue lolling out, not realizing she was giving Sam the exact opposite of what she'd asked for. Thanks to a lot of misinformation and idiot breeders, rescue dogs that looked like Back Up had a bad reputation as far as the media and the general populace was concerned. But after being impregnated several times as an incubator dog for a dog fighting ring, then left out on the street still bleeding from her last pregnancy—thank God a rescue org had found her—Back

Up now seemed way more interested in meeting new friends she could lick than tearing anyone limb from limb. If she had any blood thirst in her whatsoever, she was doing a good job of hiding it behind a perma-grin and an eager-to-please attitude.

But with her wide, square face, she looked mean enough from far away which meant she got the intimidation job done in a pinch. Sam led her to the house's front door, hoping if anyone was inside, they'd run as soon as they saw Back Up.

"Hello? Is anybody home?" she said as she came through the door. "This is Sam McKinley from the Indiana Police Department and I have a very dangerous, completely rabid dog with me—"

Sam stopped short. There was a blue-eyed white man with blond hair and a long-sleeved Indiana Polar t-shirt, sitting on the couch—no, strike that—there was a body sitting on the couch in an Indiana Polar t-shirt. Slightly slumped over to the side with a hole in its head.

Bad teeth, crazy hair, hollow eyes. Meth was written all over the scene. An addict and possibly a dealer, judging from the professional holes in his body. There were two of them, she realized upon closer inspection, one in his head and one in his chest, right above the image of a mean-looking polar bear with a hockey stick.

A rap lyric about never getting high on your own supply floated through Sam's head, even as her stomach flipped over on itself.

She might have stayed there, rooted to the spot in horror, if Back Up hadn't chosen that moment to rush past her, nose down, probably searching the house for any incriminating food she might get into. She did have her priorities.

And Sam was grateful for the distraction as she turned her face from the scene, wishing like heck she could just run out of there like any sane person would upon getting hit with the sight of a dead body. This scene was triggering all sorts of bad memories for her. But she'd told Pavel she would come for him. Sam shook off a major case of the willies. Pavel had sounded so scared on the phone. She couldn't let him down.

But where was he?

As if in answer, a whimpering sound came from the kitchen. Sam could see Back Up sniffing around a set of cabinets, below what would have been the kitchen sink before someone pulled it out completely. But the cabinets still remained, and Back Up had obviously caught the scent of something... or someone.

Someone small enough to fit inside a cabinet.

Sam knew she wouldn't be able to keep her composure if Pavel was dead, his small body stuffed inside the cabinet underneath the sink, but she headed towards where Back Up was sniffing anyway.

She took a deep breath and bent down to open the cabinet door... then let out a huge sigh of relief when she found Pavel inside, staring at her wide eyed, a burner phone clutched tightly in his small hands.

"Pavel! Thank God!"

This time when she reached for him, Pavel seemed more than eager to come to her. But then Back Up ruined the moment by charging straight at the little boy, her mouth open wide.

Pavel shrank back into the confines of the cabinet, his eyes squeezing shut with fear. "Don't let it eat me!"

"Sit, girl," Sam commanded, pointing to a spot behind her.

Back Up whimpered piteously, but did as commanded.

"Good girl," Sam told her, before turning back to Pavel. "Sorry about that. I love her, but she's never met a person she didn't want to lick. I'm always like, 'Calm down, girl, let a person get to know you first!'"

Pavel peeped over Sam's shoulder, suspicion in his eyes,

which she could now see were blue, like those of the man on the couch. Clearly it was his mother who was black.

"She just wants to lick me? Not eat me?" Pavel asked.

Sam let out a wry chuckle, despite the situation.

"No, she would never eat anybody. She looks mean—that's why I take her places with me, but the truth is she's as gentle as they come."

Back Up started in with a series of high-pitched whines, so loud, Sam had to look over her shoulder and admonish, "Back Up, he doesn't want to get licked. Not everybody's into that, okay?"

Back Up once again whimpered, hanging her head in such a dejected fashion, one would think Sam had just kicked her.

Sam turned away from her dog back to the boy. "So is it just you here? Is your mother out?"

Pavel shook his head solemnly. "No, she's dead. We all used to live together, and we were happy for a little bit. But she started using again, so Papa did, too. But she died a year ago."

Sam stared at him in mute horror. So young and now he'd lost both his parents.

Pavel blinked, and peered over her shoulder at Sam's now sullen bullie. "That's a strange name, Back Up."

"Actually it's kind of a joke from this TV show about a high school detective called Veronica Mars... ever seen it?"

Pavel shook his head.

"Yeah, it's probably a little above your viewing level. How old are you again?"

"Eight," Pavel whispered.

Another pang of regret on his behalf went through Sam. Two addict parents, and now he didn't have any family left.

"Yeah, eight's too young. Maybe when you're thirteen." Sam broke off and looked around like she was just now noticing they were in a house with the body of his last remaining parent dead on a sofa in the other room. "So it looks like some bad stuff went down with your dad before we got here."

The little boy clamped his lips together and nodded.

"The other Russians came through the door. They were yelling really loud, but I kept on hiding like you told me, even after I heard some loud popping sounds." His eyes filled up with tears. "They were gunshots, weren't they? Like on TV? Papa... he's dead, isn't he?"

Sam had to fight off her own tears, her heart was hurting so bad for Pavel. Memories of her own mother's body lying lifeless on the floor flooded her mind and it took her a few tries before she could say, "I'm really sorry about what happened to your papa." Then she said, "Looks like he was an Indiana Polar fan, too."

The boy nodded. "Papa says I'm going to be a great hockey player when I grow up. It's in our blood."

"No way! That's so cool!" Sam replied, even though she didn't know all that much about hockey beyond the pushy player she'd met at tonight's party and one viewing of *The Mighty Ducks* when she was around Pavel's age. "Maybe we should get out of here and go somewhere we can talk some more about hockey."

He peeped over her shoulder again. "The bad guys aren't out there any more?"

"Nope," Sam answered. *At least not for now.* But Sam continued to keep it casual, like she wasn't afraid for both his life and her own. "I'm starving. Are you hungry? We should go get something to eat."

It must have been a while since Pavel had last eaten, because he rubbed his stomach at the suggestion, even though his expression remained wary.

"You want me to come out?" he asked.

"Yes, I really want you to come out," she answered. "My knees are starting to hurt a little in this squat and all I had to eat for dinner were party appetizers. I could really use a good meal."

Pavel frowned, seeming to mull Sam's invitation over. Then he said, "If she really wants to lick me, I guess she can."

It took a moment for Sam to realize they were now talking about Back Up. Though really, she sensed, it was more about Pavel wanting to make sure Sam could be trusted. He was testing what she told him, to make sure she wasn't a liar. He wanted her to prove Back Up didn't intend to do him any harm.

Thankfully, unlike her story about starving when she'd actually wolfed down a sandwich on the way to the Hockey Ices Cancer event, this claim was true. She reached out behind her and motioned to Back Up. "Here girl, Pavel wants to meet you."

Back Up didn't need to be told twice. She jogged right on over and pushed her square nose into Pavel, slobbering the dirt off the boy's face with such enthusiasm that he started to giggle.

"Calm down, Back Up," Sam told the dog, tugging on her collar and pulling her back. "Don't overwhelm him with the love!"

But Pavel didn't seem to mind at all. He crawled out of the cabinet and hugged Back Up around the neck in the way of a child who loved dogs but didn't have one. He petted her large head and got several more face licks as a thank you.

Sam watched him interact with Back Up, her heart continuing to break for the traumatized child who actually looked like a carefree little boy when he was with her dog.

Pavel looked up at her and said, "Can I hold her leash when we leave here?"

Normally Sam would have said no. Back Up was a lot of dog to handle, even for a full grown adult like herself. But in this case...

"Sure, sweetie, just hold it right here," she said, placing Pavel on her left side, squeezed between her and Back Up. She placed his smaller hand in the middle of the leash and took the upper part for herself in her left hand. Then she began to walk them out of the apartment, using her body to block the sight of the boy's father as they walked by the couch.

Pavel didn't have to be told not to look. He kept his eyes on Back Up, stroking her short fur as they walked out of the house, leaving the body of his dead father behind.

Chapter Six

"WHAT'S this I hear about you taking custody of a kid in some dead meth head case?" Marco demanded two days later when she opened the door to her cottage.

Sam looked over her shoulder at Pavel who was on the couch, with Back Up's large head in his lap, watching an episode of *Peg + Cat* on her small flat screen.

She was officially his guardian now and it looked like someone had finally gotten around to telling Marco Gutierrez, the cop who'd been flirting with her since she'd opened Ruth's House Indiana which happened to be located right on his beat.

Kismet, he'd said when they'd had their first takeout date a couple of Saturdays ago. He often had to work weird hours for his beat, and she often did the same for Ruth's House. They were kind of a no-brainer, he'd told her with an endearing smile. He also had dimples. Just like her. Just like the good cop from *Veronica Mars*.

But he didn't look all that happy with her right now, and there was no trace of dimple action to be seen on his face.

Sam winced and stepped outside to talk to him.

"Please keep your voice down," she said as she closed the door behind her.

"Why the hell did you bring the kid home with you? And why am I just now hearing about this from the station social worker and not from you?"

"Marco, don't get mad," she said. "But yeah, I've signed on as his guardian until further notice."

"This isn't a shelter case," Marco pointed out. "The social worker said there was maybe some neglect but no domestic violence."

"I know that," she said. "But I've decided to help him as much as I can."

"What, by teaching him to meditate and do yoga whenever he's feeling sad about his addict dad getting shot?" Marco asked, his voice incredulous.

Sam decided not to take that question personally. She'd read all the research on how much a good mindfulness practice and yoga could help traumatized kids, but she was well-aware it might sound like a bunch of woo-woo nonsense to people who didn't spend a lot of their spare time looking for ways to further help women and kids coming out of bad situations.

She was also aware how Marco felt about drug dealers of any kind. He'd been nothing but kind to the women he'd referred to Ruth's House, but if any of them had a boyfriend or husband into the bad stuff, he'd come down hard as an anvil, especially if they came by the shelter making threats.

"I get why this would look crazy to you," she told him. "But Pavel needs a stable home and counseling and, yeah, a good mindfulness practice wouldn't hurt the situation at all. And I can give him all of that."

"Do you know how many kids need that and don't get it every year?" He frowned, worry creasing his boyishly handsome face. "Look I know you have a thing for rescue situations.

The fact that you have the world's dumbest pit bull tells me that."

"Hey! Back Up is a Staffordshire Bull Terrier," she corrected. "And she isn't dumb."

"She jumped up on me and literally tried to eat my gun the last time I was here," Marco reminded her. "She's either dumb or suicidal."

He rushed on before Sam could argue with him further. "The point is this kid is not Back Up, or even a victim of domestic abuse. He's eight years old, and he was in a cabinet the whole time his dad was getting snuffed." Marco shook his head. "Look, I don't want to be mean here, but I've got to at least try to talk you out of this. Witsec's already taken a pass. You should, too."

Sam shook her own head, knowing exactly where Marco was going with this. The same place the other police officers at his station had when she'd decided to use her social worker's license in order to assume custody of Pavel until further notice.

"There's nothing to be talked out of," she told Marco, just like she'd told those officers. She considered Marco a friend with potential to become more than that, but right about now, she was finding it hard not to get frustrated with him.

"Pavel's scared out of his mind and for good reason. He won't leave Back Up's side. He would have slept in her dog bed if I hadn't let them both bunk down with me."

"Even more reason why we should get Child Protective Services involved. Let them handle it."

Sam shook her head. "I don't want him handled. I want him taken care of."

"Yeah, but…" Marco reached out to take her hand. "Why's it got to be you?"

Sam froze. The answer to that was so complicated. Marco was a nice guy and she'd welcomed his interest in her. Working as many hours as she did, it wasn't like she met a ton of guys just dying to start a relationship with someone whose biggest dream was to open "a different kind of domestic abuse shelter" in all fifty states.

Nevertheless, there were parts of her past he wasn't privy to, parts that made it impossible for her to abandon Pavel when he needed not just anyone, but someone who absolutely understood what he was going through.

"So what are you suggesting?" Sam asked, taking her hand back from him. "That I further traumatize him by passing him off to strangers?"

Marco opened his mouth to answer just as a knock sounded on the other side of the door.

"Hold on a minute," Marco called out.

"Come on out, Pavel," she said at the same time.

The door opened and Pavel stuck his head outside. She could hear Back Up panting behind him and smiled because the dog had stuck to Pavel's side for the last few days, as if sensing the little boy needed her.

"Hi, Pavel," Sam said with a bright smile.

"Hey, little man. What's up? Settling in okay?" Marco asked with a dimpled smile of his own. Usually Sam liked how well the officer got along with children and the rest of the women at her shelter, effortlessly putting everyone he met at ease with his outgoing and affable nature. But in this case, it struck Sam as a little fake, considering he'd just been trying to convince her to pass him off to Indiana's Department of Child Services.

Pavel, who might have heard more than she would have wished, didn't even spare him a look.

"Tonight is Mount Nik's last game. May I watch it?" he asked politely, without any acknowledgment of Marco whatsoever.

"Sure, feel free to change it," Sam answered. "I've got

some paperwork I can finish up while you do that, then it's time for bed."

"I'm a big Indiana Polar fan myself," Marco told the kid. "And I'm off duty now." He smiled at Sam. "You got any beer? Maybe I could come in and watch."

"Ah…" Sam said.

"Mama, I'd like to watch it alone if you don't mind," Pavel said in the doorway.

Pavel, Sam had discovered over the last forty-eight hours, was actually a very polite little boy. At least to her. Everybody else was a different story, and he seemed even less enthusiastic to watch the game with Marco than she was to invite him in after his Child Services pitch.

"That's okay," Marco said, throwing Sam a puzzled look. "I've got some buddies I can watch it with at the bar. Go Polar!"

Pavel just disappeared back inside, shutting the door behind him.

Apparently he did not feel any solidarity with Marco whatsoever just because he was also a Polar fan.

"Wow," Marco said, running a hand over his spiky black hair.

"He's adjusting," Sam said. "And he probably didn't get much social training growing up the way he did."

"Yeah, but… Did I hear him call you Mama? You said you just met this kid, what? Forty-eight hours ago?"

Sam cringed. She'd been hoping he wouldn't ask her about that. Pavel had been calling her "mama" ever since they'd arrived at her apartment two nights ago, almost as if they'd formally agreed to the title change on the car ride over from the police station.

"He's not your kid," Marco told her now.

"I know that," she answered, even as her heart kicked up a

mutinous rebellion, pumping harder, as if to say, *That's a lie! Pavel is my son and I'm his mother. Obviously it was meant to be!*

But she brutally suppressed those thoughts and repeated, "I know, obviously he's not my son. This is just a temporary arrangement."

"Then why is he calling you mama? You've made enough calls in these domestic abuse situations to know the deal. You're not supposed to get too involved here. You pass these kids along to the foster system and that's supposed to be the end of it."

"I know that, too."

"Is it because the shelter's empty right now? Maybe you're feeling like you need a project, and that's why you took the kid into your custody?"

"No," Sam answered. Though she had to admit she'd been bored lately. The number of domestic abuse cases coming through Ruth's House had severely dipped after the Super Bowl, but March Madness was right around the corner and the NBA playoffs after that. Sadly, the one thing Sam could guarantee was that the shelter wouldn't be empty come spring.

"No, that's not it," she assured Marco. "I've got plenty of paperwork and grant applications to keep me busy."

"Then why are we having this conversation? Why won't you let me put this kid in the back of my car and take him over to DCS?"

Sam couldn't answer that without coming off as even more insane than Marco probably already suspected. She knew it wasn't wise or healthy to let Pavel call her mama, but she couldn't shake the feeling he was doing so because she needed to step up and be his mother now. At least until an appropriate one could be found for him.

Sam chewed on her lip. "Okay, fine, I'll sign off on Pavel leaving my custody as soon as you find a set of suitable parents and give me at least two weeks to thoroughly vet them with supervised visits." She put a friendly hand to his back and started escorting him to his car, which she could see parked right next to the shelter in one of the intake spaces for Ruth's House. "You have my word."

"Fine, I'll get going. But don't think I don't know what you're doing, Sam."

"Of course you know what I'm doing," Sam answered, coming to a stop beside his car. "I'm doing what's in Pavel's best interest."

Marco folded his arms. "Let me finish, Sam. I know what you're doing, but I'm not going to force the issue because you're sort of right." He rubbed a hand over the back of his neck. "The kid's been through a lot, so I'm going to call in some favors and see if we can't find some parents who meet your criteria. Until then, I guess this is as good a place as any for him. At least Ruth's House is secure." He threw a disparaging look toward the slender windows on either side of her door. "If you don't count those break-in windows on your cottage. I'll come by this weekend and maybe see about boarding them up—just until we get a bead on whoever killed the kid's father."

Her heart warmed at his words and many of the bad feelings she'd been having about him began to evaporate.

"Thanks, Marco," she said. "Thanks for your understanding."

He unfolded his arms and came closer in a move that brought to mind the hockey player who had kissed her two days ago.

"So I'm doing you a solid…" He flashed his dimpled smile. "Maybe you should reward me with a kiss?"

Unease crawled its way up Sam's back, and she had no idea why. Marco was a good guy. A good, solid guy who didn't send emissaries with balcony invites, who'd never hit her with a lewd double entendre, or even try to steal a kiss from a woman he'd just met.

Sure, he could stand to be more open-minded about the alternative healing therapies she was using at Ruth's House, and sure she didn't love that he was acting like he deserved a gold star for agreeing to let her show a little boy some compassion—

Sam stopped herself with an inner ugh of disgust. Why did she always have to psychoanalyze the guys who showed any interest in her? That was probably why she was still single at the age of thirty-four. Single and childless. Two things she needed to focus on correcting sooner rather than later, if she ever wanted her dreams of finally being a part of a loving family to come true.

She pasted a smile on and said, "One kiss coming right up."

Standing on her tiptoes, she pressed her lips to his.

The kiss was… nice. Really nice. Just like Marco.

He grinned at her when it was finished, "I'm gonna get started on finding some great parents for Pavel first thing tomorrow morning."

She grinned back and waved as he got in the car.

Marco was a terrific guy, she thought as she watched him ease around the shelter's corner and drive away. A really terrific guy.

So why had she been thinking of the Russian hockey player the entire time she'd been kissing him?

Chapter Seven

"MOUNT, WAIT, WAIT! DON'T–"

But it was too late, Brian Atwood's back hit the plexiglas wall so hard, it rattled the entire structure surrounding the ice at the Polar training facility. Introduction courtesy of Nikolai "Mount Nik" Rustanov.

"What were saying about wanting special treatment?"

Brian panted, trying to catch his breath after that hit. "We went pretty hard at your last game party last night. I was just making a suggestion…"

"You suggest we end practice early so you can sleep away your bad decisions. You think easier to ask permission for naptime now I am owner?"

"C'mon Mount, man, that's not nearly what I was trying to say," Brian said, looking both hurt and offended by Nikolai's assessment of the situation. "I'm just saying—"

Nikolai slammed the blond player into the wall again, wishing that the hockey uniforms weren't so well padded. But from the grimace on their star left winger's face, he needn't have worried. He'd most certainly felt that.

"All right, all right, I get it," Brian said through the pain. "We're not leaving early."

"No, we are not," Nikolai agreed. "In fact, we will stay extra twenty minutes because you wasted our time with your request." He all but spat out the last word before letting the entitled hockey player go with one last shove into the plexiglas.

Behind him, Gary Burton, the Indiana Polar's head coach, blew his whistle. "All right, line em up right over here. Side-to-side drills, starting now!"

Brian edged out from between Nikolai and the plexiglas, but Nikolai's dark, hooded glare followed him all the way back to the drill line-up. He hadn't been a fan of the diva hockey player with the long blond hair before he'd bought the team. And he was even less of a fan now.

He skated back over to the bleacher side of the rink, where his cousin was standing with a hot coffee.

"Maybe we trade him before playoffs."

Alexei answered with a low laugh. "You don't think Atwood got your point about not letting his fame interfere with his obligations?" His English words came out so smooth, one might not have known he'd been born and raised in Russia. Thanks to his business background, unlike Nikolai, Alexei had managed to mostly lose the accent of his youth.

"I don't like having to make the point," Nikolai answered in Russian.

"Be grateful," Alexei answered, easily flipping back to Russian, too. "He is the reason you own the team now at such a low price."

True. Part of the reason Nikolai had been able to buy ownership of the team so easily was because the last owner had blown much of the team's operating funds to sign Atwood to a seven-figure deal. That had been six months ago, and just four months before he'd been forced to formally declare bankruptcy when the new addition didn't bring in as many new fans as he'd planned. With a sizeable investment from his billionaire cousin, Nikolai had been able to snatch up the team in a sweetheart deal.

Now Nikolai was looking forward to leading the Polar into the future with a much firmer hand. But the acquisition of the team had come at great cost to his career.

"Are you angry at him or angry because he gets to play the game you no longer can?" Alexei asked behind the short rink wall.

Technically, you couldn't both play and hold a majority stake in a team, especially if you didn't want to cede your vote to someone else within your organization. He had a vision for the team, and not being able to speak or vote at NHL meetings wasn't part of that vision. So sadly, the night before had been his last game with the Indianapolis Polar.

"I am grateful for your support, cousin. Having control of this team is my dream," he told Alexei. Then he grumbled, "Not so much the paperwork."

Now Alexei really laughed. "The only cure for paperwork is family. When I come home from the office and see my Eva, my Aaron, and my little Layla, all the bad parts of business go away. Think about settling down, Nikolai. It is best thing a business man can do for himself."

"We are from the same place, but my family was not like your family," Nikolai answered. "I do not have a wish for a wife or children."

He thought about how Fedya had looked in his study. Wild eyes and obviously strung out. Like the worst stereotype of every junkie he'd ever seen on American television—but with a Russian accent.

"I see how children can become," he said.

Alexei's good cheer dimmed. "Yes, it was hard to see Fedya like that…"

Both Nikolai and his older brother, Fedya, had started out

as star players for the Indiana Polar after getting drafted as a pair from their Russian team. But whereas Nikolai had flourished, going on to win two Stanley Cups as a defenseman in the golden days of his adopted team, his brother, their original star left winger, had not been immune to the temptations America offered up to a previously cloistered athlete.

He'd quickly fallen to the vices of drugs and alcohol and within two seasons, his star, which had burned even brighter than Nikolai's, had been diminished. Eventually he'd been kicked off the Polar for missing too many practices. And in recent years, he'd sunk to a place so low, Nikolai had been forced to cut him off.

He thought back to Saturday when his formerly large brother had shown up on his doorstep, emaciated and in possession of only half his teeth, claiming to need money. Badly.

"Some Russians hired me to sell their product because their boss heard a lot about your father back when he was in Russia. I pretended Sergei was my father, too—least the dead fuck could do is give me his name for business purposes," he told Nikolai in Russian, scratching at his arm. "They gave me product to sell, and I came up with a plan—a good plan. Cut product down, sell even more, turn better profit."

Fedya acted liked this was the most inspired plan a drug dealer had ever come up with. And he actually seemed proud of himself when he said, "I sold all of it, just like I promised, and I gave money to Russian Boss. But afterwards, people started complaining about the product, and now the Russian Boss is demanding I pay him more, even though I already paid him. I wouldn't give in to his demand, but he thinks he is like your father. He might try to make example of me if I don't give him money."

A typical Fedya sob story. Bad idea explodes into a total shit storm, which his brother somehow managed to take no responsibility whatsoever for. It happened this way every single time.

Nikolai had given his brother a look colder than the Indiana winter raging outside the study's windows.

"You dare come to my home, high on drugs, asking for more money after I've already wasted so much money on you in past? No. I will tell you like I did last time you came to me. From now on, I will only give you money for rehab."

Fedya went from plaintive to petulant in an instant, Nikolai and Alexei just watched as Fedya threw a full-fledged temper tantrum. Kicking at Nikolai's desk like an oversized man-child as he accused Nikolai of being a terrible brother, and Alexei of looking down on him because, unlike Nikolai, Fedya wasn't a Rustanov. Then he had burst into tears.

Years ago, before Nikolai had learned to harden his heart where Fedya was concerned, seeing his brother unravel like this might have been enough to move him to open his wallet wide. The sight of his brother brought so low used to rip at his heart, move him to do anything to get his brother, who used to be a person Nikolai admired, to stop crying.

But Fedya had taught him a lesson about helping those who didn't truly want to be helped. Every single dollar he'd given his brother over the years had been wasted on more drugs. He'd gotten kicked out of any decent apartment Nikolai had arranged for him and either totaled the cars Nikolai had gifted him or sold them off for more drugs.

"You have five minutes to finish your crying," Nikolai told his brother. "Then security will escort you out. Do not come here again."

More cursing. This time in both English and Russian.

That was when Nikolai had gotten the text from Isaac saying the woman in the green dress had been detained at the porte-cochère valet station, right outside the front door. As good a reason as any to end the conversation with his brother.

Nikolai had headed toward the valet station with his heart full of ice, but his body was burning hot with need. He wanted to lose himself inside someone, and he'd already decided it would be her. Not the vapid fan she'd tried to pass him off to. Her.

But he'd only gotten one kiss. A kiss so unexpectedly earth shattering, he was still thinking about it three days later.

"Have you been able to find her?"

"Who?" Nikolai asked, even though he knew exactly who his cousin was talking about.

"The woman in the green dress," Alexei answered in English, his eyes highly amused.

"Your visit for my last game has been very nice, but you are eager to get back to your family, yes? When will you go to your plane?" Nikolai asked in Russian.

Alexei just smirked, and continued to speak in English. "The car won't be here for another five minutes. Until then you can answer my questions about this woman. I assume you still have not found her."

"No," Nikolai, answered, making a terse switch back to English. "Isaac is still checking. But nothing so far. We think she gave fake name to guard at gate."

"Hunh," Alexei said with a thoughtful raise of his eyebrows. "It sounds like you have a mystery woman on your hands. It must be killing you, cousin. She was very attractive, and I know you do not like loose ends."

This was true. Nikolai wasn't one to let challenges go unanswered, whether it be from an opposing team's player or their team's former spendthrift owner. And though getting turned down by a strange woman who maybe was or wasn't supposed to be at his party shouldn't have qualified as a thing that disturbed him, he'd found himself visited a few times over the past few days by mental images of him "eating her for breakfast." An idea she'd unintentionally put in his head. Even now, his body stirred in response to the mere thought of having her in this way, the flesh between his legs tightening as he imagined his tongue inside of her, her hands in his hair as she submitted to his mouth. He could almost taste her, hear her moaning cries as she came for him—

"Mr. Rustanov! Mr. Rustanov!"

Isaac's voice shattered the erotic vision. Both he and his cousin turned to see his assistant running around the edge of the rink wall toward them.

"Sorry," he said to Alexei, when he reached them. "I meant Nikolai."

"*Da*, what is it, Isaac?" Nikolai asked, not knowing whether to be irritated or grateful that the smaller man had snapped him out of his waking dream.

"Maybe it would be better if we talked privately?" Isaac suggested with a glance towards Alexei.

Nikolai shook his head. "Whatever you say to me, you can say in front of Alexei."

"Okay," Isaac said. Yet he still lowered his voice to whisper level when he let Nikolai know, "Indy PD is on the line. They say it's about your brother."

Isaac held the phone out to him.

And Nikolai sighed. "Tell the Indiana police department you will come down to the station after our practice is finished to bail him out. Whatever the trouble is that he has brought upon himself this time, he can wait until then."

Isaac nodded in agreement. "Yes, I offered to take care of whatever assistance your brother needed, but they're insisting on talking to you."

Nikolai's brow knitted. This was highly unusual. Back when Isaac had first come to work for him as his personal assistant, before Nikolai had cut Fedya off, Indy PD hadn't had any problem letting his assistant handle his brother's bail and the subsequent charges—the least egregious of which were dropped in deference to a generous on-the-spot donation from Nikolai to the policeman's ball.

Isaac gave him an apologetic grimace. "They say it's important."

He took the phone from Isaac with a frown. "*Da*, this is Nikolai Rustanov."

Chapter Eight

YEARS LATER, Nikolai could still remember the call as clearly as if it had happened yesterday. It came in the early hours of the morning, startling him from a deep sleep.

"I am sorry to wake you," his cousin had said in careful Russian. "But I must throw a party for your father."

Code for kill. His cousin had given him a courtesy call to tell him he planned to have Sergei executed. Later he would find out the very good reason Alexei decided to do this, but at the time, it wouldn't have been wise to ask over an insecure line.

"I understand," he'd said, not really needing to know the reasons why.

"I have a man ready to host a party for Uncle Sergei, but our way is to let the son host, so I am calling you…"

One of the stranger Rustanov traditions. Every once in a while it became necessary to kill a member of your own family. But in a morbid bid to honor, the option of killing the family member was always given to the killee's son.

Sergei had described this time-honored tradition to Nikolai with pride.

"If it ever happens to me, I want you to do it," he'd told his only son. *"I am Rustanov until end."*

The tradition and the conversation about it had been incredibly surreal and Nikolai had quickly put it out of his head. Especially after Alexei made the Rustanov family a legitimate business. Yet here was his cousin now, putting out a hit on his uncle, Nikolai's father.

Sergei would still want his son to do the deed, Nikolai knew. To fly all the way to Russia to put a bullet in his own father's head. Sergei would actually consider that an honorable way to go.

So, of course, Nikolai had said, "Thank you, but I do not wish to host this party. I trust your man to do a good job."

And the next time Nikolai had seen Sergei, he'd been dead on a slab. Just like Fedya was lying dead in front him right now, his face a bluish gray, with a bullet wound between his open eyes.

"If anything ever happens to me. If your father ever does as he threatens, you must take care of your brother. He is weak. Not strong like you. You are your father's son, and he is his. You must protect him. Take care of him."

His mother's words rang in his ears as he stared into his brother's lifeless eyes.

"That him?" a voice asked from somewhere behind him. Probably the detective who'd escorted him in.

Nikolai nodded, unable to look away from his dead brother's face.

"Sorry, but we need a spoken yes. You gotta say it out loud. Sorry, Mount Nik," the voice said.

A hockey fan, Nikolai noted with a grim disinterest. During his decade plus in Indiana, he'd found that fans of America's fourth favorite professional sport were everywhere. If Fedya were alive, he would have been thrilled at the recognition. During the years when he and Nikolai had still been talking,

Fedya had often taken in Nikolai the pride he couldn't take for himself.

"You showed your father good," he once said to Nikolai. *"You escaped. You did not let him ruin you like he ruined our mother. Like he ruined me."*

On the table, Fedya's body morphed into a slightly shorter and more muscular one, grey of hair, but still radiating danger even in his death. The body was now Sergei's, lying on the same kind of slab as Fedya, but in a Russian coroner's office. Also, unlike Fedya, his father had been killed in the old way, the one named after the Rustanovs and popularized by Sergei himself. One last show of respect from Alexei who'd ordered the hit, but could not get Sergei's son to make it honorable.

It had taken Nikolai three days to get to Russia and deal with the body, just as it had taken three days for the police to track him down. As it turned out, Fedya had moved since the last time Isaac had bailed him out of jail, and "hockey star brother" wasn't the kind of note kept in the non-existent file of a criminal who had been arrested several times but had never garnered an official record, thanks to Nikolai's connections. If one of the police officers in the precinct hadn't been a hockey fan and put two and two together after an internet search, they might never have made the connection, since he and Fedya had different last names.

But there had been no denying it when the white sheet had been pulled from Fedya's head. And now, as the body on the slab morphed back into his brother, he confirmed it out loud.

"Yes, that's him," he said, his voice grim.

"If you want more time to say your goodbyes, we can give you that."

"No, that is not necessary," Nikolai answered, placing another layer of ice over his heart. He'd said his goodbye to Fedya a long time ago when he cut him off. He known then that there was no way his brother would live past his forties. Known and forced himself to accept the inevitable bad end.

Nikolai took charge of the situation, turning to face the officers. "Tomorrow my assistant will come here, handle body. Is there anything else or can I go now?"

"We'll get the paperwork together for you upstairs," the older detective who'd brought him in answered. His face was creased with weary lines that spoke to how often he'd watch this same scenario unfold. "Now that you've given us a positive ID, we should probably ask you a few questions, seeing as how foul play was obviously involved. And there's also the matter of your nephew…"

Nikolai went thunderously still. "*My what?*" he asked.

~

His nephew. He had a nephew.

Nikolai was still having trouble believing what he'd been told, even as the police officer whose desk he was currently sitting at wrote down an address for him.

"Normally, I wouldn't do this," the officer, who's desk plate read "Marco J. Gutierrez", said. "But I'm a big fan. Plus, I want to see you reunited with your nephew. You know, it was me who connected the dots. Since he's half black, nobody was putting it together, even though he's got a Russian name. But he was over at my girl's house watching hockey and I remembered reading something about you having a half brother who used to play hockey, too. Did an internet search the next day and put it all together. Lucky break, huh?"

Lucky indeed, though Nikolai still wasn't clear on a few things. "Why is my nephew in custody of your girl? She is not his relation. I am."

"Yeah, try telling her that," Marco answered with a wry half-smile. "That's why I'm giving you her address, so you can go over there. You should have seen the hoops she wanted me to jump through just to find him a foster home. My girl is sweet —real cute, too, but she can be like a rabid dog when it comes to the women and kids she takes in. And she's taken a real shining to your nephew. The truth is, she might take some convincing before she hands him over to you."

The prospect of having to convince some police officer's girlfriend to give him the custody that should be his by familial right didn't sit well with Nikolai. Not well at all.

Marco mistook his frown of irritation as one of worry.

"Maybe lay on the uncle stuff real thick. Make sure she knows you had no idea this kid was in the picture, or you would have helped out."

"I would have done more than 'helped out,'" Nikolai informed the police officer.

According to the police reports, the child's mother had died of an overdose about two years ago—right around the same time Nikolai cut his brother off. Nikolai had no idea how close Fedya had been to the boy's mother, but obviously he'd taken over his custody without telling Nikolai. Maybe because he'd thought Nikolai would have judged him for having a bi-racial son. Sergei, like many in Russians in his generation, had been a vehement racist and maybe Fedya thought Nikolai would react badly to the prospect of a half-black nephew.

But more likely, he decided Fedya hadn't told him because he knew what would have happened if Nikolai had known his addict brother had full custody of a child. Nikolai not only would have taken the boy away from his brother, but he also would have made sure his brother didn't see the child again until he got clean. So of course Fedya decided to keep the boy's existence from him rather than risk losing his son.

But still, for a man-child like Fedya to insist on raising his son on his own? Stupid, Nikolai thought to himself. Stupid and unbelievably selfish. But of course, being stupid and unbelievably selfish was something his brother had excelled at, along with an uncanny ability to make the exact wrong decision at every one of his short life's turns.

"Here you go, man." The officer handed Nikolai a piece of paper with the name "Samantha McKinley" on it and an address. "And thanks. Not that I don't appreciate her commitment. I know it will come in handy if we end up having kids of our own. But it's kind of hard for us to spend quality time together when there's a kid in the background taking up all her attention. Know what I mean?"

No, Nikolai didn't know what he meant, and it sounded to him like the police officer's girlfriend would have more than one child on her hands, demanding all her attention, if she decided to marry him.

But Nikolai took the piece of paper, forcing himself to set his irritation aside. As bad as the situation was, it was something that could be corrected. Right now. He'd go get the boy from the policeman's girlfriend and by tonight, his nephew would be exactly where he should have been from the beginning: under Nikolai's roof.

Chapter Nine

"I CAN'T BELIEVE YOU, Marco! I can't believe you!"

"Sammy, don't be mad at me," Marco said on the other side of the line. "I'm only trying to do what's best here."

"What's best?" she repeated, her voice full of derision. "For who? Your favorite hockey player? I can only assume that's why you'd give this guy our home address."

"I gave him your home address. It's just yours. You only have temporary custody, and you're not the kid's blood," Marco answered. "Rustanov is."

"Maybe not. But I could have stalled, given Pavel the time and counseling he needed to properly process what happened to him before I sent him off with some guy who didn't even know he was alive until a few hours ago!"

"You're acting like it's his fault his druggie brother didn't tell him he had a kid. The point is now he knows, and he's trying to make it right."

"Trying to claim Pavel like a piece of luggage, you mean. And you just made it that much easier for him!"

Just thinking about how Marco had betrayed her and Pavel in favor of his hockey hero made her want to scream. But Pavel was in the front room with Back Up and she worked hard to keep her voice down so he wouldn't hear her in the back bedroom when she all but hissed, "Pavel doesn't need a hockey star who will hand him off to a nanny to raise. He needs *counseling*. He needs *guidance*. He needs *love*."

Sam thought about Nikolai Rustanov's derisive dismissal of love as a silly custom at the party and said, "He needs all the love he can get."

"Sam, I like you, I really like you, but you have got to start seeing reason here. You are one person and you said it yourself, you'll be stretched thin again as soon as the shelter fills back up. Rustanov can hire a battalion of yous to give Pavel whatever he needs. You should—"

"Don't tell me what I should and shouldn't do, Marco," Sam said through clenched teeth. "I don't care who he is, I'm not going to hand a traumatized little boy over to him just because they have some tenuous family connection. You have no idea what Pavel has been through. No idea!"

"And you do?" Marco asked, sounding both confused and skeptical.

Sam paused, then paused some more, her mind buffering, because how could she explain it to Marco? Her reasons for feeling so connected to Pavel were secret, and she hadn't told anyone but Josie.

"Yes, I do," she eventually said. "More than whatever therapist this hockey player's assistant picks out for him. So please, if you really like me, if you ever cared about me at all, call him off. Call him and tell him not to bother coming over here. Tell him that he'll have to go through Child Services if he wants custody of Pavel, just like anyone else would."

"Sammy…"

"Please, Marco. I know what I'm doing and I know what's best for Pavel right now. You've got to trust me."

"I do trust you, but in this case, I think you're being a

little… I don't know a nice way to say this—but you're being kinda crazy, Sammy. I mean, don't you want us to get back on track with dating? See where the relationship goes? All the places it could go?"

The stress he put on "all" left no doubt of his real meaning. During their last date, he'd hinted that the next order of takeout should include an overnight stay. Obviously he was fed up with waiting to take their relationship to the next level.

Sam's heart hardened with bitter disappointment. Marco might think she's cute, she realized, but apparently that was all he thought of her.

You're just a piece of ass, far as any of these boys concerned, and that's all you ever going to be to them.

Her stepfather's ugly words rang in her ears as she realized the truth about Marco. He wasn't a potential love connection. Not someone she could eventually marry and trust. At the end of the day, the only thing he cared about was getting her into bed.

"You're right, Marco. Obviously, I'm not thinking clearly," she said. "I mean, Nikolai Rustanov knows how to hit a ball with a bent stick really well, and all I am is a grown woman with two degrees who works with children in crisis on a day-to-day basis. What could I possibly know better than Nikolai Rustanov about what's best for Pavel? Thank you for interfering. I'm not sure how I ever got this far without your clearly superior expertise and advice."

"Now you're just being mean, Sammy."

"Don't call me, Sammy. In fact, don't ever call me again."

"C'mon, Sam—"

Sam hung up on him, and then threw her phone across the room in disgust. How dare he? How dare he?

She clenched and unclenched her fist, so frustrated it made her feel violent inside. She'd thought Marco was different from all the other guys who'd only stepped to her because she'd inherited her mother's good looks. But as it turned out, he was just like the rest. In it purely for the cookie. It was so obvious why Marco had suddenly decided she wasn't thinking clearly. Because she took a child into her home, one that would temporarily stall their fledgling relationship and disrupt any chance of sex happening in the near future.

But the joke was on him. There was nothing Sam despised more than disloyalty. From the well-meaning relatives who told an abusive husband where his wife was hiding to the cop who sent a hockey player straight to her front door. Nothing could have been a bigger turn off for Sam. Nothing.

There came the sound of knocking so loud, she could hear it all the way in the back of the house.

Sam let out an irritated sigh. Apparently the hockey player had arrived.

She walked to the front room, already rehearsing her speech about how he'd need to go through Child Services, just like any other adult seeking custody of a child they'd never met before. She'd need to send Pavel to wait in the second bedroom while she dealt with his uncle, and that might be a little hard considering Pavel had a bad case of hero worship where Mount Nik was concerned.

However the question of sending him away became moot when she reached the front room and found the table Pavel had been sitting at empty. He was supposed to be filling out a battery of tests so she could assess his skills and know how to properly advocate for him when she went to enroll him at the local elementary school next week, but he was nowhere to be found.

Back Up, on the other hand, was already at the door, muzzle up, mouth open, tongue primed to lick whoever was knocking.

"Pavel?" she called out, wondering if she'd not noticed that the bathroom door was closed when she walked past.

More loud knocking and someone on the other side shouted, "Pizza delivery!"

A temporary relief replaced the dread she'd carried into the living room. Oh good, it was just the pizza she'd ordered. She could take it and Pavel into the back room and turn on the TV for him while she dealt with his uncle—

"Don't answer the door, Mama," a voice said.

Sam frowned. It was Pavel's voice, coming from under the table.

She bent down to find him crouched beneath it, much like he'd been crouched inside the cabinet when she'd come to get him a few days ago.

The knocking must have triggered him somehow, she realized. Made him think he was back in the house where his father's horrific death had gone down.

She held her hand out to him. "Pavel, it's okay, it's just the pizza I ordered. From the same place as two days ago. You said you liked it, remember?"

But Pavel shook his head. "No, it's not. It's one of the bad guys."

More knocking. "Tony's delivery! I got the pizza you ordered right here, ma'am."

"Hold on," Sam called back. She wished the pizza guy had been considerate enough to ring the doorbell instead of knocking. The sound had probably been enough to send Pavel into a post-traumatic episode.

"You think the pizza guy hurt your dad?"

Pavel shook his head, his voice frantic as he answered. "He's not a pizza guy. He's a Russian. He's one of them."

Sam hesitated, not sure how to handle this situation. There was a lot of stuff to parse out with Pavel and she wanted to help him through this, show him how to manage his emotions when he'd been triggered. But she also needed to answer the door and hide him away in the guest bedroom before his uncle showed up.

Now the guy on the other side of the door was pounding. "Are you coming out to pay for this pizza or what?"

"I've got to pay for the pizza," Sam explained to Pavel in a low, calming voice. "I know this situation makes you feel scared and anxious, but it will be all right."

Pavel leaned forward and grabbed her forearm with both of his hands, tears springing to his eyes. "No, it won't. Mama, please don't answer that door. Please!"

She knew Pavel was having a post-traumatic episode. And she knew she'd really regret this when it came time to figure out how to get a hungry little boy to stay in his room while she talked to his uncle. But in the end, she gave in.

"It's okay. Don't cry," she told Pavel. Then she called out to the guy on the other side of the door, "I'm sorry. We won't be needing that pizza any longer. Just charge the credit card I gave you and, I guess, donate it to the next homeless person you see."

"Are you serious, lady?" the voice on the other side of the door asked.

"Yes, completely serious," Sam answered, feeling both guilty and silly as Pavel clung to her forearm, his thin fingers digging in like a tiny bear trap.

"How about my tip?" the delivery guy asked.

"I'm really sorry, but I won't be able to tip you right now. I can't come to the door," Sam said. "But if you leave me your name, I'll stop by Tony's later and make sure you get a generous tip for your trouble."

Silence. A long silence, while Sam waited for the guy on the other side of the door to give up and go away.

But there were no receding footsteps. Instead, there came more loud pounding on the door, so heavy it shook the whole frame.

"Open the door. Open the door and pay for this pizza. NOW!" The easygoing pizza guy was gone, his voice deeper and carrying the trace of a faint accent. "Open this door now, bitch!"

Sam went still as her instincts came online. Thanks to her training at the shelter, she knew when to confront an angry man at the door and when that man was high-risk enough for her to immediately involve the police. She knew exactly where she and Pavel stood with this guy.

"Pavel," she whispered, tugging at the little boy's arm now instead of vice versa. "Let's go. We need to—"

A gloved hand smashed through the thin side window to the right of the door, and went straight for the deadbolt. It was one of three locks on the door, but in this case, it was the only one that she'd locked.

Sam's heart went cold with fear. Yeah, there was no way the man on the other side of the door was the local delivery guy.

"Back Up, here girl!" she called while pulling Pavel from underneath the table.

Back Up trotted over and Sam managed to get the little boy out, just as the door came crashing open.

"C'mon!" she yelled, picking up Pavel and running into her bedroom with Back Up on their heels. She slammed the door behind all of them, looking around for a phone. She needed help, but her phone...

She cursed, the memory of it bouncing off the bed to places unknown when she'd thrown it in frustration coming back to her.

Did she have time to look for it? No, she decided. Better to put as many doors between them and the bad guy as she could. With frantic breaths, she ran into the bathroom with Pavel in her arms. Slammed that door behind her and placed him in the tub.

Pavel was crying now. "He's going to kill us!"

"No, I won't let him hurt you!" Sam said, her eyes scanning the bathroom for something she could use to defend them against the maniac at the door.

There was a metal towel rack was bolted solidly to the wall but no amount of her frantic tugging pulled it off. Sam soon gave up, her eyes once again scanning until they landed on the small window right above the tub. It was too small for her to fit through.

But maybe Pavel could.

She bent down to talk to the little boy crouched in her empty bathtub.

"Pavel, I'm going to push you through the window. Go around the cottage, and run as fast as you can to Ruth's House." She gave him six numbers, the date of her mother's death, then said, "That's the code to get in. Climb out the window and don't look back, no matter what. Just get to the shelter's back door, okay? Then call 9-1-1." Sam put her hands on both sides of the boy's frightened face. "Okay?"

Pavel nodded, solemn as a tomb. "Okay, I'll go, but I don't want you to get hurt like Papa."

She wished she could tell him she wouldn't, wished she could reassure him, but it wasn't true and there wasn't enough time. She settled on not letting her terror show as she bent down further and helped Pavel climb up on her shoulders and out the window.

His feet disappeared just as the bathroom door rattled with the force of someone banging his shoulder against it. The sound of someone trying to get in.

Back Up once again went to the door the bad guy was trying to bash through, sniffing at the crack beneath it with more curiosity than anything else. Sam loved her bullie, but this was one of the times it might have come in handy not to have a total sweetheart of a dog.

66

"Go away!" Sam yelled. "I have a rabid pit bull in here and she will tear you from limb to limb if you don't go away now!"

Back Up looked over her shoulder at Sam and snuffed like, "Who me? I'd do no such thing! In fact, dogs of my breed are way more likely to be kidnapped because we're so ridiculously friendly and trusting!"

Seriously, she'd seen teacup poodles show more menace than Back Up was displaying now. But maybe the guy on the other side of the door believed her because the rattling came to an abrupt stop.

With her heart in her throat, Sam waited. But no sound came. Minutes passed that felt like hours. And soon the fearful anticipation was replaced with dread. What if he hadn't been scared... what if he'd left? Left because he'd gotten what they'd come for?

Sam's heart seized with those thoughts and without thinking, she opened the bathroom door. She had to be sure, she just had to be...

The bedroom was now empty. Its door standing open, knocked off one hinge in ominous testament to the fact that someone had aggressively barged inside. Before leaving.

No, Sam thought to herself. No! No! No!

She ran through the broken door, down the narrow hallway, and into the living room, her shoes crunching over the broken glass as she rushed outside onto the wide expanse of lawn that sat between her and the shelter.

Only to stop short.

Pavel was standing in front of the back entrance to Ruth's House... having what looked like a solemn conversation with Nikolai Rustanov. At least she thought it was Nikolai Rustanov. He was turned to the side and had swapped his tuxedo for a black pea coat and skull cap. In fact, he was dressed all in black as if he'd set out to match the large black Escalade parked, not in one of the special parking spots for Ruth's House, but on the lawn itself with the passenger door hanging open, as if he'd skidded to a stop and leapt out.

But even turned sideways, she knew it was him, if only by the sharp planes of his face, like a gargoyle come to life.

She stood there, mouth unhinged, trying to figure out what was going on before she approached the unexpected scene. Back Up, though, wasn't nearly as wary. She barked happily and ran over to Pavel, nearly knocking the poor boy down in her eagerness to lick him after a whole five, possibly ten, minutes apart.

Nikolai watched the scene with narrow eyes, his body tense as if he were trying to figure out if Back Up was a danger to Pavel. He must have decided she wasn't, because his head swiveled towards Sam as she also came running across the lawn toward them.

The only evidence that he recognized her was a slight widening of his hooded eyes, before his face went to another setting, one that rearranged the harsh planes of his face into an expression of angry accusation.

"This," he said, his voice dangerous and low. "This is what you call taking care of my nephew?"

Chapter Ten

SAM DIDN'T KNOW how to feel about Nikolai Rustanov staring down at her. Confusion, relief, and defensiveness were all putting in bids to be her main emotion. But in the end it came down to Pavel.

She fell to her knees in front of him, hugging the little boy to her.

"Are you okay?" she asked him.

"I'm fine, Mama. The bad guy didn't get me because Uncle Nik came and chased him away." His eyes filled up with delight as he informed her, "Mount Nik is my uncle! I can't believe it."

"Me either," Sam said, trying to keep her shit together. Was it true? Were they really both still here, alive and totally unharmed? She hugged Pavel to her again. She couldn't believe how close she'd come to losing him tonight. "How lucky your uncle came here to meet you."

She could feel Nikolai's angry eyes watching her hug his nephew and knew he must be jumping to all sorts of conclusions about her fitness as even a temporary custodian. "Why don't we all go inside Ruth's House," she suggested. "Call the police and maybe we can talk while we wait for them to get here."

But Pavel pulled back, still stuck on the whole uncle reveal. "Papa said Mount Nik was his brother, but I thought he was lying. If my uncle was a famous hockey player with lots of money, why…"

He didn't seem to know how to finish that sentence. But he didn't have to. The haunted look in his eyes said more about what he had been through as the neglected son of a drug addict than words ever could. His eyes filled with tears and he buried his head in Sam's shoulder, turning them both so his back was to his uncle. His uncle, who he didn't want to see him cry.

Sam's heart broke for the boy. She'd never seen him shed as much as a tear in all that had happened and she wrapped her arms around him tight, wanting to reassure with hugs that everything would be all right.

Back Up apparently felt the same way. But since she didn't have a pair of arms she could wrap around the little boy, she settled for gently nudging his back with her wedge-shaped forehead.

"I did not know." The words came hard and flat from above them. "Your father did not tell me."

Pavel shook his head against Sam's shoulder, refusing to look up at his uncle. "I prayed for him to be real. I prayed for him to be the truth. But Mount Nik never came for me."

"Pavel…" Sam started.

"Now I am here," Nikolai said, his tone impatient. "And do not call me Mount Nik. You are my nephew. Not fan. You may call me Uncle Nikolai or Uncle, but not silly nickname."

Sam glared over Pavel's shoulder at him. Was he seriously quibbling about what Pavel called him after all he'd been through?

As if to confirm her suspicions about his abject unfitness to parent a traumatized child, Nikolai said, "You will stop crying and come now to my home. Your proper home."

Sam scrunched her face, not bothering to hide her irritation from Nikolai.

"He's been through a lot tonight," she informed the large hockey player. "He can cry if he wants to."

"It is not Russian way to cry so many tears." He frowned down at Pavel. "I see Fedya did not teach you to be man in all things. This is something I will correct."

What. The. Hell.

"Are you kidding me with this man BS?" she hissed at Nikolai. "He's been through more in four days than most kids go through in a lifetime! You might want to cut him a little slack."

Something ticked in Nikolai's jaw, but to his credit he abandoned the subject of his eight-year-old nephew's masculinity… in favor of the subject of her guardianship.

"This should not have happened. You did not keep him safe."

Pavel stiffened inside Sam's embrace and pulled away from her so he could address his uncle. "Mama was only trying to protect me. You can't be mad at her."

A new tension entered the air and Nikolai's eyes turned to her. "Why he is calling you mama?" he asked.

Okay, and now she was embarrassed on top of feeling defensive.

"Because… Well, I'm not exactly sure, but it's one of the things I definitely plan to address as we progress with his healing. You see I've been counseling Pavel in the aftermath of this traumatic event and—"

Nikolai cut her off with a dismissive sound. "You Americans and your therapy."

Sam came to her feet then, no longer able to keep herself

from fully confronting this asshole. "So what? You want him to stay traumatized?" she asked him.

"I want him to be safe!" Nikolai roared, coming toward her with his finger pointed down at the ground. "Do you know what could have happened to both of you if I not come here?"

"It's not her fault, Uncle!" Pavel insisted, coming forward to get in between Sam and Nikolai. "Don't yell at her!"

"It's okay, sweetie," Sam said to Pavel, her heart beating faster as all the alternative scenarios of how this night could have ended unfolded inside her head. Both her and Pavel dead. No one to take care of Back Up. He was right. If he hadn't come here...

An icy wind blew through their haphazard triangle and Sam shivered.

"Your uncle's just upset. As anyone would be if..." she trailed off, trying and failing to come up with some kind of silver lining for the situation. "But it's okay now."

Sam must not have been very convincing, though, because Back Up pushed her face into Sam's legs, as she often did when she sensed Sam was troubled and might need a cuddle session with her favorite bullie.

"It's okay," she said, bending down to stroke Back Up's short coat. "We're all okay."

Nikolai regarded her with those cold, green eyes. "My nephew will not stay here. You cannot keep him safe. Now he will come with me."

"No! I want to stay here with Mama!" Pavel screeched. "And Back Up. I can't go with you. I have to stay with Mama! I can't..."

As much as Pavel seemed to relish having his favorite hockey player turn out to be his uncle, he now seemed on the verge of hyperventilating at the thought of being taken away from his new home.

His rising panic diverted all of Sam's attention away from

Nikolai and back to the little boy. She squatted down in front of him, looking directly into his stricken eyes.

"It's okay, sweetie. It's okay. Just breathe. Match what I'm doing." She breathed deep, in and out through her nose. "Match my breath, honey. You can do it."

The boy did as she said, his breaths coming out short and too fast. But eventually they slowed and deepened, the panic fading from his expression. Which Back Up took as an invitation to trot forward and begin licking the tears off his face.

"Back Up!" Pavel exclaimed with a laughing screech. "No, don't lick me. Now isn't the time for licking. Tell her, Mama."

Sam shook her finger at her overly affectionate bullie. "You heard him. Back off, Back Up."

Back Up whimpered, but her words sent Pavel into a fit of giggles, making him look his very young age.

"Back off, Back Up," he repeated, appreciating the goofy word play in a way that only a child could.

She glanced at the hockey player who looked more than a little confused now, like he didn't quite know what to make of the scene or how to handle it.

"You name dog Back Up. What sort of name is this?" he asked her.

Sam shook her head at him, truly disappointed. "You haven't seen *Veronica Mars* either?!?! No wonder it got cancelled too soon."

More confused looks, then Nikolai's mouth drew back into an impatient sneer. "Pack his bag," he snarled at her. "He will come with me."

"No!" Pavel cried out. He clung to Sam's neck. "Tell him he can't take me from you, Mama!"

Sam took his hands before he could start panicking again. "Do you trust me?" she asked the little boy.

"But—" Pavel started.

"Pavel, it's a yes or no question," she said. "Do you trust me? Yes or no?"

A frown quivered on Pavel's lips but nonetheless he answered, "Yes."

Right answer. She gave him a reassuring smile and said, "Okay, good. Then stand by my side while I talk with your uncle."

"Okay," Pavel said, his voice still watery with tears.

This time when she stood up to talk to Nikolai Rustanov, she kept her arm around Pavel's shoulder and she didn't let the dark scowl on his outrageously handsome face intimidate her. Pavel needed her and there was no way she was going to let him go home with a man who thought it was unmanly for a boy who just lost his father and had come close to being killed just a few minutes ago to cry.

To his credit, Pavel stayed quiet this time, burying his face in her waist.

As if to affirm her assessment of him, Nikolai said to Pavel. "Get your face out of her waist, boy. You are too old to hide in woman. I have much to teach you." He said this with a sneer, like the sooner he got Pavel away from her, the better.

To Sam's surprise, Pavel actually did as he said, standing up straight beside her like a soldier.

The whole situation made her want to cuss Nikolai out for being an insensitive bastard. But instead, she kept her hand on Pavel's shoulder, letting him know he could lean on her whenever he needed.

"Tell me more about your house," she said to Nikolai. "I know about the ridiculous gates, but I'm assuming you've got a state-of-the-art security system, too."

"*Da*, I do. *And you don't*," he reminded her.

She just nodded with approval, refusing to let him bait her into another argument.

"And would you be willing to invest in a security guard, just until we can get the people who hurt Pavel's father behind bars?"

He crooked his head and eyed her like he was trying to decide if she was being over protective or naïve.

But in the end he said, "Of course, I will hire security guard to keep him safe when I cannot."

"Sounds good to me," she said, flashing him a bright and happy smile.

He did not smile back. In fact, there was a whole lot of suspicion in his eyes when he said, "So you agree? Pavel will come home with me now."

"Alright, alright" she said, raising her hands in a gesture of surrender, like she'd finally decided to give in. "You've made a strong case here today. We'll all move in with you tonight, okay?" She rushed on before he could protest. "But before I start packing I need to know, do you have stuff like dog food and a water bowl at your place, or should I just bring what I have?"

Chapter Eleven

THE WOMAN in the emerald dress, the one whose name turned out to be Sam, was completely infuriating. Not only had she somehow brainwashed his nephew into calling her mama, she'd also invited herself along with her useless dog to move in with him—right before she insisted on calling the police to file an official report.

And by the police, she'd meant her boyfriend. The cop who'd wanted her to get rid of Pavel in the first place.

He'd come running to the scene after the rest of the black and whites arrived, grabbing Sam and gathering her up in his arms. Lovers reunited, Nikolai thought with a dark sneer as he watched them, now standing on her front porch. Her with her hands on his chest, him with his forehead resting against hers as he said something Nikolai couldn't hear.

They were a well-matched couple. Him just a few inches taller and attractive in the same way as she. Like the proverbial Latino boy and black girl next door had decided to start going together. He even had a matching set of dimples.

Nikolai wanted to rip the guy away from her, shove him to

the ground, and warn him off going anywhere near her ever again.

She's mine. The two words popped unbidden into his head, startling and untrue.

Startling because he'd never felt possessive of a woman—especially one he hadn't slept with—before. And untrue, because obviously she was with the cop.

No wonder she hadn't taken him up on his balcony invitation. No wonder she'd run away, despite the passionate kiss they'd shared.

"You should go."

Nikolai looked down. Pavel was staring straight ahead at the woman he called 'mama' and her cop boyfriend, but he was talking to Nikolai.

"The detectives asked us all of their questions," said the little boy who looked almost exactly like Fedya had at that age, despite his kinky hair and much darker skin. "Let Mama take me to your house. Then you can deal with the bad guy."

Nikolai nodded in solemn agreement with the little boy. He might look like Fedya, but Pavel had already proven himself to be way more sensible than his addict brother, from the moment Nikolai had pulled up behind Ruth's House and seen the child running across the lawn like a bat out of hell.

Contrary to what the social worker seemed to believe, the boy was no delicate flower. After filling him in quickly on what was happening after a brief moment of recognition, Pavel had observed silently while Nikolai dragged a stout Russian in a leather bomber jacket out of the cottage. And the boy hadn't so much as flinched as he watched Nikolai chokehold the man into unconsciousness before dumping the Russian into the back of his Escalade.

And now he was calmly giving him advice about dealing with "the bad guy" before he woke up, which made Nikolai wonder how much of the hysterical little boy act had been for

Sam and how much of it was true. At that moment, Pavel reminded Nikolai less of Fedya, who'd always been the clingy sort and quick to tears, and more of himself as a young boy, watching Sergei do his dirty work with dead eyes.

"You should go," the boy said again, as he watched the cop talk to Sam, a disapproving frown on his face. "Before the bad guy wakes up. Before the cop starts asking more questions."

"ARE YOU SURE ABOUT STAYING WITH MOUNT NIK, SAMMY?" Marco asked her. All the other police officers had left by then after a set of detectives took their statements, but Marco had stayed behind to talk with Sam in an unofficial capacity—and because he was none too happy about her decision to move in with his favorite hockey player.

He rubbed her arms and bent his forehead to touch hers. "I'm glad you finally came to your senses about sending Pavel on with his uncle, but I don't understand why you have to go with them," he said.

How shocking, Sam thought. Marco was once again failing to understand how committed she was to Pavel getting the care and counseling he needed in the aftermath of not one, but two terrible events.

She brought her hands up to his chest to push him away, and reiterate how potentially traumatizing these last few days could be for Pavel if she didn't intervene. But then she decided to cut him some slack. If Marco hadn't sent Nikolai to her door, she might be dead now.

"I'll be fine," she said to Marco, resting her hands on his chest as she resisted the urge to put space between them. "And it's just for a little while, until we get whoever came after us behind bars."

A skeptical look came over Marco's face and to Sam's

relief, he drew back from her. "I'll bring you down to the station tomorrow to look at some pictures, but I don't know how far that's going to get us with both the kid and Rustanov saying they didn't see the guy's face clearly."

Sam glanced at uncle and nephew, both standing a few feet away with their arms crossed in front of them. Pavel looked like a miniature version of his uncle, even though he was light brown and wearing a neon green anorak, while Nikolai was white and wearing a pea coat.

Nikolai met her glance with a hard stare, as if waiting for her to finish her conversation with Marco was the most annoying thing that had happened to him all day. Even more annoying than having to chase away some criminal who was trying to hurt her and his nephew.

His annoyed look made her feel annoyed in turn, yet she couldn't look away from him. Why did he have to be so damn beautiful? There was something almost magnetic about his face, with all its chiseled angles and its long, sharp nose. Sam was surprised by how hard it was not to stare. Stare at him like he was currently staring at her.

"You know you don't have to stay with Mount Nik..." Marco's words broke the spell Nikolai had somehow cast over her, and Sam broke from the stare to look at the cop she now only considered a friend. He took a deep breath and said, "If you're worried about having a safe place to stay, you could come back to my apartment for as long as you need. Then you could arrange counseling sessions with Pavel until Mount Nik finds him a permanent therapist. You don't have to follow the kid."

No, she didn't, and there were plenty of places she could stay outside of Marco's apartment. A hotel or even at Ruth's House itself, since it had beds currently going unused. But she wasn't naive. The system always tried to place children with their blood relatives when they could, and Nikolai Rustanov was a local sports hero. There was no way she'd be able to retain her temporary custody of Pavel. It was either move into Nikolai Rustanov's place now or risk getting kicked out of Pavel's life all together, because he was in his uncle's physical custody.

She gave Marco a weak half smile and said, "Don't worry about me staying with Mount Nik, Marco. I can take care of myself."

"I know you can but…" Marco trailed off, and she sensed there was something he wasn't telling her.

"What, Marco? If there's something you want me to know, tell me."

He shook his head. "Nothing. It's probably nothing. It's just that Rustanov's and the kid's stories are *exactly* the same. Like they made them up together. Just maybe, I don't know… keep your eyes open for anything off, and if you feel like there's something weird going on, call me."

"Sure. Okay, I can do that."

Her easy acquiescence to his request seemed to reassure him. He cupped her shoulders and drew her a little closer. "And even if there's nothing shady going on, call me. Just because you're living with him doesn't mean we can't hang out. And it's your turn to pay for takeout at my place next time, remember?"

Sam crooked her head, trying to figure out if Marco was seriously trying to finagle her into a sleepover date she really didn't want—less than a few hours after she'd nearly been killed by some kind of Russian hit man.

"Uncle says it's time to go, Mama!" Pavel called out to her from where he and Nikolai were standing.

Marco jerked a little, as if just now realizing Pavel was still there.

"Yeah, uh, you better go, but…" He turned out his pinky

and thumb, making the universal sign for phone as he mouthed, "Call me, okay?"

Sam gave him a tight smile, saying, "Thanks for everything, Marco" before she walked away, unable to believe she'd ever been attracted to the self-absorbed cop, much less thought they'd be a good match.

She shook her head. Just goes to show how silly she'd been to think she could find a great guy and start a family like Josie had. She was on the brink of moving in with a hockey idol who'd pretty much introduced himself as Mr. One Night Stand. And he—not she—was the true custodian of the boy who'd come to feel like a child to her in an impossibly short time.

She'd never been farther away from realizing the dream she'd started spinning when she was Pavel's age, blocking her ears from the sound of her stepfather's yelling, and promising herself she'd never end up in an abusive relationship. It was as good of a time as any to accept some hard truths. She'd managed not to walk down the same path as her mother, but that didn't mean she was slated for a happy ending. Vicious thoughts circled like sharks in her head as she walked toward Pavel. Women like Josie got happy endings. Women like her— the memory of her mother lying dead on the living room floor flashed across her mind, curdling her stomach—women like her had to settle for knowing when to get out of a bad relationship while the getting was good.

Chapter Twelve

SAM HAD to give herself credit. She didn't freak out. Not while arranging to stay with Nikolai, not while being questioned by the police, and not while talking to Marco. In fact, she not only got Pavel and herself packed up in record time, but she also called for another, larger pizza from her second favorite pizza joint and stopped to get it on their way to Nikolai's house.

"It's probably a good thing your uncle had to go back to the rink to finish up some work," she told Pavel after they'd used the code Nikolai had given her to get into his colonial-style mansion. "Not to judge, but he just doesn't come across like the kind of guy who can appreciate a good pizza."

If Pavel sensed the false cheer in her voice he didn't let on. In fact, he seemed more at home sitting at the tea-stained oak top island in Nikolai's oversized kitchen than he had in her small cottage. As she ate across from him, she remembered the dirty little boy who had originally snuck into this grand house. Pavel had been showering regularly for the last few days, and she'd escorted him to a barber downtown to cut off the unruly mess on top of his head. So he'd cleaned up and he'd settled in well at her cottage. But that was nothing in comparison to finding out his uncle was his favorite hockey star and moving into his house.

If she'd been a Hollywood producer, Sam imagined she might turn the story into a Great Expectations reboot. Judging from the way Pavel looked all around him as he ate, this was a dream come true for the boy. Even if his uncle was a total jerk who didn't believe in love or little boys crying.

"What kind of food do you think Uncle Nik eats?" Pavel asked her as they hunted through the cabinets for some kind of Ziploc bag to put the remaining pizza in.

She wrinkled her nose. "I don't know. Raw eggs, lots of protein, maybe wheat germ."

"What's wheat germ?" Pavel asked, wrinkling his own nose as he checked another one of the lower cabinets.

Sam laughed. "Oh, I'm sure you'll find out soon enough."

"I don't want to find out!" Pavel said. "Please don't let him feed me wheat germ. It sounds disgusting!"

Pavel had a truly terrified look on his face as he proclaimed this, but his accompanying giggles proved him to be nothing less than thrilled to be living with a possible wheat germ drinker. Anything was better than living with an addict, she guessed.

Eventually Pavel found some tin foil and they chatted as they packed up the pizza and climbed the steps to the large suite at the top of the stairs, one of five bedrooms on the second floor. Pavel's new room was an homage to lavish taste, with crimson damask walls and heavy ebony wood furniture that looked like it was either antique or had been commissioned to look like it belonged in a home owned by Russian nobility. It was way too much for a boy Pavel's age. Even Back Up seemed intimidated, sniffing suspiciously at what looked like a hand knotted red-and-gold Aubusson rug as Sam tucked Pavel into the room's California king-sized bed.

Yet Pavel seemed perfectly at peace as she smoothed the heavy down comforter over him, like he didn't have a care in the world, even though a man had come after him with a gun just a few hours earlier.

"Do you want to talk about what happened today?" she asked, taking a seat at the side of his bed. "If you're afraid, you can come sleep with me."

Her temporary room, Sam suspected, had probably originally been intended for live-in help. It also had damask wallpaper and a comforter she suspected might cost more than most people's rents. But it was on a much smaller scale since the room was maybe 100 square feet, 200 at most. Just large enough for a full-sized bed, a closet, and an overly intricate chest of drawers.

However, Pavel just shook his head, like Sam was being silly to think he might be afraid to sleep alone tonight.

"I'm not scared. Uncle Nik will make sure nobody tries to hurt us again. He said so."

Wow. Sam silently whistled inside her head. It must be nice to truly believe your sports heroes are gods. But if believing Uncle Nik was his ultimate protector was what got him through, who was she to argue?

"Okay, well, if you need anything, I'll be right across the hallway," she told him.

"May Back Up sleep in bed with me, please?" he asked in that overly polite way of his.

"No, honey, we've talked about this. Back Up isn't exactly going to help you get a good night's sleep. That's why we put her doggie bed downstairs."

As usual, Pavel didn't argue with her and she wondered what his life had been like that he didn't seem to have a child's natural inclination to whine or keep asking for things over and over again.

Instead, he just turned over and asked, "Will you rub my back until I fall asleep, Mama?"

This request she could grant. She rubbed his back in a circular motion for a little while before bringing up a tough subject.

"Pavel, I know this is difficult for you, because both of your parents have been taken away in really cruel ways. But you know I'm not your mother, right? I'm your friend and I'll always be your friend. I'm going to do my best to stay here and help you as long as Nikolai lets me, because I'm your friend. But I'm not your mother."

Pavel looked over his shoulder at her, a frown very much like Nikolai's on his face. "Uncle is going to let you stay forever. You don't have to worry about that." He sounded so sure of this that she stopped rubbing his back.

"Pavel I think we should have a conversation about managing expectations—"

Pavel turned all the way back over and squeezed his eyes shut. "Thank you very much for rubbing my back until I fall asleep, Mama," he said.

Sam sighed, more than a little worried about the secret thrill that went through her every time Pavel called her mama. Obviously she needed to take her own advice about managing expectations. One court order for custody, and Nikolai would be able to kick her out of his ridiculous house, no questions asked.

But she and Pavel were together now. Pavel was safe—and she had enough time to teach him some mindfulness strategies for navigating his emotions and also get him started on a regular morning yoga routine. Kids were resilient and not easily broken. The little time they had left together might be enough to set Pavel firmly on a path towards healing. She hoped.

As promised, Sam rubbed his back until he fell into a heavy sleep.

Then she whistled for Back Up who'd also fallen asleep while waiting for her. Apparently the fancy carpet wasn't so intimidating that Back Up couldn't use it to get in a quick nap.

Sam escorted her bullie downstairs before retiring to her own room, where she unpacked her clothes into the dresser drawer and changed into an Indiana U t-shirt. Then with a shake of her head, she turned to face the room's absurd bed. As if to make up for the room's small size, the small bed was even more sumptuous than Pavel's. A four-poster number, covered in shimmering gold pillows and a crimson comforter. Both the head and foot boards were intricately carved and overlaid with gold paint, and the whole spectacle was surrounded by red gauze curtains that made words like "sheik" and "harem" come to mind.

Feeling like a country mouse who'd somehow ended up in the lap of ostentatious luxury, she pushed through the gauze barrier and climbed into the bed, which seemed like it was more suited to a tsarina than little ol' Sam McKinley from Detroit. But maybe some of Pavel's newfound inner peace had rubbed off on her, because soon after laying her head down on the golden silk pillow, she fell fast asleep.

Or maybe she was just in denial. Because today she'd come uncomfortably close to losing someone she couldn't keep herself from loving. Someone who felt like family, even if they had no blood connection.

And she should have known her stepfather would be paying her a visit.

Sam woke only a few hours later to the sound of Pavel's terrified voice.

"Mama! Mama!" he cried. "The bad guy got me. Mama, please help me!"

She'd jolted awake immediately, sitting up fully when she

saw her stepfather, standing at the foot of the ornate bed. His eyes were gleaming with madness, and he held a switchblade in his hand. The gleaming edge dripping with her mother's red blood. And he was holding it to a terrified Pavel's neck.

"Mama! Mama! Please help me!" Pavel cried again.

"Let him go," Sam screamed at the mad man at the end of her bed, the one who'd already killed her mother and was now threatening the boy she'd taken into her heart.

But her stepfather just grinned at her. Like she was a long lost friend. "Hey, Samantha, girl," he said. "I sure did you miss you."

Chapter Thirteen

Thirty years ago

"REMEMBER, son, before you kill someone, you must always know why you are doing it."

Sergei said these words to Nikolai, voice calm, eyes flat, as if dragging the man beside him, the one thrashing underneath Sergei's death grip, struggling to get out of the duct tape Sergei had wrapped around his wrists, caused him no exertion whatsoever. Nikolai's father barely even registered the desperate man's muffled screams behind the duct tape placed over his mouth.

As the Rustanov family's main enforcer, Sergei was well-acquainted with the disposal of bodies—dead or alive.

However, the poor fellow his father held wasn't an enemy of the Rustanov family. He was only a lowly maintenance man for the apartment building Nikolai, his mother, and Fedya lived in. The maintenance man who had been keeping Nikolai's mother company ever since Sergei had started ignoring her for a younger, more nubile woman. This wasn't the first time Sergei had done this. Nikolai had sensed from a very young age that his mother, Natasha, was more a prized possession than someone his father loved.

She was very beautiful, but from a simple shop family, one that used to pay graft to the Rustanovs to do business in their neighborhood unimpeded. She'd also gotten pregnant in high school with Fedya, only to have the boy's father move away, wanting nothing to do with a baby. So though she possessed exquisite beauty, many of her prospects were limited as a result of class and her status as a young, unwed mother.

But Sergei had taken a liking to Natasha, had magnanimously told her family they'd no longer have to pay him graft or support Natasha and Fedya with their meager earnings, before setting her up in an apartment of her own.

Natasha had told Nikolai the story of how she and his father met one night after drinking too much cheap wine.

"I was a stupid girl," she told him, her face lined with bitter shadows. "I thought he was saving me from a dull life at my father's shop. But in truth, he was putting me in a cage so he could get to me more easily. I thought I was special but I was only the first of your father's many women."

But Natasha was special in a way. Sergei had never married his mother, but he'd never let her go either. Nikolai had grown up thinking of a father as someone who spent the night in your mother's bedroom, maybe once or twice a week, for limited time periods—but then disappeared for months before coming back with flowers, jewelry, and gifts for the boys.

However this last time, Sergei had been gone for over eighteen months and Natasha had taken to saying things to Nikolai. Things like, "It looks like your father has finally forgotten about us. At least he owns the building, so we will never have to pay rent."

But Nikolai had known better. Sergei always came back, and when his mother—who was still very pretty, even with the lines of bitterness that had formed between her eyebrows and around the corners of her mouth—had begun inviting the building's maintenance man to dinner and eventually to spend the night, it had felt to Nikolai that she was putting the simple man with the simple job in grave danger.

His gut feeling had been validated when Sergei burst through the apartment door earlier that night, his arms filled with a fur coat for Natasha and top of the line hockey sticks for Nikolai and Fedya. He'd dropped it all when found the maintenance man eating at their dinner table.

It hadn't taken long after that for the rest of Nikolai's prediction to play out. The only thing he hadn't anticipated was that after tying the man up (ignoring Natasha's desperate pleas for his life) he'd commanded Nikolai to come with him.

"It is time you learned," was the only explanation he gave.

Nikolai could still see his mother at the top of the stairway, both of Fedya's hands around her wrist, trying to pull her back into the apartment as she screamed at Sergei that Nikolai was only a little boy, too young to see such things.

Sergei had ignored those pleas, too, and Nikolai had ended up walking behind his father as he dragged the maintenance man toward the end of the wharf.

Sergei sounded much like Nikolai's primary school teacher as he lectured on his favorite subject.

"There are many reasons to kill a man. Maybe he has hurt a member of your family. Then you must kill him in retaliation. Maybe he is talking to someone about your business—someone he shouldn't be talking to about your business. Then you must kill him to silence him. There are many scenarios and many reasons to kill. Too many to name. Remember, you never have to explain to others why you are killing the man you are killing. You only have to explain it to yourself. You cannot pull the trigger in good conscience until your reason is clear. That is what separates me from the young hotheads who get their families in trouble when they are out at clubs and do stupid things like shooting a bartender who got the drink order wrong. Shooting without purpose is no good and will kill you before your time."

They came to a stop at the end of the wharf and Nikolai instinctively looked over both shoulders to see if anyone else was about. But they were alone except for a few small, empty skiffs swaying from side to side, and the quiet skittering of rats lurking in unknown places. The night sky was inky black, no moon or stars in sight, as if even they did not want any part of what his father would do tonight under the dock's dim yellow lights.

"Normally I would not be so sloppy, I would take more time to do it correctly in the Rustanov way. But in this case, I kill to teach your mother a lesson," his father told him. "This means I do not have to kill this man in the usual Rustanov way. Nikolai, come stand beside me, right here."

He nodded his head, indicating where Nikolai should go, and when Nikolai was in place, Sergei released the maintenance man from inside his arm.

"You may run now," he told the smaller male.

The man, perhaps believing his fate had unexpectedly changed, that Sergei Rustanov had only meant to scare him and hadn't truly intended to kill him in front of his child, ran.

He ran as fast as he could, given that his hands were taped together in front of him. More proof that this man was either stupid or did not truly know Sergei Rustanov.

Sergei watched him run for a bit before calmly pulling a Glock 19 from his jacket holster and shooting a hole in the back of the man's head. The maintenance man dropped dead less than twenty feet from where Sergei and Nikolai stood.

"You see," he told Nikolai with a grin as the sound of the gunshot reverberated though the night sky. "In this case, it is okay to be sloppy."

Thirty Years Later

"It is one in the morning," Alexei said in lieu of a greeting when he answered his phone.

"I would not call," Nikolai answered in Russian. "But I threw a party tonight. Do you still have the maid service in Miami?"

"Lexie, is everything all right?" a tired voice asked in the background.

"It is nothing, Eva," Alexei answered. "An associate, calling about an important business matter."

Not a direct lie, Nikolai noted. For men who had been raised like he and his cousins, calls like these were a matter of business. But not the exact truth either.

Nikolai listened to the sounds of rustling on the other side of the phone. He imagined Alexei getting out of the bed he shared with his wife, and going to another part of the house to finish the call out of earshot.

"I do still work with that service," Alexei answered. "But it's based in Chicago now."

So Alexei's hit man had moved to Chicago, it seemed.

"It is fine. Chicago is closer to my party," Nikolai answered.

"Also, the service no longer caters. Family obligations."

That gave Nikolai some pause. He'd only met Tetsuro Nakamura once, when he'd handed him the audio recording of Sergei's death. But the emotionless Asian man hadn't struck him as the type of guy who would ever had "family obligations."

But then, Nikolai had never planned to have children himself and look at him now. Making arrangements to clean up this mess before he went home to his nephew... and his nephew's current guardian, the girlfriend of a police officer.

In this case, though, whether Nakamura was still willing to kill was neither here nor there.

"That is not problem. The party was already thrown," Nikolai answered. "But it was very messy. I need your maid service."

"How long did this party last?"

Nikolai surveyed the basement room, a less than classy affair, with carpet on both the floors and the walls. Not like his own home, which he had designed as one big fuck you to Sergei, who'd been from one of the richest crime families in Russia but had forced his girlfriend and child to live in a small, grey two-bedroom apartment.

That small apartment was luxury accommodations compared to this room, located below a strip club called Jiggles. Every piece of furniture looked to have been either hauled from a sidewalk or bought at a discount store's clearance sale. So cheap, it was no wonder it had only taken Nikolai fifteen minutes of "questioning" the guy who'd been sent to take out Pavel before he'd sung like a bird and gave him an address.

The drug outfit that had killed his brother was fairly new with a boss who'd come to Indiana with just a few East Coast connections and a family of thick-necked brothers and cousins. According to the hit man Nikolai had interrogated, they only had the one strip club and apparently not enough money or taste to redecorate.

Either way, it wasn't something they'd have to worry about now. The man who'd attempted to kill a defenseless woman and child earlier that evening was dead on the carpeted floor, along with his boss and other family members, after having been used as a human shield when Nikolai had kicked in the door and come into the room shooting. The only thing the hideout had to recommend it was that, thanks to all the tacky carpeting and music blasting from the club above, the short gunfight went completely unnoticed.

But there was still the not-so-small matter of clean up.

Nikolai counted eight bodies in all, and in this case, he had admittedly been a little sloppy. All of the men had been killed quietly and efficiently, but there was a strip club full of people upstairs and no way for him to sneak out fully undetected.

"Eight hours," he answered his cousin.

"The party went on for eight hours," Alexei repeated. "You are not serious."

"Eight hours," Nikolai repeated, "And there are many people here who weren't invited. This is not my house, so I need the maid service as a courtesy to the owner."

Nikolai could almost hear his cousin frowning as he said, "I will now ask you why you did not invite me to help you with set up. I would have flown back if I had known you were planning a party."

"There wasn't time," Nikolai answered. "Someone tried to invite my nephew to this party on the same night, so I had to throw the party myself. Quickly."

They'd only texted briefly about Fedya's newly discovered son after Nikolai left the police station, but Alexei cursed upon hearing the coded news of the attempt on Pavel's life.

"I understand. Hold on…"

Some shuffling and then Nikolai could hear Alexei having a muffled conversation with someone else—probably on another phone reserved for the messier aspects of his business dealings. The conversation was conducted with rapid efficiency on Alexei's part, until he broke off to ask Nikolai for an address.

Nikolai coded his answer as best he could given he lived in a city Alexei had only visited occasionally, most recently just a few days ago to assist Nikolai with some business dealings. But Nikolai's vague description clearly got the job done because after a few more rapid exchanges, Alexei came back with, "The maid service says they can clean up your party. Lock the door behind you when you leave. The service will take care of the rest."

"Thank you," Nikolai said, meaning it. There were few people he trusted in this world and his cousin was among that very small number.

"Do not thank me. We are family. Of course I will do this for you," Alexei answered. "And I would have thrown the same party if it had been either of my children."

Of course he would have.

To everyone's surprise, Alexei, who'd garnered a reputation as a ruthless businessman prior to his marriage to a spitfire from Texas, had turned out to be a dedicated and loving father. He truly seemed to enjoy his role as a parent, even more so than his role as an international oligarch. The few times Nikolai had observed him with his family, he'd been doting with just enough firmness to command his son's respect. As of late, though, he seemed be going even further into softy territory now that his wife had given birth to a little girl they'd named Layla. Nikolai had yet to meet the newest member of Alexei's family in person, but he'd been forced to listen to Alexei refer to her by the most syrupy Russian pet names, and it was obvious the baby already had Alexei completely wrapped around her finger.

His love for his family didn't make him any less commanding, though. Nikolai did as his cousin said, locking the basement door and piling the cheap furniture in front of it in order to barricade the room from the inside, so no employees with keys could stumble in on the grisly scene. Luckily there was a basement window, one he could crawl out of with the aid of a plywood chair.

He thought of his own nephew being forced to crawl at out of a small window earlier that night and felt no remorse for what he'd done to his would be killers. But he also felt no sense of relief after he made it back to his car. Because now it was time to go home and face what he could already tell would be a much bigger challenge than killing eight men.

He'd never had any interactions with children. Had never wanted them—how could he after the way he'd grown up? But now he had a ward, one he'd have to raise in Fedya's stead. And his ward had brought a woman into his house. The same one he'd been thinking about near obsessively ever since the first party he'd thrown as owner of the Polar. But she belonged to another.

He didn't know what bothered him more at this point. That he now had a child to raise, or that Sam, the woman in the green dress, would be sleeping under his roof and he wouldn't be able to touch her.

Chapter Fourteen

IT WAS VERY LATE by the time Nikolai made it home and he didn't expect anyone to be waiting for him when he walked in the front door. But soon after stepping across the threshold and flipping on the lights in the foyer, the useless dog came trotting up to him, tongue hanging out.

Despite having just met him a few hours ago, the dog seemed happy to see him.

Nikolai glared at his unwelcome guest and tried to step around her, but the dog got in front of him again. And when he tried to dodge, the dog only followed him, nudging him with her square face before dropping to the floor and showing him her belly.

Nikolai didn't have much experience with dogs, but even he could understand the message this one was trying to convey. The price for getting by unimpeded by her large body was a belly rub.

Maybe because he was tired and weary to his very bones, Nikolai bent down and gave her two short slapping pats on her pink belly. But perhaps the dog wasn't as dumb and useless as he'd previously thought, because she once again flipped over as he stood back up, negotiating her head into his palm so he was forced to pet her again. Then came more head nudges, the greedy dog all but placing the back of her ears underneath his fingertips.

Nikolai scratched her behind the ears because—well, he didn't know why exactly. At first he did it to get her out of the way, but then a calmness stole over him. The more he scratched, the more the events of tonight loosened their angry hold over him. And the more the dog rubbed her large head against his palms, the more human he felt. Not like a ruthless killer, but like a man who'd done what he'd had to do to keep his nephew safe. The only thing he had left of his brother.

A strange pain settled in his chest at the thought of Fedya, and he saw his brother, once again lying on that slab. Those Russian drug dealers had disposed of him like a piece of trash, and they would have done the same to Pavel, if he hadn't—

Don't think about it, he told himself.

"Go to bed, dog," he said to the dark grey canine, who he had half a mind to rename Useless. "No more petting. Get out of my way."

The dog must have understood he was no longer in the mood to indulge her, because she slunk away into the dark living room as if she knew she'd gotten all the petting from Nikolai she was going to receive that night.

The dog's unexpected greeting had lightened his mood, but only for a little bit. He was completely numb again by the time he stepped into his glass and marble shower. And as he watched the blood of the Russians slide off his body and down the tub's drain, he could sense his father's ghost like a heavy cloud hanging over the bathroom. Nikolai's inability to feel any emotion but grim satisfaction regarding what he'd done that night called forth his ghost as sure as if Sergei were still alive. Alive and still showing up at his mother's apartment commanding Nikolai to come with him, as he had often throughout Nikolai's teen years. The last time he'd come had been only a couple of nights before his mother's death, for what Nikolai had known would be a very messy business if he needed more than one gun to handle it.

To Sergei's credit, he'd never come back after his mother died.

As Nikolai got out of the shower and dried himself off, he could also feel his dead mother's eyes on him. Scared for him. But too scared to say anything to his father.

Nikolai's bones ached with both the memories and exertion of killing eight men with only a silenced gun, a wire string, and his bare hands—which wasn't as easy as it looked in the movies. Sergei had kept himself in excellent shape all the way up until his sudden death, and the reason for his dedication to staying fit was evident in the soreness Nikolai felt now despite his superior size and muscles.

After his shower, Nikolai threw on a pair of briefs—the only thing he ever wore to bed, wanting nothing more than to go to sleep. It was late. Very late. And he had to work the next morning.

But he couldn't make himself get into bed. There was a specific need tugging on him, as sure as a finger pulling on a toy's drawstring. Instead of going to the bed, he threw on a heavy cotton robe with the Polar's angry bear mascot emblazoned across the back of it.

He needed to see the boy and the woman now sleeping under his roof. Make sure they were safe. It was a stupid compulsion. Stupid and unnecessary. There were no Russians left alive to get past his security system. Every threat against the boy was now dead in the basement of a strip club, awaiting the arrival of Tetsuro Nakamura.

But nonetheless…

Only two of the top floor bedroom doors were closed and

he walked down the hall to the larger room on the left, as quietly as he could.

His thought had been to check on the woman first, and then the boy, but to his surprise, he found the boy in the larger room, looking like a Russian prince in all the red, gold, and ivory opulence as he snored softly. He didn't appear to have a care in the world, and for a moment the numbness inside Nikolai's chest was pierced by a strange ache.

He would protect this boy, he vowed as his heart iced back over. No matter what it took. He wouldn't let him turn out like Fedya.

With irritation he thought of the woman who'd insisted on coming here with Pavel, The judgmental look she had given him when he'd told Pavel not to cry. Fedya had been weak like that, coddled by his mother and mostly ignored by Sergei—which was close to a kindness on the enforcer's part. Nikolai could remember Fedya sniveling into Natasha's side much the same way. So Nikolai had corrected him. And Samantha McKinley had reacted to his words like he hit the boy, like he was worse than the men those women came to her shelter to escape. Like he was the exact opposite of her cop boyfriend.

Bristling with remembered indignation, Nikolai crossed the hallway to her door and put his hand on the knob. He wished he could tell her just how far he'd gone to ensure his nephew's protection that night. How he—not her cop boyfriend—had taken care of the threat against both of them—

"No! Please don't. Please don't!"

Nikolai's heart stopped beating. The words came from inside the room and we're followed by a distinct sob.

Chapter Fifteen

NIKOLAI ACTED WITHOUT THINKING, busting into the room without hesitation. He must not have solved the problem with his one man hit on the local Russian mob outfit. One of them had somehow gotten past his security forces and was now hurting her—

He stopped short when he found her thrashing around in the guest room's canopy bed, the covers completely thrown off, her oversized college t-shirt up around her waist.

He looked around to be sure, but no, there was no one with her. Just Samantha McKinley, twisting around as if she were both trying to get away and prevent something from happening.

"Please, don't do it. Don't do it! I'll do anything you want me to, just don't hurt him—"

She was having a nightmare, he belatedly realized. He went over to her and turned on the light beside her bed.

"Samantha."

"No, don't. Please. Oh my God. Don't!"

"Samantha," he said again, trying to shake her awake.

"I will kill you. I swear I'll kill you!" she growled. But the menacing affect of the words were diluted by the tears rolling down her cheeks.

"Samantha!" This time he pulled her into a sitting position and shook her harder, trying to break through her nightmare panic.

Samantha came blinking awake with a startled sound, half scream, half cry, and for many moments her wild eyes bounced around, before finally focusing on him. A shocked beat, and then to Nikolai's astonishment, her head fell into his chest as she broke down sobbing, this time with tears of relief.

"Oh my God. Oh my God. I thought it was real."

"What did you think was real?" he asked from his awkward position, one knee dug into the bed and one foot still on the ground, his hands wrapped around her shoulders. "What did you dream?"

She shook her head frantically against his chest, as if trying to rid her mind of whatever had spooked her so badly. "Nothing," she answered, still crying. "It was nothing."

Nothing had her visibly trembling all over. "Tell me about your dream. Was it about man who came to your house?"

He wondered then, for much more altruistic reasons, if he shouldn't tell her about what he'd done that night. If it meant she'd stop crying so piteously into his chest, he found himself prepared to confess anything.

"No, not him," she answered, her voice watery. "It doesn't matter. It's a long story, and I don't want to talk about it. I'm fine…" Another one of those stifled sobs, as if she were desperately trying to keep herself from breaking down even further. "I'm fine," she insisted.

"You are crying… and shaking all over," he informed her, because clearly she did not know the difference between fine and not fine.

"I know. I'm being silly, because everything's fine now. We're safe. I think it's a delayed reaction to what happened tonight." She pulled away from him, and brought her hands up to swipe at her tears. "You can go. I'll be fine in just a few seconds."

She barely got this out before dissolving into more tears.

Nikolai observed her for a hard second. "I am calling doctor."

"No!" she nearly yelled. "No doctors. I just need..." she trailed off.

"What do you need?" he demanded. "Tell me."

He purposefully kept his voice harsh. If she tried to deny him the truth one more time...

"A-a hug," she answered. Her teeth were chattering just like the night they'd met. This time he doubted it had anything to do with the cold. "But you don't seem like the hugging type, so I just n-need something to hold onto." She looked around the bed. "Muh-maybe a pillow—"

He climbed all the way onto the bed and dragged her into his arms, tucking her head into his chest. She was right, he wasn't the hugging type, but he didn't think twice about holding her. If this was what she needed, he was going to give it to her. There wasn't even an inner debate as he settled back against the gold headboard with her wrapped tightly in his arms.

She continued to cry for a long while, dampening the front of his robe. But at least she stopped trembling. Eventually her sobs began to quiet, no longer wracking her entire body. And when she spoke next, her teeth had stopped chattering.

"Thank you," she whispered. "I'm sorry you had to do that. I know it was probably hard for you, especially given your, uh, intimacy issues. But I want you to know I appreciate it. So really, thank you so much."

Her words of gratitude grated through him. What kind of unfeeling person did she think he was? Yes, technically she was right about his feelings about intimacy. He put women into three categories: those he would have sex with, those he did not wish to have sex with, and those who he could not have sex with, and the women he chose to spend time with usually didn't cry or show much emotion at all. They were like him, efficient and capable lovers who respected his disdain for drama and left without tears as soon as the act was done.

He'd never held a woman this long, much less comforted her through a crying fit. Nonetheless, he didn't like the way Samantha categorized his preference for keeping his sex life drama free as—what had she called it? Intimacy issues. The two words set Nikolai's teeth on edge. She obviously thought he was defective—defective like his father had been defective, and so emotionally deficient, he'd let a woman cry as Samantha had in his presence.

"You can go now," Samantha said, her voice awkward, as she started to pull back. "As you can see, I've calmed. But seriously, thanks again—"

He kissed her. He couldn't say exactly why. To keep her from thanking him again, or maybe—he did not want to think too hard about this—maybe because he didn't want her to remove herself from his embrace.

Whatever the reason, his hand came up to her cheek, pulled her closer, and the next thing he knew, he was kissing her. Not a soft kiss either. Not the kind of comforting peck men sometimes gave women to distract them from their hysterics.

No, he couldn't make that excuse, because when his lips landed on hers, they crashed down hard, demanding... desperate. Don't cry. Don't tell me to leave.

She didn't cry. She didn't tell him to leave.

But she did go completely stiff, a surprised gasp escaping her lips. He felt her hands come up to his chest, and for a moment he thought she would push him away. But then she moaned, turning her soft body into his and giving him better access to her lips and her breasts, which he didn't even realize he'd gone after until his hand was underneath her shirt, palming one heavy globe as his tongue ravaged her mouth.

Kissing her was unlike anything he'd ever experienced, like coming out of a Siberian prison to a home cooked meal. Yet he wanted more. More than what he was getting. Wanted... wanted...

Nikolai groaned roughly against her lips. He needed to stop. This was happening too fast and he was a systematic lover. He enjoyed conquering a woman, making her surrender to his erotic assault, sometimes more than once, before he calmly put on a condom and took what he wanted from her with the sure knowledge that she was now fully prepped to receive his larger than usual length. Like a table that had been properly set.

But this kiss... it had him pumping himself against her, his arousal thick underneath his boxer briefs and straining to get out. There came a new feeling in his chest, one he dimly recognized as the opposite of the usual ice he maintained at all time. One that caused a weird tumbling sensation inside his stomach.

He tore her t-shirt, ripping it off her body with one hard yank. She was making him feel. She was making him feel. She was making him...

Slow down, he said to himself, once again trying to rein in the kiss. But it was like trying to stop a forest fire. With a hose.

Both of his hands were kneading her breasts now—no, a trickle of logic couldn't stop what was happening between them. The only thing that could have stopped him in that moment was if she had told him to stop, that she didn't want what was happening between them to happen. Only then would he have torn himself away from this kiss, released her bountiful breasts, which seemed to have been made to fill up his large hands.

"Oh God, don't stop!" She moaned again, pressing her

breasts into his hands, her lips into his mouth, her core into his...

He had no awareness of flipping her on her back, of his robe coming off, of removing the barrier of her panties. No memory of getting on top of her.

Later, all he would remember of those moments was the feel of finally sinking inside her, the sound of himself groaning with sweet, aching relief. Because it felt like coming home.

SAM TECHNICALLY UNDERSTOOD WHAT WAS HAPPENING, BUT then again, she kind of didn't.

First had come the unexpected kiss from Nikolai right after she tried to put on her big girl pants and stop blubbering all over his robe. Instead of letting her go and running like a man on fire back to his room as she'd expected he would, he kissed her! And then there had been confusion, her mind shorting out as she tried to figure out what was happening.

Then her body caught on fire, a volcano of desperate need forming inside her core, so quickly that she didn't have time to argue with herself. Her body instantaneously responded to his unexpected kiss with a mind of its own, her breasts swelling, her core becoming unbearably hot. Even her mind abandoned her, screaming right along with every other inch of her, to let this happen. All she needed—and the only thing that would take the nightmare away, was having the Russian hockey player inside of her.

There came a ripping sound and then both his hands were on her breasts, squeezing so hard it caused her pain. But not the kind that truly hurt. It was a sweet pain that tingled all the way down to her core. She could feel his hips pumping against her body as he continued to kiss her, his erection thick and hard as it brushed against the top of her right thigh. But that wasn't where she wanted him. No, she wanted him somewhere else, and without conscious thought she adjusted herself to get him there, pressing herself into his long length... she let out a shocked gasp. She could actually feel the outline of his mushroom head behind his briefs—that was how hard he was.

Then it was too late. One press against him. That was all it took.

The next thing she knew, her back hit the bed. Her panties were yanked down and then his huge body was on top her and... Oh God... he pushed inside and he was... another cry up to the heavens as she bit down on her lip... he was so thick and heavy inside her wet folds. His large shaft spread the outer lips of her pussy farther apart than she'd ever imagined they could go and he didn't stop, not until he was all the way in, his balls coming to rest against her entrance as he gave her a moment to adjust to his size.

She didn't take that moment. Sam was so hot, so wet for him. Instead she shifted underneath him, urging him with a pelvic thrust to keep going. This wasn't natural, she thought on the razor edge of sanity. She'd never been filled like this before, and it should be hurting. But the hurt never came, only pleasure as he braced himself above her and started moving inside of her.

He was as she'd expected he'd be, despite all his talk about her pleasure the night they met. Rough. He filled and refilled her with slow thrusts, hard and raw. But Sam didn't mind, couldn't mind. It felt magnificent, and another moan tore out of her throat when he adjusted and his length began hitting her clit at just the right angle every time he plunged into her.

Apparently, that was the right answer. Sam realized he must have been looking for her hot spot when he was going at her rough and slow. Now he sped up, his powerful boy finding a rough and fast rhythm on top of hers.

Sam cried out helplessly, her body meeting his thrusts in a

dance as old as time. With past lovers, it had always taken her a while to get warmed up—sometimes too long—she'd missed out on more than a few finales with her grad school ex.

But with Nikolai, she soon realized she wasn't going to last long. The way he was pumping into her was so incredibly hot. Like having her nightmare flipped over to reveal the most erotic dream. Sam couldn't believe it. Any of it. That he actually fit, that this kind of pleasure was happening to her of all people.

He said something quick in Russian, lifted one of her legs up and over his shoulder and then continued his relentless drive into her. This made the sex even more intense—an upgrade she wouldn't have guessed possible a few seconds ago. And the new angle made it so he could go in even deeper, so deep that—

Sam cried out when electric bursts of pleasure started shooting through her core. So sharp, they were almost painful. So exquisite, it took Sam a few strung out moments to realize he must be hitting her g-spot, a place so deep and hidden she'd suspected it might only exist in legend.

But she believed now. Oh God, did she believe. Her hands found his hips and held on tight. To Sam this felt like more than sex. It felt like healing. Like Nikolai had somehow figured out the one way to keep her from completely unraveling after what had nearly happened earlier that night.

The way he moved inside her, like an animal, his strokes, powerful and crude. Yet each stroke took away the ugliness of the nightmare that had brought him to her. Sam had always taken pride in being an independent woman when it came to relationships. The total opposite of her mother, who'd only seemed to exist to be at her stepfather's beck and call. But in this case, all her independence flew out the window. She clung to him, drawing on his strength, greedily receiving everything he was giving her.

And then she came. So violently, the fiery blast of ecstasy completely seized up her body, making it so she couldn't speak, couldn't breathe. The sensation was so overwhelming, it almost felt like choking to death. The best way ever to die.

The only part of her she could still feel moving was her core, which squeezed around his thick length with fervor, milking his cock with urgent insistence.

Her mind blowing climax seemed to break Nikolai. More clipped Russian words, and then he lost all control, driving his shoulder into the back of her knee and hammering into her even faster. Like he was running to catch up with her. Getting closer… and closer… until he was right there with her.

It was a strange magic, feeling him come. His strong body jerked above her, then went just as rigid as hers had, right before he released into her with a helpless yell. His eyes were squeezed closed, she dimly noted. As if however hard it had been for her to bear the onslaught of such a pleasurable climax, it had been twice as hard for him.

Obviously she wasn't the only one who'd been over-whelmed by what had just happened between them, she thought with a small amount of pride, watching him weather the same storm of sensation.

It felt like eons had passed when he finally relaxed, his breath whooshing out as he dropped her leg. But it still wasn't over. He released her leg, but recaptured her lips, scooping her up so her breasts were flush against his chest as he kissed her with such rough desperation, Sam could tell it had been just as good for him as it had been for her.

But then he said, "Samantha," against her lips. "Saman-tha…" Over and over again. Like a prayer.

Sam froze.

She hated being called Samantha. She never allowed anyone to call her that. Not even Josie. No one. Hearing her full name on his lips completely vaporized the cloud of ultimate satisfaction she'd been floating on and she tumbled out of the sky. Falling down to Earth hard as she realized what she'd done. Exactly what she'd done.

She'd had sex with Nikolai Rustanov. Nikolai Rustanov! A man she barely knew and had only met a few days ago. And Pavel's soon-to-be guardian.

Oh, God! Oh, God! This is bad, so bad.

She pushed against his chest in a panic, desperate to get out from under him. He immediately stopped kissing her, and lifted up.

"What is wrong?" he asked her, his accent even thicker than usual as he pulled all the way out of her. "Did I hurt you, Samantha?"

"Don't call me that!" she answered, scrambling to sit up. Only to freeze again when she felt something that shouldn't have been there.

And that was when the real horror of what they'd just done hit her as hard as a tractor trailer with a full load. No, he hadn't hurt her, but even though he was fully removed from her now, not even touching her, she could still feel him. Inside of her. So much of him that he was leaking out onto her thighs.

Sam cursed and covered her face with her hands. They hadn't just had really inadvisable hot sex. They'd had really inadvisable hot sex without a condom.

Chapter Sixteen

NIKOLAI HAD ASSISTED in helping his father kill over a dozen men by the time he turned fifteen, but he'd never done anything as hard as listening to his mother cry in their apartment bathroom.

It had been a bad month for Natasha. One filled with a stomach flu that wouldn't abate. His mother, who had always been a generally healthy person, complained bitterly at first. Not used to being waited on by her sons, who cooked dinner and cleaned while she recovered.

But then the stomach flu, which Natasha had assured them would only last for a couple of days, lingered for a couple of weeks. By the second week of her illness, his mother grew quiet, her complaints coming to an abrupt stop. Eventually she'd called Nikolai into her room while Fedya was in the bathroom. She told him to walk with Fedya to school, but to leave halfway through the day and take the bus to a smaller town about an hour away from theirs. One of the ones the Rustanovs didn't bother with because it was known as a place where older people went to live out the rest of their lives in cheap apartments. His mother insisted Nikolai must go there to get the test she needed, to a place farther away where no one would recognize him as the bastard son of Sergei Rustanov.

Getting the test hadn't bothered Nikolai. Much like when he accompanied his father on hit jobs, he froze himself on the inside, divorcing his actions from his emotions. He'd refused to feel anything as he did exactly as his mother said. He delivered the test to her in a white paper bag and he'd watched her disappear with it into their shared bathroom with the dispassion of a morgue clerk.

However, the scream that came from the bathroom a few minutes later, followed by wild sobbing and a long wailing, "*Nyet!*" —those sounds he'd never forget. He could still hear them sometimes, when things got too quiet inside his head.

And he could hear them now, over two decades later, as he once again stood outside the bathroom door, this time dressed in the Polar robe he'd so quickly discarded in order to get Samantha underneath him.

Samantha hadn't been nearly as dramatic as his mother, merely covering her face before running into the bathroom without a word. The shower had come on just a few seconds after the door closed behind her. But that hadn't been enough to keep him from going to the door, from standing outside of it like her useless dog. He looked over his shoulder at the digital clock on the bedroom's nightstand.

She'd been in there for over twenty minutes, the shower running at full blast. Meanwhile, he'd been standing there, trapped in the memory of what would turn out to be the death nail in his mother's coffin.

Just as he was thinking of going to check on her, the shower finally stopped, and soon after he could hear her moving around, probably drying off. Nikolai drew himself up and waited. But then, nothing. Everything went quiet. And somehow that made it even worse than the wild sobs that had come from his mother.

He knocked on the door. "Samantha, come out," he commanded.

"No thank you, and please don't call me that," she answered through the door.

He didn't pound on the door, but his voice was fist enough as he said, "Come out and talk to me. I will wait here for you and this will be hard to explain to boy when he wakes up."

There were a few moments of silence, during which he could almost see her on the other side of the door, weighing her options, maybe wondering whether he was serious about standing out there until Pavel woke.

He was serious. Dead serious. And perhaps she sensed that, because a few seconds later the door opened and she reappeared, now dressed in a red bath towel, her long twists pulled into a large ball on top of her head. And holy shit, as his American teammates might say, but he was glad to be wearing a robe, because his cock responded badly to the sight of her in a bath towel. He was once again achingly hard and ready to take her again. Despite the circumstances, despite the fact that he'd already had her and she should be well on her way out of his system. With other women, he'd had to resist the urge to move to another room when it had been too late to send them home for the night. With Samantha, he had to resist the urge to reach out for her, to unwrap that towel from around her body, and once again bury himself in her warmth.

He forced himself to focus on her face. And was surprised to find she wasn't crying like his mother had that fateful night. In fact, her expression was totally composed, a serene work of art that put him in mind of vintage photos of Mother Teresa.

"Hi," she said, her voice calm and soft. "Sorry about that. It took me a while to clean up and process my thoughts."

"Over twenty minutes," he said.

"And I apologize," she answered automatically. "For everything. I'm fine now. You don't have to worry, though it was considerate of you to do so. But if you don't mind, I'd like to get some sleep before Pavel wakes up.

Nikolai stared at her. It was like she'd pushed a personality button, one that made every carefully considered word that came out of her mouth sound calm and gracious.

He didn't like it. He didn't like it at all.

"You are upset. About our sex… without condom."

He was upset, too. A man in his position—the owner of a team, and formerly a hockey player who'd been targeted by groupies and gold diggers alike. He'd never in his life, slept with a woman without a condom and he was deeply disturbed he'd been so caught up in getting to her, to getting inside her, that he'd violated his number one rule.

"I'm sorry," he told her now.

"I'm sorry, too," she answered. "But what's done is done. I don't need to talk about it and you don't need to worry about it."

The words, obviously meant to be reassuring were anything but.

His eyes narrowed. "If you are pregnant, what will you do?"

His question caused a momentary crack in her calm façade and she shifted in obvious discomfort. "First of all, I'm not pregnant."

"You cannot know this," Nikolai said.

"I'm not," she insisted, her voice pleasant but tight. As if all one needed to keep from getting pregnant was the right attitude and the right tone of voice. "But if I was, it would be my choice."

Nikolai's heart constricted with the thought of her…

"And your choice would be what?" he asked, needing to know.

She averted her eyes. "Well, if I was—which I'm not, but if I was, I'd, um… I'd, um…"

Nikolai braced himself to hear the ugly truth.

"I'd have to… keep it," she said quietly.

Nikolai stared at her, his mouth open.

"I'm over thirty now and though I fully support a woman's right to choose under any circumstance at any age, I—I…" Somehow this part seemed harder for her than her fierce defense of abortion rights. "When it comes down to it, I want to be a mother. I have for a while now. And if you want to be a mother like I do, you don't exercise that option." She glanced up at him, then quickly looked away. "No matter who the father is."

Conflicting emotions collided inside of Nikolai's chest like gladiators in an arena. On one hand, joy that she would go through with the pregnancy no matter what. On the other hand, it was clear she was upset that he was the father.

Him. Not her boyfriend, the police officer.

His heart, which had thawed for a few moments when they'd come together in a tangle of fire and ice, hardened again.

"In one month, I will ask you question again. If you are pregnant, you will tell me."

She looked up at him, her eyes aggressively calm, like two dark, placid stones inside her pretty face.

"I'm not pregnant," she assured him.

"If you are you will tell me," he insisted back.

"Yes, I will," she finally agreed. "But I'm not pregnant, so this conversation is, you know… pretty moot."

He wasn't sure what "moot" meant, but the promise was all that mattered. Samantha was strange, and at times infuriating, but he didn't think she was a liar.

As if reading his thoughts she said, "But again, all of this is just hypothetical. And none of it matters, because I'm not pregnant."

Chapter Seventeen

One month later

SAM STARED at the three pregnancy tests resting on top of the staff bathroom's toilet seat.

"Damn!" she whispered. "Damn, damn, damn!"

She was totally, undeniably pregnant.

If the constant queasiness that had set in a couple of days ago hadn't made it clear enough, the fact that she was four days into her usually clockwork cycle with still no period made it crystal clear. And just in case that wasn't evidence enough, she now had these three over-the-counter pregnancy tests: one with two lines, one with a cross, one stating in letters bold and plain, "Pregnant."

So no, there was pretty much zero doubt. She was pregnant.

Sam slumped back against the wall, her stomach roiling with more than morning sickness. How was she going to tell Nikolai about this?

She had to tell him. She promised she would. But, oh God,

this would make things so awkward. Even more awkward than things currently were, with her tenuously serving as a sort of de facto nanny to Pavel, two weeks after Nikolai had officially been awarded custody of his nephew. Normally, it would have taken longer than that, but the hockey star with the newly discovered half-black nephew had made front page news in Indiana, and magically, the case had been heard in record time.

So now she was only living under his roof because he hadn't kicked her out. Yet. And also because he didn't seem all that interested in raising Pavel himself. Other than insisting he be sent to St. Peter's, an all boy's school. It was one of the best private schools in Indiana, but Sam suspected his insistence on sending Pavel to this particular school had to do with them being willing to have a security guard posted outside Pavel's classroom at all times. Per Nikolai's request.

But other than that, Nikolai seemed content to let Sam deal with all his nephew's before and after school needs. Nikolai often worked weekends, too, traveling to out of town games with his team. So she and Pavel had been left to navigate Saturdays and Sundays—and any other days the team traveled —on their own with the occasional assist from her intern, Nyla. The grad student was currently working at Ruth's House for free, and was therefore happy to pick up extra babysitting hours when Sam needed to put in weekend time at the shelter.

But other than hiring a former marine named Dirk to oversee Pavel's safety outside his home, Nikolai seemed less than interested in the fact that there was now a child underneath his roof. He didn't make any effort to spend his free morning hours with Pavel, and he often worked so late that he got home after Pavel had gone to bed. Some seriously dickish behavior on Nikolai's part, Sam thought. But having made the monumentally stupid decision to sleep with him without a condom, it wasn't like she had much of a moral leg to stand on… or like she could even look him in the eye these days.

No, instead, she'd focused on doing whatever she could to help Pavel adjust to his new, luxurious lifestyle while keeping her head down as she did so. Maybe if Nikolai didn't notice she was still around, he wouldn't ask when she'd be leaving.

But now she was pregnant and that would definitely throw a big ass hitch in her "out of sight, out of mind" plan of action.

A knock sounded on the door, interrupting her panicked thoughts.

"Sam, you in there?" came Nyla's voice through the door.

Sam hastily disposed of all the sticks, sweeping them into the small wastebasket beside the toilet. "Yeah, I'm here. Do you need something?"

"We've got two intake request from Hope House. I told them we were full, too, but they're hoping we can squeeze two more in. Also, Marco's here on rounds again, and I know you asked me to handle it when he stops by but he's saying he'd like to see you."

Sam sighed. So not only was she pregnant. Not only was Ruth's House overbooked. But now Marco was literally at the door. She took a deep breath and came out to face her African-American intern, Nyla Weathers.

Nyla had five piercings in her right eyebrow, a lip ring, a nose ring, a laughing Buddha tattooed on the back of her neck, and long relaxed hair—which almost made her look traditional until she turned and you could see the hair was completely shaved off on one side. Yet she looked at Sam like she was the strange one when she came out of the bathroom.

"Hey, you okay?" Nyla asked with a worried frown. "You look, I don't know. Kind of shook. If you want I can deal with Marco." She gave Sam a rueful grin. "I've learned a lot about how to handle overbearing men since coming to intern here."

That almost got a chuckle out of Sam. This was why she'd only been half-joking when she'd suggested to Josie that Nyla could take over Ruth's House Indiana. The younger woman was capable and passionate about advocating for women and children. And like Sam, she didn't back down when presented with challenging situations.

But in this case, she turned down the offer, telling Nyla she'd call Hope House back after she talked to Marco.

Marco's face lit up when she came outside.

"Hey, long time no see," he said, cupping her shoulders. "Why haven't you been returning any of my phone calls?"

Sam desperately wanted to lie, to tell him she'd been busy, anything to not have to deal with Marco after just finding out that she was definitely pregnant with Nikolai Rustanov's child. But unfortunately, she'd seen too many women stalked to let Marco go on thinking he had any kind of chance with her.

She leveled Marco with a frank look before saying, "Marco, I haven't been returning your phone calls because I'm not interested in talking to you in a non-professional capacity. I don't want to date you."

Marco's eyebrows went up, like she'd both surprised and insulted him. "Wow, that's harsh!"

"I know," she said. And that was all she said. These were the rules of relationships in the world she lived in. Don't give men reasons, or anything that could be used against you later as a reason, to overstep boundaries. Be okay with them thinking you're a bitch, if that meant they'd leave you alone.

Despite her harsh words, Marco still didn't let go of her shoulders. "But I thought we had something, Sam. We've got a lot in common. We're both doing good in the community. You're cute," he reached up and stroked one of her twists behind her ear, "...I'm cute."

Sam had to work not to laugh. Marco, she noted, was still very charming. Just not a match for her. Plus, it showed how little Marco knew about her if he thought they had a lot in common. He was from a stable, loving, and close-knit Latino family. His desktop picture was actually one of him, his parents, and his four siblings, all smiling at the camera like they didn't have a care in the world.

Sam was the total opposite. A do-gooder who'd worked crazy hours before Pavel had come along because the alternative to that was being alone since she didn't have any family to take smiling pictures with. But Marco didn't know just how different their pasts were because she'd done with him what she'd always done with the men she dated—kept every conversation focused mostly on him.

She didn't blame Marco for not knowing much about her below the surface, but still she had to tell him, "We're not a match, Marco. And I don't want you to go on thinking we ever could be."

Marco frowned and his hands tightened around her shoulders. "Is this because of Rustanov?" he asked, his face darkening. "You two got something going on now? Is that why you're dumping me?"

She couldn't help the guilty look that crossed her face but she said, "No, we're not together."

He studied her, his suspicion obvious. "But you don't want to date me now."

"No."

His mouth flattened into an angry line. "Mind telling me what changed?"

She opened her mouth to tell him exactly why she didn't want to go out with him, prepared to give him a no holds barred list of reasons if that was what it took. But she stopped when goose bumps suddenly sprang up on her skin. Her heart filled with knowing apprehension even before she turned to look. There was only one person she knew with a stare so intense, she could actually feel it.

And yes… yes, there was Nikolai Rustanov standing at the bottom of the steps with his hands jammed in his pea coat pockets, a thunderous look on his face.

Chapter Eighteen

NIKOLAI WATCHED Samantha and her cop on the porch having what looked like a very intimate conversation as he approached the shelter. The cop's hands were on her shoulders and his forehead rested against hers. Only for a few moments, but even when he stepped back, his hands never left her, and by the time Nikolai got all the way to the porch's bottom step, the cop was still touching her. Touching Samantha. Touching what was his.

Nikolai had to work hard to hold himself exactly where he was. She was still with the cop, he realized, his chest filling up with something he recognized all too well as despair. Still with him, despite...

He abandoned that thought, feeling like a fool.

Of course she was still with him. Why had he expected anything different? Just because he hadn't so much as thought about another woman over the past month, and had buried himself in work to keep from obsessing over Samantha and the thought that she could be carrying his baby—no, that didn't mean she had spend the past month doing the same.

After all, he thought darkly, as scared as his mother had been of his father, that hadn't stopped her from seeking out other male company when he pulled one of his disappearing acts. He of all people should know that sleeping with a woman, even possibly impregnating her, didn't guarantee her fidelity.

Samantha suddenly turned, as if just now realizing Nikolai was at the bottom of the steps. And when the cop saw him standing there, his hands dropped to his sides. But even as he stepped away from Samantha, Nikolai's mind continued to burn with the memory of what he'd seen. The cop had been touching her, stroking her hair, making her smile.

Basically doing all the things Nikolai wasn't allowed to do in his current position as a much-regretted one night stand.

They both regarded him for a few silent seconds. Her with wide-eyed confusion. Him with petulant anger.

"What are you doing here?" the cop asked, his arm twining round Samantha's shoulders like she belonged to him. Like he was now protecting her. From Nikolai.

Rage flared up hot as a blue flame inside Nikolai's usually icy soul. But somehow he kept his voice level when he answered, "I am here to talk with Samantha. About a personal matter."

Marco turned to Samantha. "You let him call you Samantha?" he asked.

"No, I don't…" She rubbed her temple like the situation was giving her a headache. Then she said, "Marco, I need to talk to him. And then I need to get back to work."

Marco looked at Nikolai, and Nikolai didn't bother to keep the smug satisfaction off his face. Samantha had chosen him over Marco, and that seemed to make Marco even angrier than Nikolai's unexpected interruption.

He put Nikolai in the mind of one of the pampered Rustanov children in that moment. He had been to a couple of family events since Alexei had legitimized the family's business and insisted on bringing Nikolai into the fold. The current crop of Russian-born Rustanov children had grown up in the lap of legitimate luxury, untarnished by the old mafia family's shame. They tended to be perfectly pleasant—until they didn't get their way. Then came the Chernobyl-style meltdowns.

For a few moments, Nikolai suspected Marco might throw a temper tantrum over Samantha's brusque dismissal. But in the end, he just said, "That's okay. I'll see you later, Sammy."

He said it to Samantha, but aimed it at Nikolai.

Nikolai responded with a stony stare, his eyes locked on their iciest setting as he waited for the other man to leave,. At least he didn't kiss her before he left, Nikolai thought. He didn't trust himself to stay still if that happened.

Not today. Not after thirty days of either being ignored or avoided by Samantha during waking hours and haunted by her whenever he closed his eyes. No matter how much he tried to put her out of his mind during the day, he couldn't keep himself from dreaming about her. And the dream he'd had the night before had been the worst one yet. Them making love in his bed, her belly large and round with his baby, his ring flashing on her finger.

He'd never wanted a wife, or kids, or anything remotely approaching what he'd seen in that dream, but dammit if he hadn't woken up hard as a steel pipe. And he'd felt like an idiot, stroking himself off, unable to stop thinking about those dream images of her naked and pregnant as he did so.

That was why he was here now, using every ounce of his icy resolve to keep from exploding with rage. After a morning of barely being able to concentrate on his work, he'd gone out and bought a pregnancy test and headed over to Ruth's House —only to find her canoodling with her boyfriend.

He'd be damned if he let this go on another day. As he

waited for the cop to get back in his car and drive away, he made a solemn vow. If she wasn't truly pregnant, he wanted her gone. Gone from his house and gone from his mind.

As soon as the cop's car was out of sight, he came up the porch steps and held up the bag.

She eyed it and he had the feeling she knew what it was just as his mother had when he'd held up a similar bag to her many years ago. But unlike his mother, she didn't immediately take it.

"It is pregnancy test," he informed her. "Thirty days are up."

Understanding shadowed her eyes, but still she didn't take the bag. Instead she folded her arms across her chest and said, "I know it's been a month. But I'm in the middle of a work day and I can't invite you to have this discussion in my office, since no males over sixteen are allowed inside Ruth's House. So how about if I shoot you an email?"

His eyes narrowed. "Shoot me email," he repeated, wondering not for the first time if the woman he'd been near obsessed with over the past month was indeed crazy.

"Yes, an email," she said, backing away toward the door. "That's way better than doing this here on the steps, don't you think? So yeah, I'll do that right after I handle this very important call I need to return—"

He caught her sweatered arm, his hand manacling around her wrist. "Tell me. Now."

"No, seriously, it can wait," she said. "And it's probably better sent over email. That way you'll have all the details and be able to digest the information in your own time, at your own pace..."

She tugged on her arm, but Nikolai easily kept her there, his voice colder than icicles as he intoned, "Right now."

"Ms. McKinley? Everything all right here?"

Nikolai looked down the steps to see a little man who had

to be in his sixties or seventies. He had his hand on top of a baton, as if he planned to do something about the scene in front of him. But he didn't look like he could fend off Pavel, much less keep Nikolai from getting the information he wanted from Samantha.

Chapter Nineteen

SAM USED the interruption to gain her freedom.

"Please let me go, right now," she whispered to Nikolai, low enough that Danny, their security guard, wouldn't be able to hear her. "This isn't a good look for me or Ruth's House."

To her surprise, Nikolai instantly let her go. He even took a step back, like he didn't know what had come over him when he grabbed her.

Relief flooded her heart. Good, good, this was good. A long, detailed email was the perfect way to handle this. It would take the weird energy out of the situation, she reasoned, and put some distance between her and Nikolai so they could both think about how to handle this turn of events without angry words or hurt feelings.

Resolved, she turned toward the door.

"Please, tell me. I must know," came Nikolai's voice, harsh and choked, like he was both embarrassed and desperate to be pleading with her to tell him the truth. "You promised."

She inwardly cursed, guilt overtaking her completely reasonable decision to send him an email. Why? She had no idea. It wasn't like they were together in any kind of capacity and she was planning to keep her promise to let him know if she was pregnant… just not in person.

Yet guilt kept her from punching in the security code and pulling the door open. Even more guilt than she'd had while she was putting the kibosh on Marco.

And maybe that guilt wouldn't have been enough to get her to do this here at her place of work—and let's face it, her place of respite. But when she turned back to assure him an email was truly the best course of action, he said it again.

"Please, tell me," he said. "I can't work. I can't think."

Nikolai Rustanov didn't strike her as a man who said please very often. And she couldn't help but notice the lines around his eyes. Tight, worried lines that made him look not like the impassable mountain she'd painted him to be, but like a man. A man who might have had as many problems sleeping over the past month as she had.

"Ms. McKinley, everything all right up there?" Danny asked again.

She'd been so caught up in the moment with Nikolai that she'd forgotten the old security guard was still down there at the bottom of the steps. She'd forgotten everything but her and Nikolai and the life they'd unwittingly created together.

Damn my soft heart, she thought to herself. Then out loud she said, "It's okay, Danny. I was just about to walk Mr. Rustanov to his car. He's a friend of the shelter."

Code for big donor—not an out of sorts husband. Which wasn't exactly true, but Samantha couldn't think of a less awkward way to let the security guard know Nikolai wasn't a threat.

Danny visibly relaxed, letting his hand fall from his baton. "Alright then. I'll just take my lunch break, if you don't need me for awhile."

Sam forced a smile to her lips. "That's a great idea, Danny."

After some awkward goodbyes, she made the silent trek with Nikolai back to his Escalade. The entire block in front of Ruth's House was zoned as ten minute loading and unloading parking only. Apparently the Russian thought this would be more than a ten-minute conversation, because unlike Marco, who was always parking in the intake spots for convenience, he'd parked much further down the street in the regular parking zone. All the way on the next block, which meant they'd be able to talk in semi-private with no worries about being seen by anyone at Ruth's House.

Still, Sam felt beyond self-conscious when they reached his car and Nikolai's eyes zeroed in like lasers. Waiting.

She took a deep breath and just said it. "I'm pregnant."

Nikolai went still as a statue, his expression so neutral, it was impossible for Sam to even guess at what he was thinking. So she kept on talking.

"I still have to go to the doctor to get it confirmed, but I took three tests. All positive. So... I'm pretty sure."

Still no reaction from him. And Sam rushed on, feeling like she had to get it all out, if only so she could escape back to the safety of Ruth's House.

"But what I would have said in my email is you don't have to worry about any of this. I'm not going to ask you for anything. I have a good job and lots of resources. I'll take care of everything—"

He suddenly came back to life, his gaze narrow and suspicious.

"You are sure it is mine?" he asked.

Sam blinked. "Am I sure it's yours?" she repeated.

Now he outright sneered at her. "You and cop? Did you use condom with him?"

For a moment, the engine inside Sam's mind stalled out, choking on indignation. It took a few open and shuts of her mouth before she was able to say, "Okay, let's get a few things straight here."

She put a finger in the air to make her point. "A month ago, I was *upset*. I'd had a very bad experience followed by a very bad nightmare. I never would have let you anywhere near me if those two things hadn't occurred. Understand, you are the only guy I've ever not used protection with, and I feel pretty damn stupid about that. Especially now with you acting like I'm up in here getting pregnant all the time by guys I don't know. Like you think this is how I get my kicks and giggles. But trust me when I say, I'm just as unhappy about being pregnant with your baby as you are. If it had been up to me, this is the last way I would have chosen to get pregnant."

He flinched, like her words had more than insulted him. Like they had caused him pain. But then his jaw clenched, and he said, "It was necessary question." He gave her one of his ugly frowns. "You will keep it? Because you—how did you say —are too old to make other choice?"

Sam shook her head, feeling the usual disappointment when it came to guys and relationships beginning to set in. No, she hadn't expected a romance novel or anything when she told him the news. But she hadn't expected him to ask if it was his either or whether she was still against aborting it, which would make his life a whole lot easier, she knew.

The whole situation made her feel dirty. But she stood her ground with him.

"I'm not happy about the circumstances, but I'm happy about being a mother," she told him through gritted teeth. "And I'm keeping this baby, no matter what."

She waited, giving him a chance to try to convince her otherwise, but he just stood there, with no expression whatso-ever. Like a block of ice. Nope, this wasn't a romance novel situation at all. She wasn't that kind of girl and Nikolai wasn't that kind of man. She'd known that about him from the start, so there was no reason for the piercing hurt now radiating through her body over his total lack of reaction.

Suddenly Sam felt exhausted. Completely and utterly exhausted.

"I'm going back to work," she said, having to put real effort into keeping her voice strong. "Like I said, I'm more than cool with doing this on my own."

Then she walked away, disappointment in him and the situation and herself dogging her heels. And she wasn't surprised when this time, he did nothing to stop her from leaving.

Chapter Twenty

THAT DAY, Nikolai came home from work early. Not because he didn't have plenty to do. The Polar were due to go out on the road at the end of the week, and though they were nowhere near contention for the Stanley Cup this year, it was imperative that Nikolai observe them on the road and off this season, so he could figure out how to make them great next season.

However, as the Polar's new owner, he couldn't just worry about the team, he had to worry about the entire franchise. So he had meetings with not just his coaches and general managers, but also with PR professionals and ad companies.

Maybe he was a Rustanov after all, because he didn't mind the business aspects of the job as much as he'd thought he would. Nevertheless, not being able to play the game nearly every single day was beginning to take its own kind of toll. No longer could he take his troubles and thoughts down to the rink or take out his aggression on teammates and opposing hockey players. No longer could he "ice out"—playing and playing until all his cares froze away.

Paperwork and meetings just somehow didn't provide the

same release. Nor would he turn to drugs like his brother had. So that only left one thing: sex. In the past, he would have welcomed a road trip and the availability of women who only cared about who he was and didn't mind letting him use them as stress relief.

But in this case, he couldn't see himself employing that option on this next trip. First of all, he was the team owner now, no longer a player. And even if he had been in the position to pick up groupies, the thought of sleeping with one made him feel dead inside, even more numb than killing those Russians.

It was hard for him to admit this to himself, especially after what he'd seen on the porch of Ruth's House, but he didn't want any other woman. Not like he wanted Samantha.

And now she was pregnant. With his child. Unhappily so, he'd reminded himself the following day. Then he'd had to keep on reminding himself, over and over again, during the morning practice and the meetings he took that afternoon. But those harsh reminders hadn't been enough to stop him from telling Isaac to cancel the rest of his meetings at five and leaving early for home.

He cursed himself all the way to the house. It was like the compulsion he kept having to check on Pavel every night before he went to bed, even though he knew the boy was fine, knew the threat of the Russians had been eliminated. Knowing Sam was pregnant with his baby made him want to be close to her. Physically close. And as foolish as he felt about the whole thing, he kept his foot firmly on the gas pedal, driving faster than he should to get to her.

When he arrived home, he followed the sounds of laughter to the kitchen, and what he found there stopped his heart.

Samantha sitting next to Pavel at the island counter. Their heads both bent over a textbook, Samantha's arm resting across Pavel's shoulders. They looked like... a mother and son.

A real mother and son. The easy way they laughed together, not even a total stranger happening upon them would have doubted how close they were or known they weren't family in every sense of the word.

Nikolai was not prepared for the ache of longing that hit him upon seeing Samantha like this. An ache followed by a piercing wish for her to stand up and come around the island to greet him. Like a wife. Like someone who was happy he was home.

And in that moment, he regretted, truly regretted what he'd said to her when he visited Ruth's House the day before. *Da*, he'd had every right to ask the question, especially after the scene he'd witnessed between her and Marco. He'd still been angry about that when she told him the news, his mind reeling with the revelation that she hadn't broken up with the cop. And he hadn't been able to get past it. The sight of them together. The idea of Samantha letting the cop touch her. Maybe more.

At the time, he'd felt completely justified in lashing out. Had, in fact, been aiming to hurt her with his accusation.

But now, he felt like an idiot. Seeing her like this with Pavel, all he wanted was for her to be same way with him. A memory of Alexei's parents came to him then. The way they would sometimes kiss, soft on the lips, if Alexei's father had been away for a long time. The way his aunt's eyes had glowed with tenderness when she looked across the room at his uncle.

He wanted Samantha to look at him that way.

He did not get his wish. Back Up came trotting over to get petted, alerting the boy and Samantha to Nikolai's presence in the doorway. Upon seeing him there, Samantha's smile went away, as if a dark storm cloud had suddenly rolled in on her perfect picnic with Pavel.

Pavel immediately stopped laughing, too. But at least he said, "Hi, Uncle. You're home early."

Pavel's tone was pleased and Nikolai wished it wasn't so

hard for him to look directly at the boy. But he couldn't make himself do that often. Even with the much darker skin and the hair texture difference, his nephew looked too much like Fedya at that age. For Nikolai, it was like looking directly into a sun made of memories. Impossible to do without feeling like your eyes were burning.

So instead of looking at Pavel, he bent down and patted Back Up, who immediately flipped over on her back. Samantha's dog was the worst kind of manipulator, he was discovering. Give her even the smallest of strokes and she took you for a belly rub.

"Why were you laughing?" he asked Samantha and Pavel, as he rubbed his hand across Back Up's pink belly. The question came out harsher than he meant it to.

But there was a smile in Pavel's voice when he answered, "Because Mama is really bad at math. I didn't want to do my homework and Mama told me she'd do my homework for me, but I keep on having to correct it and put in the right answers."

"Luckily we're using pencil," Samantha said. Her voice had a different kind of smile in it.

"Luckily," Pavel agreed, cracking up again. "You're so bad at math!"

"And you're getting so good at it."

Nikolai stood there, rubbing Back Up's belly longer than necessary, awkward as a moose at a deer party. Obviously Pavel had no idea Sam was only pretending to be bad at math, and he could barely fathom such a scenario in his own past. Growing up, his mother had only to threaten to tell his father he wasn't doing something he was supposed to do, and Nikolai would do it. Right away.

But apparently Pavel had to be tricked into doing what he was supposed to do. It made him feel... he didn't know. Sometimes it felt like Pavel was a duty, something to be managed until he reached his majority. And sometimes... sometimes it felt like he was a conduit to memories Nikolai didn't want to have—memories he'd done a good job suppressing until the little boy had shown up in his life.

"Would you like some dinner?" Sam asked, her tone gracious but automatic. He got the feeling she would have offered anyone passing through the kitchen something to eat, even a servant.

"Mama and me made the noodles ourselves with your pasta machine!" Pavel told him, with great excitement in his voice. Like making noodles from scratch was the most exciting activity in the universe.

"*Da*, I will have spaghetti," he said quickly. Happy for the change of subject.

The careful smile fell off Samantha's face when he went over to the restaurant grade sink to wash his hands. And out of the corner of his eye, he noticed her hesitate before she went over to a cabinet, grabbed a bowl, and started filling it with pasta.

He sat down at the counter and watched her ladle meat sauce on top of the noodles before she came back over and set the bowl in front of him with a flat, "Here you go."

"Thank you," he answered, not knowing exactly why he'd agreed to eat a second dinner, even as he twirled the noodles around his fork.

Sam sat back down and said, "If we'd known you were coming, we wouldn't have eaten."

"It is okay," he answered, taking a bite of the spaghetti. It was good. Really good. Somehow better than what he was used to because it was plain and homemade. Not perfectly spiced to his exact specifications, like the meals Isaac delivered to his office.

He could feel Pavel and Samantha's eyes on him as he ate, as if a monster had entered their midst. And he had the feeling the quiet, filled with nothing but the sound of him eating the homemade spaghetti would have gone on forever if Pavel hadn't chosen that moment to ask, "When you were kids, did you have birthday parties?"

"Are you asking me or your uncle?" Samantha asked him.

Pavel became very interested in the problems on his math worksheet as he answered, "Both of you, I guess."

Samantha cleared her throat. "My mom made me a cake every year, and sometimes she took me out to dinner someplace like McDonald's and she'd get me a Happy Meal," she answered. "But no, never like a full on birthday party. How about you, Nikolai?" she asked. "Does Russia do the whole kids birthday party thing?"

"*Da*, we have these things, but I did not growing up," he answered.

"Why not?" she asked, looking at him directly for the first time since he'd arrived home.

He thought about the true answer, which was because at the end of the day, he was a bastard with a generally depressed mother and a father who wouldn't have shown up to a birthday party for him even if one had been thrown. And then he answered, "It is silly custom."

Pavel's cheeks reddened. "Yeah, you're right, Uncle. Birthday parties are kind of stupid. I don't know if I even want to go to the one Mateo invited me to."

A reasonable conclusion on the boy's part, Nikolai thought, but for some reason Samantha threw Nikolai a murderous look before saying to Pavel, "Birthday parties aren't so bad. We throw them for our kids at the shelter all the time and they're always a lot of fun. Maybe you should go to one and see how you like it."

But Pavel quickly glanced up at Nikolai and answered, "No, that's okay."

And so the matter was settled. Or at least Nikolai thought it was. A soft knock sounded on his study door a couple of hours later.

"Come in," he said, looking up from the work he'd brought home with him.

Sam stuck her head in. "Hey, got time to talk?" she asked.

Her voice was friendly and calm, like that scene in the kitchen hadn't been awkward at all. He frowned. He was beginning to suspect friendly and calm was Samantha's default for when she was anything but.

Nonetheless he took off his reading glasses and indicated she should sit down, which she did, looking around his study, a more somber affair than the rest of the house with dark wood paneling and a statesman like desk, so big, it had necessitated the interior designer and his crew break it down into pieces before rebuilding it inside the room.

"Wow," she said. "This is… maybe fifty times bigger than my office at Ruth's House. Sweet!"

A compliment, Nikolai realized after mulling her words over for a few moments. "Thank you," he said.

"So," she said, folding her hands on her lap. "How's it going? Everything good with the job?"

"*Da*, it is fine," he answered, knowing how Americans enjoyed their small talk. He awkwardly added, "I have much paperwork."

"Paperwork is the worst, right? I always say I enjoy everything about my job, except the paperwork. It's a real beast."

"*Da*, it is beast," he agreed, his voice stilted.

Why was it so hard to talk to this woman? He'd never had any problems talking with women before her. But everything about Samantha unsettled him, made him feel like he was once again the unacknowledged bastard of Sergei Rustanov. Not even good enough to warrant his parent's marriage.

"I came in here to talk about Pavel…" Samantha introduced the new subject like it was a delicate object, one she carefully set down on the desk between them. "He really admires you. He's very proud to have a hockey star for an uncle."

Having no idea how to answer that, Nikolai remained quiet and let her finish.

"I think that's a nice change of pace for him, because he's been embarrassed by his living situations for so long, feeling like there was something he had to hide. And now he can be proud of where he's living and who he's living with. In many ways, it's a dream come true for him."

None of these emotional truths ever would have occurred to Nikolai, but he said, "Yes, if I were Pavel, I would think so, too."

"And how about you? How do you think it's going with Pavel?"

"How do I think it's going with Pavel," he repeated, not quite understanding her meaning.

She talked slowly, like the ESL tutor he'd been given when he first joined the Polar. "Do you like how your relationship is progressing?"

He thought about this question. "It progresses fine," he answered. "Pavel is clean and fed and back in school. As you said, now he is very proud of his home and his family."

"Yes, but…" She reset, putting on another one of her bright smiles. "I'm happy that you came home early. Really happy. And I want to apologize for not giving you positive feedback on that action earlier. I wish I had responded better, I was just so surprised to see you come in. And I wish I had known you were coming home earlier so we could've all eaten dinner together."

Nikolai had to work hard to keep his face expressionless, to not let her see the pathetic soar of emotions her words sent off inside his chest. She was happy he'd come home early. Her vision about how she should have responded to it was nearly the same as his wish. Them all eating dinner together, like the happy families he'd only ever visited, but had never been a part of. The knowledge that she, too, wanted this, made the hot ache inside his chest gentle into a quiet warmth.

"It is okay," he told her. "You did not know I would come home early. I should have told you."

She leaned forward. "Is coming home earlier something you might be able to pull off more often?"

His heart nearly stopped beating. She wanted him to come home earlier more often.

"*Da*," he answered, wondering if he was in the middle of some kind of dream, if he shouldn't pinch himself to make sure. "I can come home earlier. Not on game nights or when I am on road with team, but other times, I can come home earlier and work here."

Her face lit up. "Really? Because if that's the case, maybe we could push dinner back an hour and you know… establish a family dinner routine with Pavel?"

A family routine. It was as if she knew his secret wants without having been told. And this time he couldn't keep the smile off his face as he answered, "*Da, Da*. That is good idea. I will come home early and eat family dinner."

She clapped her hands together, her genuine smile making him feel like he'd just won a trophy. She was beautiful when she was angry, but in that moment, he realized she was even more so when she was pleased.

"Okay, cool! Then I think we have a potentially good dynamic on our hands."

He had no idea what she meant by that, but he agreed, "Cool."

"And in the interest of your family dynamic, could you explain a little more about what's made you so anti-birthday party?" she asked

He froze, not liking that the subject had come back around to his past. Not liking it at all.

"It is silly custom."

"Yes, birthdays along with love," she said, her tone dry. "And you don't think that's a hard stance to take on things? Maybe something you might want to reconsider now that you've been given custody of an eight-year-old?"

A bad feeling began to boil inside his chest. "You are counselor," he realized out loud.

"Not my official title," she answered carefully. "But yes, it's one of the roles I serve at Ruth's House."

He gave her a heavy frown. "I did not ask for your counseling, but you have come here to shrink my head. Like I am hurt woman. Like I am child, same as Pavel."

She went still in a way that let him know that this was exactly why she'd come in. Not because she'd been truly happy about him coming home from work, but because she'd had an agenda.

"I…" she stopped, took a deep breath, before quietly saying, "I don't want to argue with you."

"No, you want to be counselor to me," Nikolai said, growing angrier by the second. "You think I am—how you say —traumatized. Like Pavel. Damaged."

She shook her head, her lips setting in a defensive line. "Those aren't the terms I would use for you or Pavel, but do I think you should maybe talk to somebody? Yes. You literally drove straight from the police station to get Pavel, but now you're barely interacting with him. And the few interactions you've had with him always seem to end up with him feeling ashamed. Like when you told him men don't cry, and tonight with the birthday party stuff."

"How did I shame him?" Nikolai demanded. "All I said was—"

"All you said was that birthday parties are a silly custom."

"They are silly customs," Nikolai said, his voice full of icy derision. "You Americans and your sentimental, unnecessary customs."

"Pavel's American, too," she reminded him. "And his birthday is in three months. Three months prior is around the time when regular kids start asking about what's going to happen for their birthday."

Nikolai hadn't realized that and his surprise must have shown, because Samantha shook her head at him like she was dealing with the world's biggest idiot.

"Pavel never asks for anything. Ever," she said quietly. "But maybe he's starting to trust that he's in a stable environment now, because he was obviously using Mateo's party to introduce the idea of having a birthday party of his own tonight. Until you made him feel like it was shameful for him, a little boy, to ask for something nearly every other little boy his age in America is getting. So yeah, fine, go ahead and think birthday parties are silly. But I don't care what you say, Pavel deserves a party. Deserves it more than most after what he's been through. And if you don't throw him one, I will."

That proclaimed, she stood up and slammed out of his office. Leaving Nikolai behind to feel like the opposite of a man on the verge of establishing a family. Despite the addition of a child to his household, and the eminent arrival of another one inside Samantha's womb, that dream seemed even farther away than it had before Pavel and Samantha had come to live with him.

Chapter Twenty-One

THE NEXT MORNING, Sam woke up, did a short yoga routine with Pavel before they walked Back Up around the block, and ate breakfast. A breakfast she soon regretted when she had to run out of the room to throw up. After that, she barely managed to get Pavel into the car with his security guard, Dirk, before she had to go lie down for a little bit, sweating from the exertion of her usual morning routine, though it was in the low thirties outside.

So far being pregnant with Nikolai Rustanov's baby had caused her nothing but literal headaches with bouts of throwing up in-between. And by the time she got to work, and fished two Tylenol out of the Ruth's House first aid kit, she was wondering how she was going to get through the next few weeks, much less eight more months.

And then Danny called her outside so he could put in his two weeks notice.

"Sorry about this, Ms. McKinley," he told her. "But only being able to go inside to use the bathroom was tough, and when that big bruiser came by yesterday—"

"He wasn't a threat," Sam pointed out. "He's actually

Pavel's uncle, and he was just checking in about a personal matter."

"Sure, sure," Danny said, waving off her explanation. "But my ticker got to racing just looking at that fellow. And the thought of taking him on... well, I'm thinking I might not be the best person for this job, and I've got friend who says he can get me in at the mall."

So that happened, and Sam couldn't say she blamed Danny. As much good as Ruth's House did, they had to keep costs down if they wanted to continue doing that good. This meant they only had so much money to pay security minimum wage. Not nearly enough to make even the possibility of having to take on Nikolai Rustanov worth it.

The only thing that kept the day from being a total wash was that her morning sickness truly was contained to the mornings—not all day as some of the women in the internet comments she'd read on the subject had ominously warned. She was able to eat and keep down the Cubano sandwich Nyla brought her, which meant her stomach was full and happy when her cell went off with a text message from Nyla.

"Marco downstairs. Says he needs to talk to you."

Her heart sank with apprehension. Apparently Marco hadn't gotten the message the other day, which was upsetting because the last thing she felt like doing was dealing with someone who couldn't take no for an answer.

She went downstairs anyway, knowing she'd have to figure out a way to make it clear this time. But when she stepped out onto the porch, she wasn't met with Marco's usual easygoing smile.

"Did you tell Nikolai Rustanov to have me transferred?" he demanded.

Sam blinked. "What? No!"

"Well, he did," Marco bit out. "I'm off my beat. Do you know how many years I've spent in this neighborhood, getting to know the locals, earning their trust? And with one snap of his fingers, all that's getting taken away from me."

"But…" She shook her head. "How would Nikolai be able to pull that off?"

"I don't know, Sammy," Marco answered, shaking his head. "Maybe the same way he managed to keep his brother out of the system all these years. Maybe the same way he managed to make those Russians who came after you conveniently disappear never to be heard from again."

"Wait, what?" Sam asked. She was having trouble keeping up with Marco.

"Oh yeah, you didn't hear about that? The detectives on your case go to see about this small Russian gang working out of Jiggles to find out if they've got anything to do with coming after you and the kid. But they get there and they can't find hide nor tail of the gang anywhere. Nobody at the club has seen them for days. In fact, the last time anybody's seen them was the same night somebody tried to get you and the kid. And one of the strippers said she saw Nikolai getting out of his car in the parking lot as she was coming in for her shift. Was disappointed because she rushed to get ready, hoping he'd be a big tipper, but he never came out on the floor. And according to the security outside the VIP rooms, he never showed up there, either. Could be he went straight downstairs to confront the gang. He either killed them or convinced them to leave town."

Now Sam really blinked. So that was where he'd gone the night he sent her to his home with Pavel! But a morbid gratitude filled her heart, as opposed to the horror Marco had probably been expecting. She'd been looking over her shoulder ever since what had happened, and this meant she wouldn't have to worry about her or Pavel's safety any longer, at least in that regard.

But the other matter of Marco's job didn't sit well with her.

"How do you know he has that kind of juice?" she asked

him. "And even if he did, why would he use it to get you transferred off your beat?"

Marco looked at her like she was an idiot. "Because obviously he's not just a hockey player, like he wants everybody to believe." He looked around as if he were afraid someone might overhear them, before stepping closer to whisper, "You know his cousin is Alexei Rustanov, right?"

She shook her head. "Who's that?"

"The Russian billionaire. Supposedly legit now, but his dad used to be the head of a powerful Russian mafia family. So that means Mount Nik's got mafia in his blood, too," Marco informed her with a bitter look. "And now he's using it to make sure I stay far away from you."

NIKOLAI KEPT HIS PROMISE. HE ONCE AGAIN LEFT WORK EARLY and got home just a little before six. But unlike the night before, most of the downstairs lights were off. And unlike the night before, Back Up was at the door to greet him as soon as he walked in. And also unlike the night before, Samantha was waiting for him on the foyer stairs.

He stopped when he saw her sitting on the gleaming ivory staircase. She looked out of place in her simple jeans and sweater and he suddenly found himself wishing everything in his house wasn't so grand.

Yes, all the grandeur had brought him great comfort when he'd first bought the house. There was something fitting about him—the neglected child of a murderer who'd been hidden away in a cheap apartment like a dirty secret—now having the means to live in such ostentatious luxury. But looking at Samantha in her frank, simple attire made him wish he lived in a simpler house, one where she'd feel more at home.

She stood as he closed the door behind him, crossing her

arms over her chest. That's when he realized she had something on her mind and hadn't been sitting there just to
welcome him home.

Back Up chose that moment to whine at his legs and flop
down, belly up. Over the last month, Nikolai had found the
only way to keep the bull terrier from blocking his way after he
arrived home was to pay her a regular toll of belly rubs and ear
scratches. Only then would she allow him to move about his
own house in peace.

Useless dog, he thought, even as he bent over to pet her
belly.

Then he straightened and met Samantha's eyes. "Where's
Pavel?"

"With Nyla and Dirk," she answered. "They're having
dinner now and Nyla's waiting for my call so she can bring him
home."

"Who's Nyla?" he asked, having met the latter once, soon
after he'd been hired as Pavel's driver and bodyguard.

"She occasionally babysits Pavel when I get too busy at
Ruth's House," Samantha answered. "She reads a little…
strange. But she interns at Ruth's House and she's working on
her master's in Child Psychology. So… perfect fit for Pavel."

Nikolai didn't know about that, but this Nyla person was
beside the point anyway. The real question was, "Why isn't he
here? For dinner?"

"Because I thought it would be easier if he wasn't here. We
need to talk. About Marco."

He bent back over to pet the dog again until the rage that
even the mention of that man's name inspired in him passed.
He scratched behind Back Up's ears in silence, clamping down
on his heart, until he was sure he had a hold of himself. And
only then did he stand back up and ask, "What about Marco?"

Her eyes scanned his face as if she were trying to get some
kind of read on him. "So this gaming the system and getting

people you don't like transferred? Is this the kind of thing you do all the time?"

He stood in silence, giving her nothing. This was the Rustanov way. Cold and ruthless. Never giving in, never letting your enemy see you sweat, as the Americans like to say.

"Is it an ingrained habit?" she continued. "Like you don't know any better, because that's how you were raised? Or is it a fairly new thing? Like you're so used to people saying yes to you now, it doesn't even occur to you not to grossly abuse your power?"

"Enough," Nikolai growled. "If you are angry about your boyfriend, know I do not care."

"What exactly *do* you care about, Nikolai?" she asked. "I mean other than hockey? Did you care about your brother? How about his son? Do you care at all about Pavel? Or is he just some kind of obligation to you?"

"I come here early to share meal with him. He is not here," Nikolai answered. "What more you want from me?"

Frustration flashed in her eyes, angry and hot. "I want the truth Nikolai. That guy that came after me. Did you have anything to do with his disappearance? Of him and his entire gang?"

Nikolai's jaw clenched. Apparently the cop had not taken his transfer quietly as he had hoped. An error on Nikolai's part. But it didn't matter. He refused to answer Samantha's accusations.

And Samantha took that as in invitation to throw more at him. "Is it true you have mafia ties, ones you used to get Marco transferred?"

Again, he gave her nothing. Not just because he was a Rustanov, but also because... what could he say? That he let his jealousy get the best of him? That yes, he did what he could to keep her away from her boyfriend, even though he was deeply aware it was petty and there was nothing he could truly do?

The baby growing inside of her was his. But she wasn't. So he stayed silent as he'd learned to do growing up. Stayed silent and waited for this to be over.

~

HE WAS GONE. SAM KNEW THAT AS SOON AS HE WENT completely still on her, like a living statue at the state fair. This one wasn't covered in spray paint, but nonetheless, he was a man in a suit who turned into stone when confronted in any way.

A thousand possible psychological explanations went through Sam's head for his reaction to her accusations, but at the end of her very long day, she could only focus on one. He didn't want to talk to her.

He was unwilling to communicate with her in any way. He was exactly what he'd claimed to be when they first met, a man who did not like complications, and this whole conversation along with Sam herself was a complication he wasn't willing to deal with.

"Okay," she said, making herself calm down. "Okay…"

What he'd done to Marco was beside the point, anyway. The real point here was Pavel. Making sure Pavel didn't get hurt. Making sure no matter how incapable of simple human emotions his uncle was, that Pavel got to grow up in a stable home.

She took a deep, cleansing breath, like the ones she'd instructed Pavel to take when they were in their weekly session and talking about his father became too overwhelming. Then she said to Nikolai, "I'm going to move back to my place."

The only indication that he heard her was a slight shift in his gaze from the spot beyond her head to her face.

"I think we've reached a potentially confusing time as far as Pavel and this baby is concerned, and I don't want to hurt him any more than I have to. So now that he's settled in here, I'm going to find someone else to take over his weekly counseling sessions, and I'm going to start limiting our interactions. I think…"

She said this next part quickly, so she wouldn't start crying. "I think Pavel and I have both become a little too dependent on each other and this is probably what's best for all of us, considering you and I have come to an impasse I don't think we're going to be able to navigate."

Sam waited for Nikolai to say something. Anything. For the longest time, he stood there perfectly still, his face hard as granite as he studied her from underneath hooded eyes.

But eventually he spoke. One word. "When?"

"When?" she repeated. "Well, I was thinking I'd move out tomorrow while Pavel's at school, then we'd go into a gentle transition plan, using Nyla as a partner, after that."

He regarded her for a few icy seconds before saying, "Tomorrow is too soon. Give me two days to prepare."

"O-okay," she said. "Do you need any help arranging for someone to be here when Pavel gets home from school?"

"No," he answered. Then he walked away, heading towards his study without another word, and leaving her both confused and surprised by his unexpectedly easy acquiescence. But really, she shouldn't have surprised. It wasn't like he'd asked her to come here in the first place.

She'd just given him exactly what he wanted. They'd had sex, and now she was leaving. He was probably glad to be rid of her, she thought. Which was a good thing.

So why did she feel so sad when she texted Nyla that it was okay to bring Pavel home now?

Chapter Twenty-Two

BY THE TIME Sam woke up two days later, she was still having a hard time understanding why she felt so out of sorts about the whole situation. Nikolai had technically kept his promise, showing up for dinner the last two nights in a row, eating nearly everything she put in front of him. But he hadn't exactly been great company.

He'd let her and Pavel do pretty much all the talking, only interrupting when he was done with his dinner to say he had work to do and would be in his office.

It was a start, and that was the best she could hope for. More than she would have dared to hope for a few days ago. And she had a plan to make Pavel less dependent on her and Back Up...

Oh, who was she kidding, she thought as she pulled on a pair of sweats. She was going to miss Pavel terribly. She could barely stand to think about their parting because she'd grown too used to having the little boy in her life over the past month. He'd given her a reason to not work so hard over the last few weeks, to delegate more than she had in the past, and she'd liked coming home early so she could be there when Dirk dropped him off after school.

She liked, she admitted to herself with a quiet pang as she left her room, being his mama.

But she wasn't his mama. He only insisted on calling her that. She wasn't even related to him by blood. Nikolai was. And in the end, her moving out would be the best thing for all of them.

She knocked on Pavel's door and did her best to not look like she was trying to memorize his dear little face when he opened it, already dressed in the gym shorts and t-shirt he wore for their morning yoga session.

After they were done with yoga, as had become their routine, they put on their coats, and walked Back Up around Nikolai's neighborhood. Sam actually wouldn't have called where Nikolai lived a neighborhood if it had been up to her. It was more like a small collection of mansions, all owned by local multi-millionaires and set far apart from each other on acres of land. She'd never seen a hamlet, but the word came to mind on her walks.

They weren't the only ones out walking a dog that morning, but Sam was one of the few official dog parents among the lot. She called out greetings to housekeepers and professional dog walkers and nannies alike, but her greetings to the few millionaire wives who deigned to walk their own dogs went more or less ignored. One even crossed to the other side of the street to make sure her well-groomed standard poodle had no contact whatsoever with Sam's bullie. A totally unnecessary action since the last time Sam had checked, it was physically impossible to get licked to death.

"That woman doesn't like Back Up," Pavel observed, watching another well-dressed woman walk quickly in the other direction.

"There's a lot of misinformation going around about Back

Up's breed. At first glance, she looks tough and mean, so a lot of people assume she's dangerous when they look at her and they get scared. But we're lucky because we know the truth about her," Sam said. "In any case, it teaches us we should never judge anyone by their appearance."

"Uncle Nik looks tough and mean. Do you think he's dangerous?"

The question caught Sam off guard. Pavel probably didn't realize it, but he had just introduced a topic rife with emotional landmines.

"No," she answered carefully. It didn't exactly feel like the truth. The truth was, her stomach knotted up every time she was in a room with Nikolai. The truth was, even before Marco had informed her of what he most likely had done, she could practically feel danger radiating off him and it scared her a little.

But she would be leaving Pavel in his care. Plus, as serious as he could be at times, the fact remained that Pavel was only a child. She couldn't tell him any of that. "I don't think he's dangerous." To you, she silently added.

"Then why don't you like him?" Pavel asked.

"Who said I don't like him?" she asked.

"You're nice to everyone. You even try to be nice to those ladies who cross the street to get away from Back Up. But you never try to be nice to Uncle. You never really smile at him like you do everybody else."

She wanted to say, "Yes, I do!" But then she realized the only time she'd ever smiled at Nikolai was when she was either faking it, or trying to convince him to do something for Pavel's sake. Like the other day when she'd gotten him to agree to come home earlier.

"You're right," she said. "I could maybe try to be nicer to your uncle." It was an easy promise to make, since she was technically moving out that day.

Not knowing this, Pavel beamed at her, which reminded her that she needed to schedule a dentist appointment for him before she went. She pulled out her phone and put a note in her to-do app to call Isaac about setting it up, since it needed to go under Nikolai's insurance plan. But when she went to cate-gorize the reminder under "Pavel," a wave of sadness rolled over her. Pretty soon, there'd be no need for a special "Pavel" category in her app.

"You know what we should do after Dirk drops you off tonight?" she asked Pavel. "Go to the Children's Museum."

Pavel had lived within a five-mile radius of the Children's Museum of Indianapolis nearly all his life, but he'd never been. Sure, his class would eventually take a field trip there, but Sam wanted to give him something to remember her by before she left. One last great afternoon together before she dropped the bomb that she and Back Up wouldn't be living with him any more.

After their walk, they ate breakfast. Pancakes, sausages, and eggs—a little fancier than what Sam usually made for them, and she was more than a little concerned she wouldn't be able to keep the meal down. But she wanted Pavel to have nice memories of their last morning together.

Making and eating breakfast took a little longer than usual, and Dirk pulled up under the porte-cochère while Pavel was still up in his room, gathering his back pack and other school essentials. So Sam took the opportunity to have a little talk with Dirk while they waited.

"Hey, do you mind giving me a call later on today? I have some things to go over with you about Pavel's transition."

Dirk frowned. "Oh, is that still happening?"

She gave him a confused smile. "Yeah, why would you think it wasn't?"

"Cuz I called Isaac like you told me to, and he made it sound like I didn't have to worry about it."

Alarm bells went off in Sam's head. "So Isaac hasn't found a replacement? He told me he was working on it."

Dirk just shrugged. "I dunno. I guess call Isaac—hey Pav!" he called out when the little boy came out of the house and down the red brick steps with Back Up close at his heels. "What's up, little man?"

Conversation over, Sam thought. But she'd for sure be calling Isaac as soon as she got into work that day. Meanwhile, she grabbed Back Up by the collar and took her up the stairs to the porch as the town car rolled away. She'd learned the hard way that Back Up would run after the limo if she wasn't physically held back. Despite having only known each other for less than two months, she and Pavel shared a special connection.

Best friends, she thought with a pang of guilt for splitting them up.

"Bye, Mama!" Pavel called out the open window as the car rolled away.

She waved back, reminding herself that him calling her his mother was not healthy. For either of them. This was definitely the best thing to do. Definitely. Her heart just had to catch up with her mind in this case.

She started to go into the house with Back Up, but stopped when she saw a white BMW come through the open gates, passing by Dirk's town car before it eventually came to a stop under the porte-cochère.

An older man in glasses and a black suit climbed out of the car and asked, "Is it okay to park here?"

Despite standing a few feet away, she could smell the over-bearing stench of his cologne all the way from the porch.

Sam visibly recoiled. "Kevin, what are you doing here?" she asked.

Pavel had been wrong about her being nice to everyone but his uncle. She and Kevin Boatman had met a couple of times on the wrong side of his conference room table. He was one of

Indianapolis's top family court attorneys, and he had a reputation for fighting extremely dirty. She hadn't been allowed to sit in on either of the actual proceedings for her intakes, but she'd dealt with the damage afterwards. And in both cases the women had decided to go back to their abusive husbands rather than risk the things Kevin had threatened them with behind closed doors. She didn't need much more than that to truly hate the man.

But he wasn't in his law offices now. He was here at Nikolai's house. At the front door, so someone must have buzzed him through the gate. But that didn't make any sense, because none of Nikolai's household staff were going through custody proceedings as far as she knew, and even if they were, they wouldn't be able to afford Kevin.

Which only left…

A chill of foreboding ran down her back, and she sensed someone now standing directly behind her. Someone who was usually long gone by now.

When she turned around, there was Nikolai, big as his nickname, his face stony and hard, like an iced over statue in the Kremlin's front yard.

Chapter Twenty-Three

NIKOLAI WATCHED Samantha closely as she sat down across from him in one of the study's leather guest chairs. It was her second visit to his study, but this time there was no awe in her expression as she took her seat. No bright smile dimpling her face either.

In fact, her angry eyes stayed on the lawyer, as if Nikolai had brought a lethal snake into his study, even as she spoke to him. "Why are you doing this?" she asked Nikolai.

The sincere note of hurt in her voice irritated him. She acted as if she hadn't been the one to start this, the one who'd decided to leave, taking his baby with her.

Kevin, who'd chosen to remain standing, stepped in smoothly to answer that question for him.

"As you know, Ms. McKinley, I handle all matters involving family law, which this falls under since you are pregnant with Mr. Rustanov's child."

Samantha shook her head at Kevin. "I'm only a few weeks pregnant, and he's already calling in a shark like you?"

If Kevin was insulted by her words, it didn't show on his face. "Mr. Rustanov has concerns about your future plans.

You've insinuated that you plan to retain full custody of his child."

Now Samantha looked from Kevin to Nikolai, like they were both crazy. "Yes, I'm going to retain full custody because I'm the baby's mother and because he," she shot an angry glance at Nikolai, "and I barely know each other."

"Be that as it may, if your plan is to remove yourself from this residence, then you'll need to establish a custody agreement with Mr. Rustanov before you do so."

Sam darted another disbelieving look towards Nikolai, this one soaked with derision. Then she crossed her arms over her chest and said, "Fine. What does he want? Holidays, Birthdays, every other weekend? Would he like me to arrange for a nanny for this child, too, so the baby can spend all of Mr. Rustanov's agreed upon custodial time with her?"

Nikolai flinched at her harsh assessment of his parenting skills, but her words bounced of Kevin as if the lawyer was made of Teflon.

"Actually, he'll be taking full custody of the child, and you'll be the one who needs to decide whether you'll cooperate with us."

Kevin brought up his leather briefcase and pulled out a sheaf of papers. "If you sign this custody agreement now, we'll guarantee you weekends and holidays. If you force us to take this case to a judge after the child is born, then we won't feel obligated to give you any access to the child at all."

"What?" Samantha asked, her voice hot with anger. "Okay, I understand Nikolai's good at hockey or whatever, but there's no way in hell a judge is ever going to give him full custody of a child. This isn't Pavel. I'm this baby's biological mother!"

"Sure, sure," Kevin said, folding his arms. "And you've done a lot of good work at your shelter."

"Shelters," she corrected. "I've opened two. My plan is to establish a Ruth's House in every state before I die."

"That's very noble," Kevin said with a patronizing nod. "Especially considering your background."

Samantha froze and Nikolai could see her struggling to keep her face composed as she said, "You mean the fact that I'm from Detroit? I know it's not the most upstanding city in the world, but that's not enough of a reason to deny me custody of my child."

"Yes, but unfortunately murder in the first degree, which you committed less than a year after moving to Indiana, is."

Nikolai watched Samantha falter, wondering how she'd handle what was coming next. "How——" Samantha stopped and tried again. "Why do you think I murdered someone?"

Kevin leaned down over the chair she was sitting in to address her now, his voice quiet, as if he were letting her in on a little secret.

"You should know, Ms. McKinley, this area of law gets a little tricky. You see, you murdered your stepfather on your eighteenth birthday. The courts decided to try you as a juvenile so your file was sealed and technically it would be inadmissible in court. But here's what I think you can understand about me, given my dealings with a few of your shelter clients. I'm a good lawyer. A very good lawyer. And if I didn't think there was a way to get that file unsealed, given you were technically eighteen when it happened, I would not have taken Mr. Rustanov's case. I'm not in the habit of losing, and I know I can convince a jury of your peers that not only are you a bad prospect for motherhood, but also a potential danger to your child."

Kevin grinned at her like the predator he truly was, and leaned even further down to say, "After I'm done you won't even get weekend and birthday access to your child. You killed a man, Ms. McKinley. You don't get to sit there and act like you would be a better parent to this child than my client."

For a moment Samantha did nothing, she simply sat, still as

a wood dove, as if Kevin's words had frozen her. But then she reanimated.

"Fuck you," she hissed, her eyes wide and angry. "Fuck you and your dirty lawyer tricks."

Then she turned to Nikolai, her beautiful face thunderous with rage. "You are fucked up for doing this. And obviously the only thing you care about is getting your way."

Nikolai forced his face to remain blank, despite the rage churning inside of him. "*Nyet*, you want everything go your way. Me never seeing my child, you getting to raise it with someone else."

"Yes, I'd rather this child live with someone who loves it and is capable of even being a halfway decent parent!" she screamed back. "So sorry for having the baby's best interest in mind instead of your ego!"

And then he could no longer contain himself. He leapt out of his own seat and roared, "You do not know me! You do not know of what I am capable! I will not let you keep my child from me!"

"I don't know you because you don't talk to me. Like ever! You communicate with me through your assistant and whenever I try to talk to you about anything remotely personal, you shut me out." She shook her head at him, her eyes full of disgust. "And now you've invited this snake into what should have been an adult discussion between you and me. You and me, Nikolai."

"I invited him because you forced my hand."

Her eyes continued to burn hot with rage as she answered, "I didn't force your hand. I made a reasonable decision to move out because I'm an adult who cares deeply about your nephew and I don't want to hurt him or confuse him. And I feel that way because I'm a good person—maybe not on paper," She jerked her head toward Kevin, "And maybe not according to this scumbag lawyer you've hired, but I know my worth. I'm a good person, and I'll be an amazing mother because I'll always put this child first, not my own selfish pride—"

She stopped in the middle of her passionate speech, suddenly looking stricken. Her hand came up to her mouth and she glanced around frantically, before running past Kevin and Nik and into the study's private bathroom.

Soon after, there came the sound of retching and regurgitated food hitting toilet bowl water.

A stunned Kevin looked over at Nikolai. "Well, I've gotten a lot of reactions to my proposed custody suits, but that's a first."

Nikolai didn't respond. Just stared at the door Samantha had slammed closed, her angry accusations still ringing in his ears.

"Should we reschedule for tomorrow?" Kevin asked. "I mean we still haven't gotten the paperwork signed—"

"You go now." Nikolai told him. "I will take care of rest."

"Are you sure?" Kevin asked with a confused frown. Nikolai recognized in him a kindred spirit. Someone who was used to seeing dirty work through to the end.

But in this case, his services were no longer needed. A new plan formed in Nikolai's head. One he didn't bother to explain to the lawyer as he headed out of the room to put together his weapons arsenal.

Chapter Twenty-Four

MORNING SICKNESS WAS a bitch and a half, Sam thought, as she flushed down the two deposits she'd just made, the lovely breakfast from this morning, along with her dinner from the night before. She fell back from the golden toilet—which she chose to believe was only painted that color, not made of the real stuff. A solid gold toilet seemed a bit much, even for Nikolai.

She eased herself into a seated position on the floor, resting the back of her head on the red and white marble wall. At least this office bathroom was cool. Unlike his office, which had been filled with Nikolai and his lawyer and the disgusting smell of overbearing cologne. Even righteous indignation couldn't keep her stomach at a standstill long enough for her to make her point. Nikolai was lucky she had made it to the office's golden toilet and hadn't thrown up all over his lawyer's nice wingtips. Tempting as that had been.

God, what was she going to do?

She had no idea, but at least she could take solace in the fact that she most likely wouldn't be throwing up again. Sam had given Nikolai's ludicrous toilet every single thing she'd put into her stomach over the last twelve hours. She just wished her stomach would understand that and stop churning already.

She closed her eyes, slowing her breaths down and willing the nauseous feeling to pass. Outside the bathroom, she could hear voices talking low, departing footsteps. Then it went quiet until a few minutes later when someone opened the door and turned on a faucet. Anna, she assumed, feeling too weak to check.

But she was pretty sure Nikolai must have called in his housekeeper to deal with her when a cold cloth was pressed against her head.

"Thank you," she said, breathing into the wet coolness.

But it was not Anna who said, "I will put towel on back of your neck now. It will help you."

Her eyes flew open, and yes, there was Nikolai, bent down in front of her, his long fingers keeping the cloth in place on her head.

"Lean your head forward," he instructed. But the command turned out to be just a formality, because his hand came around the back of her head, pulling it forward with brisk efficiency until her chin was touching her chest. Then he placed the cloth on the back of her neck.

Immediately the nausea began to abate, releasing it's fevered grip on her as the heaving sensation in her stomach faded away.

"Thank you," she whispered, unable to believe his simple solution was actually working.

"Take more deep breaths now," he answered.

She did as he said and caught his scent on the inhale. It was a good one. Plain, no-frills soap and something else... ice. That was it. He smelled just like the stuff he skated on... frosty. Unlike his lawyer, who'd smelled like he'd poured a whole bottle of Drakkar Noir on before coming over to intimidate her into signing a bullshit custody agreement.

As if reading her mind, Nikolai said, "Kevin is gone. I sent him away. This discussion will be as you said. Between you and me from now on."

"Oh, was that a discussion?" she asked, fighting her weak stomach to achieve a withering tone. "Because it felt like you and your lawyer were trying to explain to me why I'm not fit to be anything but an incubator for this baby."

She wanted to remain cold and removed like him, but she couldn't help it. Her eyes clashed with his, indignant and hurt.

He returned her angry look with a cool one of his own as he removed the cloth from behind her neck.

"Kevin's statements weren't personal," he said, rewetting the cloth at the bathroom's golden bowl sink.

"Really? Because they felt awfully damn personal," Sam answered, her voice thin and weak.

Nikolai made a scoffing sound. "You are not business person or hockey player. You do not know difference between game and personal."

He came back over to her and once again arranged the cloth behind her neck, and dammit, the fresh rush of cold felt so glorious, a wave of sincere gratitude went through her. An emotion completely incongruous with her hot anger.

"Kevin is, how you say—proof of concept. I needed you to know I could have full custody of baby, and you could not stop me."

And that statement solved her pesky gratitude problem. "Congratulations," she said. "You made your point."

If he was interested in gloating, it wasn't evident in the neutral set of his face. "But it does not have to go this way, there is another way it could go.

She kept her mouth closed and waited, wanting to hear what he would say next more than she wanted to shoot off another angry retort.

"You can marry me," he said.

And Sam blinked, because surely she had just heard him wrong. "Excuse me?"

"If you marry me, we will not need custody agreement. I will not need pay Kevin to destroy your reputation. I will not need—"

She held up her hand to stop his tide of potential dire predictions. "Wait, can we go back to the part where you want to marry me, because… why exactly?"

He averted his eyes. "I do not want my child to be in home where its parents aren't married. I grew up this way. My child will not."

Sam chewed over this one tiny nugget of information he had given her about his past, before saying, "You know, there are ways to raise a child successfully in two separate homes. In fact, sometimes it's better that way for everybody involved."

She thought of her own upbringing in a home that technically had two parents and shivered. Growing up, she would have given anything to have her mother leave her stepfather and raise her daughter by herself.

"We don't have to get married to craft some kind of agreement we can both be happy with," she told Nikolai.

But Nikolai shook his head. "Our child must have both parents. You should marry me, so we don't fight over baby in court. It would be, how you say, marriage of convenience. Best thing for all of us. What I want. What Pavel want. He will not care about new baby, because he will have you as his mother. My lawyer tells me I must still do legal adoption of my nephew. If you marry me, we can adopt him. Together."

Together. Her heart soared at the thought of becoming Pavel's mother, legally and with rights accorded. However, it didn't escape her that Nikolai seemed to be having trouble meeting her eyes as he offered to make her dreams of being a real mother to Pavel come true.

Sam found herself once again wondering about his childhood in Russia. What had happened that had turned him into the man bent down in front of her, the muscles in his neck straining as he offered her Pavel in exchange for marriage?

"What if I say no?" she asked him.

This question made his cold eyes finally meet hers. "Don't say no," he answered.

A bolt of fear shot through her, one he must have seen on her face, because he said, "You think I am crazy. You are scared of me now."

"I'm..." She stopped and took careful survey of her emotions. "I don't know how to feel. I don't like being threatened. And I don't like being blackmailed."

He shook his head. "I am sorry but this is way it must be."

It occurred to Sam then that she wasn't going to win this argument with him. She could talk to him until she was blue in the face about split custody and mindful parenting, but it wouldn't do any good.

For whatever reason, Nikolai was determined to be a part of this baby's life, even if it meant marrying someone he didn't love. And maybe...

She couldn't believe this thought was occurring to her even as it did, but maybe he had a point. It wasn't like her mother's relationship had suffered from lack of love—if anything, what she'd seen of marriages over the years had involved too much love. Sick obsessions disguised as romantic love.

She thought of all the men who had shown up at the shelter. Not the violent ones, but the ones who stood outside crying, pleading for their girlfriends to come out. Apologizing over and over and promising to never do it again. The dirty truth was those were the men most likely to convince their wives to come back to them. The ones who couched their invitations to return for more beatings and more emotional abuse in proclamations of love.

So she had to give Nikolai credit. At least he'd been straight-forward about his intentions in marrying her.

"So you don't think I'm an unfit mother?" she asked him, just to be sure.

"No," he answered instantly. "I did not tell Kevin to say those things to you. I have seen you with Pavel and I know you will be very good mother. This is why I want to marry you."

Once again, not exactly the most romantic thing she had ever heard, but considering the situation, maybe it was time for her to give up on her old notions of romantic love.

She went over her list of the classic signs of abuse and was surprised to find that though Nikolai's offer was unorthodox, it wasn't exactly abusive.

Still, she tested the water to make sure.

"Marco," she said, floating the name like a toy boat into their conversation.

His face hardened. "What about him."

"If I marry you, would you use whatever connections you have at Indy PD to put him back on his regular rotation?"

"Why?" he asked, his voice hard with suspicion.

"Because Marco doesn't deserve to lose his beat, that's why," she answered.

Nikolai's jaw set. "I do not want you with someone else while pregnant with my baby."

She shook her head. "This is none of your business, but just to cut this line of argument short, Marco isn't my boyfriend. In fact it's fair to say he never was. We went on a few dates, but we never slept together. And quite frankly, I don't ever want to sleep with him." She told him like she'd told Marco, "We weren't a good match."

Nikolai's eyes ran over her face as if trying to gauge whether she was telling to truth or not, and Sam released an annoyed sigh. "I don't think this arrangement is going to work if you can't take me at my word on things—"

"I believe you," he suddenly said, voice grim as a storm cloud.

Sam eyed him suspiciously. "And you'll make sure he gets put back on his rotation?"

Something ticked in Nikolai's jaw, like she was making a very large ask, but nonetheless he said, "*Da*." Then he asked, "We have deal?"

Sam eyed him nervously. She needed a reason to say no, but try as she might, the more she mulled it over, the more sense Nikolai's proposal made. She'd get to be a mother to both Pavel and the baby inside of her, and she already knew Nikolai's M.O. It wasn't like he'd be interfering much with how she raised the children. Her children. A tentative hope sprang up in her heart. This really could be the most reasonable solution to their current situation.

Only one question remained. One that made her hold her breath as she asked it. "This marriage of convenience? What exactly would it look like?"

A confused look from Nikolai.

And she tried again. "Like what would you expect of me other than providing Pavel and this baby with a loving upbringing?"

His eyes flared, a certain heat appearing in their green depths without warning. "I want you as real wife in my bed," he answered, bald and to the point. "If this is your question, that is my answer."

Sam's throat went dry at the thought of sharing Nikolai's bed, not just for a night, but into the foreseeable future. She stirred down below, her breasts going impossibly heavy as her traitorous body became aroused at the thought of occupying the bed of a man who was basically blackmailing her into marriage.

"And what if I don't want to be with you that way?" she

managed to push out past the dry desert her throat had become.

He leveled her with a piercing stare and asked, "You do not want me that way? As husband in our bed?"

"No." She forced the lie through her lips as quickly as possible. Because even if it wasn't the truth, it should have been, and it would be—as soon as she got her treasonous body on board.

His eyes shuttered. "If you don't want me, fine. We will sleep in same room, like husband and wife. But I will not touch you, unless you want me to…"

Sam clenched down below at the thought of his hands on her in an intimate way again. And she couldn't help but think of the way he'd driven himself into her their one fateful time, making her explode with pleasure.

"…I can be gentleman," he finished, bringing her back to the here and now. Where she'd just finished throwing up and shouldn't even be thinking about sex with a man who was asking her to pledge her life to him, to sleep in the same room with him, not because he had feelings for her, but because he wanted a certain kind of set up for their unborn child and his current ward.

"Do you feel better?" he asked her.

She blinked, "What?"

He nodded towards the hand towel still resting on the back of her neck. "Are you sick still?"

"No," she answered. Actually her nausea had completely disappeared. "I feel fine now."

He nodded as if her stomach had simply obeyed one of his commands. "You will take day off. Rest," he instructed.

But she shook her head. "No, we're expecting a big shipment and we're at capacity right now, so I want to make sure it all gets put away so we have everything we need when we need it. And our security guard gave me his two-weeks notice a few days ago, so I have to start actively looking for a replacement."

She waited for him to tell her she couldn't go to work. She found herself wanting an excuse to go back to actively disliking him. Something clear she could grasp onto like a controlling behavior or some sign that he'd become emotionally or physically abusive in the long run.

But instead he once again averted his eyes, before asking, "You really don't want me?" The question was quiet... embarrassed.

And the vulnerable note in his voice sent her head into a complete spin. Her common sense and her gut warring over every psychological detail of her true heart's answer. In the end, she opened her mouth, but nothing came out.

And apparently that was answer enough.

He stood in one abrupt movement and said, "I go on road tomorrow. You will give me your answer by time I get back Sunday night."

Then he walked out, leaving her behind, stunned and still unable to answer his question. Even in her own mind.

Chapter Twenty-Five

"YOU DID WHAT?!?!"

Sam winced. She wondered if this was going to be a trend on phone calls with Josie from now on. Her casually dropping a bomb. Josie screaming at her to repeat herself.

"I decided to marry the hockey player."

"The one who doesn't believe in love?"

"Yeah, that one…" Sam said.

"I'm assuming you have a good reason for this sudden decision."

"Several actually," Sam answered. "Pavel, and… well, um… I'm pregnant with his baby."

This time Sam made a pre-emptive move to protect her left eardrum, holding the phone as far away as she could. But that still didn't mute Josie's, "WHAT!?!?"

Sam explained to her best friend the way she'd been explaining it to herself over the past week, using phrases like "best thing for the baby" and "best thing for Pavel." She even threw Back Up into the sales pitch, explaining how happy she'd been having acres and acres of backyard to run around—and perhaps, more importantly, another person to give her belly rubs.

Despite her marketing efforts, Josie still didn't sound convinced when she was done. "This all sounds great for Pavel, Back Up, and the baby. But what about you?" Josie asked. "How about what's best for you?"

"I'm getting Pavel and a baby," Sam answered. "I couldn't be happier about that. Josie wait 'til you meet Pavel! He's so wonderful. You'll understand why I'd do anything to stay with him."

"Anything, including marrying a guy you don't love?"

"Not everyone can have what you and Beau have. You and Beau barely managed to have what you have," Sam reminded her friend, referring to their tumultuous courtship with dark tones.

"Yeah, but..." Josie let out a sad sigh. "You're so great, Sam. And you're always putting others before yourself. I just want to make sure this isn't you sacrificing what's good for you for what's good for everyone else."

"Trust me, I'm not sacrificing myself," Sam said. "Considering the circumstances, this seriously is the best solution I could hope for."

"If you say so," Josie answered, not bothering to hide her skepticism. "I just want to make sure you're all right."

"I'm great, Josie," Sam assured her. "Better than I have ever been. I promise."

Which was true, she told herself. She had Pavel and a baby on the way, and even if that meant marrying a detached, uncommunicative Russian, it was still more of a family than she'd ever been blessed with before Nikolai Rustanov barged into her life.

It was enough, she told herself, just as she'd been telling herself for the past week.

It had to be.

"Okay, then, I'm going to choose to believe you," Josie said. "I'm happy for you, Sam. I truly am."

"Thanks, Josie," Sam said softly. She didn't realize how much she'd needed her best friend to accept the situation until a tide of relief rolled over her. Her shoulders relaxed, and she finally allowed herself to breathe easy again.

But then Josie asked, "So when's the wedding? I'm too far along to fly to Indiana, but maybe our home aide can drive Beau and me up there for the big day."

A huge wave of guilt rolled over Sam, and she found herself wincing again as she glanced down at the white petal shift dress she was wearing.

LESS THAN AN HOUR AFTER HER PHONE CALL WITH JOSIE, AND two Sundays after receiving the least romantic proposal ever, Sam married Nikolai Rustanov.

She walked into Nikolai's office, Pavel on one side of her and Back Up on the other. She repeated the necessary words to the justice of the peace Isaac had found to officiate their wedding. She signed the license afterwards, along with Nikolai, the JOP, and Isaac, who—as far as she could tell—had only been invited because he'd arranged everything, including the dinner the five of them shared afterwards.

And what a jovial affair that was. Sam in a state of shock, hardly able to believe she'd gone through with this. Pavel watching her with solemn eyes, as if he suspected she was on the verge of a nervous breakdown. Back Up whimpering at Nikolai's knee, having decided to choose the absolute worst person in perhaps the entire world to beg from for scraps of dinner.

Read the room, Back Up, she thought at her clueless bullie. *Read the room.*

Nikolai regarded Back Up with hard eyes and pointed to a corner at the far side of the room. With one last sad whine, Back Up left, her disappointed head hanging before she flopped dejectedly in the corner.

Pavel started to get up and go to Back Up with a bite of his uneaten steak, but his uncle stopped him with, "You will not feed dog, Pavel. She will eat food Anna put in kitchen for her."

Pavel opened his mouth to argue.

But Nikolai gave him a look, much the same as the one he'd given Back Up, and Pavel wasn't a fool. He kept his mouth closed and slumped down in his chair.

And then there were two disappointed beings in the room as both Pavel and Back Up sulked under separate dark clouds.

Sam didn't blame the judge for suddenly remembering an appointment and excusing himself from the awkward gathering twenty minutes into the meal. Isaac was the next to go, claiming he had just begun training for the Indianapolis marathon and wanted to get up early the next morning for a long run. Sam had to admit she was jealous as she watched Nikolai's assistant go. She wished she could run away from the dinner, too. The dining room was an intimidating mix of crimson damask, oriental carpets, heavy dark furniture, paintings that took up entire walls, and gold-plated everything else. She missed the relative coziness of the state-of-art kitchen and felt uncomfortable in such ostentatious surroundings.

But at least Pavel and Back Up stayed loyal. Unlike the judge and Isaac, neither of them left the dining room until dinner was over and Sam insisted a yawning Pavel go to bed.

And then came a heartwarming moment when Pavel hugged her and said, "We're a real family now. I'm glad you can be with me forever, Mama."

"Me too," Sam said, hugging him back. *Totally worth it*, she thought in that moment.

After they finished hugging, Pavel turned to Nikolai. "Congratulations, Uncle," he said with a stiff nod.

"Thank you," Nikolai answered, just as stiffly. He glanced at Pavel and then quickly looked away as if the sight of the boy hurt him somehow.

Perhaps picking up on that, Pavel didn't linger. He called to Back Up and they were gone a few seconds later.

Sam hadn't had the energy or the heart to keep up the pretense after that, saying, "Well, I'm super tired. I think I'll be retiring now."

He gave her a short nod in that dismissive way of his which grated on her. And she left the room. It was one thing to get dismissed like that when she was basically a squatter, living under his roof for Pavel's sake, but she was his wife now.

His fake wife, she reminded herself as she climbed up the stairs to the sanctuary of her room. Their marriage license was only a piece of paper meant to seal a deal. There was no reason to expect him to change his ways just because they'd undergone a Facebook status update. She thought of the talk she gave women who weren't married to their abusive boyfriends. Her "marriage-won't-change-him-he'll-basically-always-be-an-abuser-unless-he-gets-serious-help" talk.

Nikolai Rustanov wasn't abusive, but he'd never change. He'd never magically one day stop being dismissive or autocratic or... the thought blew through her mind like a sad wind... someone capable of loving her the way Beau loved Josie.

She thought of her earlier phone call with her best friend. No, not everyone could have what Josie had with her husband, Beau: mutual understanding and a deep and abiding love after overcoming their demons. Some people—people like Nikolai and her—had to do the best they could with the demons still riding on their backs.

She divested herself of the evidence of their sham

marriage as soon as the small bedroom door closed behind her. Balling up the dress, which she already knew she'd never wear again, and throwing it in the corner.

Now all she had to do was change into her pajamas and hide out in her room for an hour or so until she was sure Nikolai had gone to bed. Then she'd sneak downstairs and unwind with a few episodes of *Veronica Mars* in Nikolai's entertainment room, which was another perk she could add to agreeing to this marriage of convenience. His state-of-the-art entertainment room had a 72-inch OLED television and barcolounger stadium seats. There was even a fireplace, and she could already see herself making the room nice and toasty while she binged on *Veronica Mars*. Tonight she didn't want to think about anything but clever girl detectives who always managed to get themselves and their loved ones out of bad situations. That and a glass of wine would be exactly what the doctor ordered… if only she could drink.

Sighing, Sam went over to the ludicrous ivory white dresser where she kept her simple clothes, including the IU sweats she'd been wearing as pajamas. Truth was, she'd never been much of a drinker (nothing like seeing how much alcohol could fuel physically abusive marriages to turn you off the stuff), but she did like a glass of wine after a long day. And this had been a very, very long day, she admitted to herself as she opened the bottom right drawer—

Only to find it empty. She looked at the vacant space for a confused, shocked moment. Then with an ominous feeling of dread, she pulled open the drawer beside it, the one that had been filled with her sweaters. That one was empty, too, as were all the drawers in the ridiculous piece of furniture. And as was the walk-in closet—even the shoes she kept lined up underneath her bed for easy access were no longer there.

"What the…" she said out loud.

Nikolai answered her knock on his door with an expression she would describe as amused, verging on smug. As if he'd been expecting her. Probably because he had.

The jerk, she thought, as she opened her mouth to demand answers. But the angry words got clogged in her throat when she saw he only had on a pair of boxer briefs. And though she was pissed—really pissed—it was impossible not to admire his strong shoulders and large biceps, the muscles that rippled down his torso, before stopping right above his—

Sam quickly brought her eyes up from the dangerous bulge inside his briefs and forced herself to keep her eyes on his face as opposed to his magnificent body as she asked, "Where's all my stuff?"

"Hello, Samantha," he said, giving her wedding dress a once over so sensual, she wondered if he could tell she hadn't bothered to with a bra when she'd hastily put it back on before coming down the hallway to confront him.

"Don't call me that," she said, crossing her arms over her chest.

"You do not want me to call you Samantha, and I do not want to call you by boy's name," he said, his gaze becoming a lazy perusal. "I will have to simply call you 'wife.'"

He pulled the door open wider for her, revealing a bedroom dripping in gold

baroque fixtures, dark red furniture, marble floors… and one incredibly large bed.

"Come in, Wife."

"Where's my stuff?" she demanded again, refusing to look at the bed.

"In our room, where it belongs," he answered. "Anna brought your things here during wedding."

"What?" Sam took a step back in shock.

Nikolai's hooded gaze suddenly froze over, as if her surprise offended him, and Sam wondered what he'd expected her reaction would be.

"You share my room. That is our agreement, *da?*"

Yes they had agreed to that, she thought, thinking back to their conversation in his office bathroom. But… "I thought you meant after the baby came."

"You thought wrong," he said in cold reply. Then he stepped back and opened the door wider. "Come in."

Chapter Twenty-Six

FORCING the issue of Samantha coming to his bed had seemed like a good idea. At first.

Nikolai was perfectly aware she'd believed she wouldn't have to come to his room until after the baby was born. But the thought of her sleeping down the hall, so grateful she could spend the next eight months away from him, stuck in his craw with a bitter after taste he could not abide.

No, if she wanted to deny the attraction between them, to pretend what had happened the night their baby was conceived had been a case of him taking advantage of her scared state, then she would have to do so in his bed.

And he'd felt vindicated by the flash of desire he'd seen in her eyes when he'd come to the door in his briefs. However, she'd only allowed him a short moment of restored pride before visibly recoiling when he announced Anna had already moved her things to his room.

Apparently his new wife didn't agree that he was "The Most Desirable Hockey Player on the Planet" as *Bleacher Magazine* had named him in the previous year's "Hottest Players" issue. He opened the door wider anyway. Nikolai didn't back down on the rare occasion a hockey player bigger than him came his way, and he refused to let his new wife's reluctance to share his bed deter him.

Sam came into the room, eyeing him like he was a tiger and this was his den.

"Your clothes are in there," he said, indicating the large antique wardrobe he'd cleared out for her things.

With much huffing and puffing, she pulled out some clothes before disappearing into his bathroom.

Nikolai turned off all the lights except for the lamp on his nightstand and got into bed, settling in for a long wait. Nikolai's master bath was somewhat of an architectural marvel with its marbled walls, heated floors, and crystal chandelier that perfectly underlit a thirty-foot frescoed ceiling. In his experience, woman who went in to "freshen up" stayed a little longer than expected to gape.

Sam, however, was in and out in under five minutes, reappearing in a pair of unflattering red sweats with Indiana University's famous logo emblazoned across its bosom-obscuring front.

"I'll be sleeping on top of the blankets," she informed him as she climbed into his bed. Then she immediately gave him her back.

Nikolai gritted his teeth and turned off the lamp for another first: sleeping, and only sleeping, next to a woman.

But she was here, he told himself as he yanked the covers up over his shoulder. By his side and in his bed, which was where a wife belonged. That was enough for now, he thought, lying awake in the dark long after she'd fallen asleep. It would have to be.

BUT IT WASN'T ENOUGH.

The next morning when Nikolai woke, he found himself in bed alone. His wife's scent, a mixture of whatever she used in her hair and the perfume she'd spritzed on for the wedding, lingered, filling up his nose. But her side of the bed was now empty.

Dread icicled its way up his chest. He was a naturally early riser and Sam had never gotten up before him. Not once.

He rushed out of the room, not stopping even long enough to throw on a robe. Alarm bells rang loud in his head as he bounded down the hallway and pushed open the door to his wife's old room. She wasn't there, and the icicles inside his chest turned sharp, spiking into his heart as he went across the way to Pavel's room, throwing open his nephew's door.

Pavel's room was empty, too.

Nikolai bolted downstairs, needing them to be at breakfast. Hoping to the God he'd never bothered with that they were in the kitchen, eating bowls of cereal.

He stopped short in the kitchen doorway, his heart freezing with horror inside his chest.

Because the only one sitting at the island was his father, Sergei.

His father smiled at him in that predatory way of his. "Nikolai, you finally woke up. I thought you would sleep all day."

"Where are they?" Nikolai demanded.

"Where is who?" Sergei asked him in Russian. "Only I'm here. Come with me now. I have a job for you."

"Tell me where they are," Nikolai growled, stepping forward, only to feel something slick underneath his feet.

He looked down. Blood. A puddle of it, covering his bare feet. For a moment, Nikolai couldn't speak for the fear clogging up his throat.

But eventually he looked back up at his smirking father. "If you've hurt them…"

"You will what?" Sergei asked with an arrogant laugh. "Kill me? You had your chance and now you are powerless to do that to me, boy."

It was hard to fully process Sergei's words through his near blinding rage, but Nikolai managed to choke out. "Where are they? Tell me."

Sergei's voice suddenly turned dark. "You know where they are, you sniveling boy," he sneered. "A black grandchild and a black wife for my only son? You knew I wouldn't allow that. They are exactly where they should be now. At the bottom of river with four shots in each of their bodies."

His father, who'd taken nearly every other family member who mattered to him had now taken his wife. His nephew. And his unborn child.

"No!" Nikolai roared. Despair tore through his insides and his entire body went cold with the realization he'd never see Pavel or his wife again. Never hold the baby he and his wife had created in his arms.

The next thing Nikolai knew, his hands were around his father's thick neck "Bastard. Bastard!!"

His father only laughed, as if Nikolai's choking hands were but a necklace around his muscular throat. "No, there is only one bastard here."

"Nikolai..." Samantha's voice said somewhere in the distance.

Nikolai let go of his father's neck, his head whipping from side to side. That was his wife's voice. But how? She was dead!

"Nikolai!" Her voice again, so close, but he couldn't see her.

Sergei laughed behind him, a mean, cackling sound. "It is her ghost, boy. I put two bullets into her chest and two more into her kneecaps. The Rustanov way. I was not sloppy this time. And then I did same to fake Rustanov you were trying to make your son."

"No!" Nikolai yelled, his chest exploding with grief and guilt that he'd let this sadistic demon anywhere near Samantha or Pavel. That he hadn't able to protect them from Sergei, just like he hadn't been able to protect his mother and brother.

"Nikolai!" his wife's ghost called to him again. She sounded frantic, worried.

More derisive laughter from Sergei as if Nikolai in his despair was the funniest thing he'd ever seen. "You will never have what you want, boy. You will never have a family. You will never be rid of me," he informed Nikolai.

Then his father slapped him.

But this action only served to confuse Nikolai. Not because it happened, but because the slap wasn't that bad—almost on the dainty side. Also, Sergei didn't slap. He backhanded.

That one detail alone made Nikolai realize…

He opened his eyes and found Samantha hovering above his prone body, her face pinched with worry.

"Are you okay?" she asked. "I'm sorry about slapping you. I tried everything else to wake you up, but—"

In one abrupt move, he sat up and hauled her into his arms. She was alive! The first light of morning had come through the bedroom's arched bow windows, casting a yellow halo around her beautiful face. And she was here, in his bed with him. Still.

"It's okay," she said. "You had a nightmare. It was just a nightmare."

Her arms came up around his shoulders and to his great embarrassment, an involuntary shudder went through his entire body. Then another. And another.

He'd thought she was dead. He'd thought his father had killed her. He was trembling now, he realized. Like the scared boy his father had accused him of being in the dream. The opposite of the man he wanted to be for his wife and Pavel.

"It's okay," she whispered into his ear. "Just hold on to me until it stops. I'm here for you. I'm here."

As much as he wanted to end the hug, to pull away and show her he wasn't some helpless boy, he couldn't. Just couldn't. In fact, he held on to her tighter, desperately grasping at every word she whispered into his ear until he stopped shaking. And even after that, he kept holding her as his heart rate slid back down and eventually he was able to breathe again, not suck in air like a cosmonaut with a broken helmet.

"It's okay. It was just a nightmare, just a nightmare," she said again when he'd finally calmed down all the way.

She leaned back from him and stroked the hair that was now damp with cold sweat away from his forehead. "Do you want to tell me about your nightmare? It might help to talk—"

He captured her lips, his desperate mouth licking into hers with an urgent need that couldn't wait for permission. One hand anchored at the back of her neck, keeping her lips fused to his as the other hand grabbed on to her hips, tugging her left leg over his waist so that… yes, her hot center was now exactly where it needed to be.

A complete erection soon followed, so instantaneous, the pain of it sent him into auto-pilot. He flipped her over, putting her beneath him. She was alright. It had only been a nightmare. But he had to make sure. He needed to get inside her, to bury himself in her sweet warmth.

"Let me in," he heard himself begging. "I need you. I need you, *zhena*."

Her soft moan was all the permission he needed.

One moment there was still a pair of sweat pants between them and the next, they were no longer a concern, pushed down and yanked off. He disposed of his own briefs and then he was back on top of her, guiding himself into her slick, clenching wetness and taking what he needed to erase the nightmare.

Her hands gripped his side and her legs veed wide to let him in, accommodating him on top of her in a way he'd had no reason to hope for. Gratitude, piercing and unexpected, welled up inside him and he closed his eyes as he rolled into her tight sanctuary, reveling in her body.

And what had started with him getting what he needed from her suddenly did a 180. Nikolai fell over her, claiming her lips again as he slowed down his thrusts. He wanted to pay her back for the gift of her soft comfort. He wanted to make her feel good, better than good.

He was soon rewarded for his efforts when she groaned. "Oh, God, that's so good. So good. Fuck me, fuck me. Please keep going. It's so good…"

And though he'd been wild to have her just a few minutes before, to drive himself into her until he reached completion, he found he didn't mind the slower pace at all. He relished her helpless cries and the way the heels of her feet dug into his buttocks as he forced the top she was wearing up and over her breasts.

She wasn't wearing a bra underneath and Nikolai took a moment to admire the sight. One moment. Before devouring it. He inhaled one perfect globe into his mouth, biting down as he worked the hard bud with his tongue, all the while stroking into her, stroking into her until…

She came apart with a sharp gasp, her fingernails digging into his sides as she went rigid underneath him with her climax.

Maybe he would have been able to last longer if he hadn't had the nightmare. If her cries of completion hadn't been the proof he needed to fully believe she was truly there with him, alive and unharmed, maybe he could have gone on like that in her warmth just a little while longer.

But as it was, he didn't want to be away from her. Not even in this. His head lifted from her chest and he erupted, once again filling her with his seed, so much so that he could feel the hot, slick action on his own shaft as he emptied out inside of her.

When he fell back on top of her, he was once again shuddering, but this time not because of any nightmare.

This time it was because of a dream come true.

"*Zhena…*" he said, kissing her neck. "*Moya zhena…*"

Chapter Twenty-Seven

"JENNA," Nikolai said against her neck. Sam stiffened, her eyes flying open. Who was Jenna? And why was he calling her by another woman's name?

But then he kissed her neck. And said, "Moya Jenna."

No, not a name, she realized. Russian, he was speaking to her in Russian.

She opened her mouth to ask him what "jenna" meant, only to have it seized again. But this time his kiss wasn't desperate or harsh, like the one that had shocked the hell out of her earlier. This one was a soft exploration, almost as if he were trying to get to know her better through her lips.

The kiss made her feel like she was in high school again, tentatively leaning forward to surprise her AP Chemistry lab partner, Anthony Collison, with a kiss the bespectacled black nerd hadn't been expecting. Nikolai's kiss made her feel like she had back then, when she truly believed something beautiful might be waiting on the other of all the ugliness at home.

Hopeful. That's how Nikolai's kiss made her feel.

At least for a second or two. Then her stepfather's slurred

voice broke through her afterglow. *"You think that boy's in love with you? Check your damn head, girl. He using you for that ass,"* he said when she announced she'd be moving in with Anthony. *"He want to put that ass on tap!"*

Nikolai finished the kiss with a satisfied smile. There was no trace of the man who'd shaken in her arms, helpless shudders racking his entire body.

"Thank you," he said, his voice low. "For helping me with nightmare."

He sat up. "Pavel will be up soon, but after he goes to school…" He gave her knowing look. "We do this again, *da?*"

"You're just a piece of ass, far as any of these boys concerned, and that's all you ever going to be to them," her stepfather said inside her head. It had been the last thing he'd said to her before she moved out.

Shame, ugly and hot, rolled her stomach.

Nikolai frowned at her. "You have morning sickness again?"

"No," she answered, rubbing a hand over her aching chest. "I… it's just…" With shaking hands, she pulled her college sweatshirt back down over her breasts and climbed out of bed.

"You're right," she said, tugging on the sweatshirt and wishing it were a few inches longer so it could cover her naked bottom. "I- I should get up. G-get myself ready. M-make Pavel breakfast."

Nikolai regarded her from underneath his hooded stare. "You have much trouble speaking sometimes after we kiss. You are like woman from kind of film—you know, kind of movie where woman falls in love with man and then trips and falls down many times. How do you say that kind of movie?"

"Romantic comedies," she mumbled, pulling on the sweatpants she found discarded next to the bed as fast as she could. "Rom coms."

"Yes, *rom coms*," he said from the bed. "You have trouble with your words like those women. Why?"

"Probably because I haven't had my coffee yet," she answered, keeping her eyes down as she headed toward the bathroom.

"Or maybe it is because… *zhena*, turn around. Look at me."

There was that name again. But this time she heard the nuance. A zh sound, not a J. What did it mean? she wondered as she turned to look back at him.

Which was a total mistake. All the breath left her body. There was sexy, and then there was Nikolai Rustanov sitting on top of that big bed of his. His hair tousled on top of his head, his chiseled chest on full display, his legs spread apart so you'd have to be blind as Beau not to notice the large erection in between his legs. Standing at attention, and still glistening from having been inside her.

Despite the pounding it had already received that morning, her sex throbbed in response to the sight of him. She refocused on his overly handsome, but not nearly as discomfiting, face and waited for him to say whatever he wanted to say.

But he didn't speak for a few long seconds, just stared, his eyelids so heavy they verged on dangerous, even though he was technically smiling. Technically. The sides of his mouth were quirked up, so she guessed that counted.

"I make you nervous," he finally finished, scanning her body with smirking assessment.

"Ya think?" she answered in her best Captain Obvious voice. "I mean, you've got the muscles, the looks, and the, you know…" she circled her hand around her face. "The whole dead-eyed stare thing going. I think you make a lot of people nervous. On purpose."

His gaze shifted to the side as if he was giving her words

careful consideration. "Yes, I often make women nervous." His eyes came back to her. "But I do not want to make you nervous, *zhena*. That is not what I want to do with you."

More staring.

And Sam's heart actually skipped a few beats, her own gaze hopelessly locked onto his. To the point that it felt like he was letting her go when he finally broke the stare off with a stretch of his heavily muscled arms.

"I will take my exercise, and you can take shower." He smirked at her. "But *zhena*, do not fall like woman in rom com. This could hurt our baby."

"I'll try to stay upright," was the best she could come up with under the him-very-naked-on-the-bed circumstances.

She disappeared into the bathroom for a long shower and pondered his parting words, "Do not fall..." Sam was fairly certain he meant it literally. But she chose to read between the lines. Do not fall… in *love*. Especially not with him.

And as she washed him off her body, she was haunted once again by a remembered conversation, this one much more recent, having only taken place less than two months ago.

"Love. Love is a silly custom you don't believe in? You seriously just said that? How can you not believe in love?"

"Trust me, you do not have to believe in silly custom to give woman much pleasure. Come upstairs. I will show you."

And show her, he had. Twice.

LUCKILY THERE WAS NOTHING LIKE A HECTIC MORNING OF getting a little boy through his yoga practice and off to school, followed by an oh-so-sexy bout of depositing the rich food she'd eaten at her wedding dinner into one of the downstairs toilets, to clear her mind. By the time she got over the dry heaves enough to drive herself to work, she was more than ready to think about anything other than Nikolai Rustanov and the morning sickness-inducing baby he'd put inside of her, courtesy of the last time she'd let a kiss with him go too far.

However, her Don't Think About Nikolai plan hit a bump soon after she arrived at Ruth's House. An Asian man was waiting on the front steps, a very handsome Asian man in an expensive-looking suit.

Sam was perplexed. He looked way too wealthy to be a social worker and way too classy to be a lawyer. And she seriously doubted he was the abusive husband or boyfriend of one of the women at the shelter. Not that Asians were immune to abusive relationships, but in her many years of working with abused women, she'd discovered some cultures were simply more private about their relationship troubles than others and, as a result, a lot less likely to call attention to themselves when the shit hit the fan.

"Hello?" It came out more a question than a greeting.

"Hello," he replied, coming down the steps to meet her on the sidewalk. Upon closer inspection, she was pretty sure his suit had been hand tailored to his body's specifications. And he walked with a slight limp. An old injury, she guessed, one that for whatever reason hadn't set right.

"I'm Suro Nakamura," he said with a bow. Unlike Nikolai, he spoke perfect English with only the slightest accent to indicate he wasn't from the States. He came to a stop a few feet beside her, turning his body sideways between the house and the road so she was forced to do the same if she wanted to address him.

"Okay, Mr. Nakamura," she said, feeling all sorts of unsettled as she noticed how his eyes did a continuous slow back and forth between the house and road, like a tracking light scanning the perimeter. "What can I help you with?"

Suro arched an eyebrow at her. "This is actually about how I can help you. I'm here in regards to your security needs."

"Oh," she said, her mouth falling open with surprise. "You're here about the security guard position?"

She could hear the skepticism in her voice and she didn't want to be rude, but this guy looked nothing like the usual rent-a-cops she'd met before. He didn't have the build of an ex-high school football player whose muscle had turned mostly to fat. And he was simply too young to be a retired police officer like Danny had been.

An aura of cool remove surrounded him, one that put her in mind of—well, of Nikolai. Nikolai at his worst, when he was doing his "no feelings, no feelings at all" thing.

"I thought the agency wouldn't be sending anyone over until tomorrow," she said.

"I'm not here with an agency, but as a favor to Nikolai Rustanov."

She cocked her head to the side. "Nikolai sent you?"

"Yes, he's asked me to assess your security needs, so I'll need to take a look around your shelter."

"I don't think so," she said, her brain still trying to catch up with the fact that Nikolai had sent someone to her shelter to assess her security needs, like… like he had anything to say about it. "First of all men aren't allowed in the shelter and second of all, I think your suit might cost more than we normally pay our guards in a year. As capable as I'm sure you are, we can't afford you."

A slight smile turned up the corners of his mouth as he conceded, "No, you probably cannot. But I won't be the one serving your needs, only finding four men who can."

She blinked. "Four men?" she repeated. Ruth's House had never had more than one day or night guard on duty at any given time.

"Mr. Rustanov was very clear about wanting your shelter to

have twenty-four hour protection. Front and back."

"Yes, but… we get by with what we already have. And twenty-four hour security protection isn't exactly in the budget."

"Consider it a gift from Mr. Rustanov. A security endowment."

Sam opened her mouth. Then closed it. Then opened it again. Then closed it, truly frustrated because… yeah, it was a gift she hadn't asked for and no, she didn't like having decisions forced upon her.

But unfortunately, Nikolai had hit her right in her weak spot. She didn't want to give in, but she had a duty to her shelter. If anyone else had given them a "security endowment," she would have thanked them with a handwritten letter, then again in person with a plaque, and then yet again with a mention in their bi-annual donor newsletter.

She also would have called Josie in a fit of delight to tell her the good news. The only reason she didn't now, and knew she wouldn't later, was because this generous gift came via Nikolai Rustanov, who was apparently trying to—actually she wasn't quite sure what he was trying to do with this extreme gesture.

"May I show you something?" Suro asked, interrupting her conflicted thoughts. His face had gentled, she noticed. Less all-business mode, and more sensitivity than she would have guessed him capable of possessing at first sight.

He pulled out his phone and came to stand beside her. Then he swiped a picture on to the phone's rectangular screen. A little girl with creamy brown skin, a bubbly expression and chubby legs and cheeks appeared. She looked to be about two, on the thin edge between baby and toddler, and she was nothing less than completely adorable.

"This is my daughter, Gracie," Suro said with a smile in his voice. He swiped the screen again to the picture of a little black boy. This one was definitely a toddler, standing up strong and confident with a dinosaur toy raised above his head. "And this is our adopted son, Spidey."

Before Sam could ask if he'd really named his adopted child, Spidey, Suro swiped again. This time to a picture of two young teenagers, one Asian, one black, sitting at a piano together with intent expressions on their faces. "We call these two the twins, but they're technically my son and stepdaughter. They formally introduced me to my wife."

He swiped the phone to reveal one last picture: a pretty woman with dreadlocks, smiling sleepily up at the camera as a newborn Gracie slept on top of her, her small head nestled into the woman's shoulder. "And this is my wife, Tasha."

He gave the picture a thoughtful smile before tucking the phone back in his inside pocket. "I'd do anything to keep my family safe and if Tasha were working at a place like this, I'd make sure she had security I could trust. Let Mr. Rustanov do this for you."

The slideshow had been cute. Too cute. It had left a sweet ache in Sam's heart that made her rub a hand over her chest for the second time that morning.

Suro was probably right about Nikolai doing this because he wanted to protect his family. But he was wrong about Nikolai doing it for her. He'd hired a security guard for Pavel, and she supposed this was his way of making sure the baby inside her womb received the same standard of protection.

Nonetheless, the fact remained: she'd be an idiot to turn down such a gift. She'd always put the Ruth's House shelters first, and she was prepared to downshift her pride if it meant the women who came to her would benefit from Nikolai's commitment to providing security for their baby.

She forced a smile onto her face and asked Suro, "Since we're going all out on security, do you think it's possible to get four women guards in here? I've been asking the agency we use here and in Alabama to provide us with women for years now, but it's kind of a "take what you can get situation" at the wages we've been paying."

Suro nodded, family man gone and all business now that she had agreed to let him assess Ruth's House Indiana's security needs.

"I'm sure that can be arranged," he answered.

Chapter Twenty-Eight

"CANA YOU PASS me the salt, Pavel?"

Nikolai watched his nephew pass his wife the salt shaker sitting in front of his own plate. So close, in fact, that the obvious thing would have been for her to ask Nikolai for the salt. But his wife had been using Pavel as a go-between all night. In fact, she hadn't said a word to Nikolai, beyond hello, since he walked in the door.

Nikolai added a bit of pepper to the lemon chicken his wife had made with a tight jaw. It was Monday, technically the night after their disastrous wedding dinner, but despite what had taken place between he and his wife that morning, nothing had changed. She barely looked at him throughout the meal. And just like every other night they'd had dinner together so far, she and Pavel did most of the talking, leaving him to sit there with a strange emptiness in his stomach, wondering if he'd ever be able to do the things that came to her and Pavel so naturally. Wondering if he'd ever be able to act like he was a member of a normal family.

If Pavel had wanted to talk about the best gun for killing a man quietly, Nikolai could have held forth on that topic all night. But for most of the meal, his nephew and his wife talked about some TV series that sounded both inane and complicated. A show called *Avatar*, which Pavel loved, even though it wasn't based in any way whatsoever on the James Cameron movie of the same name. At least not so far as Nikolai could tell.

In any case, his wife and nephew had yet to choose a topic he could feel comfortable talking about. But he was no longer a little boy, forced to exist on the periphery of the Rustanov family, he reminded himself.

His father was dead. And his Russian relatives for the most part were proud to have a famous hockey player in their family tree now. He had a big house and more money than he knew what to do with. He owned a professional hockey team, he thought to himself, biting down fiercely on a piece of chicken. He refused to be intimidated by the small talk of one small woman and one even smaller boy. Also, he'd be damned if he was going to let Samantha avoid him by talking to Pavel all night.

When their conversation about the boy avatar versus the girl avatar came to a close, he forced himself to jump in.

"Pavel, how is your schooling?" he asked, his voice terse.

Pavel's eyes widened as if a statue had suddenly come to life at the table. "How is my schooling?" he repeated carefully. "It's cool, I guess. I'm still behind in math. But Mama's a good tutor. She's been helping me."

"Good," Nikolai said. The one word landed like a stone in the middle of the table, and he looked from side to side, having no idea what to say next.

But then Pavel asked, "Were you good at math when you was in school, Uncle?"

"'Were in school', Pavel," corrected Samantha from the other side of the table.

"Were you good at math when you *were* in school, Uncle?" Pavel repeated dutifully.

Nikolai answered with a slight shrug. "When I was your age I was already on hockey team. Maybe it did not matter so much how good I am with numbers."

Pavel gaped at him. "You and my dad was-," he darted a guilty look at Samantha, "I mean, you and my dad *were* already playing hockey when you were my age? Like professionally?"

"No, not as professional, but maybe, how you say, *potential* to become professional. Our coaches put us on path to become star hockey players. Math was not so important."

Pavel thought about that. Then he asked Sam, "Mama, since I'm going to be a professional hockey player, too, can I stop doing my math homework?"

"No," he and his wife answered at the same time.

Nikolai added, "You like your dream, like telling everyone you will be hockey player like me," he told the boy with a sniff. "But you cannot think yourself into becoming professional hockey player. You do not have what it takes to make this happen."

Pavel's eyebrows squished together, his mouth turning downward into a sad frown, and Nikolai could feel his wife's eyes on him, harsh and judging.

"But Papa told me I was going to be a great hockey player cuz it was in my blood," Pavel said with a voice that was half tremble, half whimper, as if Nikolai had just dashed the biggest dream he'd ever had. "And he wasn't lying about you, so I thought for sure he wasn't lying about this."

"Fedya did not lie, but he did not tell you truth either," Nikolai informed his nephew. "You should not want to be like Fedya. Talent but no discipline. You should want better for yourself, but you want easy dream."

Pavel didn't answer, but his eyes were bright with unchecked anger even as his bottom lip quivered. Nikolai could tell the boy was working hard not to cry... or punch his uncle.

"Pavel," his wife said quietly. "Breathe. Breathe slowly, until your ready to look at what your feeling right now. It's just a feeling in your body. One you can just observe without acting on it."

Nikolai had no idea what that meant, but apparently Pavel did. The little boy took several deep breaths. And then his eyes shuttered, as if he'd come to some sort of conclusion.

"Uncle doesn't think I'll be a hockey star like him," he said to Samantha with a quiver in his voice. "He doesn't think I'm good enough because I'm not a Rustanov like him. Because Papa was an addict."

Before his wife could chime in with one of her nonsensical suggestions, Nikolai slammed his hand on the table, forcing the boy's attention back to him.

"Do not put false words in my mouth, Pavel. You are child. Your job right now is to listen to adults, not say we say what we don't say."

Now Pavel shook his head. "But I don't understand. You said—"

"I said you do not have what it takes. *Yet*. Pavel, have you ever played hockey?"

"You mean on ice?" Pavel asked.

"*Da*."

"No, just in the living room with Papa," Pavel admitted with a frown, as if just now considering that having never actually learned how to properly play or skate might be an impediment to the bright future his father had promised him. "So that means I can't be a good hockey player like you?"

Nikolai glanced at his wife. Her hands were clenched tight around her silverware, her body slightly leaned forward as if she was primed to physically jump between him and Pavel if Nikolai said the wrong thing.

"No, I'm saying you are not good hockey player yet," Nikolai answered his nephew. Then he heard himself say, "I must teach you, and *then* you will be great hockey player like your papa."

Pavel's eyes lit up like Nikolai had just given him the best Christmas gift ever. "Seriously? You, Mount Nik, are going to teach me to play hockey?"

"*Da*," Nikolai answered, his voice gruff. He looked across the island at Samantha and said, "Starting tomorrow, Dirk will bring him to me after school. I will make him work hard, so he can have his dream and not lose it."

"But what about homework?" his wife asked. "His math…"

"We can do it after dinner!" Pavel all but yelled. "I promise I'll do my homework after dinner every day, no complaining, if you let me play with Mount Nik. Please, Mama, please!"

Pavel actually had his hands clasped together, and he shook them like a supplicant at the feet of a Mary statue. "It'd be me practicing with Mount Nik! Mount. Nik."

Sam's nose wrinkled and Nikolai could tell she didn't quite understand why this was so important to Pavel, but eventually she caved with, "Okay, but if you ever don't do your homework, I reserve the right to cancel your next practice."

"If he doesn't do homework, I will cancel all of his practices for week, so lesson is learned," Nikolai assured her.

Pavel came out of his seat as if he hadn't heard either of their caveats.

"This is the best day of my life!" he yelled, throwing his arms in the air. "Thank you, Uncle. Thank you!"

Back Up loped over, licking at Nikolai's shoes as if to say she approved of this arrangement.

Nikolai answered Pavel's enthusiastic thank you with a stiff, "You're welcome, Pavel." Then he picked up his fork to finish his dinner. Maybe, he thought to himself, maybe this wasn't the worst idea in the world.

He'd been afraid to spend too much time with the boy before. He looked too much like Fedya, and it still caused an uneasy sensation inside of him when he let himself look at Pavel too long.

But perhaps this would be a good thing. Maybe spending more time with the boy would… help with the other things he didn't like to think about too much. The things that made it feel like the ice rink inside his chest was cracking apart when he thought too much about the demons that had led his brother down the path of addiction.

But maybe this would help with that—inoculate him, so he could look at the boy without thinking of his doomed brother. He eyed Pavel, still waving his skinny arms in the air as he informed Samantha that he was going to be the best hockey player ever because Mount Nik would be his coach. In any case, practicing would put some muscle on the boy, Nikolai thought to himself. He'd need those if he truly wanted to make his NHL dreams come true.

"Good job with Pavel tonight," his wife told him, when she visited him in his office after putting Pavel to sleep that night.

She dropped into one of his guest chairs, and as she did so, Nikolai took her in with hungry eyes. Her twists, which she'd gotten redone for the wedding, were hanging down and she was dressed in jeans and a simple sweater. A cold weather wardrobe choice for sure, but just looking at her made Nikolai think of sunny days, and when her eyes raised to meet his…

That ice breaking feeling again, like a warm front was moving across his chest as he let himself take a tiny moment to revel in the fact that she now belonged to him. That the woman in the green dress was now his wife.

"He was still talking about your offer to train him when I tucked him in. He's saying Back Up will probably want to come, too, so do you want me to text Isaac about the arena's policy on dogs or do you want to handle that?"

"I am boss. He may bring dog if he wishes," Nikolai answered.

She grimaced a little. "Okay, but be sure you don't create a monster there."

He crooked his head to the side. "You do not think I know not to indulge my nephew too much?" he asked.

She gave him a teasing smile. "No, I'm not talking about Pavel, I'm talking about Back Up. Start taking her to your skating rink and she'll expect to come everywhere with Pavel from now on."

So she wasn't questioning his parenting skills, only his decision to let Pavel bring her useless dog along. There came an unexpected release of tension in Nikolai's stomach.

"And the security person you sent to the shelter, Suro Nakamura?" Her voice was tight, and he tensed again, waiting for her anger.

But then she lowered her eyes and said, "Thank you. It's a very thoughtful and generous gift. I'll be sure to send you a donor acknowledgement letter for your taxes at the end of the year."

"You're welcome," he answered. Then he waited, sensing there was another subject looming on her agenda, one he wouldn't necessarily like.

He was right.

"About what happened this morning..." she said.

Sam wasn't fooled this time when Nikolai's face went totally blank. She knew better now. The last time he'd gone completely neutral on her, the most rabid family lawyer in Indiana showed up on the doorstep a few days later.

This time the shuttering of his hooded eyes sent a chill down her back. But she swallowed to get some moisture going in her mouth and pressed on. "That was a really intense nightmare you had. It sounded like you were scared. Really scared."

His gaze went cold, his eyes two green circles on a bed of ice. "I'm fine. It was only nightmare."

She inclined her head. "It didn't sound like nothing. Was it about your brother? Sometimes grief gets processed through our dreams, especially when we don't take the time to acknowledge it. That's what happened to me when I had my nightmare. I was basically processing what had happened that evening."

He said nothing.

"Or maybe it was about your father?"

More nothing.

And Sam began to feel very foolish for trying to talk to him, for coming in here with the intention of lending an ear to someone like Nikolai Rustanov.

"Okay," she said with a sigh. "I won't pry. I'm just saying if you ever need to talk to somebody, I'm here for you."

"Is there anything else?" he asked. His tone made her feel like she was talking to a living icicle.

She cleared her throat. "Actually, as matter of fact, there is something else. After what happened this morning, I'm thinking I should go back to my room—"

"Nyet, that isn't what we agreed," he said before she could finish.

She nearly rolled her eyes. Exactly what she'd expected him to say. "Fine, well we agreed I'd share a room with you. Not a bed, just a room. So I'll be sleeping on the couch tonight."

His eyes flared with frustration, probably because she'd

introduced this subject too late in the night for him to get someone in to take the couch out of his room.

"And if you take out the couch, I'm just going to sleep on the floor," she let him know so she wouldn't run into the issue with him the next day. Then she waited for him to issue some kind of edict about her sleeping where he told her to sleep.

But the next words out of his mouth were a question.

"You do not wish to share my bed?" he asked, his voice low and gruff. Then he averted his eyes. Like Pavel did whenever he asked a question and feared he would be hurt by the answer.

His question caused Sam to falter a bit. She wished Nikolai would stop doing this. Going vulnerable on her when she least expected it.

"I, um…" She quickly pulled on her counselor hat again. "I think sex confuses things, especially in a relationship like ours. Which was established for reasons of convenience. I don't want anyone to get hurt."

Especially me, she thought with a pang, before rushing to a finish with, "This morning was a mistake on both our parts, and I think it would behoove both of us to never let it happen again."

An icy pause.

Then Nikolai reached into the top drawer of his desk and pulled out a pair of reading glasses before picking his smartphone up off the desk.

"Excuse me. English is not my first language. I am looking up this word 'mistake.'" He frowned. "Ah, here it is. The internet says mistake means 'an action or judgment that is misguided or wrong. Synonyms: error, fault, omission, slip, blunder, miscalculation, misunderstanding, oversight, misinterpretation…'" he carefully sounded out the next word. "so-lee-cism—I say this word right?"

"I- I don't know," she answered. The truth was she'd never

heard of the word, but she didn't need to know how to pronounce it in order to realize he was making fun of her. "My point is—"

"I thought I knew what mistake means, what all these words except so-lee-cism mean. But maybe we have two different definitions. I will look at this other word, behooves." A few thumb taps and his eyes scanned the resulting page. "Hmm, this makes things you say even more confusing. You think it *appropriate* and *suitable* for husband and wife with baby on way not to share bed?"

"We're not—we're not a *real* husband and wife," she reminded him. "We're more like project partners, and I don't sleep with my project partners. So if you have an event or a work obligation you need me to attend, fine. That's what I signed up for. But I'm sleeping on the couch."

Another icy pause. Then he bit out, "I will not sleep in our bed without you, *zhena*."

For some reason his referring to her by that name again made her lose the firm grip on all the calm she'd been determined to maintain when she walked into his study to have this conversation.

"I'm already letting you use me as an incubator," she told Nikolai in a harsh, ugly voice. "I shouldn't have to explain to you why I don't want to be used as your fuck toy."

Silence dropped down like a curtain and Nikolai stared at her for several long, heavy seconds, before saying, "You did not seem to mind being my fuck toy this morning, *zhena*," he said, his voice low and calm. "What were your words? 'Fuck me. Fuck me. Please keep going?'"

He lifted his eyebrows in mock consideration. "But maybe I do not understand these words correctly either."

Sam dropped her gaze, her cheeks burning angry and hot. But she didn't waver. "I'm sleeping on the couch from now on," she said, fighting to keep her voice level. "Don't try to bully me out of it."

She said that last quiet thing and then she left his study feeling like the biggest fool imaginable for getting herself entangled with a man who had an ice rink where his heart should be.

∾

To Sam's relief, Nikolai didn't try to stop her from sleeping on the ornate, red and gold chaise lounge in his bedroom that night. In fact, he left her alone. Literally. He still hadn't come up to the room by the time Sam fell into a fitful sleep on the couch, which was comfortable enough—especially for a chaise lounge—but not nearly as comfortable as his luxurious bed had been.

Sam woke the next morning to an unexpected sight. Nikolai's empty bed, sheets smooth, blanket in place, pillows still plump, the whole tableau an obvious testament to not having been slept in.

Sam sat up on one elbow. *So then where did Nikolai sleep last night?* she wondered.

An unexpected jealously gripped her, its bony green hand squeezing her heart.

Had Nikolai gone out to find what he wanted in the arms of another woman? One who had no problems with sex without love, or sleeping with a married man? The thing was, she couldn't see Nikolai sleeping in the guestroom or his office —he was a natural competitor and he would never cede his turf. And they'd never discussed the intimate terms of their marriage beyond the fact that she didn't think it was a good idea to be intimate with him.

Anyone looking at the situation from the outside in—a woman who refused to sleep with her own husband—might take his side on this. He wasn't getting what he needed at home, so he went somewhere else for it. She'd met enough marriage counselors to know that open marriages were a thing that worked for some couples.

But not her. The thought of sleeping with another man made her stomach turn in a way that had nothing to do with her recurrent bouts of morning sickness.

She sat up on the couch and threw off the blankets. More proof that she'd made the right decision in refusing to sleep with him again, she decided as she got up. She headed to the bathroom with her chin raised, thinking she'd be damned if was going to let this situation throw her off her healthy morning routine. She'd get dressed, go get Pavel for their morning yoga session, then they'd walk Back Up around the neighborhood and eat breakfast together, and she wouldn't give any more thought to her cheating lothario of a husband—

Sam suddenly pitched forward violently, and she had no doubt she would have broken something when she hit the floor…

…had Nikolai's mountainous body not cushioned her fall.

"*Zhena*, I told you to watch yourself," he said, reaching up and easily rearranging her, so she was lying on top of him. Her face right above his. He gave her a tired half smile. "No falling I told you. Remember?"

She blinked down at him. "What are you doing sleeping on the floor?!?!"

"I told you. I will not sleep in bed without you."

His expression was so neutral, he almost look bored, but she could feel his length against the top of her thigh coming to hard, thick life.

"Be more careful," he said, lifting her up like she weighed nothing and setting her aside. He came to his feet, looming over her. "Soon, baby will be hurt if you fall."

"I- I usually am—I mean, I'm not the falling type. It's just,

I didn't know you slept on the floor last night…" She struggled for more words, but only came up with another, "I didn't know…"

He looked down at her with another of his heavy frowns, "Take your shower, *zhena*. I will take my workout."

Then he left the room without another word.

Chapter Twenty-Nine

A LITTLE OVER a month after having drawn her line in the sand, Sam was still wondering who was getting their way in this current situation. Because it certainly didn't feel like her.

The morning of Pavel's birthday, she woke to the same sight she'd been waking up to for the last five weeks. An empty room. Her husband already gone for his morning workout, which would be directly followed by his commute to work, since he'd started going in even earlier to make up the extra time he spent training Pavel after he got out of school.

She sat up and stretched, but the movement in no way addressed all the little aches and pains that came from sleeping on a chaise lounge while four months pregnant. Yet another reason she was seriously doubting her winner status these days.

Two months ago she'd been sure Nikolai would eventually tire of sleeping on the floor and might even send her back to her former room in a fit of frustration. But he hadn't sent her back to her old room. And though she never saw him when she went to bed or woke, she'd become used to either stepping over or walking around a sleeping Mount Nik during her increasing number of late night bathroom visits.

"Can Uncle come with us to the Children's Museum after school today?" Pavel asked while they walked Back Up that morning. "I don't think he's ever been either."

Sam had to work not to laugh. The little boy made it sound like his uncle having never been to the Indianapolis Children's Museum, the largest of its kind in the world, was the saddest thing he'd ever heard. "He probably has to work, honey."

"Maybe not," Pavel said. "The season's almost over, and the Polar didn't make the playoffs this year. Uncle says it's going to take a year or two before they win another Stanley Cup cuz building a great team takes time and the right players."

Sam had to resist the urge to roll her eyes. The "uncle says" stuff had reached a fevered pitched ever since Pavel had started spending most of his afterschool time with Nikolai.

However in this case, Pavel didn't know the reason she was taking him to the Children's Museum after school as opposed to on the weekend as she'd originally planned was because Isaac had sent her an email asking her to do something with the boy until five pm. Apparently, Nikolai had a meeting he had to attend during their usual practice time.

Sam had quickly agreed and tried to focus on the fact that Nikolai had been consistently spending time with Pavel up until that point, but she couldn't help but be a little disappointed. Of all the days for him to schedule a meeting during his regular skate time with Pavel, did it have to be on the boy's birthday?

Not that Pavel was allowing her to make much of a big deal out of him turning nine. He'd forbidden Sam to throw him a party, and the only reason he'd agreed to let her take him to the Children's Museum on his birthday was because they already had a family membership, so it wasn't like Pavel was giving into some silly custom.

God, she wished Nikolai hadn't said that to him. In many

ways, Pavel was thriving. He was steadily gaining weight, he'd nearly caught up in math, and he'd even made a few friends at his new school. But he still seemed truly afraid of going against his uncle in any way, abiding by all of Nikolai's rules and personal beliefs like they were sacrosanct.

This refusal to acknowledge his birthday was not good, Sam thought as she waved the little boy off to school with Dirk later that morning. Not good at all. They should all be celebrating and thanking the heavens for him making it to the age of nine, especially after the year he'd had.

But she made herself take a calming breath. Things with Pavel were so much better than they'd been four months ago, she reminded herself. And they'd only get better with time. He had a routine and stability and she was there to look out for his best interests. Eventually everything else would fall into place, with or without Nikolai's blessing.

She hoped.

Accompanying Pavel to the Children's Museum gave her an excuse to take off from work early, which she almost never did on Fridays, since those could be high intake days. But Ruth's House was currently at full capacity, and though Nyla was still in school, she was proving to be more than capable when it came to taking over in Sam's stead.

Sam was beginning to trust her nearly as much as she'd trusted Josie back when her best friend had only been a volunteer. And that gave her a lot of peace of mind as far as her upcoming maternity leave was concerned.

Dirk arrived with Pavel to pick her up from Ruth's House at three on the dot that afternoon. She'd told the bodyguard she could take him herself, no need for him to stay past his allotted hours, but he'd insisted. "Mr. Rustanov pays me to shadow the kid—plus, I've never been to the Children's Museum and Pav says I'm missing out. Sounds like fun."

So that was how she ended up digging for dinosaur bones,

riding an indoor carousel, and exploring the Reuben Wells locomotive with Pavel and his bodyguard, who was ostensibly there to have fun but glowered at every person who came anywhere near Pavel as if they were enemy forces in disguise. Including the children, who seemed to find the bodyguard's menacing presence fascinating. A few of the parents and care-givers, in contrast, escorted their children far away from Dirk's "don't even think about fucking with this kid" vibe, which seemed to suit Dirk just fine.

"You don't look like you're having much fun," she said with a wry smile, as they lingered for the hourly water clock lecture in the museum's atrium lobby. Pavel was on the floor with the other children, while she and Dirk stood off to the side with the rest of the adults.

Dirk wasn't even pretending to listen to the many inter-esting details about the water clock as he scanned and rescanned the stairs and all the entrances and exits. Sam was beginning to suspect he hailed from some kind of Special Forces background, and that all this open space made him nervous.

"No, I'm having a great time," Dirk answered. Completely monotone.

His phone made a dinging sound and it must have been important, because he actually stopped eye sweeping the lobby long enough to take a look at the text message.

"All right. We gotta get out of here," he informed her as he re-pocketed the device.

"Excuse me?" Sam asked, thinking she must have heard him wrong.

"That was Isaac. Rustanov's meeting's been cancelled. If we get there in the next twenty minutes, he can still get some ice time in with Pav. You don't mind tagging along, do you? I don't think I can get him there in time if I have to drop you off."

First of all Sam didn't like the thought of Pavel having his museum trip cut short, and on his birthday no less. And second of all, she could think of about ten thousand things she'd rather do with the rest of her afternoon than watch Pavel play hockey with his uncle. But in the end, she guessed she must really love the kid because she let him decide whether they should go or not.

Pavel didn't even take a moment to consider. "Uncle Nik," he answered immediately. "I gotta practice my goal shots some more. Uncle says if I can get one past him, he'll buy me a pair of Bauer Supreme MX3s."

Sam had no idea what Bauer Supreme MX3s were, but assumed they must be ice skates and valuable ones at that if Pavel was willing to cut short his Children's Museum trip.

Once they got to the Polar's training facility, a concrete and red brick building with cars filling nearly all of it parking spaces, Dirk led the way.

"Isaac said to take you straight back to the Polar's rink. Rustanov's waiting for you there. C'mon, I'll show you the way."

Sam understood why Dirk thought they might need an escort when they got inside. They passed a smaller rink with children playing hockey, and a larger one with thin girls, some in workout pants, some in sparkling costumes, spinning and leaping on the ice.

"Uncle says if the baby you have after this one is a girl, he's going to enroll her in figure skating here," Pavel informed her. "He says Russian girls have ice skating in their blood."

He said what now? Sam wanted to reply. The big sixteen-week ultrasound where the doctor should be able to tell the baby's sex wasn't for another three weeks—after the close of the Polar's season, as if the baby had been perfectly planned to fit into Nikolai's schedule. But the genetic screening blood test Sam took a couple of weeks ago had come back with an

XY sex indicator, so it was a pretty sure bet they'd be having a boy.

But if Pavel was quoting his uncle correctly, Nikolai was already thinking about and having a second biological child with her. She couldn't tell whether the shiver that suddenly went down her back was because she was walking through a skating facility with only a light jacket on, or because of what Pavel said. Or because the thought of having another child with Nikolai, a little girl with his strong resolve, didn't exactly repel her.

Pavel came to an abrupt stop. "He's not here," he said, his shoulders slumping with disappointment.

Indeed, the rink they were apparently headed toward was completely dark behind the plexiglas windows.

Sam frowned but kept her voice reassuring as she rubbed the little boy's back. "Maybe he's still in his office." She pulled out her phone. "I'll text Isaac."

But Dirk kept walking and beckoned them forward. "Isaac said to meet him here at 5:00 PM on the D.O.T. It's 4:59 PM and I'm not getting in trouble because I missed the drop off."

Dirk's insistence on getting to the darkened rink on time surprised Sam. He was usually pretty flexible, but she supposed that was because she and Pavel were almost always where they were supposed be, when they were supposed to be for "the drop off."

Irritated, but not wanting to cause Pavel's bodyguard any unnecessary stress, she put a hand on Pavel's back and guided him forward.

"It's okay," she assured him. "He'll probably be here soon, and we can just wait for him in the—"

Dirk flipped the lights on to reveal a large rink filled with smiling people. Many of whom she recognized as classmates of Pavel's and their parents. There were also a couple of guys in full-on hockey gear, including a long-haired blond she'd seen on a few Polar's posters. One of their star players, if she recalled correctly.

"SURPRISE!!!" they all yelled in unison.

It was a birthday party, Sam realized then. A birthday party for Pavel, who was just standing there beside her, frozen in shock.

Until his Uncle, who'd been standing in the middle of the crowd, skated forward and beckoned him forward with a solemn "Happy Birthday, Pavel."

After that, Sam knew for sure what she'd only suspected before. All Pavel's talk about not wanting a party had been a bunch of hooey. And it was totally disproved when he didn't just walk, but flew across the ice towards his uncle, hugging him around the waist so hard, it was a wonder Nikolai was able to stay balanced on his skates.

At first Sam thought Pavel was laughing with delight when he buried his face in Nikolai's side and his shoulders started shaking, but then there came a sound. A ragged keening that could not in any way be mistaken for laughter. Pavel was crying, she realized, crying so hard his whole body convulsed with it.

The rink grew quiet and for a moment, the only sound that could be heard was that of Pavel's wild sobs, which were obviously about so much more than being surprised with a birthday party. Nikolai looked up at her, a heavy frown on his face, as if he blamed her for this unexpected response.

"Pavel, stop this," he said to the boy. "Stop this now."

Sam came forward, prepared to intervene so Nikolai wouldn't make him feel ashamed about crying.

But then Nikolai gently patted the overcome boy on the back. "Come Pavel. It is time to stop crying," he said quietly. "We all came here for you. Come, take your party."

To Sam's surprise, Pavel let his uncle out of the fierce clutch, sniffled once, and then did just that. Skating off to join his cheering friends who seemed more than willing to overlook a little crying if it meant skating on the Polar's ice rink with a few of the team's players, no less.

She turned her gaze back to Nikolai and saw he was watching her watch Pavel finally get the party he deserved with a satisfied smirk in his eyes. And she wondered if he'd done this for Pavel. Or just to prove her wrong.

Either way, she couldn't begrudge him the results. Pavel was flipping out, especially when the long-haired blond skated over to him with a pair of slick black skates, which from Pavel's jumping up and down action, she could only assume were the coveted Bauer's Pavel had mentioned earlier.

No doubt about it, whatever Nikolai's true intentions, he'd made Pavel the happiest boy on earth. And she couldn't help the warm feeling that erupted inside her chest, despite the smirking look he was giving her.

In fact, she wondered if she was ever going to figure out how to dislike Nikolai Rustanov as much as her good sense told her she should if she didn't want to get hurt.

Chapter Thirty

"THEY GET ALONG," Nikolai's cousin, Alexei, observed as they watched Pavel and Alexei's son, Aaron, take part in a shooting drill game. It involved the Polar's star left winger, Brian Atwood, who was acting as goalie.

Aaron was a couple years older than Pavel, but anyone who saw them together at the party likely assumed the light brown boys had known each other forever, the way they talked trash and encouraged each other during the drills in equal parts.

"*Da*," Nikolai agreed.

At that moment, Pavel got a shot past Brian—most likely because he was the birthday boy and Brian was trying to get back into Nikolai's good graces, so that he wouldn't go through with his threat to trade him to the worst team in the league.

But Aaron treated it like a great feat, dropping his own stick and yelling, "Yeah, cuz! That's how us Russians do! Act like you know!"

Then he began chanting, "Russia! Russia! Russia!"

Pavel's classmates, who were still trying to wrap their heads around the fact that there were not one but two biracial half-Russians at this birthday party, stared.

And Alexei's mouth twitched, his eyes glimmering with amusement, as explained, "The boy takes after his mother."

Nikolai's own mouth twitched as he looked to the other side of the rink where Eva was standing with Samantha. The two women had started talking shortly after the cake had been served and much like Pavel and Aaron, they'd immediately hit it off. A half an hour later, they were still chatting away.

Nikolai wasn't surprised. His wife and the Texan who, much to Nikolai's consternation, insisted on calling him Nikki and his nephew Pavvy, had a lot in common beyond the color of their skin. Including backgrounds in social work, gregarious spirits, and Russian husbands. Of course they had decided to become instant best friends.

His wife had a way of immediately connecting with other women, Nikolai noted. That was probably what made her so good at her job. It also didn't hurt that she seemed to have a warm smile for everyone she met.

At least everyone but him, he thought, his mind darkening.

"So you married the woman in the green dress," his cousin said beside him. His eyes stayed on the two half-Russian boys on the ice, but his voice took on a certain chill. "Yet you did not invite your favorite cousin to the wedding. Only to this child's birthday party."

"Our wedding was small and quick. This party is much more important. It was time for Pavel to meet you and your family."

"More important than your wedding? Hmmm," Alexei chewed on that for a moment and Nikolai felt himself tense up. But then Alexei smoothly continued, "Aaron is glad to have another boy on the American side of the Rustanov family, so we appreciate the invitation to Pavel's birthday."

Nikolai had always liked and respected his cousin, but his easy acceptance of Pavel as an official Rustanov, despite the fact that he had no official blood ties to their family, made Nikolai admire him that much more.

"Pavel feels the same, I am sure," Nikolai answered in Russian.

They stood there for a few moments, watching Aaron and Pavel play with matching fondness, but then Alexei opened his mouth again and totally ruined the moment.

"How far along is she?" he asked Nikolai.

Nikolai respected Alexei too much to pretend he didn't know what he was talking about, even though he'd never told his cousin Samantha was pregnant.

"Twelve weeks," he answered. "The blood test says it will be a boy."

Alexei nodded and said, "*Pozdravlyayu.*"

Congratulations in Russian.

"*Spasibo*," Nikolai answered, hoping that would be the end of this line of conversation.

But after a few moments of thoughtful silence, his cousin said, "Did you get this woman pregnant on purpose?"

Nikolai's chin dipped low in embarrassment and growing anger, but he answered his cousin truthfully. "Of course not on purpose. It was a surprise. You know I did not want children."

Alexei tilted his head to the side and gave his cousin another thoughtful look. "I told my Eva I did not want children. I told her this from the start."

"So you understand," Nikolai said.

"I told her this, but then I made her pregnant. It was also a surprise. A surprise I have never had with another woman."

Nikolai who was already well acquainted with Alexei and Eva's dramatic back story, pursed his lips and asked, "What is your point?"

"I did not like growing up in the Rustanov family. The constant danger, the bodyguards, all the killing. It colored the way I saw the world, and I would not wish that for my children.

That is why I refused to have any. But maybe Eva changed my mind, without me knowing it."

Alexei continued to watch the children skating, but his eyes were in a faraway place as he said, "I did not like growing up a Rustanov, but at least my parents were kind to me. At least they showed me what it was for two people to love each other. That helped."

Nikolai didn't reply this time. It was the first time his cousin had ever alluded to the difficulties of growing up a Russian mafia scion, and though Nikolai respected his cousin for turning the Rustanovs into a legitimate business family, he still found it hard to see things from Alexei's perspective.

Back then, Alexei's life had seemed perfect, a Russian version of a Norman Rockwell painting. His parents doted on him, and gave him good memories of them to carry forward even after their untimely deaths. It was the complete opposite of how Nikolai had grown up, making it difficult for him on the few occasions his father had brought him to the Rustanov's palatial estate in Rublevka.

Alexei regarded him with a sad smile. "I will make a confession to you now. Your father scared me as a little boy, and also as a young man. I often took solace in the fact that he was only my uncle, and I felt very sorry for you and Fedya, especially after what happened with your mother. Even sorrier now, because Fedya did not make it."

Nikolai flinched, Alexei words a sharp knife twisting in his gut. He'd always suspected his cousin regarded him as an object of pity, that finally accepting him into the Rustanov family was an act of pity, and now here was his confirmation.

But the flinch was the only thing Alexei got from him. After that small movement, Nikolai blanked his face and said, "Thank you for your thoughts. But I keep the past in the past. My father does not concern me now."

"So you say," Alexei continued to regard him, his eyes

narrowing slightly. "You know, I made a lot of mistakes with Eva because of my past. Mistakes I deeply regret now that she is the mother of my children."

Alexei shook his head, wincing as if the memories of his and Eva's tumultuous relationship still caused him pain. "I do not know what is wrong between you and this woman, but I see she does not talk to you, does not look at you while we are all here together. Whatever it is that is wrong, you need to fix it. Before the baby comes."

Alexei and Nikolai were no longer boys. Alexei was no longer a mafia prince, and Nikolai was no longer in line to replace his father as the Rustanov family's enforcer. Alexei had no right to talk to him this way. No right at all.

Nikolai's fist clenched at his side.

"Hit me if you want," Alexei told him calmly. "But it is still the truth. You must fix this. She is a good woman. Funny, like my Eva. And you are full of pride, like me. But trust me, pride has no place in relationships and I promised you this, if you do not get over yours, you will lose her."

The thought of losing Samantha, of her taking the baby with her as she had threatened before, tore at him worse than a nightmare and it rooted him to the spot in horror. Because Alexei's words didn't feel like a warning, but a promise.

A promise of things to come.

"I would like another piece of cake," Alexei decided out loud. "And then I will take my family and we will go. But think about what I said, Nikolai."

Alexei left then, heading towards the cake table, and Nikolai was left alone. Still a little boy, still unable to defend himself when confronted with an opponent he couldn't punch or knock down or kill.

He watched Alexei walk away, his words of answer stuck in his throat. *I am trying. I am. But... I am not sure it can be fixed.*

"Mr. Rustanov?"

Nikolai turned around to see Isaac standing there.

"Just checking in," his assistant said. "The party's scheduled to end in twenty minutes. Is there anything else you want me to do before I give everyone a fifteen warning?"

Nikolai thought about it. Thought about what his cousin had said, and answered, "*Da*, I have one thing more for you to do."

"HELLO, MRS. RUSTANOV!" ISAAC'S VOICE CALLED OUT BEHIND Sam, just as she was about to take Layla into her arms.

Alexei and Eva's one-year-old had somehow cuted them into a game of pass-the toddler-back-and-forth, and it was now Sam's turn to hold the adorable nugget for up to a full minute before she started squirming to be handed back to her mother.

Or maybe more, Sam thought, cuddling the toddler in her arms. Depending on whatever Isaac had to talk with Eva about.

Eva grinned at her, though. "I think he's talking to you."

And Sam turned to see that yes indeed,, Isaac was clearly waiting for her attention.

"Oh… hi, Isaac. You can just keep on calling me Sam. Just Sam, seriously," she said, wondering if she'd ever get used to people calling her by Nikolai's last name.

Isaac gave her an uncomfortable smile. "Okay… Sam," he said. "Mr. Rustanov has an all-day event he'd like you attend the Friday after next, and he asked me to make sure you clear your calendar for it."

Sam remembered what she'd said to Nikolai the last time they'd had a full conversation. *We're more like project partners and I don't sleep with my project partners. So if you have an event or a work obligation you need me to attend. Fine. That's what I signed up for. But I'm sleeping on the couch.*

Apparently Nikolai had taken her at her word. "What kind of event?" she asked Isaac.

Isaac shook his head with a shrug. "You know, he actually hasn't told me yet, just asked me to give you a heads up. Also, I'll need your passport for security clearance purposes. I assume you have one. Can you send it in with Mr. Rustanov in the next day or so?"

"Sure, " Sam answered. "But I need to know what the event is. Like, what should I wear, because I'll probably need to shop…"

"Nope, I'll take care of all that and coordinate with Nyla on childcare," Isaac answered, already backing away. "Just clear your calendar. Thanks!"

He was gone before Sam could ask any more questions or tell him Nyla was officially an intern, not her assistant. Again. Isaac was forever insisting on "coordinating" through Nyla, as if it were somehow anathema to him to talk directly to Sam herself. He was like the walking personification of "have your people call my people."

"Sounds like you've got a hot date," Eva said with a wink. "Good idea to get them out of the way now, because trust me, hot dates become mighty hard once breastfeeding comes into play."

Sam shook her head, "Oh, it's nothing like that. It's probably just an NHL thing or something. Nikolai doesn't do hot dates. Or any dates whatsoever."

Eva lifted a brow. "Wow, really? Now that I've finished breastfeeding, Alexei's always pressuring me to let our nanny take over for the weekend so we can do a hotel getaway."

Sam really liked Eva, she really did. Not just because they were both black women married to Russians—which had been huge but pleasant surprise—but also because she had a wicked sense of humor that reminded Sam of how she used to be back in Alabama, when she'd only had the running of one Ruth's

House on her plate. But as much as she liked Eva, it was hard to keep her jealousy at bay when she said things like that.

Before she met Eva and her husband, she blamed Nikolai's cold behavior on his cultural background. But his cousin, Alexei, who shared the same culture and was even part of the same family as Nikolai, was incredibly devoted to his wife. So in love with her that Sam wasn't surprised when he appeared out of nowhere with another piece of birthday cake.

"Share this with me, *kotenok*," he said.

Eva groaned, "C'mon, Lexie, you know I'm still trying to lose all this baby weight."

"I like your baby weight," he all but growled at her, pulling her closer with one large arm. "Tonight after the children are asleep, I will show you how much I like it."

Eva giggled and shook her finger at him. "You are like the anti-Weight Watchers! I'm going to tell on you to my meeting leader."

"Eat the cake, *kotenok*. For me." Then he leaned down and let loose a stream of Russian words that didn't sound at all cold. No, not cold at all—especially with the way he was looking at Eva as he said them.

Eva groaned again. "You know I can't think right when you start talkin' all romantic in Russian. That is so unfair!" she said.

Then she opened her mouth, and Alexei popped a piece of cake inside.

Sam, who still had little Layla in her arms, watched the exchange from the corner of her eyes in self-conscious silence. They were a totally cute couple, but completely sickening to watch. Overly sweet, and even worse, they made Sam wish for things. Things she knew she could never have. Like Nikolai's heart.

Chapter Thirty-One

THE NEXT TWO weeks passed in a blur of Sam working like a dog not to have to go back on her promise to keep the Friday she promised Nikolai free. They were at full intake status with requests for two more beds. And Nyla had finals coming up next week, as well as an entire Saturday, Sunday, and Monday of babysitting for another family who sounded like they were going on some kind of super glamorous vacation, so her intern hadn't been able to help out as much as she usually did.

"But I can come in if you really, really need me," Nyla offered when she called on Wednesday to beg the next two days off. "I'm so excited about coming to work there full time after I graduate, I'm totally willing to blow off studying as long as you're okay with having someone who may or may not get her degree as your assistant director."

Sam was okay with it in theory, but she couldn't do that to Nyla. She let the poor girl off the hook and was just glad she'd hired on a permanent weekend director for the center a few weeks back, using the now unnecessary security budget.

As it was, she didn't have much time to be curious about Nikolai's event until she came home late that afternoon to a dress bag lying across the bed she still wasn't sharing with her fake husband. It was from Bonnington's, a national boutique store she only vaguely recognized because she'd walked past the one in the Keystone Crossing mall a few times. The store always had at least two or three dresses in the window that were almost always on a scale so gorgeous, she didn't think she'd have anywhere to wear one, much less be able to afford it. But apparently wherever Nikolai was taking her, it was that kind of event.

She opened the bag and pulled out the most beautiful cocktail dress she'd ever laid eyes on. It was simply cut with an empire waist and belled three-quarter length sleeves. But its shape was the only simple thing about it. It consisted of metallic gold lace with large fuchsia and gold buttons in the back that were either made from real Swarovski crystals or doing the best imitation she'd ever seen. If Russia still had tsarinas, it looked exactly like what one would wear to a Very Important Event.

Where the hell was Nikolai taking her? The Oscars!? She got out her phone and pushed Isaac's contact number. No answer. But less than two minutes later, he texted, *"Sorry. Swamped. Is it important? I can call you back later."*

"No need to call," she typed back. *"Just need the details for tomorrow's event."*

"Okay, will try to get that to you before I go home tonight."

But the night came and went with no texts from Isaac whatsoever.

Nikolai came to bed—or in this case, the floor—earlier than usual and she thought about asking him about it. But instead, she just stared at his back, unable to figure out how to cross the distance between them enough to even ask a simple question.

Things had been so awkward between them over the past

two weeks. Him continuing to sleep on the floor. Her feeling like an idiot because now that her first trimester morning sickness phase had passed, she was in the second trimester "lots of energy" phase with a hot side of "ooh, what's that you say, pregnancy hormones? You're feeling weirdly horny?"

You'd think now that he was no longer playing hockey, some of that heavy muscle would have turned into fat. But no, he was still cut all the way up in a way that made her body scream to purposefully fall on top of him whenever one of her increasingly frequent late night sex dreams were interrupted by a need to go to bathroom. She'd never been so tempted in her life to ignore her counseling background and just go on ahead and let a man use her as his toy.

But she couldn't get back in the bed. She had a degree in psychology, for God's sake. She knew his sleeping on the floor was a total manipulation, designed to get her to agree to be his marital fuck buddy until he got tired of her and moved on to someone else. Probably as soon as she was big as a house and no longer appealing to him.

No, she decided, squeezing her eyes shut against the sight of his heavily muscled back. Better to let things remain as they were. She wouldn't be moving back into the bed, no matter how many times she had to step over Nikolai's ridiculously gorgeous and totally magnificent body.

She'd never surrender.

She fell asleep with that mutinous thought and when she opened her eyes again, Nikolai's floor pallet was gone. Cleaned up and put away like he'd never been there.

After showering and putting on her new maternity yoga pants and t-shirt, she knocked on Pavel's door... but didn't get an answer.

Strange, but sometimes he woke up and went downstairs to hang out with Back Up in the TV room. A chance to veg out with the TV, which he wasn't allowed to do much these days now that he lived with Sam and her "one hour of TV per day" rule.

But when she went downstairs, he wasn't in the TV room. She tried the kitchen next, and the sight of the empty room caused Sam's heart to flip over inside her chest. What if Marco had been wrong about the Russian who had tried to kill Pavel being permanently gone? What if the thug had come back and somehow managed to make his way past Nikolai's security system? What if...?

In the distance, she heard the sound of Back Up's feet, nails clicking against the foyer's floors, along with the pant that came after a good, brisk walk around the neighborhood.

Relief flooded through Sam, even as she went out to the foyer to chastise Pavel for taking Back Up out without her. He'd been hinting that he wanted to do this for weeks now, but she'd been clear with him about the importance of having an adult along when he took the dog for her walks.

But when she came into the foyer, it wasn't Pavel she found holding Back Up's leash, it was Nikolai. Nikolai let the dog off her leash as if they were old friends, before producing a treat out of his pocket and saying something to her in what sounded like halfway affectionate Russian as he let her eat it out of his hand.

For a moment Sam could only stare. How could he make a heavy sweater worn over a denim shirt look so appealing? He should have been less attractive outside his usual work wear. But this much more casual look made her breath quicken, and she suddenly became hyper aware of her own heartbeat, thumping loud and fast as her entire body clenched hard with lust.

All because he'd walked the dog.

Stupid pregnancy hormones, she muttered to herself, before forcing herself to focus on Pavel who was hanging up his anorak on a coat rack.

"So you guys took Back Up out for a walk without me? I'm so hurt," she said to the little boy.

She was just teasing, but a stricken look came over Pavel's face. "Don't be angry, Mama, and I'm sorry for skipping yoga, but Dad and me had some stuff we needed to talk about."

"Dad?" Sam asked. When had Pavel started calling Nikolai dad?

Nikolai stood. "My lawyer called. Our official court date to adopt Pavel is in two weeks, day after our ultrasound. So I tell Pavel he must decide what to call me. Fedya is his father and will always be his father, but I will be his father, too."

"So I'm going to call him Dad, not Papa," Pavel told her. "That way my papa in heaven won't be mad, right?"

"Right," Sam agreed, as her heart swelled with happiness. Pavel deserved no less than a male guardian who not only wanted to be his legal father, but his father in name, too. "That's great. Really great. I'm glad you guys were able to come to good compromise on that."

"Yeah, and maybe Uncle—I mean Dad, you, and me can all go to the Children's Museum after our court date. He still hasn't been, you know," Pavel said. "Dad can we do that? All of us go *together*?"

Pavel put a strange amount of emphasis on the word 'together,' Sam noticed, and Nikolai seemed to be giving the boy a censoring look as he said, "I will talk with your mother about it on plane tonight. Right now, it is time you go become ready for school."

"Okay, *Dad*," Pavel agreed with a goofy grin. It was easy to tell Sam wasn't the only one who was elated Nikolai had made his claim on Pavel official. The boy ran up the stairs to his room and Back Up, who apparently never got tired of watching Pavel do mundane things like getting dressed, quickly followed.

Sam smiled after them, her heart full of love and happiness

for Pavel—but then she remembered what Nikolai had said in answer to Pavel's question about going to the Children's Museum.

"Wait, did you say we were going on a plane tonight?" she asked Nikolai.

Chapter Thirty-Two

YES, he did say that. As it turned out, they'd be flying overnight to Nikolai's event on Thursday, spending the whole weekend wherever it was, and arriving back in Indianapolis late Sunday night. That meant she'd be spending two whole nights and two whole days with Nikolai. The man she'd sworn to stay as far away from as possible now that her pregnancy hormones were out of control and practically begging her to do things she really shouldn't. With a man who'd straight up told her he didn't believe in love.

With true dread in her heart, she stepped out on the porch of Ruth's House after wrapping things up at work, awaiting the arrival of Nikolai who'd said he'd be picking her up himself.

To her surprise, though, when she got outside, she found Marco walking up the sidewalk towards the house instead of Nikolai.

She frowned. She'd gotten use to seeing Marco on rotation again—Nikolai had kept his promise. But ever since the news of her and Nikolai's marriage and impending baby had hit the wires, things between them had been—well, awkward to say the least.

But here he was now, coming up the walk in his civilian clothes, nice slacks, and polo shirt. And he had flowers in his hand. Even more unexpected, he was walking in from the street and not from the side of the house.

"You parked on the street?" she asked him.

"Yeah," he answered, stopping at the bottom of the steps. "Nyla kept giving me a hard time about parking behind Ruth's House, so…"

He didn't finish, just held up the flowers. "Um, is she here?"

Sam blinked. "Who? Nyla?"

"Yeah," Marco answered, suddenly taking a huge interest in the sidewalk. "Last time I was here, she said she had finals coming up and I thought I'd bring her these. Like, you know, to say good luck."

Normally Sam would have treated this news with extreme sensitivity, but this was Marco. And Nyla.

"Wait, you're bringing Nyla flowers? Nyla Weathers? The one with all the piercings in her ears—and face?"

Marco looked everywhere but at her, and Sam had a feeling he'd be beet red if not for his olive skin tone. "Yeah, it's not a big deal, Sam. The earrings come out. I think." He rubbed a hand over the back of his neck. "But we have some things in common."

"Things like what?" Sam asked, honestly curious.

Marco shifted. "Things like Death Buddha," he answered, referencing the weird metal band Nyla had spent a year following around the country before she'd decided to be a grown up and go to grad school. "We're both big fans and they've got a show coming up. I was thinking we could go together. I was thinking maybe I'd ask her about that tonight."

He peeked up at her, "Think I should?"

Sam had to fight hard to control her laughter. Yes, she

thought. This made a certain kind of sense. Marco, so loyal to his hood he insisted on staying on his beat after Nikolai had tried to get him kicked off of it. And Nyla, who Sam had complete trust would run the shelter well while she was away on maternity leave.

Suddenly Nyla's generous offers to deal with Marco's daily visits so Sam wouldn't have to didn't seem quite as altruistic as they had before.

"Actually, I think you should," she said to Marco, happy to give the new couple her blessing. "But Nyla's not here. She's studying. Her last final is tomorrow, then she's babysitting for me on Friday."

Marco grimaced. "Oh…"

It was easy to tell in that moment that Marco had spent some time working up the courage to come over here and ask Nyla out.

"I guess I'll try again on Monday," he said.

"Yeah, Monday."

In the distance, Nikolai's Escalade pulled up and Sam said, "I've gotta go."

Marco looked over his shoulder at the Escalade. "Yeah, I guess you do. Thanks for the talk, Sammy."

"No problem," she said. She came down the steps, prepared to walk past him, but at the last minute she said, "I can't give you Nyla's address…"

"I know," he answered. "I can always look her up in the database—"

"No, you can't, because girls like us consider guys showing up unannounced stressful and creepy," she said. "I should have told you that before."

And Marco looked down again. "Yeah. I guess that could come off kind of wrong."

"But I can text you her number," Sam told him. "And maybe you can text her, offer to bring her by something to eat.

I remember being where she is right now, and getting food was a total hassle."

Marco smiled. "That's a great idea."

"If she takes you up on your invitation, then you've got a green light to ask her out. If not, you should probably back down. So, do you still want her number?"

Marco looked from side to side like he was trying to decide between the blue and the red pill. "Yeah," he said finally. "Yeah, I do."

So that was how Sam ended up keeping her fake husband waiting while she sent her ex-almost boyfriend her soon-to-be assistant director's number. Then of course she had to wait to see how it turned out.

Marco sent the text and less than a minute later, he grinned as he read out loud. "'Dude, you're saving my life. How soon can you get over here with a burger?'"

Sam clapped her hands, truly happy for him and for Nyla.

Marco shook his head. "I'm just happy she asked for a burger. I was worried she'd be one of those vegetarians, and I'm already going to have a hard time explaining all the face jewelry to my mom if we start dating."

Marco escorted Sam to the Escalade where Nikolai still sat, waiting.

"Hey, Mount Nik," he said, acknowledging Nikolai with a small wave before continuing on down the street towards his own car.

Nikolai didn't return the greeting and Sam noticed that his hands were gripped so tight around the Escalade's wheel, his knuckles were white. But he hadn't gotten out of the car, hadn't yanked her out of the conversation with Marco. And Nikolai didn't make any attempt to follow Marco as he climbed into his vintage Mustang.

Progress, Sam thought to herself as she climbed into the

passenger seat, which she supposed was why she decided to tell him...

"You'll never believe this... I was helping Marco set up a date with Nyla! How wild is that?" Then she rushed on with, "I hope I didn't make us late for the flight."

The only indication he'd registered what she'd said about Marco and Nyla was that his hands visibly loosened on the wheel.

"No," Nikolai answered, his voice completely casual. "Plane will wait."

THE PLANE TURNED OUT TO BE NOT A COMMERCIAL AIRLINER, but a private jet with RUSTANOV ENTERPRISES painted across the side in large black letters.

"A late wedding gift from my cousin," Nikolai explained while she gaped at the jet awaiting them in a hangar behind Indianapolis International Airport.

"Is that where we're going?" she asked, as they walked up the air stairs to the plane's main entry door. "To Texas? To an event for your cousin?"

"No," Nikolai answered. And that was all he said.

Sam opened her mouth to once again try to extract some answers other than "you will see" and "no" to her questions, but her thoughts trailed off when she saw the inside of the plane.

The front quarter-half of the cabin was taken up by sumptuous, side-by-side leather seats like those she'd seen in the first class section of the commercial airplanes she'd flown. But instead of seats, the other side of the plane was taken up by a conference table and a thin couch. That seating area, Sam noticed, was just wide enough to sit on—but not wide enough to stretch out on without fear of rolling off in the middle of the night.

"Hello, Mr. and Mrs. Rustanov," a cheery voice said behind them.

They both turned to see a smiling male flight attendant holding a tray with two glasses of what looked like champagne.

"Don't worry, it's sparkling cider," the attendant said, handing the flute to her with a wink. "And congratulations, to you both!"

"Thank you," she said, taking the glass.

The flight attendant went on to introduce himself as Dave before asking if there was anything they needed before he went to prepare dinner, which he'd be serving at a small dining table just behind the row of seats.

"I'm good, thanks," Sam answered, settling herself into her seat. She jiggled the lever at the side, pushing her back against it.

"Is everything all right, Mrs. Rustanov?" Dave asked.

"Please, call me Sam," she answered, ignoring Nikolai's displeased look. "And it's nothing. I was just hoping these seats leaned back a little further, maybe turned into a little bed." She had heard some seats in first class converted into beds on some airlines, but apparently these didn't.

"No, our seats don't convert because there's a bedroom just on the other side of that door," Dave explained, pointing to a closed wooden door at rear of the cabin. "So when you're ready to go to sleep, let me know and I'll fluff the pillows for you." He winked again.

Sam's cheeks flamed as her dream of getting a semi-comfortable night's sleep died a quick death.

After an extremely awkward dinner, she opened the upper compartment above the seating area and found what appeared to be a plush lap blanket in a neat fold. She opened it with an angry snap, hunkered down into the back row's window seat, and pulled the blanket over her, squeezing her eyes shut. Sam hoped this would be enough for Nikolai to take the hint and leave her alone.

There came the sound of heavy footsteps, then Nikolai's voice above her. "That seat looks not comfortable. You don't want to sleep in bed, *zhena*?"

"No, just like you don't seem to want to tell me where we're going. Or why," she answered, keeping her eyes closed.

"You are not same as other women. You don't like surprises," he said.

This time Sam did open her eyes, if only to let him see how not amused she was by this entire situation.

"I don't like being confused, and I don't see why you can't just tell me where we're going."

"Like I say, you are woman who does not like surprises. I will, how you say, make note for future." Judging from all the twinkling going on in Nikolai's eyes, Sam was fairly certain he was incredibly amused by the whole situation. But then again, he was the one holding all the cards, wasn't he?

She closed her eyes again with an annoyed huff. "Goodnight, Nikolai."

Silence. And then she felt the seat beside her compress underneath Nikolai's weight. Her stomach tightened. Apparently, Nikolai was fully prepared to take an aisle seat if it meant getting the last word on their sleeping arrangements.

"Good night, *zhena*."

ONE MISERABLE NIGHT OF SLEEP, TWO MORE MEALS, AND about eight back-to-back episodes of *Veronica Mars* later, they eventually made it to the tarmac of Athens airport. Athens, Greece.

"Welcome to Greece, *zhena*," Nikolai said, waving an arm

toward the city's skyline beyond the airport, as if it was his gift to her.

Sam, who had been half-way afraid they were headed all the way to Russia, gaped in amazement.

Greece!

She'd never been farther than Canada in her life, and even then it had been for work—a special seminar in Calgary on how to provide counseling services to women with refugee status. Not exactly a glamorous getaway.

Sam watched as the plane slowly came to a stop. What kind of work obligation could have possibly brought Nikolai to Greece? Then she remembered what her friends on social media often went abroad for.

"So... I'm assuming we're here for somebody's wedding?" she asked Nikolai, as she divested herself of the winter coat she'd put back on before deplaning. No need for coats here. The air was warm and balmy—at least in the seventies.

"No," Nikolai answered, producing both of their passports out of nowhere. He took her by the elbow. "Come, *zhena*. We must go through passport control and customs before we meet car."

Well, that explained why Isaac has asked for and never returned her passport. But...

"Why are we here?" she asked for what felt like the millionth time.

"I think you will soon—how you say—figure it out," Nikolai answered.

But she didn't figure it out. Not that she didn't try. She scoured her head for possibilities and put them to Nikolai: a charity event, a movie premiere, a hockey game—even though she was fairly certain hockey wasn't a thing in Greece. Every guess was met with a firm "no" on Nikolai's part, as if she wasn't even in the vicinity of the right answer. And by the time they pulled up in front of a multi-tiered, white stucco and stone hotel, she was even more frustrated than when they'd departed Indiana.

The sun had begun its descent when they left the airport and by the time they got out of the town car, it was low on the horizon, making it so she couldn't see much beyond the hotel's covered car port. She had a quick thought that she should have worn sunglasses, then another bitter one about how she couldn't be blamed for not bringing them since the only instructions Nikolai gave her was to bring whatever "woman things" she might need to survive a weekend.

Sam searched the hotel's quaint blue-and-white facade for any indication of why Nikolai had brought her here, hoping for some kind of clue like a small sign announcing that the reception for whatever would be in the main ballroom. But there weren't any of those types of signs to be found—and the few signs she did see were written in Greek, which looked closer to Nikolai's Russian Cyrillic alphabet than her own Roman one.

She sighed, thinking as much as she admired *Veronica Mars*, her own detective skills were completely lacking.

"Come, *zhena*," Nikolai said again, interrupting her thoughts and beckoning her forward.

Speaking of mysteries, she was going to have to figure out what "zhena" meant as soon as she was back in Indiana and had internet access again. Another oversight on her part. The planned trip had been so short, she'd assumed they'd be staying in the United States and she hadn't bothered to bring her laptop since she had her smartphone. But here they were in Greece. And here she was without an international data plan, rendering her smartphone useless until she could find Wi-Fi.

After a quick luggage exchange between their driver and a man in a starched white uniform, she and Nikolai were led past the check-in desk, up three short flights of stairs, and through a set of arched doors painted a vibrant blue.

The scene that met her when she walked through the blue

doors made her heart stop. It was a spacious and gorgeous white room with sea blue furniture that matched the blue infinity pool just beyond large balcony windows. And beyond that…

Sam went to the windows to stare wide-eyed at the Athens peninsula spread out to the left and right of them. A lush scene, dotted with hotels and trees overlooking a sea so blue, it seemed to glow underneath the city's lights.

It was easily the most beautiful view she, Sam McKinley—now Sam Rustanov—had ever clapped eyes on. And suddenly, all her questions dropped away, replaced with something else she didn't think she'd be feeling toward Nikolai Rustanov at any point over this weekend. Gratitude.

She turned and watched her husband exchange a few short words with the uniformed man, before closing the door behind him.

"Thank you," she said when they were alone in the room. "Thank you so much for bringing me here."

He gave her a look she was beginning to recognize, the one he gave her when she'd confused him. Probably because they'd only just now arrived and she was thanking him like he'd already given her a whole weekend in paradise.

"I've only ever lived in Alabama, Indiana, and Michigan," she explained. "I'm just happy to be somewhere so beautiful."

He considered her statement for a moment before saying, "You're welcome. Now we must take showers and change. Then we have dinner."

Less than an hour later, Sam found herself in the gorgeous dress Isaac had bought for her, at the best Greek restaurant in the entire world. Granted, the only Greek food she'd ever eaten was at the Mr. Gyro in Lafayette Square, but shoving bite after bite of the delicious lamb dish in her mouth, she couldn't believe there were any Greek restaurants better than this one on the face of the earth.

"Oh my God, why does anyone ever move from here?" she asked. "If I was Mr. Gyro, I never would have left!"

She glanced up to see if Nikolai was enjoying the meal as much as she was. She thought her golden dress was a show-stopper, but Nikolai was equally holding his own in an elegant black suit paired with a crisp white shirt. He cut a striking figure seated across from her. However, he didn't seem to be enjoying the meal as much as she was. He was just sitting there, his chin resting on his fist, eyes bemused as he watched her eat.

"Why aren't you enjoying this?" she demanded, nodding toward the family-style meal. "Everything's delicious!"

"I'm sure it is," he answered with a nod. Then he leaned forward to say in a husky voice, "But I prefer watching you eat, *zhena*. This sight pleases me very much."

A shiver went down her spine at the thought of him being pleased by the sight of her eating. But she wondered aloud, "I-is that a cultural thing? Um, liking to watch people eat? M-maybe it's something they do in Russia?"

She was stuttering again, she noted with an inner wince. Like the rom com character Nikolai had accused her of being.

He frowned at her, as if he were trying to figure out if she was joking.

But Sam continued. "Like your mom—was she a good cook? Did she like to watch you and your brother eat?"

Sam cringed as soon as the question left her mouth. Yes Sam, good job, she thought to herself. Don't just shut down his game, rain it out by asking him questions about his childhood. The same kind of questions he always refuses to answer.

She braced herself for the cold shutdown and waited for the heated look to leave his eyes.

It did. Immediately. And he leaned back, as if suddenly wanting to put more distance between them.

But then he said, "My mother was very good cook. She

loved cooking. She loved watching Fedya and I eat. *Da*, maybe I have little of her in me."

She nearly dropped her fork, she was so shocked by his answer. That he actually had answered!

He looked away, his jaw clenching. "I do not talk about her," he said, as if reading her stunned thoughts. "But my mother is same as your mother, *zhena*. Dead."

She lowered her fork and confessed, "I know. I Googled you." No surprise, there hadn't been any mention of his possible mafia ties, but... "A few articles mentioned your mother died when you were young."

He shifted in his seat. "Seventeen. Not as young as Pavel."

"No, but that's young enough," she said, thinking of her own mother's death. "Was it hard when you lost your father, too? The internet said he died a few years ago."

Nikolai looked further into the distance, like this whole conversation was leaving a bad taste in his mouth. A taste even all the delicious food sitting on the table between them wouldn't be able to take away. But nonetheless, he once again answered, "No. World is better off without my father."

Harsh, but it wasn't a sentiment she could hold against him. The world was better off without her father as well. Her stepfather, too. She guessed they had more in common than she ever could have imagined.

His unexpected answer made her feel bad for purposefully introducing a dark subject just to get around his mild flirtation. There was a dark cloud hanging over the table now, and she attempted to clear it away by segueing into a less painful topic, one that seemed to have brought him quite a bit of amusement over the last twenty-four hours.

"So here we are, two orphans in Greece, living it up before your big event, which is..." she teased, waiting for him to shut her inquiry down again.

But when his eyes met hers they were quizzical, not

amused. Like Sam asking the same question she'd been asking him over the last twenty-four hours had somehow confused him greatly.

"What?" she asked, using a hand to check for food on her face. She'd gone hard on a flaky pastry dish filled with meat. Maybe her mouth was covered with it now. But no, no food, which prompted her to ask, "Why are you looking at me like that?"

"*Zhena*... you still have not figured it out?" he asked.

She stared at him, perplexed.

"Do you remember what you said first time we met at party? About dates?" he asked. Then he lifted his eyebrow, as if he were waiting for the other shoe to drop.

After a quick memory search, her own words came floating back to her, *When I'm working late, I'm always like, wouldn't it be cool to be one of those people who goes on dates? Seriously, how nice would that be? To like, you know, go to a dinner and a movie.*

That was when the other shoe finally dropped with a great, big thud. She gaped at Nikolai. They were on a date! An actual real life date. In Greece!

And as if to confirm her thoughts, Nikolai said. "This is dinner. Next comes movie."

Chapter Thirty-Three

DA-YAM!!!! Sam thought as she walked out of the restaurant after finishing one of the best meals she'd ever eaten. *Nikolai Rustanov had game.* For someone who'd sworn up and down he didn't date when they first met, he was proving he was more than adept making a date happen. In a BIG way.

Her state of shell shock must have been written clear across her face, because he placed her hand in the crook of his arm before they got to the gravel lane outside the restaurant, which sat at the top of a slight incline. "Hold on to me, *zhena*. This is not good place for falling."

Her cheeks heated, but she did as he said since she couldn't necessarily trust herself not to trip. And she was glad when they made it all the way to the bottom of the hill without incident.

"Just so you know, I don't trip all the time," she said, taking back her hand at the bottom of the inclined road. "Just around you."

"Because I make you nervous."

Yes, that was exactly why, but Sam folded her arms across her burgeoning waist and said, "Because you do things like sleep on the floor, which is like a huge—some might say Mount Nik-sized—safety hazard. Especially for a pregnant woman trying to go to the bathroom in the middle of the night."

If he felt any guilt whatsoever about compromising her safety, it didn't sound like it when he replied, "I'm ready to return to our bed whenever you are, *zhena*."

If anything, he sounded the exact opposite of guilty. Flirty Nikolai was back.

"You know, this isn't going to work," she told him.

"What?" he asked.

"This. Taking me to Greece, showing me a good time so you can get back in my pants. You're manipulating my emotions with a big gesture, and using scale to get what you want. Don't think I don't get that."

Get that and totally falling for it, she added to herself. Between her pregnancy hormones and the pleasant surprise of an exotic trip, she had no idea how she was going to keep her Celibate Bride Defense going when they got back to the hotel room.

Say something smug, she mentally begged him. *Convince me I'm right to be way suspicious of your motives in bringing me to this insanely gorgeous country with its incredibly yummy food.*

But all Nikolai said in that moment was, "Here we are."

"Here" turned out to be an empty, amphitheater-style movie theater. Thanks to an almost full moon and cloudless sky, she could see it was made out of the same bleached white terracotta as the hotel and surrounded by what she guessed were olive trees. A warm breeze blew through the space bringing a heady floral scent with it, like a blessing from the Greek gods.

So. Freaking. Romantic.

Sam shivered as even more of her defenses came crumbling down.

"Here, *zhena*." Nikolai took off his jacket and put it around her shoulders.

They stood there for a moment, facing each other like they had that night at the party, the last time he'd given her his jacket, Sam's heart helplessly beating with the thunder of a thousand horses.

She knew she should give the jacket back to him. Her dress was on the shorter side, but long-sleeved. It wasn't like she needed it in such a temperate climate. But his jacket was warm, and she liked the spicy, dark scent of the cologne he'd decided to wear tonight.

It didn't make her want to throw up. Like, not at all.

"Thank you," she said softly.

"You're welcome," he answered, leaning forward. And for a moment she thought he would kiss her again, wondered how she would resist kissing him back if he did.

But he didn't kiss her, just whispered in her ear, "Will you give me your hand, *zhena*?"

Tomorrow. Tomorrow she was going to wake up early. Go down to the front desk and look up the meaning of that damn Russian word. She swore this to herself solemnly.

Then she gave him her hand.

He led her to the two best seats in the house, which wasn't hard to do since they were literally the only two people there if you didn't count the handful of theater staff.

"When does the movie start?" Sam asked, after a movie attendant came by with two sparkling waters and a small white bag of caramel popcorn.

"Soon," he answered, holding the popcorn out to her. "This is how people do on dates. They share popcorn, da? That is what it said in woman's magazine Isaac got for me."

She stared at him. "You did *not* have Isaac get you a woman's magazine."

"How else do I know how to do this dating?" he asked.

She shook her head, feeling both amused and overwhelmed. Oh, she was in trouble. She didn't have any idea if he was being this charming on purpose or if he really had no idea how appealing he was right now with his innocent I-read-this-is-how-you-do-it-in-a-magazine shtick, but either way, she could sense the boundaries she'd set down between them blowing away in the warm Grecian breeze.

Especially when his large hand closed around hers, enveloping it in warmth.

"S-so what's showing tonight?" she mumbled, hoping to change subject from unbelievably romantic dates she had no business going on. And to distract herself from the way her whole body became attuned to his as soon as they touched.

"This week it is *The Wrong Girl 3*."

Sam tried not to let the disappointment show on her face. Not that she didn't appreciate the popularity of the film, based on three books about a girl living in a post-apocalyptic future, whose mother marries a maniacal despot out of desperation. But teenage girl, abusive stepfather—it was a little close to home and certainly not the movie she would have chosen to watch in her free time.

"But tonight, theater shows different movie," Nikolai told her.

"Which one?" she asked.

As if in answer to her question, the screen suddenly came to life with the opening strains of "As Time Goes By" followed by the Warner Bros. Pictures logo. And then, a plaintive voice saying, "I need your help, Veronica!"

Luckily they were the only ones in the movie theater, because Sam screamed out loud. It was the *Veronica Mars* movie! And on a twelve-foot screen, no less!

Yeah, that sealed it. She leaned over and dipped her hand into Nikolai's white paper bag of caramel popcorn, feeling she had no choice but to confess, "Best. Date. Ever."

Chapter Thirty-Four

"DID YOU ENJOY THE MOVIE?" she asked Nikolai as they
made their way back to the hotel a couple of hours later. She
was glad for the long walk back because she wasn't quite ready
for the night to end.

Not only because this had seriously been the best date in
the entire history of all dates that had ever gone down, but also
because she didn't know how she should handle the hotel room
sleeping arrangements. The room had a blue couch, long
enough for her to stretch out on, and she'd made a point of
placing her suitcase next to it before they went out to dinner,
her way of letting him know nothing had changed between
them except the locale.

But that was before she'd discovered Nikolai's event was
really a date... really, more like a mini-honeymoon. Whatever
you wanted to call it, it was the best one she'd ever experienced. And though she wasn't one to be pressured into doing
anything she didn't want to do, well, c'mon! It was kind of
hard not to want to do pretty much anything with him after a
date like the one he'd just taken her on.

"*Da*, I liked movie," he said. "But I am more wondering why you like her so much—this Veronica Mars character."

"I guess I like the idea of a girl taking control of her own life, using her wits and unique skills to one-up the bad guys. Also, she's really spunky, the way I wish I had been when I was younger."

"Me too."

"What?" she teased, scrunching her nose up at him. "You wished you had been a spunky girl?"

"I wished for more control when I was young, *da*." His face darkened. "My home life was not happy."

She waited for him to say more, but this time he didn't surprise her. Just continued walking, letting the subject fade away before asking, "How is your morning sickness?"

"Much better now," she answered. "I haven't felt nauseous for the last ten days, so I think it's finally letting up."

"Book I am reading says you should eat many small meals throughout day. Eating like this will keep your stomach happy and give you nutrients you need."

She did a double take. "Wait, you *read* that? In a book?"

"*Da*," he answered, sounding confused by her confusion.

"You, Nikolai Rustanov, are reading a book about... what? Like a guide to pregnancy?"

He stiffened beside her as if he'd been caught do something embarrassing. "*Da*," he admitted.

"But why?" she asked, finding it hard to imagine this hulking male beside her was actually reading a book like *What to Expect When Expecting* when she hadn't even started reading pregnancy books herself.

"Because..." He went quiet, and for a few moments there was only the sound of her wedges and his shoes, crunching against the gravel. "Because I am not bad man like you think. I was not bad caretaker to Pavel because I wanted to be. I was not good parent because… because I don't know how to be good parent. My mother and father maybe not so good at job."

Her mind went into buffer mode, she was so shocked he was once again sharing something real with her. But thank God she was a natural counselor, her autopilot soon kicked in. "So because you had bad parents, you think you're doomed to be a bad parent? Is that why you were keeping your distance from Pavel when we first came to live with you?"

He nodded, his eyes seemingly glued to the street beneath his wing tips. "He is maybe not lucky boy. At first I think, I will give him money and room to live in, that is all he needs. But when I see you with him, way you are with him, way he is with you, I realize I cannot give him what you give him because I do not know how."

He expelled a harsh breath, as if saying this to her was actually a major effort on his part. *Maybe it is*, she thought, waiting for him to finish, completely fascinated.

He continued to look down at the ground as he said. "When you tried to leave my house, take my baby with… When you said to lawyer I am bad parent, I… I…" he shook his head seemingly unable to finish that sentence. "After that I told Isaac to buy for me books about how to be good father. It is hard because maybe my English is okay for talking, not so good for reading, and they have many books translated to Russian for woman but not for man."

Sam stared at him, her eyes wide as her hands unconsciously came to rest on top of belly. "Are you trying to say you want to be a father? A good father to this child?"

Silence, then a quiet, "*Da*," as if he'd had a hard time working up the nerve to say that one word. "I want to be good father. Good father to both Pavel and our baby."

He finally met her eyes, his own filled with utter sincerity. "I'm hoping I can read enough books in time."

Dammit. And there went Sam's last line of defense. She'd

let Pavel into her fortress willingly, happily. But Nikolai's simple wish struck an impossible chord, one that crumbled the last wall she'd constructed around her heart to keep out men like Nikolai, cracking it open with a sudden flood of compassion.

She couldn't help it. She didn't know what had happened to Nikolai as a child, but she knew it couldn't be good. And her instincts were telling her that this man walking beside her, the one Indiana hockey fans called Mount Nik, was way more vulnerable than he'd previously let on with his balcony invitation and his bedroom manipulations and his hard stares.

With her heart beating in her throat, she said, "I'm assuming you read all the stuff your lawyer dug up on me?"

A pause, as if he was considering whether to tell her the truth or not. But eventually he answered with a quiet, "*Da.*"

"Then you know I wasn't exactly raised in a great situation either. My mom had the potential to be a good parent, but she had zero self-confidence and she was really pretty, which turned out to be a fatal combination. She got involved with some awful guys. My dad was the first of them, and the biggest favor he ever did her was catching his life sentence without possibility of parole while she was pregnant with me."

Sam thought about the man she'd only known through prison pictures. He'd died in a prison riot when she was ten, but it wasn't like that really mattered in the grand scheme of things. His imprisonment meant her mother had been given a long enough respite from his violence to give birth to her. But that respite had been brief in her mother's otherwise permanently stormy sea. After that, she'd never been able to carry a pregnancy to term again.

"After my father, it was one guy after another beating her up. My stepfather was the worst of them, so of course he was the one she married. He got some work in Indianapolis soon after and we followed him to Indiana when I was sixteen."

"Did he hurt you?" Nikolai asked, his voice a cold wind on a warm night.

"No," she answered. "He came at me a couple of times, but my mom taught me well. Go and hide when he started drinking, she'd tell me. Remember when I described how I found Pavel hidden in the cabinet that night? That was me all the time. I was like the queen of cowering while my mother was getting hit."

She let a few beats go by before asking, "Did Slimy Kevin's fact-finding mission say why I shot my stepfather on my eighteenth birthday?"

He didn't answer, so it must have. Yet she still felt compelled to explain, to tell him all of it. To make him understand what happened.

"Growing up, I thought my mom was so weak and I got sick of it. All the drama, patching her up after my stepfather was finished. I couldn't wait to get out of there. When I was seventeen, I met this guy name Anthony... and he felt sorry for me, I guess. He convinced his parents to let me stay with him, just until I finished school. I got a thirty-one on my ACT, so I automatically got a full ride to IU. So it was only supposed to be for a few months."

Her face darkened, remembering. "It wasn't the best situation. I felt really ashamed all the time, being around Anthony and his perfect family. All of them acting like Anthony was a saint for dating me and convincing them to let me stay there— which he was. I'm still very grateful someone showed me that kind of compassion. I just... I just wished things were different. I spent a lot of time back then resenting that I'd had to impose on him and his family like that. And I hated my mother for putting me in that position."

She sighed thinking of how judgmental she'd been before getting her degree in psychology, before she'd been able to understand something had happened to her mother to make her think these were the only kinds of relationship she deserved. But Sam pushed through her personal shame to continue with the story.

"My mom called me on my birthday, begging me to come over to eat my cake. She always made me a German chocolate cake on my birthday. I can still remember her limping around a few times while she was making it, but she always did it, no matter what. I told her not to bother, but she begged me to come over. Begged me. I still can't believe I made her beg…"

Sam had to pause while another wave of shame knocked her around. "But eventually, she wore me down. I agreed to come. I only planned to stay for a few minutes. One slice of cake I told myself…"

The memories choked her up, clogging her throat with tears. She stopped.

"Tell me rest." Nikolai's voice was quiet, but strong in its command.

She had to finish the story. Not just for him, but for herself. Sam took a deep breath, made herself calm down "So yeah, when I got off the bus, I took a detour to my favorite neighborhood sub shop. Ate a whole twelve-inch meatball grinder so I'd be nice and full when I got to my mother's and wouldn't have to stay too long. If I hadn't stopped to do that, maybe I would have gotten there in time, but I did and when I came through the door, my stepfather was standing over her body with a knife."

The image of her mother lying on the floor, her beautiful face frozen in a rictus of terror, like she'd known this would be the last beating, the one that ended her—that image came back to her like a perfectly preserved movie scene. So much blood…

"I know the statistics now," Sam said, gritting her teeth against the pain of the memory. "I know physically abusive relationships often escalate to murder. That forty-percent of murdered women worldwide are killed by their partners. That many women like my mother don't think they're deserving of good relationships, and their spouses alienate them from everyone they know, make them feel worthless, like they're all alone... so they don't seek help."

Sam shook her head. "But back then, I didn't take the violence seriously. It was just this big thorn in my side, something I imagined my mom enduring for the rest of her life, because she was too dumb and weak to leave my stepfather. So I did the worst possible thing. I left her alone. I was her last resource and I left her alone with him. Made her beg me to come home."

Sam's voice cracked, as regret over her ignorance flared anew inside her chest. It took a few more shallow breaths before she was able to talk again. "Anyway, they didn't live in a great neighborhood and like a lot of people, my stepfather kept a gun in their apartment. Near the door, in fact, so it was easy..."

Sam grimaced. "I don't remember much, just being angry, and then the gun was going off, and I guess I was a better shot than expected, because the bullet hit him in the face."

Sam wrapped Nikolai's jacket tighter around herself, suddenly cold. "So that's how I ended up getting tried for murder. Because technically, he'd already killed her. There was no reason for me to kill him. Even my boyfriend couldn't deal with that. He visited me once in juvie to say he was sorry but his parents didn't think he was equipped to continue associating with somebody who had my kind of issues. He made it real obvious he thought I was a nut job for killing my stepfather," Sam thought of her stepfather's prediction when she moved out to live with Anthony. "Too much trouble for a piece of ass, I guess."

She recovered with a brave smile, "But luckily I had good grades and a decent court lawyer. She got them to try me as a juvenile, and the judge was a woman who believed the story she made up for me about self-defense. So I got very, very lucky."

She sighed and finished with, "And that's why I'm here today, walking around Greece with you instead of rotting away in the penitentiary system, just like my father. And that's why I started Ruth's House, so no woman anywhere would ever be left alone with her abuser like my mother was. And that's why I do things like teach yoga and mindfulness along with providing counseling services, to give women the tools they need to get out of bad relationships and stay out of them. But trust me…"

She forced herself to look directly at him now. "I've got baggage, too, but here's what I've learned working at Ruth's House: your past doesn't matter. Only what you do today matters. What you continue to do tomorrow. If you want to be a good father to Pavel and to this baby, you can do it. I know you can. You just have to try."

And there it was. Her long, sordid story laid out for him in full, so he could see she wasn't some perfect parent, pre-made. That she was a human, who'd done some truly terrible things before getting to the place where she could properly mother a child.

She'd hoped her story would inspire him, but judging from his reaction it did the exact opposite. He glanced over her, opened his mouth… closed it again. Then he looked away. Just like Anthony had looked away from her when he'd been dumping her across a gray metal table.

His inability to speak, to so much as look at her, made Sam's heart sink.

Why had she told him everything? He already knew most of it anyway from the court papers. So why hammer it home here and now? This was why she never told anyone about her past. Well, except Josie—and even then, that was after years of knowing her, after hearing Josie's own tragic story. But she'd only known Nikolai for a few months, and the fact remained that she barely knew anything about him. Yet she'd told this huge Russian guy everything—all because he'd read a couple of parenting books.

She couldn't have been more pissed at herself.

They walked the rest of the way back to the hotel in awkward silence.

Chapter Thirty-Five

IF SAM HAD BEEN LOOKING for ways to kill the romantic mood Nikolai created before they got back to the hotel, she could not have picked a better tactic. By the time they returned to the room, their merry romantic comedy of a night had turned into a Swedish film. Sam could have sworn she heard the mournful strains of a funeral dirge as they entered the room they would be sharing.

Someone, probably a maid, must have come by while they were out. A couple of lamps now bathed the room in soft, flattering light, and there were dark rose petals scattered on the large square bed, along with chocolates on each pillow. The hot tub which stood encased in white stone about two feet away from the bed was bubbling. Even if there hadn't been a standing ice bucket with a bottle of champagne and two flutes tucked inside, she would have been able to easily guess that the room had been specially prepared for romance.

Nikolai walked over to the tub. The pronounced beep of him hitting its off button cut through the room, and the bubbling sound came to an abrupt halt.

Sam took a seat gingerly on the sea blue couch and

watched Nikolai take off his jacket, vest, shirt, shoes, and pants with stoic efficiency before giving them the closet treatment.

Then he walked over to the bed.

Sam held her breath…

For naught, as it turned out. Nikolai's next action was simple enough. Pillows and petals went flying as he displaced the romantic detritus and climbed underneath the covers. By himself.

It was exactly what she'd wanted, exactly what she'd said she wanted. Him in the bed, her on the couch. No one on the floor, making her feel like she was keeping him from his creature comforts just because she didn't want to confuse an already emotionally fraught situation with sex.

But for some odd reason, Sam's heart sank as she watched him get into the bed.

"Sounds like a hot date."

Eva's words came back to her with a mocking twist as Sam reached behind herself and unbuttoned her own dress. After several minutes of button wrangling, she walked over to the closet where whoever had set up the room for romance had set their two suitcases, side by side on white luggage racks. His chrome-colored, large polycarbonate Tumi suitcase right next to the purple cloth one she'd gotten on sale at Target for thirty bucks before leaving Alabama.

Opposites in every single way, she thought to herself as she unzipped her bag… only to discover in her hasty packing job, she'd forgotten one very important item. Pajamas.

She silently cursed, going over her options. Jeans, a swimsuit, and a couple of t-shirts that would barely cover her bottom, if at all. Her eyes searched the blue bar above the racks. No hotel robes. In the end, she pulled out a t-shirt, thinking him seeing her bikini underwear probably didn't matter now anyway. The mood was now deader than dead in their shared hotel room. Thanks to her.

As arguments for getting some went, this had been a doozy, and as Sam put on the t-shirt, she wondered who else but her would have felt compelled to share the ugliest piece of herself after one of the most romantic dates she'd ever been on. She remembered how Josie had quite wisely called her after getting in an ugly fight with Beau about her staying out all night.

"He triggered me, and I know it's partly my fault because I haven't told him about my past, but I can't bring myself to tell him, because I guess some fucked up part of me would rather him think I'm sleeping with somebody else, than tell him the truth. But I don't know how I can go on with him if I don't tell him. It's too unhealthy. So I need you—I need you to help me tell him. Can you do that for me, Sam?"

Of course she'd come through for Josie, even joked about it though she'd had a few reservations about getting involved. Usually people asked her to help them leave bad relationships, not start new ones.

Back then, she'd been a little baffled by and rather curious about Josie's situation. But now she understood exactly where Josie had been coming from.

Right now, she'd rather Nikolai still thought of her as a hotheaded woman dead set on rejecting his sexual advances. Not some emotionally traumatized psycho with a sad back-story. As vain as it probably was, she liked the Sam she'd crafted out of her mother's ashes and she now wished more than anything that she'd gone on letting him believe she really had killed her stepfather in self-defense, that she really was the perfect mom in every way.

And despite her vow to stay as far away from Nikolai as possible, to not be swayed by his romantic vacation tactic, her body burned with what might have been. How this night could have gone if she hadn't decided she just had to confess to killing her stepfather in cold blood.

Sam tied up her twists, grabbed an extra cover from the closet's top shelf, and dragged it over to the couch. She'd leave the lights to Nikolai. If he was still awake, the remote to turn them all off was on his nightstand. If he was already asleep, then she didn't mind sleeping with a few lights on. Either way, there was no way she was going to extend the awkwardness by going around the room manually turning off the lights.

She settled across the couch, grabbing one of its throw pillows as she did. Its satiny finish made her feel a little guilty. It was so pretty, like a work of art not actually meant for anything other than decor, and definitely not meant for sleeping on. But that was too bad because she wouldn't have been able to get in bed with Nikolai at this point anyway. The awkwardness of doing so would have been too damn excruciating.

As soon as she laid her head down, all the lights clicked off, sending the room into darkness. So Nikolai must not have been asleep. Yet.

Sam breathed into the foreign night, listening to the sound of waves crashing outside the window. She found no peace in either activity, and doubted she'd get much sleep tonight. The couch, with its fine finish, was slippery in a way that made her fear she'd slide off if she so much as turned over. And her thoughts—well they were racing and in full panic mode.

Maybe tomorrow morning she could arrange for another room, or even better, her own flight back to Indiana. She had a few dollars in savings. Why not use it for a last-minute intercontinental flight? How much would that cost? If it was in the hundreds, she could swing it. But if it was in the thousands... well, she just might have to call Josie and ask for a loan, which would be another bad conversation, two months after the one about her marrying a Russian hockey player she barely knew because he'd knocked her up—the one that had ended with, "sorry, Josie, but the wedding is today and you're not invited."

Sam cringed in the dark. No, maybe not Josie, especially considering her and Beau's baby would be arriving any day now, but maybe—

"He hurt me."

The three quiet words made Sam blink in the darkness, wondering if it had been Nikolai who said them, or if some other man with a thick Russian accent had come into the room.

But then his voice sounded again in the dark. "My father never hit my mother. But sometimes he hit me. Mostly me. To punish her or... he said he was training me. But I never want to train Pavel this way. I will never train him or our baby this way."

She believed him and wanted to interrupt with some stories of men from abusive backgrounds who'd gone on to become perfectly good parents. But she sensed there was more he had to say, so she stayed quiet and let him continue.

"With my mother—he never put hands on her. More abuse of... how you say abuse of mind?"

"Emotional abuse," she supplied.

"*Da*." His answer came back terse and thick. "He refused marry her, because of Fedya. He said she didn't deserve marriage, even though she was mother of his child. He left her alone in apartment with us. For weeks, sometimes months. But if she tried to move on to another man..."

He grew quiet for a few seconds before finishing with, "He made it bad. Very bad. She learned not to take other man. She learned to wait for him always—at least I thought she learned this. But she was beautiful woman. Very beautiful woman, like you are beautiful woman. Men gave her attention, and I think she was lonely."

Sam's heart beat faster, sensing this story was not going to have a happy ending, but she gave him the respect of silence. Listening without comments, so he could get it all out, like he'd let her get it all out.

His Russian accent grew even thicker as he continued with his story. "One day she asked me go get pregnancy test from store. I do it and she went into bathroom to take… my mother was not weak woman. She had strong voice, strong will, even when my father tried make her submit. She never cried, but I can still remember her that day. Crying behind bathroom door."

Tears sprang to Sam's own eyes in that moment, thinking about the unfairness of the situation. A woman whose boyfriend refused to be a true partner to her, but also refused to let her move on.

"She died week later when she tried to get rid of it. She could not go to clinic, because my father—he was well connected. He would know if she went somewhere official. So she went to bad place to get rid of baby. I took her to this place. She went into back room and she didn't make it out alive."

Sam could no longer hold back her words. "I'm sorry!" she whispered in the dark. "I'm so sorry."

"I do not tell you story so you feel sorry for me, *zhena*." He answered, his voice one part stern, and another part annoyed. "I tell you so you understand. I did not protect her from my father. I should have killed him after she took test to keep her safe. She is dead because I did not do right thing."

"No, she's dead because she was in an abusive relationship," Sam told him, sitting up on one arm, even though she couldn't really see him in the dark. She had to let him know. "It's never the child's fault."

"I was seventeen. Almost same age as you. And I was big. Larger than you are now."

"Still a child," she insisted, realizing for the first time as she said it that this was true in her situation as well. "Size has nothing to do with it. Nobody that age is emotionally equipped to deal with those kinds of circumstances. And it's not like killing your father would have made your life any easier. Trust me on that one."

A moment of silence... then, "I do. I do trust you, *zhena*."

Her heart stop beating. He trusted her. For a victim of domestic violence, that was huge, almost the equivalent of saying "I love you" because it was harder for people who'd grown up like she and Nikolai had to trust. She'd been dealing with trust issues all her life. Was still dealing with them, in fact. Which was why throwing herself heart and soul into her two shelters was almost easy in comparison to having a normal, healthy relationship with someone.

But Nikolai was telling her right here in this hotel room that he trusted her.

She couldn't have been more honored. "Thank you," she whispered.

No answer. For a very long time. So long, Sam was beginning to think maybe he'd fallen asleep when he said, "You say we have nothing in common. You say this why we can't be together as man and wife. But maybe... maybe we have much in common. Maybe that is why I can't stop chasing you, even when you push me away. Maybe that is why I feel like I would do anything, offer you anything, if you would agree to share this bed with me."

He let out a harsh, ragged breath. "Tell me what you want, *zhena*, and I will give it to you—"

She was across the room before he even finished the sentence, struggling to get her leg not only over the high bed but also over his big body. But then she didn't have to struggle because she was lifted into the air, hauled right on top of Mount Nik, his large hands grabbing on to the sides of her face as they erupted into a frenzy of kissing.

Chapter Thirty-Six

NIKOLAI DIDN'T ATTEND CHURCH. Had never thought much about whether he believed in the God his mother had paid homage to most Sundays, depending on whether Sergei was in residence or not.

But having his wife finally come to him felt like nothing less than a prayer answered. To feel her on top of him, her hips grinding on his boxers as their tongues tangled... he came back from their hour of sorrowful tales instantly. Hard as stone and wanting—no needing—very much to be inside of her.

He flipped her over and his hands went to work, dealing with anything that got in his way. The t-shirt blocking his access to her round breasts got shoved up and the band of her bikini briefs got shoved down as he took one breast in his mouth and laid one hand over her core.

His. She had given himself to her. Come to him willingly, and the desire to both possess and revel in her sent his mind into a tangle of conflicting needs.

He decided to satisfy both, moving down her body and taking her with his mouth. Her taste exploded across the flat side of his tongue as he licked her slit, lapping and lapping, until she was squirming beneath him.

"Oh, God, that feels so good. Please don't stop!" He could feel her hands in his hair, urging his mouth deeper into her wet pussy. "Don't stop… don't stop… don't…"

He did stop. Abruptly. Ignoring her cry of protest, he braced himself on his arms, hovering over her as he asked, "Did you just now have nightmare, *zhena*?"

She squinted up at him in the dark. "What? No!" she answered, her voice foggy with confusion.

"Did I…?" he asked. "Did I just now have nightmare?"

"No," she answered carefully, sitting up on her forearms and looking at him with a perplexed expression. "I don't think so."

"You had no nightmare and I had no nightmare?" he asked her. "You must be sure before we continue."

"Oh, I see," she said, understanding dawning in her voice. "I finally gave in and now you're rubbing it in."

"Not rubbing in," he answered. "You—how do you Americans say—hurt my feelings."

She laughed, a light sound in the dark room.

And he waited for her to realize he wasn't joking.

Eventually she did. "You're serious?" she asked, squirming to sit up some more, as if this conversation made her uncomfortable and she wanted to get in a less vulnerable position.

"Yes, very serious," he answered, leaning into her, not too hard but firmly enough that she fell back off her forearms. After that, it was easy to get her back beneath him. And keep her there with a well-placed thigh. "No more rubbing in of anything. Not until you tell me you want this. Want me."

He laid the ultimatum down between them like a stick of dynamite. Potentially explosive in ways both good and bad.

She licked her lips and tried to sidestep it.

"You know I do," she said, tilting her hips toward him. "You can feel how much I do."

As a tactic, it was a very good one, Nikolai thought. Feeling how wet she was through the thin cloth barrier of his briefs, his cock punched out to get to her. But he didn't give in. Instead he worked to keep the strain out of his voice as he told her quite seriously, "This is what you must say: 'Yes, I want you, *muzehnek.*' Give me words, *zhena*. Give me words or we won't continue."

He could sense her studying him in the dark, imagined her eyes narrowing as she tried to figure out if he was serious about not continuing if she didn't tell him exactly what he wanted to hear.

He was and she must have read the answer in his still body because she tilted up again, pressing her slit against his erection as she said. "Yes."

She was a clever minx, he thought. Hedging in such a way that made it that much more difficult to insist on her total acquiescence. But she was his wife, and now that he finally had her in his bed, he would allow no more misunderstandings between them. No more room for misinterpretations.

"'Yes, I want you, *muzehnek'*—give me full sentence."

She let her head fall back with a frustrated huff. "I'm not even sure I can pronounce that last word."

He pressed himself into her, letting her feel his fullness against her naked, wet core. "I believe you can, *zhena*."

She moaned. "Fine—yes, I want you, *muzehnek*."

She said the words in a rush, but her pronunciation was near perfect and he found himself smiling as he asked her, "How?"

"What?"

"How do you want me, *zhena*? My mouth, my fingers, my...?" He rocked against her again and gave her a slang

Russian term for penis, more than certain she wouldn't need a translation.

She sounded skeptical when she answered, "You'd seriously be okay if I said your mouth or your fingers at this point? Like if I got mine and didn't let you get yours afterwards?"

"If you don't want me other way, I will be... disappointed, *zhena*, but it doesn't change question."

She wiggled underneath him as if she was actually giving his question some careful consideration, and for a moment he wondered if he hadn't misplayed his hand. His wife was compassionate, one of the most compassionate women he'd ever known. Nonetheless, she could be a she-devil, especially when it came to him.

But eventually she said into the narrow strip of dark between them. "I want you." Her voice was slightly above a whisper. "No more games, please. I really, truly want you right now. However you want me, I want you."

Of all the things she could have said. Of all the ways she could have begged, this was the one that made him lose his iron grip on the situation.

His briefs came off and then he was inside her, penetrating her so deep, he could feel her stretched wide around every inch of him.

Feel her and hear her soft mewls in his ears as he took her without any further debate. Took her hard, took her fast, his hips pumping wildly as she received him with greedy undulations.

Neither of them lasted long after it started. His *zhena* came with a sharp gasp, her nails biting into his ass, pulling him further into her as she spasmed around him. Then he felt himself spilling into her with a great yell, his ejaculation more powerful than any he'd ever experienced before.

So powerful, he couldn't find words as it flowed over him. Actually he did find words, one word, over and over again,

"*Zhena... zhena... zhena,*" until he was fully done, until he had nothing left to give and collapsed beside her.

But even then, he didn't stop saying the word. In fact, he was fairly sure he was still saying it as he pulled her into his now sweaty embrace and fell into a deep sleep with his wife in his arms.

With his wife in his bed.

SAM HAD NO IDEA WHAT TIME IT WAS WHEN SHE WOKE UP, BUT she knew it had to be way past her usual 6:30 AM morning stretch and get out of bed time, because the sun was shining brightly through the hotel room's picture window. Also because there was a huge Russian in bed with her, the top of his thick thigh pressed against the back of hers, his chin resting on top of her head, his arm heavy across her waist. It immediately became obvious why she'd overslept and what had happened. Again.

And as Sam took in the view beyond the window, an impossibly blue sky overlooking a deep azure ocean with the outline of islands off in the distance, she waited for the usual doubt and self-recrimination to set in. But it didn't.

In fact, there was only one question in her mind now, asking itself loud and clear. What the hell does *zhena* mean? And she carefully attempted to extract herself from the bed so she could go find the answer.

As soon as she moved, the heavy arm on top of her went into lockdown mode, pulling her back to her husband's hard chest like an industrial magnet.

"Where are you going?" he asked behind her.

So apparently Nikolai was awake. She felt him swell against the curve of her back.

Very awake.

"Funny, you should ask," she said, squirming.

"Are you uncomfortable, *zhena*?" he asked, low and husky behind her.

"You're sort of poking into my back," she said, moving the lower half of her body forward a little.

He readjusted himself to make her more comfortable. At least she thought that was what he was doing. When they resettled, the new "more comfortable" position had his hard length resting against the bottom of her soft womanhood, the tip in just the right position to...

"Did you have nightmare, *zhena*?" he asked quickly.

"No," she answered just as quickly. Then she gasped when he pushed into her with embarrassing ease, because she was still wet from what he'd done to her the night before and, okay, maybe because she was more than a little turned on.

"I did not have nightmare either," he informed her as he began stroking into her from behind with slow, languorous rolls. "But you are very wet, *zhena*. Maybe you had other kind of dream?"

"Pregnancy hormones," she gasped out breathlessly. "I think it's the pregnancy hormones."

He chuckled against the back of her neck. "You should have woken me sooner. Ask for my help with pregnancy hormones," he said. He increased the speed of his strokes then. But only a little. Only enough to make her even more aware of the urgent need he was building like a fire inside her.

Her head fell forward, her chin resting on her chest as he filled her up from behind. Oh God, he was so big, stretching her to near impossible lengths. Yet it didn't feel uncomfortable to her. In fact, it felt like he belonged there.

She moaned, both wonderstruck and terrified by the aching hole he'd created inside her. The one that could only be filled by him.

Yet he still asked, "Do you want this, *zhena*? Do you want me?"

"Yes," she half-cried, half-moaned. And this time he didn't have to instruct her any further for her to say, "Yes, I want you, *muzehnek*."

She surrendered quickly this time, not wanting him to toy with her again. Not knowing if she could stand it, with the pressing need to climax riding her hard. But she was amply rewarded for her speedy concession. His hand dropped down to the front of her, and the ball of his palm met the button at the top of her slit, rubbing it in the same lazy manner he was stroking into her from behind. Leisurely, like this was the Nikolai Rustanov version of a stroll through the park on a Sunday afternoon.

But the double attention soon drove her over the edge. "Oh, my God... I'm... I'm..."

She never finished the sentence. Her head kicked back and her back arched as the orgasm ripped through her, hot as a fever and so electric, she could still feel it still tingling inside her even after she was done.

She waited for Nikolai to finish, too, like he always did, but instead he pulled out of her and flipped her over. Sam laughed, her head falling back against the pillows, as she waited for him to slide into her again. But... nothing happened.

And when she opened her eyes, she saw he was now standing on his knees between her veed legs, his sex hard and glistening with her recent cum, his hands heavy on top of her knees. He stared down at her, face grim.

"Is there something wrong?" she asked him.

"You are pregnant," he answered with a heavy frown.

Well, that tossed her sexy spirits right into the dumpster. He might not have noticed the swell of her stomach the night before, she realized then, but in the harsh light of morning, it was easy to see how her formerly flat stomach was now bulging out.

There was nothing wrong with her body. She knew that. It was just doing what it was supposed to do in order to make room for the baby growing inside of her. Still, his words made her feel self-conscious, like the least attractive woman on the planet. Not to mention the desperate picture she was probably painting, lying there with her legs spread wide, while he was getting all sorts of turned off by her body.

She sat up. Remedying the situation as best she could by drawing up her knees so he no longer had a close-up view of her stomach, breasts, or sex. Problem solved.

But Nikolai reacted liked she'd just handed him the gravest insult. "Why do you hide yourself?"

She had no idea how to answer that and it was an effort to keep her voice level as she replied, "I'm obviously not what you're used to, and I guess I'm trying to say you don't have to finish if you don't find me attractive in the light of day."

Confusion flickered in his eyes. "*Zhena*, I try hard to understand you, but I think I must not be translating your words correctly. Why you say I don't find you attractive? I find you very beautiful. I told you this from start."

"Yes, the start. When I wasn't pregnant."

He shook his head. "You think pregnant stomach makes you not attractive?" he asked, as if he were honestly struggling to understand her meaning because of their language differences.

God, this conversation! Why couldn't a pit just open underneath her so she could get out of it already?

"I don't know," she mumbled. "You just went very still and when I asked what was wrong, you said I was pregnant. What was I supposed to take away from that?"

"I don't know, too," he answered with an angry frown.

"But *zhena*, I am very tired of you always thinking worst thing of me."

"What else am I supposed to think? Look, I know I'm pretty, but I also know I'm not perfect. I'm not a stick and I've got a lot of junk in my trunk, and now a belly. And I'm sorry, but how am I not supposed to think the worst thing after you say you can't get yours because I'm pregnant."

"*Zhena*, look at me," he said, his voice low and quiet.

This time he didn't wait for her to obey his command. He took her chin in his hand and forced it up so she was looking straight into his angry gaze.

"*Zhena*, I want fuck you. It is not pretty thing to say, but it is true. Even when you hate me, even when you accuse me of false thing because you think I'm not good man. Even then, I want to be inside you, fucking you. I sometimes wish this is not true. Sleeping on floor I wish this much."

Sam froze, beyond stunned. Not only because his words were harsh, maybe the least romantic thing that had ever been said to her, but also because... her body totally responded to them, stirring anew, her breasts swelling against her thighs, her legs pressing against the crook of her arms because they wanted to open.

Open for him.

She looked away, knowing she wouldn't be able to meet his eyes as she said the next words. "You're right. We do have a lot in common. That's exactly how I feel about fucking you. And it's something I really, really wish weren't true."

She still wasn't looking at him, but she could feel the heat of his gaze on her in the silent seconds that followed.

Could feel his tension and that he was keeping himself coiled tightly even before he said, "*Zhena*, you are pregnant and I don't want to hurt you," he said. "So I stopped. I want to fuck you badly. Too badly. I was trying to want you less before I took you again."

Another harsh explanation. But dammit, if it didn't bring a smile to her lips. His confession made her feel beautiful… powerful. Like she was the one in control here, not him. And that was a new feeling—especially when it came to Nikolai.

"Poor Nikolai," she said, uncurling her body. "You're all riled up. Maybe you should sit down…"

She pushed against his chest, and he went down, falling backwards just like she wanted.

"And now maybe you should lean back against the footboard," she instructed, crawling into position between his legs. "Put your hands beside you and keep them there."

He hesitated, but did as she said, probably wondering if she was really going where it looked like she was going.

He didn't have to wonder long. She took his large member in her palm and began stroking him, her fisted hand going up and down.

She could feel him watching her do this, and somehow that turned her on even more. So much so, that when pre-cum started to pearl out of the top of his mushroomed head, she found herself leaning forward without any conscious thought to lick it off. Just one lick, meant to clean more than anything.

But Nikolai's sharp intake of air emboldened her. She let her mouth go down further and opened her throat so she could…

He groaned above her, like she was torturing him.

But that must not have been the case, because soon she felt his hands on either side of her head, encouraging her on as he said, "*Zhena*… you kill me. *Da, zhena. Da!*"

She loved the way his voice strained when he said that. It sent an erotic power thrill through her entire body. He was too large to take in all the way, but she did the best she could, fisting the bottom of his shaft and keeping her throat open so she didn't gag. Every time she ran her tongue over a new batch of pre-cum, it felt like an award for driving him crazy.

She tried to keep a cool head as she dominated him with her mouth, but tending to him made it that much harder for her. Her pussy soon swelled with rekindled arousal and her fingers rose up to her newly soaked core, massaging with a mind of their own.

Wrong move.

"*Zhena*, what are you doing?" He bit out the question, his voice stretched to his very limits, as if the sight of her touching herself actually pained him.

Her temporary power grab soon came to an unceremonious end.

Nikolai pulled himself out of her mouth, hauled her up the length of her body, and slammed her down on his wet erection.

"Look what you make me do, *zhena*. Look what you make me do."

He grabbed a fistful of her twists and used them to anchor her in place against his chest as he moved her entire body up and down on his staff, so rough, she could feel every forced thrust at the back of her tunnel, but so tight, she could also feel it at the front of her slit, in the place that mattered most.

Even though this was supposed to be about him getting his, the position he'd put her in was too much. She soon came a second time, with a helpless cry as her whole body melted into his. Which only made him hold her tighter as he thrust up into her, his hips pistoning at an impossible speed.

"Look at what you make me do—" He released into her with an angry yell that went on for a very long time, before he ended it with a much softer, "*Zhena*."

"*Zhena, zhena…*" he crooned, his rough hands falling out of her hair. "I am sorry. I tried to let you, but I couldn't. Did I hurt you?"

She laughed. "No, you definitely didn't hurt me."

He didn't join in. Just said, "We are past first trimester. Books says sex is okay after that." But he still sounded worried.

"I'm fine. More than fine, I swear." Sam threw him a teasing smile, wondering if she'd ever stop finding the fact that her rough hockey player was reading and apparently abiding by pregnancy books so amusing.

If he was like this now, what was he going to be like when the baby actually came? Would he be the one telling her what kind of diaper cream to use or weighing in on her breast-feeding options? This little quirk, she thought with an inward smile, could get annoying very fast. But it wouldn't make her love him any less—

She paused, her insides curdling.

"What is wrong?" he asked. "Why do you suddenly freeze?"

"Um…" she said, scrambling to think of an excuse that didn't involve her feeling something for him that he didn't feel for her.

"Did I hurt you? The baby?"

"No, no," she assured him out loud. At least not physically, she thought to herself.

She gave him her smile. Her best Sam smile. "I was just wondering what was on the agenda for breakfast. I am eating for two now…"

Chapter Thirty-Seven

THE ANSWER to that question was a whole lot. She came out of the shower to a veritable feast. Breads, pastries, smoked meats, savory pies, fresh fruit, and an assortment of teas, all set up like a colorful brochure for Greek brunch on a white table standing between two sea blue rattan chairs.

"Eat. Now." Nikolai issued the command as he headed out of the room. "I must make business call, but don't wait. *Eat.*"

Apparently, Nikolai took claims of needing food very seriously, and that caused her stomach to twist as she watched the door close behind him. She'd only said she was hungry to get him off the subject of what had her so shook.

No, not past tense, even after a long shower, she was still feeling it. And now she stood there, staring at the food. Completely shaken by his overwhelming gesture of making sure she was fed before he went to make his call.

Her heart beat erratically, continuing to fill up with a love so big, it made her clutch at her stomach.

Nikolai had read her case file, but a case file didn't tell you the real stuff. Like how she'd never been taken on a date by any man—much less one involving her favorite movie in an exotic location. No file would have pointed out to him that she had taken care of her mother for much of her life and then gone on to a career that involved taking care of other women just like her. She'd never cooked for herself before moving into his house, and only did so now because it was important to get good, healthy food into Pavel.

He had no way of knowing such huge, romantic gestures combined with something as simple as ordering her a crap ton of food would send her straight over the edge.

This was too much, she thought to herself. Too much…

Panic squeezed her chest tight and made her feel like the room was closing in on her.

Air. She needed air.

With her heart beating loud in her ears, Sam pushed through the balcony's French doors. Once outside, she ran past the infinity pool to the white railing, gripping it tight as she dragged ragged breaths into her lungs. Willing herself to detach, to not feel what she was feeling. Willing herself to not have fallen head over heels in love with Nikolai Rustanov.

But it was impossible. He'd played his hand too well. Stepped to her better than any other guy ever had, including himself a few months ago. It was like a new Nikolai had taken her on this date, and this new Nikolai had found the special key. The one that unlocked all her doors, so he could just let himself into her heart. Easily. And now he was making himself at home, as if he'd always belonged there.

What had changed, she wondered. Why had he done all of this for her? It was like after telling her love was a silly custom and standing by that conviction when he asked her to marry him, he'd done a complete 180 and spent the last twenty-four hours practically forcing her to fall head over heels in love with him. But why would he do that? Why would he—

"*Da*, I did what you said, exactly what you told me."

Nikolai's heavily accented voice floated up to her, as if called forth by her panicked questions. Sam looked all around, but couldn't see him.

"*Da*, it worked. Exactly like you said."

Nikolai's voice again. Sam realized it was coming from below. Nikolai must have gone down the stairs to make the call, not realizing she'd be able to hear him if she came out to the balcony. But of course, why would he think she'd be on the balcony when he'd left her in the hotel room with enough food to provide all of Ruth's House with a morning brunch?

An unfamiliar sound suddenly split the air, deep and almost growly. Laughter, Sam realized after a confused second. Nikolai was laughing at something someone was saying on the other side of the phone!

"*Da*, she now acts like real wife in all ways, just as I wanted." Nikolai sounded smug, like he'd just won the sex lottery. "You are better business man than me. Thank you for your good advice. I think I have no more problems with her. She is how you say—in my pocket now."

Sam stumbled back from the railing, pain exploding inside her chest and head as complete understanding set in. With sudden clarity, she recalled Pavel's birthday party. Watching Nikolai talk with his cousin, the expert businessman, with such a grim expression that she'd been somewhat concerned there was something terribly wrong with the team.

Shortly after she observed that conversation, Isaac had asked her about clearing her schedule. And two weeks later, they'd flown to Greece in his cousin's jet.

It now dawned on her that it hadn't been the team they'd been discussing with such grim faces, but her. How to fix it so Nikolai got exactly the kind of wife he wanted. One who put out. The perfect piece of ass.

How to make her surrender.

And despite the fact that he was long dead, she could hear her stepfather's cruel laughter ringing across the gorgeous Greek sky.

Chapter Thirty-Eight

NIKOLAI JOGGED BACK up the stairs with an unfamiliar lightness in his heart. A lightness that made him want to whistle. A lightness that made him wonder if he had time to keep the long delayed promise to his wife before the next leg of their trip. The one about making sure she liked how he would eat her for breakfast.

But the scene that greeted him when he opened the door brought him up short.

"*Zhena*, what is this?" he demanded.

Instead of sitting at the table as he'd expected, he found his wife fully dressed in a short-sleeved blouse and pencil skirt. Her purple suitcase was out on the bed and she was throwing things into it. Her things from last night, including the designer gold dress, which she crumpled into a ball before tossing it into her case.

She didn't answer his question, just went into the bathroom and came out with a bunch of toiletries.

"Why do you pack?" he asked.

No answer, and the toiletries joined the dress inside her suitcase. She went over to the couch and came back to the bed with her wedged heels from the night before. Still not answering him. Still not looking at him.

But this time he went over to the bed, closing the suitcase flap before she could put in the shoes. "Talk to me, *zhena*. What is this?"

She stopped, her heels in mid-air, her lips pressed into a thin line that made her look older than she was. Older and more weary.

She fixed her eyes on the view beyond the balcony's French windows as she said, "I miss Pavel and Back Up. I've never been away from them this long. I'd like to go home now."

She said this in a dull monotone, as if they'd stayed too long at a party. Nikolai shook his head, not understanding her. Or any of this for that matter.

"We have one more day," he reminded her. "Plan is for us to go to Poros." He pointed out the picture window. "An island across sea. We will rent scooters, eat at café, go to beach, and watch sunset from famous clock tower."

He didn't know where this new Sam had come from. Brusque and dismissive, as if last night had not happened. As if what had happened between them this morning hadn't happened either. But he wanted the woman he'd woken up with. His Sam. His *zhena*.

He came around the bed, desperate to make her understand what he had planned for them.

"On Sunday morning, we will wake up early. I will keep my promise to eat you for breakfast, we will come back to Athens after that, and then we will fly home. Please, Sam, let us eat breakfast. Go to Poros."

She glanced at him, her eyes conflicted.

But when he tried to take her hands in his, she snatched them back, taking a stiff step away from him as if he were a poison she didn't want to touch.

"I'm sorry, but you asked for one day and now it's been

two," she informed him in that same dull monotone, her lilt completely missing. "I wasn't planning on making it three, so if your cousin's jet isn't available, I can make my own way to the airport and you can go to Poros. But I'm going home."

He stared at her. Stared at her and willed her to look at him, to give him some clue as to why she'd suddenly turned on him like this. After all they'd shared, why was she acting so coldly toward him, as coldly as he used to act toward women he cared nothing about? Why was she now acting the exact opposite of a real wife?

His long, silent stare seemed to push her over the edge of her tolerance.

She cut around him and went over to the phone on the nightstand. "Fine, I'll just ask the concierge to call me a car or something—"

She gasped when his hands landed on her shoulders, spinning her around so her back was to the wall.

"You are pregnant," he said to her, placing a hand on the wall on either side of her head so she was trapped. *"With my child."*

She gripped the receiver, which she'd hung on to, tight in her hand. "Let. Me. Make. My. Call," she commanded. Not backing down. Not showing an ounce of fear beyond that initial gasp.

Myriad possibilities for keeping her here, for making her stay long enough for him to recast the spell that had finally brought them together the night before, ran through his head. And if that didn't work, there were always threats. Threats that would make her wish she had never dared to cross him. He could have Marco transferred again, refuse to let her adopt Pavel. He could...

...stop this, he thought, a sad realization sweeping through him. Because none of those threats would make her want to be his real wife. They would only prove to her that he was the same as his father.

He stepped back and let her out of the trap he'd set up with his arms. "I will not let you make own way home. Of course I will make sure you return safely. I will make arrangements. Can you wait small time for me to take shower?"

Her nose flared with defiance, like she wanted to argue further with him, but in the end she nodded. "Okay," she said.

And that was the last thing she said to him before they left Greece.

NIKOLAI TRIED TO KEEP HIMSELF FROM STARING AT HIS WIFE while they ate lunch on the plane ride home, but found he couldn't. She looked like a portrait in the seat across from his, her eyes on the window to the left of them, so far away they didn't seem to track the white clouds below, or notice that Dave, the flight attendant, had set down a plate of food in front of her.

He should have been enraged, and he was a bit. The way she'd cut off the trip with such a weak excuse—that had been salt on the old wounds he'd cut open last night. For her. He'd taken a chance and finally opened up to someone, a woman of all people. And for a moment, he'd felt truly rewarded when she'd come to him, called him *muzehnek*—only to knock him from her sky the next morning, like Icarus flying too close to the sun.

He gripped his silverware tight, thinking about her demand to come home this morning. He wanted to punish her for what she'd done. For cutting the trip short. For not eating enough breakfast then or enough lunch now.

But mostly he wanted to punish her for making him feel like this.

Watching Sam look out the window made his entire chest ache. Something between them had died this morning, he realized, and he had no idea why.

"Is there anything else I can get you?" Dave asked, his return breaking through the heavy cloud that had settled over the silent table.

The attendant blinked with surprise when he saw Sam's untouched plate of flat iron steak, smashed potatoes, and kale. "Was the meal not to your liking?" he asked.

Sam, who always seemed to have a kind smile for everyone who wasn't him, rushed to reassure the distressed attendant. "No, I'm sure it's fantastic. I just had a lot to eat back at the hotel."

A total lie. She'd only nibbled on her breakfast back in the hotel room. He'd watched her not eat enough as he made the arrangements for them to come home early, and now Nikolai had to resist the urge to command her to finish her meal.

Instead, he handed his own empty tray to Dave and said, "Leave her tray on table."

Dave nodded, picked up Nikolai's tray only, said something about being in his small attendant cabin toward the front of the plane if needed, and then he was gone. Leaving Nikolai alone in the large main cabin with his wife...

Whose eyes went straight back to the window as if they had a rubber band attached.

A fresh torrent of rage surged through him. And for a moment, he regretted everything about going along with this silly plan to fix things with her, for ever trying to convince her to look at him differently.

He gripped the sides of his chairs, deciding he didn't have to put up with this. He would go back to his seat. Devise a new plan. Figure out how to get back the woman who'd come to him last night. Make her talk to him, tell him why she was behaving this way.

"We need to talk."

The unexpected sound of Sam's voice lifted his eyes back to her, and he was surprised to find her now looking back at him from across the small table.

"*Da, zhena.* Let us talk," he agreed. "Tell me what this is about. Please."

Her gaze shifted away for a moment, as if his impassioned words were embarrassing. As if she were embarrassed for him.

"I have a little experience with international break ups and I know they can be… messy. I didn't want to have this talk with you in the hotel room, in another country where I didn't know the laws or have any recourse if you decided to, um… use your resources against me."

He shook his head at her, confused. All he really heard in all she said were two words. Break and up. "You want to leave me. Again."

She sighed. "Nikolai, last night. Was any of that real? Like, were you serious when you told me you wanted to be a good father to Pavel and this baby?"

"*Da*, of course. How can you doubt that?" he answered.

Her lips twisted as if he'd said something extremely naïve. "I get that a lot of what you said is probably true. Your background and the fact that you've had no therapy whatsoever probably makes it hard to distinguish between right and wrong. I'm a friend to people like you, Nikolai, and I will always do my utmost to understand what you're going through. I'll always try to be the best friend I can to you considering the circumstances. I hope you understand that."

She was acting like he was some kind of lost cause. Someone who couldn't be fixed, even by her.

"I don't want friend," he answered. "I want wife. You are my wife."

"But I don't want to be," she said, quick and to the point, like a doctor delivering bad news. "Not anymore. Not like this.

I want a divorce. And I want you to prove you meant what you said last night, by not siccing Kevin on me. I want you to agree to split custody and I want you to let me stay in Pavel's life because he needs me, and I love him, and it would be wrong on your part to punish him because you're angry at me."

Nikolai blinked. It was like she'd pulled a grenade out, set it down on the table, and casually pulled out the pin.

"No," Nikolai said as something inside of him blew up.

"Nikolai. It's the healthiest thing to do," she said, clasping her hands together tight. "The best thing for all of us. Please just let me go. I'm not the one to make this perfect family obsession you have happen, and there are plenty of woman——"

He picked up her tray and threw it across the cabin. "I don't want other woman. You are my wife. You!"

"But I don't want to be!" she screamed back at him. "I don't want to be. So let me go! For the good of everyone, including you. If you really meant all those things you said last night, just let me go."

She wanted a divorce. She didn't want to be his wife. Nikolai breathed hard, his heart constricting, because he didn't know what to do, how to handle this.

The problem was she was right. He'd do anything for Pavel. Anything for this baby. And the only way he could make her stay involved hurting her and her career irreparably.

But she was the mother of his child and at the end of the day, he must not have been as much like his father as he feared, because the thought of hurting her in any way——no he couldn't. He let out a heavy, sad sigh.

"Okay… okay," he said. "I will give you divorce. Split custody. Whatever you want, I will do."

His words of concession made her close her eyes, and she breathed a sigh of relief, as if her most fervent wish had just been granted.

Seeing her do this cut Nikolai to his fucking core.

"I'll just... I'll just clean up the tray," she said. "Before Dave comes back."

"Did you have nightmare, *zhena*?" he asked before she could turn away from him.

His question brought her eyes up, and she frowned at him. "Nikolai, don't..."

"I will give you divorce, but first you must answer my questions. Did I have nightmare?" he asked.

She shook her head, refusing to answer.

"If you want divorce, *zhena*, you will answer me," he said. "Tell me truth, what did I do? Why don't you want to be my wife anymore? Whatever it is, I will fix it."

She looked at him for a hot, angry second before saying. "You can't fix it. It's unfixable. I can't make you—"

She stopped and shook her head again.

"What?" he asked. "Tell me."

Ignoring him, she went across the cabin and busied herself with picking up the tray. But he didn't give up. He continued to fight for her even though she didn't seem at all interested in fighting for him.

"Last night meant nothing to you, *zhena*?" he asked.

No answer.

"It was you. You who came to me."

She rubbed a hand over her eyes as if she were exhausted, as if this entire conversation had made her weary. "Don't," she said quietly. "I already feel like enough of a fool for doing that. Don't use last night against me...."

She seemed on the verge of saying more, but then she trailed of, and he could see her taking deep breaths. Purposefully calming down. But he did not want her to calm down. He wanted her to talk to him.

"You will not breathe," he told her. "You will not make yourself calm. You will talk to me. Yell at me. Say whatever it is you don't say this morning in hotel. Give me words. I deserve them."

This only made her breathe even slower and deeper, and a few seconds later, when she stood up to face him again, she was the very picture of calm.

"No," she answered. "You don't deserve anything from me. We're getting a divorce. We're splitting custody of this baby like adults, and we will work out an arrangement for Pavel. You'll agree to this because you're not a sociopath, and that's what a non-sociopath would do in this situation. So that's the end of this discussion."

She was right. She knew it. And he knew it. He wasn't going to hurt his children, and he would agree to the divorce. He would agree to split custody. Later.

But right now, he'd be damned if he was just going to let her cut him up and walk away with a few yoga breaths.

Now it was he who became calm. Deadly calm as he closed the space between them and said, "You should have eaten your lunch, *zhena*."

She threw him an annoyed look. "I wasn't hungry."

"This would be easier if you had eaten your lunch."

Before she could ask the next obvious question, he had her trapped against the door that led to the rear bedroom cabin. Then he began his torture. With a single kiss.

Chapter Thirty-Nine

SAM CURSED herself for letting her profession cloud her instincts. She'd been prepared to stand strong against any argument Nikolai might offer against letting her file for divorce. She'd readied herself for yelling, threats—and though she suspected deep down in her soul that Nikolai would never lay a hand on her, there was a part of her that always braced for possible punches. Seventeen years with her mother and over a decade working in domestic violence shelters. There were just some things you couldn't unlearn.

But she'd never learned how to deal with being kissed. At least not kissed the way Nikolai kissed her. Hot and urgent, like it was the end of the world and they'd both be blinked out of existence if she didn't return his erotic overtures.

It screwed with her senses, never failed to take her reasoning skills offline. And instead of pushing him away, she found her hands clutching at his sleeves, bunching the material in her hands as his mighty body pressed hers hard into the cabin's rear door.

Why did kissing him feel like such consolation now? Like

she'd been out in the desert during their argument and he was now welcoming her home?

"*Da*, she now acts like real wife in all ways, just as I wanted."

The sudden memory of those words made her heart scream with sadness, and in a fit of self-disgust she ripped her lips away from his and pushed against him.

But it was like pushing against a stone wall. Nikolai barely moved. "*Zhena*, don't... don't push me away." His voice was ragged against her lips. "Talk to me. Tell me what I did. Tell me how to fix it. *Please*."

She could stand up to any command this man gave her and throw it back in his face, but when he begged...?

She shook her head, wishing he were a different man. That she was a different woman, one who could be okay with a relationship built on sex without love. On manipulation with the ultimate goal being her complete surrender. She thought of the woman she'd fobbed off on Nikolai the night they met and knew there were a lot more like her waiting in the wings. Women who would be happy to have a rich husband, one who also happened to be amazing in the sack. There were a lot of women who would be satisfied with that, no love required.

"You can't fix it," she told him again, her body pulsing with desire. "This is the end, Nikolai. Please just let me—"

He hit her with another sizzling kiss, this one so hot, it pushed her head back against the door and made her back arch.

Nikolai quickly took advantage of her lifted pelvis, plunging his hand down inside her waistband. "Ride my hand, *zhena*."

Oh God, she was lost, she realized, feeling her body become soft and pliable as soon as he touched her. Sam didn't realize she was obeying his command until he said, "Yes, just like that."

"Last time," she gasped, flailing at straws to get out of this with some pride intact. "One last time and never again."

His powerful hand pumped into her with relentless strokes. "*Zhena*, you're so wet, so hot for me, every time I touch you—" he broke off with a frustrated growl. "How can you want to leave me? How can you?"

Of course the answer to that question was complicated, but the orgasm that soon overtook her wasn't. She bit down on her lip to keep from crying out and letting Dave know exactly what they were now doing in the back of the plane.

"So wet, *zhena*, so wet," he whispered against her ear as she climaxed all over his fingers.

Before she could come all the way down, he lifted her up and carried her over to the couch just a few feet away. Pushing away the Russian newspaper he'd been reading earlier in the flight, he sat her down on the cushioned seat. But instead of entering her like he usually did after he'd gotten her to come once, he began slowly unbuttoning her short sleeved blouse.

"What… what are you doing?" she asked.

"If this is last time I can have you, I want to remember it," he answered.

So he was taking her condition on having sex with him seriously. A dribble of sad gratitude trickled through Sam's heart, despite the shame of knowing she still couldn't resist him when it came to this. Never in this.

Nikolai's hands worked and soon her top was all the way off, followed by her bra, which was removed with an easy flick of the wrist. His eyes heated up when the bra fell away, revealing her breasts, swollen with tightly beaded nipples at the center of their aureoles.

"*Zhena*…" he said, his tone regretful as he dealt with everything below her waist: her skirt and panties, her casual flats.

Soon, she was fully naked, without a stitch of clothing to

hide behind. But he was still fully clothed. And she had the feeling that was exactly how he wanted it.

His eyes roamed over her breasts and stomach before finally landing on her sex, which was still glistening with the orgasm he'd given her.

Only after he'd looked his fill, did he unzip his pants.

"*Zhena*, you will tell me why you made us leave Greece, why you want divorce." He took her roughly by the hips and pushed into her with an, angry jerk. "You will tell me."

Sam gasped at the suddenness of his intrusion. Rushed to widen her legs in order to accommodate his large girth. But it didn't hurt. No, it didn't hurt, even when he started pumping into her with vicious, punishing strokes. Even like this it felt unbelievably good to have him inside her.

In fact it might be better this way, she thought to herself. She didn't want to remember the Nikolai who had supposedly been afraid of hurting her this morning, running game like a pro seduction artist. She wanted to remember him like this, merciless and vengeful. Crude. The exact sort of guy she had no business falling in love with.

"Do you see how you can't help yourself with me, *zhena*? How powerless I make you with my touch?" he sneered into her ear, like the jerk he truly was when he wasn't playing head games with her.

But his next words were sharp with hurt. "We are perfect fit. Why do you leave me? Why?"

Tears pooled in her eyes. Oh God, why did he always have to make everything so hard? He was just manipulating her again. She knew that. Doing whatever it took to get his way. It only sounded like he was sincerely hurt, she reminded herself.

He interrupted her mind's scramble to harden her heart to his questions by once again grabbing her by her twists, so she had no choice but to look at him. "Talk to me, *zhena*. I want you to talk to me." He punctuated each question with a hard, desperate stroke. "Tell me why you won't stay."

She closed her eyes, not wanting to be swayed by what looked like real anguish on his face. She knew better. It's just another manipulation, she told herself. Yet another damn manipulation.

"Why do you hide from me, *zhena*?" he asked. "Why can't you talk to me?"

She whimpered, hot and sticky pleasure making its way through her core, despite the seriously messed up nature of this sexual transaction.

"You will tell me reason," he growled, pushing into her harder. "Tell me."

"No," she moaned, finding it harder to hold on to her determination with every thrust.

"*Tell me.*"

She clamped her mouth shut and shook her head back and forth.

"TELL ME!!!" he roared, pushing into her with one final thrust.

It was like pushing the button on a detonator. The orgasm exploded inside of her like a bomb, making it impossible to hold on to herself, to her pride, to keep what she'd been refusing to tell him inside any longer.

"I heard you!" she cried as she came apart for him. "I heard you on the phone with Alexei at the hotel. I heard what you said about me!" And then she couldn't talk anymore.

The orgasm lasted a very long time, her body convulsing with the aftershocks of her climax even after she thought it was done. But eventually she fell right back to down to earth, her post-climax euphoria rapidly fading only to be replaced with a deep sense of humiliation.

And then there was Nikolai pulling out of her and falling onto the couch beside her like she'd just punched him.

Chapter Forty

NIKOLAI SAT ON THE COUCH, and so did Sam. For several minutes it was very quiet in the plane, with nothing but the soft whooshing of the aircraft eating up the miles.

It didn't take long for the chill to set in. Sam was still completely naked and her confession hadn't exactly left her feeling warm and fuzzy. More like cold and ashamed.

But before she could reach down to gather her clothes, he came out of his fugue. "You heard phone call?" he said.

"Yeah… I heard it." Sam reached down to pick up her blouse and put it on without the bra, just wanting to cover herself up, to hide from this conversation and Nikolai in any way that she could. "I heard it all. About how I'd fallen right into your trap to make me perform like a real wife in bed." A fresh dose of humiliation surged through her and she grimaced.

"And that is why you hate me? Because I take advice about how to make you real wife?"

"I don't hate you," she whispered as she did up the last button. "I hate the way you make me feel."

He looked over at her then, his eyes deeply troubled.

"What? Why are you looking at me like that?" she asked him.

"I also think this to myself," he answered. "Several times I think it. I hate way you make me feel."

"No, Nikolai, it's not the same," she said with a bitter shake of her head. "I'm frustrating to you because I won't act the part you want me to play. Because I won't surrender and be the perfect wifey and let you fuck me whenever you want. The way I feel about you, that's different."

He stilled. "Different how?"

She sighed, and decided to tell him all of it, to kill every last ounce of pride she had.

"The reason I can't have a sexual relationship with you is because it would hurt me too much. It's stupid. I know it's stupid. But I've fallen in love with you and I'm going to work on not being in love with you, but I can't do that if we're having sex, or if we're still married, so I can't be married to you anymore…"

Nikolai's mouth worked and at least six different kinds of distress registered across his face, before he finally choked out, "You love me?"

"Yes, I love you," she admitted with a shake of her head. "Because I'm a masochist, who apparently doesn't know how to not become overly attached to every walking sob story that comes across my path."

Nikolai frowned in that Russian way of his. "So this love has happened before. Man tell you he has bad past and you love him?"

"No," she answered, wishing she was anywhere but stuck thousands of miles in the air having this conversation with Nikolai. "I've never been in love before. Believe me, if I'd thought it would be a possibility with you, I wouldn't have agreed to the marriage in the first place. But I've started two domestic violence shelters. And it still breaks my heart whenever one of my intakes goes back to her abuser. Every single time—but keep in mind, I still want to open forty-eight more Ruth's House shelters."

She looked away from him. "I fell in love with Pavel pretty much from the first moment I saw him in your laundry room, all dirty and skinny. And I couldn't adopt Back Up soon enough after I read the little card outside her cage at the rescue fair, talking about the abuse she'd suffered." She took a deep breath, and forced herself to meet his eyes again. "Obviously, I have a problem…"

"Obviously," Nikolai agreed. A look of deep consideration came over his face. "So you are saying you love me like you love Pavel and Back Up. Because I am broken man and my story makes you sad."

"Yes, I guess so," she answered. "Though, I maybe wouldn't have put it in such a harsh way. But yes, I stupidly let myself fall in love with you. Maybe I could have prevented it from happening if we'd just kept it contained to sleeping in separate places back in Indiana, but c'mon… Greece… and the *Veronica Mars* movie… and your gruesome back story… and then you ordered me breakfast! Why did you have to order me breakfast? Nobody's ever done that for me before, and it really messed me up."

"So you are in love with me now because of date, my sad story, and breakfast I order." He considered this information with a heavy frown, then he shrugged and said, "Okay, I take it."

Her near-crushing heartache turned into deep confusion. "What? What do you mean?"

"You will stay with me, no divorce, and I will take your love."

She tilted her head to the side. "Okay, that's not exactly how it works."

"No?" Nikolai asked, with what sounded like genuine confusion. "How does 'it work?'"

"I'm in love with you and I'm putting some distance between us because I don't want to be in love with you."

"Why not?" Nikolai asked.

"Because it hurts too much."

"Why?" he asked again.

Was he serious?

"Because you don't love me back!" she answered, stringing the words out carefully since obviously Nikolai was even lower on the emotional intelligence spectrum than she'd originally feared.

Nikolai's brow wrinkled and he turned fully towards her, laying his arm across the back of the couch.

"*Zhena*, I have important question for you. When you said I could learn be good parent, did you mean it?"

"Yes, I meant it," she answered immediately, though she had no idea why he was asking this in response to her confession of love.

"So why you think I not learn to love you?"

Before she could answer, he looked down, almost as if he were frustrated with himself for not being able to solve a tricky math problem. "No, I not ask right question…"

He looked back up at her, his green eyes the opposite of ice now. So heated, they seemed to burn.

"I will answer now question you asked me before," he told her. "Yes, *zhena*, my father was enforcer for our former Rustanov mafia family. Yes, he taught me everything he knew. I did not, how you say, follow in his footsteps. I became hockey player. But I did remember these things. I did use them to kill those Russians. I killed them to protect Pavel, and I killed them to protect you."

Sam stared at him wide eyed. Why was he telling her this now? To get her to stop loving him? To convince her she'd made a mistake by bringing her heart into it? If that was the case, then he'd used the wrong tactic.

She looked down, then back up again to say, "I see where you're going with this, but unfortunately that only makes me love you more. Nobody's ever gone out of their way to protect me before."

Nikolai looked at her for a few moments and let out a sad sigh, as if she were the most pitiful woman he'd ever encountered—which maybe she was. Then he said, "When you did not realize it was date until I say to you, '*Zhena*, this is date,' I thought maybe you are smart in some ways, and maybe not so smart in others. But now I see question I should ask you is are you same as your mother?"

Her heart stopped, her back going up straight. "Why would you ask me that? Because I'm not upset about you killing the Russians? You think I want to be in an abusive relationship?"

"No, I asked you, because you thought I told you about my killings to make you stop loving me. This is why I ask," Nikolai answered, his voice harsh and angry. "Are you same as your mother? Do you think you are—how did you say—undeserving of loving relationship?"

Sam froze. "I…"

She wanted to say no. She wanted to say she used to dream about being in a loving relationship, of having a family with someone she loved, so obviously she thought she deserved one. But she ended up telling him the truth instead.

"I don't know," she whispered.

Nikolai reached out to her then, cupping the side of her face gently with his large hand. "I will tell you another secret now, *zhena*. I was not talking on phone with cousin. I was talking with Pavel."

"Pavel? But why?" she asked, sitting back in stunned surprise.

And his hand fell from her face.

"Why did I ask nine-year-old boy how to make you my wife in every way? Because I was desperate," he answered with a miserable look. "So I ask Pavel his help. And he told me story. He said when you saved him, he thought, 'She is good person. I wish she was my mother.' So he called you mama, because he wanted you to be mama to him, and after we married you became his mama. This made him very happy. So when I ask him advice, he told me to do same. He said to be nice to you, treat you like real wife and he said if I do this, you become my real wife, same as you became his real mother."

Sam stared at him in horror and he shifted his gaze away from her. "You look at me like this because I took advice from child."

"Not because you took Pavel's advice, but because you asked a child how to get me into bed!"

Nikolai screwed up his face. "You think this is about sex only?" he asked. Then he reset with an annoyed huff. "Okay, you have been in Indianapolis less than year. Maybe you don't understand yet. I am big deal. I could have many girls at any time."

"Oh, I get that, Nikolai," she answered with a pained expression. "I totally get that."

"Then why you think this way about me?"

Nikolai asked this question, both his tone and his face filled with hurt, and it disarmed Sam. Not only because she wasn't used to him showing emotion, but also because... "Because yeah, maybe you think you can learn, but I'm not sure you can. I don't even know if you're capable of love. You said it was a silly custom. Remember?"

"I know what I said!" he snarled. "But you—how you say —should observe things I do, not things I say!"

Now it was him taking a deep breath before he said, "I wanted you from first time I see you. From beginning. I told you that. First time I touch you, I have no control and I put baby inside you. I slept on floor because I couldn't be in our bed without you. Your dog is no good guard dog and she make me rub her belly too much, but I pet her because she is yours. I took you to Greece, watched your strange movie about female detective. I told you things. Things I told no one before, not my cousin, not God, no one."

He now looked at her like she was the one who'd done a cruel number on his heart and not the other way around. "I do these things because I want you to love me. Love me like you love Pavel. Love me like you love your useless dog. I do everything to make you love me. And now you say you can't be sure I can learn love you?" he asked, his Russian accent thicker than she'd ever heard it before. "How you not sure? How can you not see I already learn this? How can you not see I already love you?"

And that was the kill shot.

Nikolai swung his hockey stick and the puck went right into the goal. No matter what the damaged girl who still lurked inside of Sam was trying to tell her about the chances of someone like Nikolai loving someone like her... when she thought about it, really thought about it, she could no longer go on believing this man who had killed for her, who had protected her in every way, who had fulfilled her every need—even the ones she didn't know she had—did not love her.

As Nikolai would say, of course he did.

She looked at him with tears and wonder in her eyes. So afraid to believe after all she'd seen and been through that the man sitting next to her was really offering her a happy ending. But...

"You love me?" she asked. Her heart trembled, as did her hand when she reached out to cup his cheek like he'd cupped hers a few minutes ago. "You love me like I love you?"

He immediately covered her hand with his much larger

one, and pressed his face further into her palm, as if her touch, and only her touch, could soothe the wild hurt inside him.

"*Zhena, zhena...*" he said, his voice cracking with emotion. "How you not know?"

She had no idea, and tears began to roll down her face because she was so ashamed. Ashamed of not guessing it sooner, of cutting their trip short.

"I'm sorry. I'm sorry for not realizing."

The apology was barely out of her mouth before she was in the air, being ferried across the cabin in Nikolai's fireman carry and through the door to the neglected rear bedroom. His manner was urgent, but when they got to the bed, Nikolai set her down gently, once again unbuttoning her blouse, this time with great care, before he stripped out of his own clothes.

Sam watched him get naked with heavy anticipation, all the while her mind screaming like a teenage girl, *"He loves me! He loves me! He really loves me!"*

As if reading her mind, he said, "*Da,* I love you, *zhena.*" Then he crawled into the large bed and covered her body with his before bracing himself above her on one arm. "But I must get inside you now. Please, I beg you."

To his credit, he waited for her answer, keeping his hard length still at the entrance of her once again very slick folds.

"I want you inside of me," she answered. "I love you so much, Nikolai. Please—" She didn't have to finish her own beg. He reached down between them, and then...

Sam threw her head back with a moan. He was inside her. So thick and heavy, she could actually feel the pulse of his member against her inner walls. He rolled into her, carefully at first, until he found a rhythm that kept the stem of his cock against her clit as he thrust into her.

It was good, so good. Even better than before, because she didn't have to bite her tongue about the way he made her feel.

"I love you so much, Nikolai. So much. I'm sorry I didn't realize…"

"*Muzehnek*," he said harshly into the back of her neck. "Call me *muzehnek* when you say you love me from now on."

"I love you, *muzehnek*," she repeated, though she still had no idea what that word actually meant. Her heart soared into the sky. It was if she'd had a rubber band around it for all her life, and now Nikolai Rustanov had finally set it free.

But the words didn't have the effect she expected. Instead of going all out, Nikolai came to an abrupt stop, reaching out to cup a hand around her neck, anchoring it so she could look at nothing else but his grave face as he said, "I love you, too, *zhena*." Harsh and low, like he'd never been more serious about anything in his life. "You believe me, *da*?"

She nodded, too choked up to answer with words.

But Nikolai wanted the words. Seemed to need them as he insisted, "You believe me and you will stay with me? Always?"

"*Da*," she whispered.

A happy smile spread over Nikolai's face like sunshine on a gloomy winter day. It felt like that one word from her had made him the happiest man on earth, and that in turn made her feel like the luckiest woman in the world.

He started moving again, filling her deep and tight, as he silently drove himself into her, his hand still cupped around her neck. No more words were exchanged after that, and eventually they fell over the edge together, in silent communion, as an ocean of complete and utter ecstasy washed over them both.

He kept their bodies connected for as long as possible, bracing himself above her, and gracing her lips and neck with tender kisses until he finally went soft inside of her. Even then, he didn't seem to want to let her go. He lay down, still holding on to her, even as he positioned himself behind her. He settled a hand over the gentle swell of her stomach, as if he were sheltering both their child and her in his large arms.

And Sam had to blink back more tears. She was still having trouble processing all of this. That she had somehow stumbled into a loving relationship with a man who understood her on the deepest levels, a beautiful man who forced her to communicate with him through mind-blowing sex—

"I will never call you Samantha," he said behind her. "Never again."

"What...? What changed your mind on that subject," she asked.

"Pavel told me reason. About your stepfather calling you by that name. I don't care if it sounds like I love another man. I will only call you Sam in future. Sam or *zhena*."

She was going to get Pavel something insanely nice for Christmas this year, Sam decided. Like his own pony. Or maybe a trip to Disneyworld.

"Thank you," she whispered in the dark.

"Please do not thank me for this. Of course, I would do this for you."

He asked nicely, so she didn't thank him again. Instead she gave thanks to Pavel and whatever other spiritual force had decided to bless her with this man.

The sky had darkened outside the plane's small window, leaving the little room dim, with only the barest hints of sunlight. Sleep began to drag at Sam's eyes,

But there was still one thing she had to know before she let her inner dreams take over the one she and Nikolai had created in the real world.

"What does '*zhena*' mean?" she asked. "Is it some really cutesy term of endearment? Like flower, or honey, or kitten?"

His unfamiliar laugh sounded then, a deep rumble against her back. "Do you remember what I said to you when you come to my door on our wedding night?"

You do not want me to call you Samantha, and I do not want to call

you by boy's name. I will have to simply call you 'wife'... Come in, Wife."

Now Sam laughed, realizing out loud, "*Zhena* is Russian for wife! And *muzehnek* is Russian for husband."

"*Da...*" he answered.

And this time she said it with him, "Of course!"

Epilogue

"I THINK I should move back to the guest room."

Nikolai lowered the Russian version of *What to Expect the First Year*, which he was almost done reading. He put it on his nightstand before turning in bed to face his wife who was sitting up in their bed.

"*Zhena...*" he growled, fully prepared to do battle.

"No, no, just hear me out. You've got a lot going on right now with the new hockey season starting this month, and I know I've been keeping you up. If I moved back to the guest room, then you wouldn't have to put up with me tossing and turning because I can't find a comfortable position. And also, you'd have more space in bed. I mean.... look at me. I'm basically a beached whale."

He did look at her. Nearly full term with a thin sheen of sweat covering her forehead, despite the fact that it was fall and the air conditioner was set at a freezing sixty-five with the fan rotating on high overhead. Luckily he was Russian and could handle the lower temperature. He'd had to give Pavel one of the winter quilts, and had thrown an old blanket over Back Up.

So yes, his wife was huge, and a bit sweaty. But he'd still put her up against any rail thin super model as the most beautiful woman in the world.

"You are uncomfortable, *zhena*," he said. "I will help you."

"No, you don't have to——"

Too late. He rolled over to her side of the bed, and his head was between her legs before she could finish her protest.

"You really don't have to do this every time I complain about…" Sam moaned. "Oh God, why are you so good at that?" she asked. Her hands came to rest in his hair, and he could see her head falling back against the pillow rest she jokingly referred to as "her other *muzehnek*."

It wasn't a joke he was particularly fond of but it showed how much he'd grown that instead of throwing the thing out when his *zhena* wasn't looking, he used his ire as an excuse to redouble his efforts to make her comfortable in ways that a standing pillow could not.

Tonight was no different and he was soon rewarded for his efforts with his favorite sight: his wife rubbing on her full breasts with her eyes closed, tweaking her distended nipples as he worked her over with his tongue. These days he knew when she was getting close, when she started moaning, *muzehnek*, over and over again.

And though this had started out as a way to make her more comfortable, by taking her mind off the heat only she could feel, he found he still had a distinct problem with wanting to fuck his wife. All the time.

"*Zhena*…"

He didn't have to finish. She heaved herself up and flipped on to her hands and knees, throwing a few pillows under her full belly. The books had warned him he might want her less as she got bigger, but as he put himself inside her hot, slick womanhood, he knew it to be nothing less than his most erotic dreams coming true. He couldn't imagine ever wanting this woman less. She'd wormed her way into his soul, and even when they were in the same room together, it felt like something was missing when he wasn't inside of her.

He shoved the pretend *muzehnek* off the bed and started moving behind her with urgent thrusts, his hands tight on her hips. As always with her, it felt right. Like coming home to a warm fire after a lifetime of feeling left out in the cold.

"I love you, *muzehnek*," she cried underneath him.

Love. He'd been so scared of it before, and now these were his favorite four words on the planet.

He leaned down over her, careful to support himself on one heavily muscled arm in order to keep as much of his weight off of her as possible. "I love you, too, *zhena*."

Then they exploded together, twin suns forming in a perfect universe.

However, he didn't let himself linger inside of her, no matter how much he wanted to. The baby was large, maybe too large for her small body he sometimes worried, and he didn't want to cause her even a second of a discomfort by keeping her in this position too long. He allowed himself one appreciative glance at the view of her from behind, her ample ass in the air, the braids she'd gotten put in recently to see her through her maternity leave fanned out over her arched back. Then he set to rearranging the pillows like a nest around her, in just the way his wife liked, because he knew she'd soon be asleep.

Sex was the best way to help her "feel comfortable" on these hot fall nights. It was also the best way to help her fall asleep. In fact, there'd been a night earlier in the week when she'd been already softly snoring by the time he'd gotten the last pillow arranged.

But not tonight. Tonight she sat down inside the newly made pillow nest, grimacing with her hand on the side of her belly.

"He is upset with us again," Nikolai guessed. Sometimes,

the baby they'd already decided to name Alexei, staged protests when their lovemaking got a little too vigorous for his taste. Baby Alexei had no idea how little his demonstrations deterred his father, since Nikolai adored feeling his son move inside his wife's belly. Loved the confirmation that he was alive and well.

But this time when Nikolai reached out to touch his wife's belly, she shook her head, pushing away. "Don't. I think... I think I'm having a contraction."

His eyes widened.

"No actually," Her face seized up in pain and she fell over on her side. "I know I'm having a contraction. Ow...!"

WHEN SHE'D FIRST MET NIKOLAI RUSTANOV, SAM HAD TURNED down his advances without a second thought, because she'd been so sure he would hurt her.

And she'd been right.

She'd been utterly and completely right, Sam thought as she breathed through another contraction. She hated Nikolai Rustanov, really hated him.

Except when she loved him. Like when he was holding her hand through contractions and promising her he'd get her something to eat, whatever she wanted as soon as she was all done. And when he kissed her forehead, saying he understood why she'd told another man—the male anesthesiologist—that she loved him, and that he wouldn't hold it against her later.

Then she hated him again when the drugs wore off a few hours in—apparently there wasn't a one-hundred-percent guarantee that epidurals would completely take. And soon the contraction pains were back with a vengeance. Even worse this time because she'd been laboring through the night, and she was so tired.

Then she loved him again, when it turned out he'd read so

many books on the birthing practice he was more than able to coach her through breathing through the worst of her contractions—like a really stern Russian doula who treated her like one of his hockey players. But hey, she had been so counting on the drugs coming through, that she hadn't even bothered with Lamaze classes. Beggars couldn't be choosers. She loved him so much.

Then hours passed and she hated him again, because why hadn't he used a condom? And why did his big ass baby boy have to be taking his sweet time getting here? She hated him. Truly hated him.

Eventually the contractions became too much, and she started crying with snot and everything, babbling on about being so tired and couldn't they just cut it out of her already? Nikolai climbed into bed behind her, hugging and rocking her back and forth through the pain.

He soothed her and calmed her down, and unlike a particularly unhelpful nurse from earlier, didn't tell her stories about how women in Japan gave birth quietly and without a lot of drama. In fact, he'd had that nurse replaced with another labor and delivery nurse who tutted with sympathy and patted her hand, telling her what a good job she was doing with a totally straight face, even though they were fourteen hours in and she was a blubbering mess.

She loved Nikolai for that, loved him deeply... until the angel nurse put on a pair of devil horns and told her the baby was crowning and it was time to push.

She shook her head. "No, no, I can't. I don't have anything left in me."

"You must, *zhena*," he said behind her.

"No, I hate you."

"You love me."

"No, I hate you," she cried, exhausted and nearing hysteria. "Why did you do this me?"

"*Zhena, zhena,* listen to me. Do you remember when we went to Greece?"

"The first or the second time?" she asked, thinking of the second trip just a few weeks after school had let out, when they'd taken Pavel, Back Up, and Dirk. They'd stayed for a whole week, tooling around Poros, while Pavel, as promised, had happily played in the pool with Dirk looking on all day.

"The first time," he answered. "The meal we had. You said it was best one you ever ate. I told Isaac call restaurant as soon as they admitted us here, and he arranged for special delivery."

"You're kidding," she said, shaking her head.

"No, *zhena*. Five minutes ago, Isaac texted me. He got your meal from airport. It is waiting for you outside this room as soon as you are done."

"You're lying," she said with tears in her eyes. She was so hungry. They hadn't let her eat anything but ice chips for the last fourteen hours. "You're telling me whatever it takes to get me to push."

"I would not lie to you," he said, his voice quiet but fierce in her ear. "I love you, I love Pavel, I love our dog, Back Up. I am so happy to have you all as my family. It is more than I deserve. But please make me more happy, *zhena*. Please push and bring us this baby."

Sam shook her head, wondering how she and Nikolai could be from two opposite countries, two opposite races, and two opposite backgrounds but be so much the same. She blubbered, "I love Pavel. I love Back Up. And I love you, *muzehnek*. So much."

Then she bared down.

Less than thirty minutes later, Alexei Joseph Rustanov was placed in her arms, eyes squeezed shut and squalling.

However, he calmed down quickly and with one look, all was forgiven. Something in Sam's heart fell loose the moment she took him in. Little nose. Ten little fingers and toes. Full lips like his mother and a long straight nose like his father. He was nothing less than…

"Perfect."

She looked up to see Nikolai standing beside the bed, his eyes suspiciously shiny.

"Do you want to hold him?" she asked.

And for the first time in the last fifteen hours, he actually looked a little afraid.

"Go on," she said, holding the baby out to him. "It's all right. You read up on how to do this, right?"

He must have, because he took the baby from her like an expert, cupping his head and bringing him in close.

Then there was no doubt about what that shiny stuff was in his eyes, because the tears really came down then, as he babbled to the baby in Russian, seeming not to care that the OB and two nurses were all watching the tough former hockey player blubber all over his new baby boy.

Sam watched the scene with a smile, the last of her doubts about him, about her, about them, blowing away like dandelion seeds in the wind. Nikolai was truly going to be a great father, a loving father, who Pavel and their son would be proud to call papa. She was sure of it.

Just as she was sure that finally surrendering to the Russian hockey player was the best decision she'd ever made.

Sigh!

Nikolai and Sam remain one of my most frustrating and favorite couples of all time. There were times during the telling of this super emotional story that I thought they might never figure out their happily ever after. But oh my gosh, they finally did, and I'm now just so glad that Pavel, Little Alexei, and Back Up have the loving parents they deserve.

I hope you enjoyed the second story in the Ruthless Russians series, too. If so, please do this amazing family the boon of leave a review on Amazon, so that others might find their way to their one-of-a-kind story.

And don't forget to check out the entire Ruthless Russians series:

HER RUSSIAN BILLIONAIRE
HER RUSSIAN SURRENDER
HER RUSSIAN BEAST
HER RUSSIAN BRUTE

If you loved these Ruthless Russians, you'll also love my best-selling **RUTHLESS TYCOONS series**, four blazing hot stories, featuring revenge and second chance love.

Thanks again for reading HER RUSSIAN SURRENDER. And keep swiping for a special preview of HER RUSSIAN BEAST.

So much love,
Theodora Taylor

HER RUSSIAN BEAST Special
Preview

Psycho Sexy Rustanov

HIM: She showed up in my dark world and pulled me into her light. And then she ran away. For six long years she kept herself hidden from me. She is my wife. My siren. My everlasting obsession. Did she really think I would just let her go?

Nyet.

She belongs to me, and now that I have found her, I will make her pay for destroying me.

HER: He's the domineering monster I had to escape. The only place him and me work right is in bed. And now that he's found me, he's determined to take every scrap of dignity I have left.

So why can't I stop wanting him? Needing him? Aching for him?

He's my husband. My keeper. My Russian Beast. And I don't have a chance in the world of getting out of our twisted relationship with my heart intact.

Chapter One

"HEY! Hey! Hey, Beast, look at me! Look at me!"

His vision cleared, and the world came swimming back to him on a drunken wave of adrenaline and anger. He emerged from the Darkness to find himself in a hot concrete basement. The place reeked of blood and sweat, and a circle of yelling men surrounded him.

But in front of him stood a girl. A vision of loveliness with dark tumbling curls, golden brown skin, and eyes the color of champagne.

"Hey, Beast, welcome back," she said with a teasing smile.

Behind her, the crowd booed, same as they always did every place he fought. He wasn't the pretty guy in the underground fighting movie who fought Goliath and won. He *was* Goliath, the villain everybody wants to see brought down. He was used to hearing his fight name get cursed in every language, but this crowd's booing seemed especially loud.

And now that the Darkness had receded, he could see four bodies on the floor. One a bloody pulp. The other three knocked out cold. That explained the booing. The other three must have tried to pull him off the bloody pulp and gotten

K.O.ed for their efforts. Which meant the men who'd bet against him hadn't just lost money on *this* fight, but on the next three, too.

He knew this not because he was particularly adept at reading underground fight scenes, but because it had happened before. Enough times that he now knew exactly what had happened, even though he'd gone Dark.

But there were still other fighters left. He could sense them even if he couldn't see them in the messy circle of disappointed cowards who'd hoped to win big tonight with their pretty underdogs. Yes, he was back, and he was ready to fight again.

He raised a gloved fist and started to call out for another fighter to approach him.

"Wait, wait! Hold up!"

The girl got in front of him again, and to his shock, she laid her small hands on his arms. As if it were just the two of them in this dark basement and she was pulling him in for an intimate conversation.

"Stay with me here for a little bit, okay?" Her voice compelled him. Made him want to do as she asked for a second or two.

But she wasn't a fight. And he needed another fight.

Nose flaring, he swung his gaze away from her, scanning the crowd for someone else to fight. And he spotted him. Tall and wide with a Greek nose and jawline, his next challenger was dressed in fight shorts and sparring gloves, which meant he probably knew a few different fight styles. A worthy opponent, even if he was currently talking to Cyrus, the Greek who ran this basement fight gig, shaking his head in a way that insinuated he had no wish to be The Russian Beast's next victim.

As he watched the fighter try to talk his way out of the match, the Darkness compelled him forward, blanking his mind of everything but the need to put his gloves on something. To hear the music of cracking bones beneath his fists.

He pulled away from the girl and started toward Cyrus and the reluctant fighter…

Only to find the girl in front of him again.

"Hey, hold up! Hold up!" she said, putting her hands on his chest this time. "What you trying to do? Get me fired?"

Her words confused him, brought his eyes back down to her. She was small, but not small he saw now. Dressed in tiny shorts and a tank top so skimpy, he could see the outline of her push-up bra. She was short and her breasts were most likely small without the extra padding, but everything else on her was big and lush. Lush dark curls tumbling all the way down to her shoulders. Lush curves, barely constrained by her ring girl ensemble. Lush lips, smiling up at him like they knew each other. And more than that, were already old friends.

Not many women smiled at him like that. Especially the ones who didn't know his last name, the only real acknowledgment his father had ever given him. Even the women his half-brother had sent to "help" with his recovery after Turkey, had only barely managed to cover up their terror with simpering smiles. Which was why he'd used them then tossed them out of his hotel room immediately after.

Without his last name, he was too frightening. Mountainous body, hawk nose, knived cheek bones that put girls in mind of long ago Mongolians who would not only burn your poor European village to the ground, but also claim every woman in it as his own. Even the gentle tilt of his mother's Buryat eyes didn't help, because his pupils burning black as coal let them too easily see the Siberian beast buried just beneath his surface.

But this woman smiled up at him, her champagne eyes crinkling as she nodded at his forehead. "That cut above your eyebrow. I need to patch it up before you can fight again. I'm not just the ring girl, I'm the nurse, too—and the clean up crew, but that's a whole 'nother job," she said with a roll of her eyes.

He stared at her. This woman sounded American. But not like the rich ones his brother kept company with. More like the ones on television. But not exactly. Her voice had a husky quality to it that made him think of the girls who sang in the basement bar where his grandmother used to work.

"It is scratch," he heard himself saying to her, his eyes going back to the next man he would fight, even if that man didn't want to.

"Cool, then I'll have you back out here in no time. Just come with me."

"It is *scratch*," he said again. And this time he didn't wait for her answer, just started toward the Greek fighter again. The Darkness guiding his every step.

But against all odds, she got in front of him a third time.

"I said no!" she yelled, shoving him backwards. "You don't fight until I look at that cut."

The boos cut off with an abrupt gasp, and both he and the rest of the men in the room looked at her like she was crazy. Which she would have to be to shove a six-foot-six fighter known in underground fighting circles throughout Europe and Asia as The Russian Beast.

There were grown men who wouldn't dare do what she'd just done. But her beautiful champagne eyes held his in a defiant stare down as she declared, "Listen, I ain't afraid of you! I ain't afraid of nothing. So you can either come with me now or fight *me* next. It's up to you."

His eyes slitted. She could not be serious.

With an annoyed glare, he simply picked her up and set her aside in one easy motion, then started forward again.

"Oh, for *fuck's* sake…"

The next thing he knew, her body collided into his. Two arms wrapped around the back of his neck and pulled him down with what could only have been all of her strength. At first he thought she was trying to bite him—the classic defense of the weak—but then...

Then she kissed him.

The entire world stopped when her lush mouth found his, lips giving him determined claim as her soft curves pressed into his hard body. She kissed him. Long and tough. She kissed him like she already knew him and was merely waiting for him to know her back.

The beast inside him faltered...

And the formerly pissed off crowd erupted into cheers, egging them on in a confusion of surprise and visceral lust. Somewhere in the distance, he heard the heavily accented voice of Cyrus the Greek saying, "Take him somewhere else, Sirena."

And then the kiss was over. She slid down his body, the back of her feet landing on the floor.

"C'mon," she said softly, beckoning him forward with eyes that almost seemed to glow in the barely lit space. "Come with me."

Sirena. That is good name for her, he thought. Because like a sailor enchanted, he let her take him by the hand and lead him out of the fight circle.

Chapter Two

"JUST TAKE A SEAT RIGHT OVER THERE," she said once they got to her room. She let go of his hand and indicated the little wooden chair she used as an informal nursing station.

He gave her a long, dark look before apparently deciding to indulge her and sit down. She couldn't keep herself from staring as he did. He had a huge tattoo that took up nearly his entire back. What looked like a Siberian tiger, rendered so realistically, it seemed to animate with the bunching of his muscles as he lowered himself into the chair.

"So, I'm guessing you ain't exactly a fan of 'your mama' jokes," she said, coming to stand a few feet in front of where he was sitting.

The fighter's black eyes cut up to hers in a glare of confusion.

"The dude you was fighting tried to talk some trash about her before the fight." She decided against repeating word for word what the large Albanian fighter had actually said. The promise he'd made in English, the agreed upon common language of the fights. That he would beat the Russian *dog* and then go find his mother to give her the fucking she deserved for bringing such an ugly beast into the world. The crowd of betting men had eaten it up with a loud cheer.

But a switch had clicked off behind the eyes of the dude everybody was calling The Russian Beast. A deadening like nothing she'd ever seen before.

Now the Albanian was laid out on the concrete floor outside her tiny room, battered and broken, with no guarantee he would survive the night. And it was on her to keep the Beast distracted until Cyrus's two goons could remove the body.

"Extra hour pay for tonight if you get him to stop," Cyrus had said, right before he shoved her into the fight circle with the huge muscle-bound fighter. You know, the one who'd just knocked out the last three guys who tried to stop him.

Luckily, she really hadn't been kidding about not being afraid of anything. But she still couldn't believe he was here. In her room. Threating to splinter her little wooden chair with the sheer heft of his body. She couldn't stop herself from stealing several glances at him. He was huge and nothing like the other fighters she'd seen come through this place.

He looked big and Slavic, but the tilt of his eyes told her he might also have some farther East Asian in his background. He had ink black hair tied into a tight knot at the base of his neck —a strong 'fuck you' to would-be competitors, because most fighters wouldn't dare go into a no-holds-barred fight with long hair. Talk about an instant vulnerability! But this dude definitely didn't have to worry about being taken down in a fight because of his hair. Instead of swagger, he oozed absolute certainty, and she didn't have a doubt in the world that he could beat down any man who came at him.

She could feel his cold gaze on her as she rooted through her waist pack with deliberate slowness, searching for the mini flashlight she used to see cuts better.

But she could only pretend for so long. Eventually she had to find the flashlight and come stand in front of him to perform her bullshit exam. The dude was beyond huge. Nearly as tall as her, despite the fact that he was seated and she was standing. She moved between his legs in order to get a good look at his cut. Those glittering black diamonds he called eyes tracked her every movement as she came in closer. She felt like she was being observed by a straight-up predator.

The weight of his stare did something to her insides. Made that pretty song she'd heard the other day chew on her chest even louder, just begging to get out.

Trying to ignore the song, she took him by the chin and lifted his face further into the light.

"You're right, this cut ain't that deep," she said after a quick inspection. She clicked off the flashlight and returned it to the waist pack before pulling out a small band-aid.

Outside, the sound of the men cheering on a new set of fighters erupted. Which meant they must have successfully removed the body. The Albanian was probably on his way to get unceremoniously dumped somewhere. If the dude was lucky, outside a hospital. If not…

As if reading her thoughts, The Russian Beast asked, "Why are you here with me? Other fighter is much worse."

"True," she agreed, smoothing the band-aid over his itty bit cut—the only indicator he'd even been in a fight. "But he's beyond my nursing skills. Cyrus wanted me to see to you."

He stared at her for a dead-eyed second before saying. "He doesn't want me to fight his Greek. Not good for bets. So he sends you to distract me."

"Wow," she said, stepping out from between his legs. "Has anyone ever told you you're real perceptive, Mr. Beast?"

"I do not usually talk enough for people to say this about me," he answered.

"Really? Why not?" she asked, genuinely curious about the answer, which was way more curious than she'd felt about anything in a real long time.

"Because I scare them. People do not wish to talk to that which scares them."

"Oh, I get it," she said with a shrug. "Well, like I said, you don't scare me, so talk away."

Another slitted look, like he was trying to figure her out. And then. "No more talk. I need to fight now."

"But you just said yourself Cyrus doesn't want you to."

He came to his feet, already rolling his neck. "What Cyrus wants does not matter."

She believed him. This hulking beast didn't look like he gave two fucks about Cyrus or anything else but his next fight.

"How did you get that?" she asked, nodding toward the ugly scar running a diagonal line across his heavily muscled gut.

He glanced down as if just now realizing the scar was there.

"Fight," he answered with a sneer. "It is just scratch."

"Looks like more than a scratch to me."

A dark second ticked between them. And then he said, "I have to fight now."

"Want to or have to?"

He stared at her, his black diamond eyes blank. And she clarified. "Most guys come in here *wanting* to fight. But you got something inside you, don't you? Something that makes you *have* to do this?"

She must have hit it on the head, because he looked away. Dropping his black stare from her to the dingy linoleum floor.

Was he ashamed? She wondered. Upset she'd seen through all his hulking insistence to his real motivation? Not his mother's honor. But that he had a dark rage burning inside of him. Her heart went out to this Russian then, like it used to go out to the road dogs her and Trevor made a habit of rescuing.

Dear oldest daughter, you can't keep bringing these sad animals home, her mother would say when she and Trevor showed up at the door, Trevor carrying yet another dog some cruel person had left at the side of the road.

Their little house lay on the very outskirts of the small Virginia town they'd moved to when she was seventeen. The perfect place for folks from the surrounding bigger cities to dump aging or hurt pets they no longer wanted. She'd felt compelled to start rescuing those poor dogs from the beginning of their tenure in the little brick house, sometimes going as far as to nurse them back to health before taking them on to the local shelter. Her little brother, Trevor, had been the perfect assistant for her unofficial fostering service. Big and mentally disabled, his kindness continued to know no bounds even after the age when most boys became cruel with raging hormones.

And now here was a man everyone called The Russian Beast, hurting bad from something—she could tell—and fighting demons only he could see. She stepped closer to him on instinct.

But then he asked, "How much?"

"Excuse me?"

"I have been to these fights before. I know how it works with Cyrus's ring girls. Especially the ones he lets room here."

Her eyebrows shot up. "Oh, you want to have sex with me." She threw him an apologetic look. "Yeah, Cyrus told me that's a good way to make extra money down here, but I'm still…" she searched for the right words to describe her current mental state and could only come up with, "…not quite there yet. Maybe next time."

His dark eyes flickered with angry confusion. "Next time I can have you. This is what you are saying."

"Yes, maybe next time," she answered. "Like I said, I'm still working up to it."

"You are being serious? You are not like Cyrus's other ring girls? You do not take fighters into your bed after the fights?" he asked, obviously not believing her.

"So I'm assuming you've been in this room before?" she asked, her tone wry. "With all those other ring girls?"

He just continued to stare down at her, his unrelenting gaze heavy as stone. "My brother tells me my English is good. Better than his when he was my age. But I do not understand you."

She tilted her head up at him. Liking him. Liking the way he made her laugh, even if it wasn't anywhere near intentional on his part. "I'm saying it sounds like you've fucked a few girls before me in this bedroom, Beast. Is that clear enough for you?" she asked.

He actually seemed to consider her question. Then surprised the hell out of her when he quietly confessed. "Sometimes the fighting is not enough. Sometimes I need more."

"More," she repeated. "For the demons you mean?"

He nodded, looking wary like he expected her to run or something.

But when she continued to stand there, waiting to hear what he'd say next, he surprised her again by asking. "Sirena. That is your name, *da*, little ring girl?"

"Yep!" she lied with a pleasant smile. "Sirena Gale. My passport got stolen a few days ago, so I figured that was Life telling me to start over. So now I'm Sirena Gale, ring girl-slash-nurse maid. At least until I find the funds to move on."

He frowned. "Your passport was stolen, but you are not upset."

She shrugged. "It's cool. I came over here to be somebody else for a little while. Now I can be."

"But you are not ready to sell your body?"

"No, not yet," she answered with another shrug and a smile.

Her answer made his glower go even darker. "I do not like being teased."

"You should reconsider your position on that, Mr. Beast,"

she replied with a grin. "Teasing's kind of fun under the right circumstances."

Now he regarded her with a suspicious glare. "Do you know my real last name?"

"It's not Beast?"

His square jaw gritted back and forward. "You are teasing me again."

She grinned. "You got me."

But he didn't smile back at her. Like at all. "No, I do not have you. *Yet*."

THE GIRL STANDING IN FRONT OF HIM, SO CLOSE BUT SO FAR away, was not making this easy for him. With her sultry eyes and her teasing voice. But his erection was pounding now inside his shorts, and he was done with her games.

"Tell me this, Sirena," he said. "You guessed the truth about me having to fight, but do you really understand about me now? What has to happen if you do not get out of my way and let me return to the circle?"

He got a brazen satisfaction out of watching the girl visibly swallow in response to his question, her throat working up and down. And just in case she had any remaining illusions, he told her the hard facts of their situation without any softness whatsoever.

"Fight or fuck, Sirena. That is only choice you will ever have with me."

Her eyes widened slightly, but she remained where she was. And he had to admire her for not fleeing like a small animal. As most girls would do given a set of similar choices.

Now it was he who stepped closer to her, head dropping so he could get a better look at her as he said, "You lie about your name, are you lying about other thing?"

"Other thing?"

"When you say you aren't afraid of me."

"No, I ain't lying about that."

"Perhaps," he said, bringing his large hands up to her waist. "You should be scared of me."

"Hmm," she said, tilting her own head to once again meet his gaze square in the eye. "But I'm not."

"But you should be," he said, even as he tugged her closer, pulling her body flush with his so she had no choice but to feel what was going on behind his fighting shorts. The pulsing erection that had apparently replaced his need to fight.

But... "I'm still not scared," she informed him.

"You should be."

"But I'm not."

And before he could answer, she curled her hand around his neck and kissed him, sipping at his sweat, lust, and rage like a curious cat.

He froze, the Darkness inside of him not quite knowing what to do with this bold girl's kiss. But then...his Darkness exploded into flame.

He kissed her back. Savagely lifting her head higher as he gave her lips rough claim. Kissed her and kissed her until everything around them disappeared: The grimy basement room, the noise of the fight taking place on the other side of the door, the wild sadness that had been dogging him for the past year.

Kissed her until she understood.

She wasn't a whore, but tonight she would give her body to him. Tonight she would become his possession.

Chapter Three

HE WOKE the next day to the sound of an angel singing. Had he gone to heaven?

Of course not. He didn't believe in heaven. And even if he did, he doubted such a place would let him in.

Nonetheless, he could clearly hear the angel singing in this room. He sat up and found her by the space's only window with a white mug in her hand, watching the feet of pedestrians pass by as lyrics spilled out of her mouth.

It was a soft song with a strange vernacular. He was only able to catch a few of the English words. Something about summertime and living easy. Although it was not summertime, nor from the looks of her unheated basement room did her living seem easy. But still he recognized the song as opera—beautifully sung, which was surprising since he was fairly certain she couldn't possibly have any formal training.

"You sing like angel," he told her when she was done.

"Oh, I didn't know you was up," she said, startling at the window. A sultry smile lifted her lips, and to him it sounded like she was still singing when she said, "Thank you for that nice compliment, Beast."

He sneered as he looked around the cold room. She was the only pretty thing in the small, gray place with a solitary mattress, a cheap dresser drawer, and a sink for washing up. It reminded him of home. The one he'd shared with his grandmother in Siberia. And he hated it.

"It is fact not compliment," he told her, tone harsh as the gray winter morning outside the window.

"Oh, even better then," she answered, laughing. "A fact from you feels exactly like a present come early on Christmas Eve."

And he once again found himself squinting hard at her. She was still not scared of him.

Even after last night.

"The last ring girl must have had a real steady clientele," Sirena had joked, pointing to the basket of condoms on top of the dresser drawer as he carried her to the bed.

He didn't laugh as he plucked one foil package out of the basket. Couldn't laugh at the thought of Sirena eventually becoming like the last girl and pointing other men to the basket.

The Darkness threatened and he had to blank his mind in order to deal with this silly girl who didn't know any better than to be scared of him in her tiny room.

He'd taken her hard the first few times. Brutal, his desire for her not allowing for any of the prettiness women liked. But she'd received him each time. Her lush curves pillowing his heavy body, making him think of that place in which he didn't believe as he spilled into one condom after another.

But it was never enough. He kept pulling out, only to have himself immediately rise again. Wanting her. Needing her back beneath him...

They'd spent nearly the entire night fucking. Him unable to stop rising for her. Her murmuring English words in his ears as he pushed his big body into hers.

"Yes, baby. Fuck yes. Just like that. So good…I ain't never…oh…make me feel…make me feel."

"How old are you?" he'd asked her at one point, beginning to wonder if her many "I ain't nevers" were a joke.

"Nineteen. No, wait…twenty," she answered with a smile. "My birthday was in August, but I don't like that month so I keep on forgetting."

Twenty. Not even old enough to drink in her home country. That explained her eagerness and wonder with him, if not his own desire at the relatively hardened age of twenty-one to keep possessing her again and again. Never sated. Satisfied for long, pleasure-strung moments, but never full.

He'd fallen asleep inside her, cock still jerking for more.

He hadn't understood then in the dark of night, and he still didn't understand now in the dim gray light of day. He never stayed overnight. Especially with whores. The Fight or The Fuck—those were his two options when the Darkness was riding him. And he was always out the door as soon as either was done.

But here he was waking up in this strange American woman's bedroom. And here she was, smiling down at him, like he'd pleased her beyond belief just by opening his eyes.

"Want some Greek coffee?" she asked. "I can get you some. I also waitress at the restaurant upstairs."

Four jobs. Four fucking jobs, yet she lived like a dog.

He came to his feet, not knowing what to do with the emotions riling inside of him, feeling the need to fight even though there was nothing in this room to punch. Not even a pillow.

This wasn't the usual Darkness, he realized. But some other unnamable thing. It made him want to say things to her, do things to her. Do things *for* her.

"I will go now," he told her, rejecting the weird compulsions inside of him. "Good-bye."

"Okay, kinda abrupt," she said with a soft laugh. "But you've got to go. I get it."

Good. She got it. At least one of them did, he thought. He looked around. Where was his bag?

"Your gym bag's right there." She pointed to the wooden chair. "I went out and got it from Cyrus after you fell asleep. I had to get up early to clean the basement anyway."

He was glad she got his things, but unprepared for what the thought of her cleaning out there while he slept in here did to him. He stalked over to the chair and snatched up the bag. He didn't even bother to go through it to make sure his wallet was still there. Cyrus knew his last name. He wouldn't dare.

Shouldering the bag, he started toward the door, refusing to look at her. He didn't trust himself not to take her back to bed if he did.

But she once more got in front of him, splaying her hands against his chest. "Wait, before you go…"

She curved a hand around the back of his neck and brought him down for another kiss. This one chaste, just a tender press of her lips to his as she rose up on her tiptoes.

Yet it made his heart roar the same as if she'd used her tongue.

"Thank you," she said against his lips. Swaying with the effort to stay on her toes.

"For what?" he asked with the strange feeling that he should be the one thanking her.

"I heard that song out on a walk a few weeks ago, just spilling out of somebody's open window. It's been stuck inside my chest this whole time. Chewing on me. But I couldn't…I couldn't figure out how to sing it. And then this morning it was just there. Cuz of you, I think. So thank you for that, Beast. I do appreciate it."

She pressed her lips to his once more, and then she stepped back, grinning. He didn't know her, but he felt like he did in that moment. She was that girl, he realized. Pretty, popular, so utterly confident in her every move. Back in Siberia he'd seen girls like her, but never spoken to them, and they, in turn, hadn't so much as attempted to speak to the wild half-Russian boy who even the teachers treated like a feral animal.

But this girl continued to grin up at him, her sparkly champagne eyes twinkling. "See you later maybe?"

This time he didn't answer. Just left with the answer ringing firm inside his dark mind.

No. She'd unsettled him so much, he knew even before the door closed behind him that he'd never let himself see her again. The one who'd named herself after a creature who lured men to their deaths.

Chapter Four

HER MAMA MARIAN had been telling her for as long as she could remember that her daddy—the guy who'd knocked Marian up less than three months after her arrival at college in North Carolina—was the son of a siren.

"You see, dear oldest daughter, he'd been sent by his mother to repopulate the world with siren singers. This is why so many of the true singers come from single parent homes," Marian told her a few days after she got her first period. *"But anyroad, three things are guaranteed for you in this life, my dear. You'll always be able to swim, sing, and seduce. Do with that what you will."*

This had been her mother's idea of the "you're a woman now" speech. But okay, whatever. Everybody back in her small town knew Marian was crazy, and now she herself was becoming pretty sure her mother had overstated the power of her mythological DNA.

Yes, she could swim like a fish, even though she never recalled learning how. And yes, she could sing pretty good—copying any song she heard, note for note, no matter the language, and often doing the singer one better. Though that usually felt less like a blessing than a curse. For as long as she could remember, if she went more than five days without singing, it began to feel like something was chewing on her, inside her chest. That's one thing the books never tell you about having singing talent. The songs can be brutal, threatening to eat a girl alive if she don't let them out.

Which was one of the reasons she'd taken the ring girl-waitress-nurse-maid job in the first place. Sure it was a lot of work, but she got to sing the Greek national anthem on fight nights. Her father's song, as she'd come to think of it. So it meant all the songs she hadn't wanted to sing since Trevor died didn't hurt quite so bad inside her chest.

However, it looked like Marian had grossly miscalculated her powers of seduction. Boys had come easy in high school. Doing most anything for as little as a kiss, even though she was other, in more ways than one—her sister Willa and her being the only two brown kids at Greenlee High School.

The only reason she didn't have boys swarming all over her now in Greece was because after what happened with Trevor, she'd stopped wanting anything to do with them. So she'd flipped off her siren switch. Learned how to talk and act in ways that didn't make men want to do things for her.

In fact, it had been so long now since she'd flirted, she'd been halfway wondering if she was doing it right with The Russian Beast. But then he'd pulled her to him. Practically told her she either needed to let him fuck her or let him fight.

She'd surprised herself by opting for the former, but she certainly hadn't regretted it. In fact she'd spent all day happily tired and sore, but looking forward to the next time with him. Had put her ring girl outfit on over what felt like a new body and strode into the basement crowd to sing her anthem along with a cheery Greek Christmas song she'd heard in a department store.

You'd think the fact that it was literally the night before

Christmas would have thinned out the crowd, but there seemed to be even more men gathered in the basement that night. Cheering for the blood of the fighters on the eve of their savior's birth.

But he wasn't there. She scanned the crowd for him throughout the night, but never saw him. And when Cyrus came over and told her to announce that the last fight was coming up, she released a disappointed breath.

"That's how that one goes," Cyrus told her as if reading her mind. Or her body, which felt like an open outlet, just waiting for her new lover to plug himself back in. "He comes in for one night, then we don't see him again for awhile. Weeks…last time, months."

So he was gone and most likely wouldn't be coming back for some time. So much for the power of her siren grand-mother, she thought to herself. The one time she'd truly wanted a boy, the supposed power had completely failed her. He'd given her all the feelings she'd been missing over the past year and then disappeared back into the ether.

Maybe he was descended from some sort of mythological creature, too, she thought with a grimace. Like an incubus. If the delicious soreness between her thighs from last night was anything to go by, that really might be it.

"You given any more thought to my offer?" Cyrus asked. "It's Christmas Eve, and the men are happy but lonely tonight. They will line up at your door to have you. Sixty percent for me, forty for you. I give you good deal. Could be very prof-itable night if you say yes."

She shook her head. This again. Cyrus had been asking her this question every night since she started working here. And every time, she'd just looked away and told him to let her think about it.

Up until last night, she'd thought all she'd needed was

more time. More time to go deader inside, until she truly no longer cared who fucked her.

It's just a body, she'd told herself. One that belonged to someone she could barely stand after Trevor's death. Why shouldn't she use it to make some more money?

But then *he* had happened. A night of pleasure so intense, she'd found herself doing something she hadn't done in the year since she ran away from home. *Feel.* Feel something other than numbness or when she let that numbness slip even a little, the wild grief that made her know she either had to stop feeling or jump off the Acropolis's high rocky outcrop. For what she did. For what she let happen. Sometimes it felt like the only thing keeping her alive was the numbness and knowing Trevor wouldn't want her story to end that way.

The weeks she'd been working here, she'd truly thought it would be just a matter of time before she took Cyrus up on his offer. But after last night…

"No," she answered the small Greek man with a firm shake of her head. "I don't want to do that."

Cyrus, who was usually such an affable guy, actually looked surprised. "Why not? Because of The Russian Beast? Was he too much for you? He hurt you?"

She shook her head. No, it'd been quite the opposite. He'd made her feel. Made her want things for herself. Which was why she couldn't imagine sleeping with another man tonight, much less several, and then passing on the majority of the cut to Cyrus.

"How about 50/50 then? You are friend. I give you this deal."

"Seriously, that side hustle's not for me," she answered, letting her voice go hard. "Find somebody else, because it ain't going to be me, Cyrus."

Cyrus didn't answer, but a terrible look came over his face, red and furious…. She could tell he wasn't pleased, and she welcomed the roar of the crowd that came with the latest knockout.

Using the downed fighter as an excuse to rush away, she decided she'd need to gather her things and get out of here. Not at some future date when she'd saved up enough money for an apartment. But first thing in the morning.

Luckily she didn't have much stuff to take with her. After her bags were stolen last month, she'd been left with just the clothes on her back. So she had some toiletries and a few outfits—one of which she was wearing and technically belonged to Cyrus.

Whatever. She was more than happy to leave that one here, she thought as she rushed to her bedroom door. She'd just finished mopping down the venue and putting everything in the basement back in pre-fight condition. So, you know, still grimy but not so bloody and cluttered.

But just as she put her hand on the knob of the door, a voice behind her said, "So you think you can take advantage of my hospitality, American girl?"

She turned around to see Cyrus, which wouldn't have been so bad. He was slimy but small. She maybe could have taken him. But he had the large men she privately referred to as Goon 1 and Goon 2 flanking his back. Two former fighters who exclusively wore turtlenecks overlaid with thick silver chains. They were too old to participate in the fights anymore, but still tough enough to handle anyone Cyrus felt was getting out of hand.

And apparently Cyrus felt she'd gotten out of hand. They stood behind Cyrus, hands to fists, as if daring her to run.

Fuck.

She clamped her lips and pasted on a conciliatory look. The kind she used with women who couldn't be swayed by her siren. And she already knew she couldn't use the siren here. It would only make an already volatile situation worse.

"Cyrus, you're mad. I get it. I tell you what. I'm going to pack a bag and get out of here right now. If you don't want me in your room no more, that's fine. I'm gone."

"You think you can leave here without paying me what you owe?"

She blinked because, "What do you think I owe you, Cyrus? Last I checked, I've been working my fingers to the bone here for not a lot of money."

Cyrus's lips twisted in a contemptuous smirk. "It would have been less if I'd known you weren't going to come through."

Her brain boggled at the thought of anyone getting paid less than she did to do what essentially amounted to four jobs. But she had nothing but the little ring girl outfit on her back and he had two goons at his.

"Okay, how much do you think I owe you? We'll work out a deal."

He moved so fast, she didn't have a chance to defend herself. The next thing she knew, a fist was coming at her. Then a burning hot pain radiating across her face. Cyrus had just punched her, she realized as she fell to the ground. Straight punched her like she'd been watching men punch each other in the ring for weeks now.

But they weren't in the ring. And Cyrus wasn't backing off like a fighter was supposed to after he'd knocked his opponent to the ground.

Instead he stood over her, wheezing hard, looking like he was pissed because she'd made him exert even that much energy.

"Give me the needle…" he said, holding out his hand.

Goon 2 passed him a syringe, already filled. Like he was a nurse and this was Cyrus's version of the E.R.

Drugs, she realized through the ringing in her ears. He was going to drug her. "No…" she mumbled, trying to get up. Trying to fend him off. "No…"

"Shut up, bitch!" Cyrus answered, fisting the syringe. "You brought this on yourself."

He bent down, and she started to crawl backwards, frantic to get away from him. But then she didn't have to, because Cyrus suddenly disappeared from her line of sight, taken out by a large blur.

"*Ohhee! Ohhee! Ohhee!*" she heard one of the goons call out. Greek for "no."

Then came two muffled popping sounds. She jumped when both of Cyrus's goons landed in front of her. Wide-eyed with small holes in the middle of each forehead.

What the…?

She sat up fully. Just in time to see Cyrus on his knees, the large man now looming over her boss like he'd been looming over her. Though it was hard to see anything in the dimly lit room, she knew it was The Russian Beast. By his hulking form, by the stillness of his body, by the absolute cold front coming off of him as he stared down at the sobbing man. He was holding something in his hand. A gun, she realized with a wide-eyed gasp.

"Please! Please! I didn't know she was yours! I'll make it right. Whatever you want. I'll give her to you. Promise. I'll make it ri—"

An orange spark lit up the room along with the sound of a muffled pop.

Cyrus's body flew back with the force of the bullet hitting his forehead, then The Russian Beast came to stand over him.

She could see his face clearly now, cast in partial light. Hard as a statue's as he squeezed three more orange sparks out of his gun. Three more bullets made their way into Cyrus's chest, making his dead body jerk with the violence of their impact.

THEODORA TAYLOR

The next thing she knew, The Russian Beast was standing in front of her, his huge chest heaving. He was breathing hard. But not with exertion.

No, he looked nothing but angry. Nostrils flaring in and out as he held out his hand and said to her, "Come."

342

Chapter Five

"COME," he said to her.

And she found herself taking his hand and letting him pull her to her feet. In a daze, the siren followed the beast out to the street and into the back of a cab.

Inside the car, she clung to his large hand with both of hers. But his face remained unreadable, no emotion to be found about what had just happened or what he had done. So she watched him watch nothing but the passing scenery as the cab took them through the congested streets of Athens, into the historical neighborhood of Plaka. Above them, the Acropolis was lit up like a shining beacon to tourists everywhere. A sure sign, even more than street's strictly engineered switch to neoclassical design, that they were now in a neighborhood she couldn't possibly afford.

That had been one of the first things she'd learned when she'd finally used the passport she'd gotten after graduating from high school. When she'd finally followed through with her plans to get out of Greenlee County, spurred on by her brother's tragic death. Anything too close to a tourist site or with a decent view was out of her price range.

But apparently that wasn't the case for The Russian Beast. Her mouth dropped open when the cab deposited them outside a hotel that looked like an ancient Greek palace made new. This definitely wasn't any kind of student hostel situation. In fact, it boasted columns so high, she could barely see their tops, even when she bent her head all the way back.

No, this place was definitely out of her price range. But she followed him through the middle set of columns anyway.

Inside she could feel the stares of the other hotel guests, and couldn't help but feel self-conscious in her skimpy ring girl outfit. She also became keenly aware of her face, which had to be sporting a black eye if the pulsing pain coming off of it was any indication.

However the hotel employees were nothing but deferential to The Russian Beast, inclining their heads as they said, "*Kalispéra*, Mr. Rustanov." Good evening, Mr. Rustanov. So she guessed Rustanov was his last name, not Beast. Though why he'd asked if she knew it, she had no idea. Was she supposed to know that name? Was he famous?

She didn't understand. Any of it.

After a short elevator ride, they finally arrived at a door made of a rich, dark wood. She braced herself, but was still a little overcome with the opulence of the hotel room, which made her fully understand the term "presidential suite" for the first time. The room—which was more like a full-on apartment, in her opinion—had a living room fit for a statesman, with luxurious leather furniture, heavy carpets, and a dining area that could easily seat six. Beyond the floor-to-ceiling windows, she could see a balcony with a hot tub and…

Her eyes widened. Was that a private swimming pool? Yes, it was. And in the distance, the Acropolis shone like a nighttime portrait. Forget price range. This place was out of her imagination's range.

A low growl interrupted her blatant gaping. She looked across the huge room to see an insanely large dog with white and black fur standing outside a closed set of sliding doors like a canine sentry. It stared at her with demonic blue eyes, as if it were trying to decide whether or not to kill her.

"That is Sascha. Siberian husky, wolf mix. Do not try to pet. Not safe."

The Russian said something to the huge hound in a strange language. She'd never heard the language before, but she was almost sure it wasn't Russian. Whatever it was, it did the trick, because the growling stopped almost immediately. And it didn't start up again when The Russian disappeared through the sliding doors, which apparently led into a bedroom.

Still, Sascha continued to give her the evil eye until The Beast emerged a few moments later with a gray t-shirt.

"Put this on," he commanded, thrusting it at her. And to her surprise, he turned around to give her privacy.

She did as instructed, and found that the t-shirt came all the way down to her knees without clinging to anything what-soever. The night before, he'd all but ripped the ring girl outfit off of her, but tonight it seemed like he could barely look at her and wanted her completely covered up.

"I'm done," she told him.

"What do you need to fix your face?" he asked, turning back around.

Her face. She could feel it throbbing with the heat of damage done, and she wasn't going to forget the way the other hotel guests had stared at her anytime soon. They'd probably thought he was the one who gave it to her.

"I apologize if I embarrassed you down there," she said, cringing at that thought.

Something ticked in his jaw. "What do you need to fix your face?"

"Um…just some ice and a towel," she answered, pressing her fingertips into the large bruise. "Nothing feels broken."

He left the room without another word. Leaving her alone in the suite with the dog she wasn't supposed to pet.

"Are you really that dangerous?" she asked it.

Sascha stared back at her. Eyes inscrutable.

But she had a feeling about this one, so she sang to it. "Yellow," by Coldplay. One of the songs she used to sing to Trevor to lull him to sleep. Sascha seemed like a Coldplay fan.

As it turned out, she was right. By the time The Russian came back with the ice, she was sitting with her back to the sliding doors with Sascha's head in her lap.

However, both she and the dog stood up somewhat guiltily when he came back into the suite.

"Hey," she said.

He just grunted and pushed the ice bucket into her hands. He pointed at the sliding door, "You can sleep in there. I am going out."

"Okay, thank you—"

He was heading back to the door before the words were even out of her mouth. And this time he slammed it behind him.

So apparently he wasn't completely unaffected by what had happened that night, she thought in the wake of his departure. He'd come to the basement, probably looking for another hook up, and had found her in need of saving instead. Total mood killer. And now not only did he not want a repeat of last night, he was also plainly struggling with the decision to let her stay here in his beyond-grand hotel room. She totally got that.

But she must have had a little more pride left than originally thought, because for a moment she considered leaving. Disappearing back into one of the poorer parts of the city and getting out of his obviously annoyed hair.

But it was four in the morning. All she had in the world now was the waist pack with the little money she'd made working for Cyrus. And her head was swimming—she could only hope not with a concussion. Sure there was her pride, but she was also the daughter of a nurse. She knew she needed to ice her face. And sleep.

Deciding to do at least that for herself, she opened the sliding doors and entered a sophisticated bedroom done up in deep browns and fine white linens. Another entry in the "this is how you do rich-ass hotel rooms" catalog, and her heart nearly cried out a happy gospel song when she saw what looked like the softest bed ever. When she woke up, she'd figure out a new plan, she promised herself. Or just start wandering the streets of Greece again until she found another place to land.

She found a hand towel in the small alcove that sat between the bedroom and the bathroom, and made herself a decent enough ice pack. Then, pressing it to her face, she climbed into the huge bed and let herself sink into it with a sigh. Only to find she couldn't sleep.

Funny that unlike her reluctant host, she wasn't remotely bothered that he'd so ruthlessly shot Cyrus and his goons. But the fact that he wasn't sleeping beside her, making her feel the things he'd made her feel last night when he'd taken her again and again like he couldn't get enough…that bothered her.

And though this was the most comfortable bed she'd lain in like, ever, it took her a long while to fall asleep.

WHICH WAS WHY SHE WAS SHOCKED TO WAKE UP TO THE SIGHT of The Russian Beast. But not so beast-like anymore. He was clean-shaven now, and had replaced last night's black track suit with a pair of gray wool trousers and a black sweater, which made his eyes look even darker. And instead of a knot, his long hair fell in a silken, jet-black waterfall past his shoulders.

"Hi," she said, sitting up on her forearm. She could only wonder what she looked liked. Dressed in his bulky t-shirt, wild curls in a frizzy tumble on top of her head—since she hadn't tied it up last night.

"What's up?" she asked, trying not to feel self-conscious.

"I come back to room last night. No Sascha. I look for him on balcony, in other bathroom, and then I find him in here. My guard dog curled up beside your bed."

Oh, so Sascha was a boy. She hadn't bothered to check last night.

"Sorry," she said with a chagrined smile. "I kind of have a way with animals—especially if they're male. My mom says my grandma on my father's side was a siren."

He stared at her for a long black-eyed second and then said, "Or maybe he recognizes kin. He is dog. You live like dog. He comes in here with you."

She tilted her head. Okay, this guy...he had a way of insulting her, so brazenly, it was hard for her to actually feel insulted. Just bewildered. "So you came in here to compare me to your dog?"

Another dark look, and despite the much more sophisticated clothes, he put her in mind of a frustrated beast. Nostrils flaring in and out as he glared at her.

"You are quarter siren, but you live like dog in that basement. Do you know about men like Cyrus? What they do to siren girls like you?"

She shook her head, once again not knowing whether to feel insulted or bewildered by his obvious anger.

"They give you drugs. Then they give you to somebody who breaks girls like you as job. Rape you over and over and keep you on drugs until you are addicted and will do whatever they say for next hit. What did you think happened to girls who came before you?"

"They quit because of the obviously shitty working conditions?" she answered, truthfully.

"No, they do not quit," he answered, tone scathing as acid. "They were *broken*. Cyrus lets men use them after fighting is done. That way all money comes back to him, even if house loses on fights. He lets men use them until they are too old or too far gone. Then he gets new girl. You were new girl."

She expelled a breath, strangely more upset for the women who'd come before her than herself. "Those poor girls. Is there any way to help them?" she asked him.

He flinched. Almost like her question had taken him by complete surprise. "No, there is no way to help them."

"Oh," her shoulders sank. More souls to add to the list of people she couldn't help.

The memory of Trevor's broken body lying in the road came back to her on a flash then. Along with the image of her sobbing. Begging him and anybody else who would listen not to go, to stay here with her, not to die—

She broke out of the memory, clinging to her numbness like a lifeline.

"Okay, well, thank you for the advice," she said to the intense man sitting in front of her.

She swung her feet around so she could get out of the bed. "No more taking jobs at underground fighting rings. Message received. Thank you. Sincerely, thank you for all you did. I'll be getting out of your hair now."

But as soon as she stood up, so did he, effectively blocking her exit with one move of his giant body.

"You are scared of me now," he said, bending his head to look down at her. "After you saw the real me. Who I really am."

It was statement not a question, but her answer would have been the same either way. "No, I'm not scared," she told him. "Just grateful. And sad for those other girls. And I don't want to overstay my welcome here, so I'll just be going."

But instead of stepping out of the way for her to leave, he stepped even closer. Towering over her as he said, "You should be."

"Sad?" she asked.

"Scared. You should be scared of me. After last night."

She smiled then, broken and wry. Yeah, she supposed she should be. But...

"I'm not," she said, looking up to meet his gaze. Bold as she used to be. Before Trevor. "I don't care how many dudes you kill. I ain't going to be scared of you."

A few dangerous seconds ticked by, and then he sneered, "You are stupid girl. But you make my dick hard."

Her eyes widened. "Okay, well, I guess that's supposed to be some kind of compliment."

"I will make you offer," he continued, still sneering. "Instead of dying like dog in some Greek's basement, you will become my pet."

"Your *pet*?" she repeated, looking down at Sascha.

"No, Sascha is guard dog. Not pet. The men in my family..." He sliced his eyes to the side as if trying to figure how to explain this to her, even though English wasn't his first language. "The men in my family. We are known for keeping a certain type of woman. A woman we take care of, who in return takes care of the needs every man has. We give this woman many things, and she gives us whatever we want from her, anytime we want it. Do you understand my meaning, Siren?"

She nodded. "Yeah, I think I do. You all have a whore on the side," she summarized, voice blunt. "It's like a family tradition, and you want me to be your whore."

"No, Siren, let me make this clear. Not my whore. My *pet*. If you are to sell yourself, I would have you sell yourself to me. But I do not pay for sex. I pay for ownership."

Ready to finish this dark, psycho sexy story?
Visit Amazon to read the rest!

HER RUSSIAN BILLIONAIRE

Russian oligarch, Alexei Rustanov, wants nothing more than to leave his past behind, including the sexy and sassy Texas beauty, Eva St. James, who so callously broke his heart back when he was a poor grad student. But when he runs into her at a wedding eight years after their tumultuous break-up, passions ignite and Alexei decides he will settle for nothing less than red-hot, dirty, and oh-so-erotic revenge.

HER RUSSIAN BRUTE

Ivan Rustanov is a total jackhole. He has no conscience, and now he's forcing me to stay in his remote mountain home as his prisoner until Spring. He's no holds barred, and dangerous and wants me in his bed, but that will NEVER happen. I hate him. Or at least I should. Shouldn't I?

Characters From HER RUSSIAN SURRENDER

Characters featured or mentioned in this novel

HIS ONE AND ONLY (Beau and Josie)

HIS PRETEND BABY (Nyla)

THE SCOTTISH WOLVES

Her Scottish Wolf

Her Scottish King

Her Scottish Warrior

BROKEN AND RUTHLESS

KEANE: Her Ruthless Ex

STONE: Her Ruthless Enforcer

RASHID: Her Ruthless Boss

THE VERY BAD FAIRGOODS

His for Keeps

His Forbidden Bride

His to Own

RUTHLESS TYCOONS

HOLT: Her Ruthless Billionaire

ZAHIR: Her Ruthless Sheikh

LUCA: Her Ruthless Don

HOT AUDIOBOOKS WITH HEART

The Owner of His Heart

Her Russian Billionaire

His Pretend Baby

His Everlasting Love

Her Viking Wolf

HOT CONTEMPORARIES WITH HEART

The Owner of His Heart

The Wild One

His for the Summer

His Pretend Baby

His One and Only

HOT HARLEQUINS WITH HEART

Vegas Baby

Love's Gamble

HOT SUPERNATURAL WITH HEART

His Everlasting Love

12 Days of Krista

(only available during the holidays)

About the Author

Theodora Taylor writes hot books with heart. When not reading, writing, or reviewing, she enjoys spending time with her amazing family, going on date nights with her wonderful husband, and attending parties thrown by others. She now lives in Los Angles, California, and she LOVES to hear from readers. So….

Friend Theodora on Facebook
https://www.facebook.com/theodorawrites

Follow Me on Instagram
https://www.instagram.com/taylor.theodora/

Sign for up for Theodora's Newsletter
http://theodorataylor.com/sign-up/

Made in the USA
Middletown, DE
23 September 2020